THE TRUTH ABOUT LORIN JONES

ALISON LURIE

THE TRUTH ABOUT LORIN JONES

AVON BOOKS ◢◣ NEW YORK

AVON BOOKS
A division of
The Hearst Corporation
105 Madison Avenue
New York, New York 10016

First Avon Books Trade Printing: May 1990

AVON TRADEMARK REG. U.S. PAT. OFF. AND IN OTHER COUNTRIES, MARCA REGISTRADA,
HECHO EN U.S.A.

Printed in the U.S.A.

OPM   10   9   8   7   6   5   4   3   2   1

For Barbara Epstein

"They say the owl was a baker's daughter. Lord! We know what we are, but know not what we may be."

— *Hamlet*

THE TRUTH ABOUT LORIN JONES

1

Polly Alter used to like men, but she didn't trust them anymore, or have very much to do with them. Last month, on her thirty-ninth birthday, it suddenly hit her that — though she hadn't planned it that way. — almost all her dealings now were with women. Her doctor, her dentist, her accountant, her therapist, her bank manager, and all her close friends were female. She shopped at stores run and staffed by women, and when she had a prescription she walked six blocks out of her way to have it filled by the woman pharmacist at Broadway and Eighty-seventh. For days at a time she never spoke to an adult male.

When her husband left eighteen months ago, Polly hadn't expected her life to turn out like this. Miserable and angry though she was, she had looked forward to the adventure of being single again. But as her friends and the media had already warned her, there weren't any good men over thirty in New York, only husbands and creeps. She'd refused to go out with the husbands, and her other encounters had been such disasters that it made her laugh now to remember them, though at the time she had sometimes cried with disappointment and rage. After about six months she had realized she'd much rather stay home and watch television with her twelve-year-old son, Stevie, or go places with her women friends.

Of course, until recently Polly had spoken to men at work. But now she had a half-year's leave from the Museum and needn't go there except to use the library. Three months ago she had lucked out: she'd been awarded a grant and given a publisher's advance for a book on the American painter Lorin Jones, born 1926, died 1969 almost unknown; now — partly thanks to her — becoming famous.

As it turned out, this commission had a striking, almost supernatural appropriateness. Though Polly had never met Lorin Jones, she'd been following in Lorin's path all her life. Lorin had grown up in a New York suburb; Polly (twenty years later) in a neighboring suburb. Both of them went to school in Westchester; both, after college, lived on Bank Street in the West Village. Their paths must have crossed, probably many times. When Polly was a toddler, she and her mother might have passed Lorin and hers on the street in White Plains. Or, on some steamy summer afternoon while Polly made castles in the sand at Rye Beach or waded in the warm ebb and flow of the Sound, her subject may have been sunning or sketching nearby. Later, when she began to visit museums and galleries in New York, Lorin might have been among the other spectators; she could have been buying pantyhose at the same counter of Bloomingdale's, or sitting next to her future biographer on the Eighth Avenue bus or at a Museum of Modern Art film showing.

Photographs of Lorin Jones from that period showed a strikingly beautiful young woman, in the French beatnik fashion popularized after World War II by Juliette Greco: ghost-pale, with heavy waves of shoulder-length dark hair, thick bangs, high cheekbones, and huge silk-fringed dark eyes. She had a Modigliani figure, long-limbed and high-breasted, and was dressed usually in black. Whenever Polly looked at these photos she had a sense of déjà vu. Damn it, she knew she'd seen this woman somewhere, at some time. If only there had been a sign: some loud clanging bell, some flash of light to warn her that their lives would be intimately connected!

The flash of light came later: in the summer of 1970, a year after Lorin Jones had died. It happened one morning in a Cape Cod guest house when Polly was on her honeymoon. She came down to breakfast, and there on the wall over the knotty-pine sideboard, lit by a silvery wash of reflected light from the bay, was one of Lorin's semiabstract landscapes.

"Yes! That's it!" she had cried half-aloud, her gaze, her whole consciousness, drawn into the veils and swirls of color.

"That's how I'd like to paint," she told her new husband later over the muffins and beach plum jam. "He sees the world the way I see it." Stupidly, though she already considered herself a feminist, Polly had assumed that "Lorin" was a man's name; she still believed that a great painter must be male. How much time had been lost through that ignorant error! If she'd known the truth she would probably have tried to find out more about Lorin Jones then, and Lorin's submerged reputation might have been retrieved years sooner. The idea still made Polly angry.

But then a lot of things made Polly angry. Since childhood, her short-fuse temper had got her into trouble. It flashed out suddenly and unpredictably, and usually extinguished itself just as fast, leaving her to flush and apologize. But sometimes, even after she'd calmed down outwardly, she was still hot inside, and a deep fuming stubbornness prevented her from admitting that she'd been rude or wrong.

One of the things that continued to make Polly furious was what the male establishment had done to Lorin Jones while she was alive, and for years after she was dead: how it had exploited her as a woman and neglected her as an artist. The most infuriating and saddest thing of all was that Lorin had never realized she was going to become famous. She didn't foresee that she would be the surprise star of Polly's first Museum exhibition, "Three American Women," and that the prices of her paintings would rise astronomically. She didn't know now that she was soon to have a one-woman show at a major New York gallery and be the subject of a full-length biography.

Instead, Lorin Jones had died in 1969 of virus pneumonia in a hospital in the Florida Keys, more or less forgotten. If only she could have seen what was coming! Or if only she could have lived a little longer! The new feminism would have saved her; she would have found friends, allies, supporters, courage to go on. Every time Polly thought of this she felt rage and a painful, wrenching regret.

Sometimes she had a fantasy in which she traveled back into 1968 or 1969 to find Lorin Jones. She imagined flying to Florida, driving down the Keys, locating the cottage on Aurelia Lane, rapping on its door. Lorin would come out, looking like that last sunstruck black-and-white snapshot: still beautiful, but pale and wasted, her face white within a blurred moss of dark hair, the expression of her eyes concealed by a blindfold of shadow. She would lean against one of the sun-blistered pillars of the porch, her bare thin forearms crossed over a man's white shirt, one long hand holding a cigarette from which a smudge of smoke rose. "Goddamn it," Polly would say to her. "You've got to take more care of yourself. You've got to quit smoking, get more sleep, eat better, see a doctor about that cough. You can't give up now; you're a very great painter. You're going to be in art history. Please, Lorin! You've got to hold on."

But Lorin Jones would not answer. She was dead and gone; and all Polly could do now was to find out everything about her and tell it the best she could, sparing no one. Then the truth would be known, and not only Lorin's life but Polly's too would be justified and made whole. And maybe, even, no other American woman artist would ever again have to suffer what Lorin had suffered.

If Lorin Jones had had loyal women friends, like Polly's friend Jeanne, one of them might really have done what Polly had imagined doing. But so far Polly hadn't been able to locate any woman who knew Lorin well in her later years. It was beginning to be clear that after her marriage she didn't have many close friends of either sex; that she was, or rather became (Polly largely blamed Lorin's husband for this) a shy, solitary person — in the end, almost a recluse. Not only had this probably contributed to her untimely death, it had made the task of her biographer much more difficult.

Though Polly hadn't had much to do with men lately, all that was about to change. Over the next six months she would have to interview several of them — and not just any men, but the exact same ones who had discouraged and denigrated and exploited and neglected Lorin Jones. It was their fault, ultimately, that the world would never see the beautiful paintings Lorin would have made if she'd lived.

Among them were:

1. Lorin Jones's dealer, a suave elderly person named Paolo Carducci, founder and owner of the Apollo Gallery, which after 1964 had refused to show Jones's work.

2. Professor Leonard Zimmern, Lorin's half brother, who seemed to be more or less devoid of feeling for his sister, since he had by his own admission hardly seen her over the last few years of her life. After she died, though, he had been quick enough to go down to Key West and collect her unsold paintings, of which he was the legal owner.

3. Lorin's ex-husband, the famous art historian and critic Garrett Jones, who had been all gracious elderly charm at the time of Polly's show, eager to lend pictures and photographs, to locate and speak to other collectors. To hear him talk now, Garrett had always done all he could for Lorin and her career. But the record suggested otherwise. While they were married, Lorin had paintings in group shows at the Apollo Gallery in 1954 and 1955, and in 1957 and 1960 she had two successful one-woman shows. She had another show in 1964, the year after she and Garrett separated, and then nothing. Polly had no proof that Lorin's former husband had deliberately wrecked her career, but it would have been pretty damn easy for him to do so.

4. The man with whom Lorin Jones had lived after her marriage broke up, an unsuccessful ex-hippie poet called Hugh Cameron, who took Lorin to Key West and then left her when she was ill and dying. Polly had never met Cameron, but she had heard plenty about him.

Of course, there was no guarantee that any of these men would even begin to admit their guilt; probably they would lie like hell in order to protect their own self-esteem and reputation. If Polly had any choice in the matter she would have had nothing to do with them. But because no one else knew the facts, she would somehow have to get them to tell her the truth about Lorin Jones.

How this could best be accomplished was now being discussed by Polly and her friend Jeanne, in Polly's untidy New York apartment on a hot late-summer evening. Polly was still sitting at the round oak table, her elbows on either side of a handmade brown pottery mug, her small square chin propped on her fists. Jeanne, who had made the tasty supper (cold chicken, tabbouli, and cucumbers in yogurt, followed by lemon sherbet), was sunk among cushions on the sofa, smoking one of her endless cigarettes. She never stood when she could lounge, or sat when she could recline.

If an uninformed observer had been told that one of these two women was a lesbian, Polly would have been the natural candidate. Though she had hardly thought about what it might be like to make love with another woman until she became friends with Jeanne, her short untidy hair and face scrubbed clean of makeup suggested scorn of feminine artifice; her checked workshirt and jeans and scuffed Birkenstock sandals, the uniform of both male and female gays in New York that summer, gave her a definite tomboy look.

On the other hand Jeanne, who had been erotically interested in her own sex since she was eight, was soft and generously rounded — an Ingres blonde, delicately powdered and rouged, in a scooped-neck pink T-shirt and a rose-flowered Laura Ashley skirt. Her voice was high and gentle, and none of her lovers had ever thought of calling her Johnnie, or even Jan. Lesbianism for Jeanne meant moving as far and fast as possible away from bisexuality, not toward it. In her view, it was natural for a woman who loved women to recoil physically from the masculine in any form. As a separatist she avoided the opposite sex whenever she could; she was still very disappointed that the Long Island college where she taught history and women's studies had recently agreed to admit males.

Though Jeanne also distrusted men, she disagreed with

Polly on the proper method of dealing with them. If avoidance was impossible, she counseled guile. Polly's instinctive preference, on the other hand, was for confrontation. When she did those interviews, she said now, she wanted to be open about her own feelings.

"Yes. Of course, you would want that." Jeanne gave a small indulgent sigh. She had once suggested — and maybe correctly — that it was Polly's openness about her feelings that had kept her an assistant curator for five years.

"That's what seems natural to me."

"Sure, it seems natural," Jeanne agreed; her intonation suggested that there wasn't all that much to be said for nature. "Confrontation is always natural for you. But if you want results, you've got to keep your cool."

Jeanne often urged Polly to keep her cool, cool off, or simmer down — not always with success. Outwardly she herself was not particularly cool, but rather mildly warm. She appeared to most men to be a sweet, pretty, easygoing sort of woman. Inwardly, however, she concealed a revulsion that went back to her deprived and abused childhood.

"Look, Polly," she reasoned, dragging on her cigarette. "You know you're going to have to spend hours, perhaps days even, with those people. If you want them to talk to you, you'll simply have to prevent them from guessing what's in your mind."

"I'm not sure I can do that."

"Of course, it's not going to be easy," Jeanne continued. "I know you." She smiled. Though several years younger than Polly, she habitually took toward her (and toward all her close friends) a stance of maternal experience. "I think maybe the best thing for you would be to resolve right now to say as little as possible. Next time, simply turn on your machine, ask your questions, and whatever they answer, you just nod and grin. Let them blather on and condemn themselves. . . . And they will, I'm sure of that."

"I don't know." Polly frowned and shoved her heavy mug away, splashing the table with lukewarm coffee.

"What don't you know?"

"What you said — it just sounds wrong to me. I mean, women have been smiling and lying to men for centuries. I figure it's time for us to stop all that crap. I want to make it clear that I know what those guys did to Lorin Jones; then they won't be able to waffle."

"Waffle?" Jeanne laughed. "They'll waffle whatever you do. But the proper way to treat a waffle is with syrup."

"I can't sweet-talk people; it's not my thing. I've got to let them see where I'm coming from."

"Oh, Polly." Jeanne sighed. "You know what your problem is? You still believe deep down that if men really understood how we felt they'd be surprised and sorry. They'd repent and reform, and we'd all live happily together ever after. You've got to realize that they already understand quite well how we feel. And none of them give an *S-H-I-T*." Jeanne never uttered an obscenity; she preferred to spell out the words as if some invisible child were listening.

"Mm," Polly murmured, accepting Jeanne's account of her views but not Jeanne's conclusions.

"You'll have to be on your guard every minute. And prepared for the worst."

"Yeah? And what's the worst?"

"I know what men are like." Jeanne put down her cigarette and turned to look at her friend. "I know they'll all try to seduce you, figuratively. Or even perhaps literally."

"Aw, come on." Polly shook her head.

"It's true. And for two reasons: first, because they're all going to be in your book. Naturally they'll want to go down in art history as good guys."

"Well, maybe so," Polly said, suddenly feeling powerful. "But that doesn't mean they'll make a pass at me."

"I bet they will," Jeanne said. "Some of them, anyhow. That's the way men's minds work. And second, they could try to seduce you just because that's the traditional male response to an attractive unattached woman. It doesn't matter if she's gay or straight. A woman who doesn't need men — they'll do anything to destroy her, prove she doesn't exist. When they hear of someone like you, or me, they say to each other: 'All she needs is a good lay.' "

"Sure, some men do, but —"

"You remember what happened to Cathy when she was up in Vermont? If Ida hadn't come back from the village in time, their redneck neighbor, that Cathy thought was such a nice guy, would have more or less raped her. He would have told himself she was asking for it, because she always invited him in and gave him a cup of coffee after he finished mowing their field."

"Yeah," Polly said. "Still, I figure I'm pretty safe. Paolo Carducci is over seventy and has a heart condition, and Garrett Jones is over seventy and married." She laughed.

"Yes; but from what you told me, he used to have quite a reputation. All I'm saying is, watch out." Jeanne extinguished her cigarette delicately in her saucer.

"Okay, I will."

"That's right. Well, I guess I better be getting back to Brooklyn before the muggers start their night's work." Jeanne gave a long sigh.

"You could stay over if you liked," Polly said. "Stevie's room's free now." She sighed in her turn; Stevie, now thirteen, had just left to visit his father in Colorado.

"Oh, thank you; I'd love to, it's so peaceful here. But I can't tonight. I think Betsy's going to call." Jeanne stood up; her usual serene expression had been replaced by one of tension and anxiety. She had recently become involved with a young married woman who taught part-time at her college, and who had what Jeanne described as a neurotic, abusive husband.

"Good luck," Polly said.

"Thank you," Jeanne replied distractedly. "Maybe some other time."

Alone, Polly scraped tabbouli into a bowl and covered it with plastic wrap. As she opened the fridge to put it away she was reminded that somehow she had to use up the crunchy peanut butter, grape jelly, raisin bread, milk, Pepsi, and hot dogs left behind yesterday by Stevie. There was no use saving any of it as she'd ordinarily do, because this time he wouldn't be home in a week or so; he'd be gone the whole fall term. Logically, Polly could see the point of this. It would give Stevie a chance to know his father better, and free her to travel and do research for her book. But illogically she felt awful about it. Her son had been gone only twenty-four hours, and already she missed him terribly.

And what would happen to Stevie while he was away? Raising her eyes from the sink, Polly stared past the smudged glass in the direction of Colorado. Her view was restricted, for though the building was on Central Park West, her apartment didn't face it, but confronted another building the color of birdshit and a vacant lot littered with broken glass and stunted sumac.

When Stevie looked out of the windows of his father's new architect-designed split-level in Colorado (clearly pictured in the background of a snapshot of him taken earlier that summer), he wouldn't see a dirty brick wall and piles of trash, but a wide-open vista of mountains and plains and long drifting Ansel Adams clouds. Would New York, and this apartment, seem cramped and dirty then, a place he didn't want to come home to?

Jeanne thought it was a good idea for Stevie to stay in Colorado for four months. She believed he needed a maturing experience; also she believed that Polly had invested too much in him emotionally. She thought it was a mistake to care too deeply for male children, or become too close to them, since they would inevitably grow into men — that is, into aliens.

But whatever Jeanne said, Polly couldn't think of Stevie as an alien. He wasn't like most males; he had been raised on nonsexist principles from birth, read aloud to from *Stories for Free Children,* given dolls as well as trucks to play with, taken to women doctors and dentists. For years his freedom from prejudice had been Polly's greatest pride. Over Christmas and spring vacations, and for two weeks in July when he went to stay with his father, she held her breath, fearing that he would come back infected with ugly paternalist ideas; but he never had. But what would happen when he was exposed to these psychological germs not for a week or two, but for nearly four months?

Jeanne didn't understand what she felt about Stevie, and she probably never would, Polly thought, because she had no children of her own. She didn't understand, either, what it meant to be married; how much you invested, how long and desperately you tried to make things work out. Often, when Polly related something Jim had once done or said, she saw a particular look, between amusement and impatience, cross her friend's gentle, rounded features. *Rather slow, weren't you? Rather dense?* this look said.

What if Jeanne was right? Polly thought as she rinsed a plate. What if even now the child she loved was turning into a man like other men?

There were so goddamn many dangers in this culture. Magazines, books, newspapers, television were heavy with overt and covert sexist propaganda, and Polly wouldn't be around now to point it out to Stevie. Some of the kids he played with had already been brainwashed, she'd seen the signs. And Stevie's father, Jim Meyer, was in many ways the most dangerous companion he could have, because his sexism was so well concealed. After all, Polly herself, though an adult, had been deceived by him. For fourteen years she had believed him to be a decent, generous, sensitive, nonchauvinist man.

Jim Meyer had first appeared one afternoon at the auction gallery where Polly then worked. He was a tall, solid man about her own age, with regular features and wide gray eyes rimmed with sooty, transparent skin, giving him an intriguingly — and as it turned out, deceptively — sophisticated and world-weary air. (Stevie had inherited this characteristic; even after nine hours of sleep he and his father both looked as if they'd been up all night.)

Jim had come in to arrange the sale of some valuable but not very interesting nineteenth-century paintings and furniture that belonged to his grandmother, who was moving to a nursing home. Polly was drawn to him at once, not only by his looks, but by his good manners. Since she was obviously working for a living, and not a society girl amusing herself while she waited to make a good marriage, many of the people Polly had to deal with at the gallery treated her like a typist or even like a housemaid. But Jim was considerate, even deferential. As it turned out, he was incapable of being rude to anyone.

Though she was attracted to Jim Meyer, Polly didn't expect much to come of it, partly because he was a medical researcher. From years of living with her stepfather, Bob Milner, she had formed the false opinion that scientists were like icebergs. Nine-tenths of them was under the surface, and most of that nine-tenths was ice. She didn't get her hopes up when Jim kept returning to the gallery on various excuses; she assumed that he came to see his grandmother's paintings and furniture before they disappeared forever. His attachment to them made her both sad and impatient — though of course she'd seen the same thing in other consignors.

"That big shipwreck picture, you know, it used to hang over the hall table in the Maine house, next to the barometer," he told her one day, for the second time. "You see the woman screaming and drowning there in the corner, and the big wave coming for her? When I was a kid I used to imagine I was just outside the painting, in a rowboat, and I was going to throw her a rope —"

"Listen." Unable to stop herself, Polly interrupted the story, though the sale catalogue in which this picture appeared was already at the printers. "Excuse my asking, but why are you selling this painting, if you like it so much? . . . I mean," she went on when Jim didn't answer, "couldn't you work something out with your grandmother? For instance, maybe you could have it appraised, and then buy it from her gradually."

"I guess I could. But the thing is, I don't figure I have a right to a picture like this. It ought to be in a museum or somewhere it could be appreciated properly. I don't really know anything about paintings."

"Says who?" Polly asked, turning around from the shipwreck to confront Jim.

"I don't know. I guess it was my mother who pointed it out first. 'Jim's a scientist,' she always said. 'He has no feeling for the arts.' "

"Oh, bullshit. Listen, it's not like that. There isn't any race of special privileged people who deserve to own paintings because they're so damned sensitive and aware. You like this picture, you should hang on to it."

Jim Meyer, typically, gave no sign that her argument had convinced him; but the following day, to the great irritation of Polly's boss, he withdrew three of his grandmother's pictures from the sale. He also invited Polly to dinner to thank her; and that was how the whole thing started.

All Polly's feminist friends liked Jim because he was so agreeable and good-looking and well informed, so obviously crazy about her, so respectful of her work. When she admitted that back in high school and college she'd wanted to be a painter herself, he was impressed and enthusiastic. It was a goddamn shame that she'd never had the time to go on with it, he said.

For the first time in nearly twenty years, as Polly had later explained to her therapist, she felt really happy and secure. Jim appeared to be all any liberated woman could want. He read the books and articles Polly lent him, and agreed with their conclusions; he supported the hiring and promotion of women at his lab. He tried unfamiliar dishes, and went with her to look at the work of new artists.

In return Polly made an effort not to shock Jim's colleagues and family with her language, or lose her temper. In fact, Jim was so patient with her outbursts that she gradually gave them up. Yelling at him was like punching the tan beanbag chair in their bedroom; he didn't argue or answer back, only sagged and looked deflated.

There was only one problem: though she loved and

trusted Jim, he didn't always turn her on. His gentle and affectionate lovemaking was sometimes almost on the verge of boring her.

For years, Polly tried with some success not to notice this. She blamed herself for still being susceptible to a stupid false adolescent idea of the desirable male — the Gothic myth of the Dark Stranger: reckless, willful, undependable. In the daylight hours she mocked this myth, deploring those of her friends who seemed to have bought into it. But sometimes late at night, as she lay in bed beside Jim Meyer and listened to his regular, almost apologetic snoring, the phantasm returned, and carried her into hot, windy, luridly lit regions whose existence her husband did not suspect.

Jim was completely faithful — unlike Polly, who twice when her husband was away at conferences let the hot winds blow her into bed with the wrong sort of man. After these episodes she was furious with herself and nervously guilty. She longed to be exposed and forgiven; but she had the good sense to realize that confession would hurt Jim far more than it would help her.

Though Polly went on working at the auction house after the wedding, with Jim's encouragement she had begun to hope that she was an artist after all. Four months before Stevie was born she quit her job and tried to start painting. She cleared most of the boxes out of the narrow little room with the north light that had been meant for a maid when the apartment was built, and set up her easel.

But she had waited too long. Standing up for hours at a time exhausted her and made her legs ache and her belly feel swollen and heavy. When she sat down she couldn't reach the easel properly. Her arm and leg muscles twitched like worn-out rubber bands; she grew restless and then angry. The one or two canvases she completed seemed to her ugly, clumsy, and empty of meaning.

Polly assumed it would be easier after the baby came, but it wasn't, though Jim not only paid for a part-time housekeeper, but took equal responsibility for the remaining housework, and spent as much time as Polly did with their son. Stevie was a great kid; but he took up a lot of emotional energy. When she went back to the studio after feeding or changing or cuddling him, the spontaneity of her impulse was gone; she found herself scrubbing at her work and fucking up something that had begun well.

It was a bore staying home all day, too, talking only to Stevie and the housekeeper, both of whom seemed to have a mental age of about four: Stevie of course precociously. She missed being in touch with the New York art world; she missed using her mind and having grown people to talk with. So when Stevie started nursery school she took a part-time job at the Museum, which in a few years became full-time. Soon she was going to meetings, working on catalogues and exhibitions, seeing artists and dealers and collectors and critics. She painted less often; then not at all. The studio, though it was still called by that name, became a storeroom again.

As soon as Stevie was a little older and needed her less, Polly told herself and everyone else, she'd get back to her art. Meanwhile her life, if not exciting, was fun and satisfying, her marriage solid. Or so she thought.

Then, a year ago last spring, when Stevie was twelve, everything fell apart. One day when Polly was showering after work Jim came bursting in on her. She knew something extraordinary, maybe something horrible, must have happened, because he was usually so careful of her bathroom privacy. At first, all she felt was relief and joy when there turned out to be no disaster. Instead, Jim had just been offered an important job and a really big research budget in Colorado. With an impulsiveness Polly hadn't seen in years, he threw out his arms, embracing both her and the yellow shower curtain printed with abstract designs, exclaiming that he couldn't believe it, God, he had never expected anything like this.

For a while Polly shared his euphoria. She had been feeling a little stale; Denver would be an adventure, a change. It would be good to get out of Manhattan, which was becoming more crowded, expensive, dirty, and dangerous every year. And, as Jim said, it'd be great for Stevie: he could meet real kids and have a normal American childhood — which simply meant, Polly thought now, that he could have the kind of childhood Jim had had.

Then, slowly, it dawned on her that she wasn't going to find a decent job in Denver. For Jim, it would be "the chance of a lifetime," as he put it, sliding into cliché in his enthusiasm — but it wasn't the chance of Polly's lifetime. And after all, Jim didn't have to go to Denver. He already had colleagues he liked, a good lab, adequate research funds. Whereas she had just got a raise at the Museum, and was working on an important exhibition ("Three American Women"). Was it fair to ask her to give all that up?

Jim, it turned out, thought it was fair. If Polly didn't get a job right off, she could go back to her painting; wasn't that what she'd always wanted? Anyhow, with the money he'd be making she wouldn't need to work anymore. They could live well, travel, have full-time help. It was true, Polly said (or lied? — she didn't know now), she did want to paint, but for that reason, too, she had to stay in New York, where the artists and galleries and collectors were.

While she still thought the matter was under discussion, Jim came home one afternoon and announced a unilateral decision.

"I can't stall them anymore, Polly," he explained, sitting down suddenly in the hall in a narrow-backed, hard Art Deco chair that nobody ever sat in. "I heard today that if I don't take the Denver job they're going to offer it to Frank Abalone. And hell, he'd really mess it up. He's got a name in some circles, but essentially he's a fraud, only nobody can prove it. Nobody even dares to try, after the way he ruined that lab assistant in L.A. I told you about that, you remember?"

"I remember," Polly said, standing in the kitchen door with a head of half-washed escarole in one hand. "But hell, it's not your responsibility, you know, what happens in some lab in Denver."

"Yes it is, though," Jim said. "It's my profession." He

swallowed, looked at the new beige twist carpeting for a bit, then up again. "Anyhow, I told Ben I was going to take the job."

"You told him you were leaving, just like that?" Polly stared at her husband and the chair that nobody ever sat on and thought: It was a sign; I should have known.

"I had to, Polly. They'll have to start looking for someone to replace me as soon as possible."

"I can't believe it." Polly's voice rose; she had an impulse to throw the wet soppy head of lettuce at her wet soppy husband's head. "Oh, shit. I thought you understood how I felt — Goddamn it, you said — I thought you'd do anything for me."

"I would, honestly," Jim insisted. "Anything but this."

The next few weeks were horrible. Slowly but relentlessly, like a dirty oil stain seeping through the back of a badly prepared canvas, the apartment on Central Park West became fouled and darkened with distrust. Polly and Jim began to have long, increasingly exhausting conversations after they were in bed, lying side by side for hours but hardly touching. Finally, at two or three A.M., they would make love in a weary, desperate way. Afterward she would lie as still as possible, not moving, with the sleepy, blurred thought that as long as she held Jim within her body, he couldn't leave her.

It was at this point that Polly began seeing the therapist. She didn't know yet that her marriage was breaking up; all she knew was that she and Jim had argued about his going to Denver until both of them were worn out, and now she was angry all the time and Jim was more and more silent and withdrawn. She knew they had to talk to someone else, to ventilate their feelings; that was why she made the appointment for them with Elsa.

The trouble was that when air got into their feelings it turned into a cyclone and blew them apart. Jim was revealed to Polly as a pathetic, selfish windbag, with a mind so closed that he wouldn't even go back to Elsa after their first three visits; he claimed she wasn't on his side. But Polly hung in there, and Elsa supported her through the worst months of her life.

Gradually she began to see how she had been deceived. Underneath his friendly, compliant manner, her husband was another MCP like all the rest. Worse, in fact, because at least the others were up front about it. With Jim there were never any remarks about women being weak-minded or unreasonable, there was no bluster or shouting. He was what an article she read later called a "passive-aggressive" male: a twentieth-century husband with the emotional tactics of a Victorian wife. He did exactly what he wanted, and made Polly look terrible at the same time.

Jim wouldn't, he simply wouldn't fight. When she shouted and started throwing things he remained infuriatingly sad and silent. He almost never raised his voice, even, so everyone thought of him as terribly good and patient and mature. It was Polly who seemed to be in the wrong, who seemed selfish and childish and unreasonable. It was Polly whom Stevie blamed for his parents' troubles. ("Why are you always yelling at Dad?") It was Polly whom her own mother argued against. ("Really, dear, you're beginning to sound like one of those radical students that have been giving Bob so much trouble lately.")

Meanwhile Jim went around looking ill and caved-in, begging her to change her mind and come with him, promising her anything else she might want: a separate studio, frequent trips to New York and Europe. The first six months they were apart, for what he told everyone was a "trial separation," he kept phoning, writing, pleading. He even finally pretended to understand her position. ("I guess you have to do what's right for you and your art.")

That first summer alone in New York was terrible for Polly. Rage and depression consumed her. If it hadn't been for Elsa, she probably would have cracked up, or given in and gone to Colorado. For the first few weeks she didn't even have Stevie, who had been sent to stay with his grandmother so that he wouldn't have to witness his father's departure and the departure of half the furniture.

The apartment was not only empty of furniture that summer; it was empty of friends, because everyone Polly knew, with the single exception of Jeanne, had turned out to be on Jim's side, and even if they felt like seeing Polly, she didn't want to see them. They claimed to be neutral, but they all kept telling her what an exceptional person Jim was, and saying that she ought to hang on to him even if it meant leaving the Museum, because good men were scarcer than good jobs. If she really cared for him, they said, she'd reconsider. They told her how much she was hurting him, how much he loved her; they said he'd probably never get over it. (What a laugh. Fourteen months after Jim moved to Denver he was remarried.)

When she talked it over with Elsa she came to realize that in the past thirteen years she'd acquired a new set of friends: better off, more conservative politically, and more apt to be conventionally married. Though she still considered herself a feminist, she'd lost touch with most of the members of her old consciousness-raising group, who didn't get on with Jim; she saw them only once or twice a year now, and always alone. "I had lunch with Wild Wilhemina today," she would report disloyally afterward, using the nickname she'd invented to amuse him. "Oh, really?" Jim would reply, grinning in anticipation. "What's she into these days?"

Without realizing it, Polly had accepted Jim's mild but persistent idea of who they were; of who she was. She had betrayed her old friends for him; and she had betrayed herself. She herself had become conventional. She hadn't noticed this because it had happened so slowly, and because she was bamboozled by superficialities. She had thought that she was different from the wives of Jim's scientific colleagues: she believed her free, sometimes foul language, and her Mexican embroidered smocks and African jewelry and brown-rice casseroles outweighed the fact that she lived on Central Park West and read *New York Magazine* the day it came, while *Mother Jones* and *Ms* slumped unopened for weeks in the wicker basket in the bathroom. Probably Jim's friends had been quietly laughing at her all those years.

The worst discovery of the summer was that, as if Jim's parting wish had been a curse, she wasn't able to paint. Alone in her studio weekend after muggy weekend, with the boxes of toys and winter clothes shoved aside, she stared at canvases that seemed to have dissolved into ugly messes of color like spilt or vomited food: a half-scrambled egg dropped on the floor, or regurgitated pizza. Somehow Jim's departure had destroyed her creative will. And even if she could have finished something, it wouldn't have had any future. The loose, painterly style she had developed in college wasn't fashionable anymore. Unless you were already famous no gallery wanted abstract work now; they were looking for hard-edged color-field painting or photo-realism.

Sometimes, alone in the apartment, unable to work, Polly gave herself up to storms of dizzying rage: cursing, smashing of glass, scalding, angry tears — all of them echoed, as July baked into August, and Elsa went on vacation, by bad summer weather: thunder and sheet lightning and a hot dust-laden breeze that didn't clear the air. But in the end it was her rage that saved Polly from despair. In the temper she had tried so hard to control for years she found her strength. Goddamn it, she had reason to be angry. Goddamn this world, goddamn Jim Meyer. It was then, on a hot thundery evening, alone in the apartment after having refused for the second time to meet the husband of a friend for "lunch," that she resolved to stop trying to please men.

The good effects of this decision were immediate. For one thing, it was a relief to stop searching faces at parties and openings to see if, maybe, here was someone interesting and unattached — (There never was, anyhow.) It was a relief to give up distorting her face and body: to eat whatever the hell she liked; to throw away the fashionable pointed shoes that hurt, and the tubes and bottles of colored grease and soot with which, though she'd called herself a feminist, she had continued to paint her face.

Over a few weeks Polly's whole appearance changed, or rather changed back. In school and college everyone had called her "cute": she was small and sturdy, with a solid rounded figure. She had thick untidy short curls, a naturally high color, big light-brown eyes, and a lively, sensual, puppy-dog expression. Now this self reappeared, not much the worse for wear. She strode purposefully on flat heels, stopped shaving her legs, never went to the hairdresser, and made no further effort to starve herself into thinness. Men on the street still gave her warm, interested looks, but she ignored them. She wasn't ready to go out with anybody yet; maybe she would never be ready. Maybe that side of her life was over.

Last month, in their final session, Elsa had suggested that eventually she would be able to relate positively to men again. But Polly wasn't counting on it. Even if she did meet a man who seemed possible, it wouldn't be any use. If she couldn't trust Jim, what man could be trusted? In the end no good had ever come to her from them, unless you count erotic pleasure. And Polly suspected now that erotic pleasure was the bait to a trap, a way to get the squirrel into the cage so that it — or rather, she — could spend the rest of her life running around a wire treadmill, breathless with love and fear.

owner and director of the Apollo Gallery, New York,
Lorin Jones's former dealer

Yes, in nineteen-fifty-four. She had two little oils in our Christmas group show that year, as you say.

Both of them sold quite soon. Of course, as an unknown, her prices were minuscule. But I think it did give her considerable encouragement.

Through Garrett, yes. Though naturally, if I hadn't seen something interesting in her work, that would have made not the slightest difference.

Well, it's hard to say. These intuitions are so very private and intangible. But I was correct, you see, wasn't I?

Two watercolors and a large oil in nineteen-fifty-seven? I imagine that's right. But I'll ask Jacky Herbert, my assistant, to check our files and give you all the details.

Yes, I think you could say that both the one-woman shows were successful.

I don't believe everything was sold, no. But on balance we did rather well. But again, you can get the data from Jacky.

That's a rather difficult question. Perhaps it's best to say that I didn't feel she was ready for another exposure yet.

No, it wasn't exactly a matter of her not having enough paintings on hand.

Very well, to be frank with you, yes. As Garrett says, there was a definite falling-off in the quality of her work. And a gallery like this has a reputation to maintain, you must realize.

It's hard to answer that. I think what I saw was a certain confusion, a lack of control, a series of experiments that didn't seem to be going anywhere.

Of course, it might have been temporary, but unfortunately —

Naturally, you have a right to your opinion. But I believe it's generally agreed that those late paintings —

How do I explain it? Well, I'm afraid it's something one occasionally sees in an artist's work. There is a brilliant debut, but no staying power. Take, for example . . .

Yes, to tell the truth, I do think that it happens more often with the women.

No. As a matter of fact, in my honest opinion, there's never been a woman artist of the very first rank.

Certainly, Cassatt did some rather fine things. But even her best work is a bit derivative, isn't it? And when you compare her to her contemporaries, her masters: Manet, Renoir. Well, now, really —

O'Keeffe? Yes, she's very popular just now. And of course she was a remarkable personality. But just between us, Miss Alter, isn't there something a little forced there, a little slick? Those smooth flat surfaces, those creamy pastels; rather like the American advertising art of the thirties, I've always thought.

No, I was very glad to show Lorin's work. She had a definite talent, and her paintings were accessible. A dealer can't always fill his gallery with masterpieces, you know.

Well of course there are many anomalies in nature. I wouldn't want to predict that there never will be one. But essentially I think it goes against the grain. It is the same in music and the theater. Women have been magnificent performers, oh yes. Singers, concert artists, dancers, actresses; because it is natural for the woman to display herself. But as composers, or dramatists — well, you know as well as I do —

In literature, yes, to some extent. But then a novel or a poem is a kind of performance, is it not? And even so, the highest level of achievement is very rare. You see, it goes against the grain. A real woman, like my wife, she doesn't have the impulse to create works of art; she is a work of art.

Yes, I have heard that argument.

Please, don't mistake me. I said nothing about critics; women have excelled at criticism for centuries, unfortunately.

If you want to believe that, of course it is your privilege.

I really can't answer that question, I'm afraid.

I have no idea; and I do not sit here to listen to insults of my profession.

All right, Miss Alter, you are sorry; very well. But excuse me, I don't give you any more time now. I'm expecting a client.

I suppose you could try calling my secretary next week. She may be able to set up another appointment.

2

Two weeks later, in one of those West Village bistros that strive to resemble a country-house garden, with sand-blasted brick walls, rough scrubbed pine chairs and tables, and rampant ivy and pink geraniums, Polly sat opposite Lorin Jones's half brother, Professor Leonard Zimmern. It was the first time in months that she'd been alone in a restaurant with a man, and not her own idea. She had proposed interviewing Zimmern in his office at the university, but he had refused, saying that there would be too many damn interruptions. Maybe so, but it would have been more professional.

From her dealings with him at the time of the show, "Three American Women," Polly knew Lennie Zimmern to be a difficult person, moody and given to cutting remarks. He was tall and thin, with a short pointed gray beard like a man in an Elizabethan miniature, theatrical dark eyebrows, strongly marked features, and a sharp, ironic expression. So far today he had been agreeable enough; but why the hell shouldn't he be? He was Lorin Jones's nearest surviving relative, and the owner of all her unsold paintings; it was in his interest that they should become better known and therefore more and more marketable.

As soon as they had been served coffee, Polly opened a spiral notebook containing a list of prepared questions, ranged in decreasing order of harmlessness according to the advice given her by a friend who was a professional jour-nalist. Then she set her tape recorder on the plastic placemat with its view of Warwick Castle. Lennie, like all her pre-vious interviewees, flinched slightly at the sight. He sat back and straightened his spine, confronting her more squarely.

For a while everything went well enough. Lennie answered the easy questions without hesitation, supplying dates, addresses, and the names of relatives and schools. But when Polly started to ask about Lorin Jones's parents he began to speak more slowly and give short, unhelpful replies. ("Sorry, I don't recall . . . I don't remember, really . . . It's a long time ago.")

"Can't you tell me any more?" she asked as persuasively as she could. "You said just now that you visited your father's new family fairly often."

"Not all that often. It was a long trip from Queens, and my mother wasn't all that keen on my making it." He smiled sourly.

"But you must remember something of what it was like there."

Lennie smiled briefly sideways, not exactly in Polly's direction, and shook his head.

"Really? . . . I find that hard to believe." She waited, but he merely shrugged and took another sip of espresso. "I'm beginning to get the feeling that you don't want me to write about your sister," she said finally, not quite in control of her tone for the first time.

"I don't want you to write the kind of personal things you've been asking for; no. In my view, it's far too soon for anything like an analytic biography."

"But you said — you agreed —" Remembering what had happened with Paolo Carducci, she tried to keep the indignation out of her voice. Jeanne was right; she wasn't going to get anywhere that way.

"I agreed to the idea of a book on Laura, yes. But what I assumed you had in mind was a study of her paintings — an extension of what you wrote in the catalogue."

"Well, of course I'm planning to discuss the paintings," Polly said, trying to remain calm.

"I think you should concentrate on that." Lennie smiled in an irritating way. "On the professional side of her life."

Don't tell me what to concentrate on, Polly thought angrily. But she feigned docility and began to ask about

Lorin Jones's early years. Did she show artistic talent as a child, did she win prizes, did her parents and her teachers recognize her ability and encourage her? "Yeah, I think so," Lennie kept saying; but he wouldn't provide any details.

"You're not helping much, you know," she told him finally.

"I know. I'm trying, but you've got to remember we grew up apart, and I was nearly five years older than Laura. It wasn't until she'd finished college and was studying in New York that we really got acquainted."

"So you didn't know her all that well as a little girl," Polly said, trying to give the appearance of believing this.

"No. But I don't think anyone did. Laura was extremely shy, you know. Especially with older people. When I visited my father's house, most of the time she'd be up in her room, or out in the garden playing with her dolls under the lilac bushes. Or making up stories and singing them to herself, or drawing — yeah, I do remember her drawing sometimes."

"And would you say she was a happy child?"

"Happy?" Lennie squinted past Polly and the bleached brick wall of the restaurant, into some lost space.

Now he's going to tell me, Polly thought; making an effort, she said nothing more. But when Lennie looked back at her, his jaw was set. "As I believe I mentioned before," he said, heavily ironic, "I don't see the point of questions like that. Who knows what happiness is for anyone else?"

"Mmh," Polly agreed, disagreeing.

"Anyhow, it's unimportant, in my view, whether or not an artist was happy as a child. Or as an adult, for that matter." He gave a harsh laugh. "Suppose Laura wasn't happy? Telling everyone about it now won't do her any good. And people who are still alive could be hurt."

"People who are alive?" Polly asked, thinking at once of Lorin Jones's principal persecutors. "Do you mean her dealer, or Garrett Jones? Or do you mean Hugh Cameron?"

"I don't mean anyone. That was a general comment."

Lying, you're lying, Polly thought with rage, but managed with great effort not to say. "I see."

Lennie laughed sourly. "If you want to know, I wasn't thinking of any of them. I suppose I was thinking of myself. I'm in no hurry to read about how mean I was to my little sister."

"And were you mean to your little sister?" she asked as casually as possible.

"About as often as most boys, I expect." Again he gazed past Polly. *Give them enough rope,* Jeanne's voice whispered inside her head, *and they'll hang themselves.*

"Well, go on," Lennie said abruptly, using the rope she had given him as a lash rather than a noose. "What are you waiting for?"

"Nothing — I —"

"If you're expecting some sensational tale of child abuse, forget it." He grinned mockingly at her. "That's what you were hoping for, wasn't it? Your eyes were positively popping."

Polly's hands tightened on her notebook, becoming fists. "If you don't want to answer a question, then don't," she said as politely as she could manage, which was not very politely.

Lennie stopped grinning. "Let me make my position clear, okay?" he said in a weary lecturing voice. "I'm not principally concerned for my own reputation." (The hell you're not, she thought.) "But I really despise the current fashion for exposing the private lives of artists and writers. Nothing is gained for literature when we learn that someone cheated on his taxes or his wife. That's not the point; the point is the text, the work."

"But what we know about an artist's life can usually tell us something about the work," Polly protested.

"So you say. But how often does it really? If you want to know what I think —"

"Yes, sure," she lied.

"I think this passion for revealing the most intimate and embarrassing details about well-known people is a by-product of envy. They must be exposed as flawed or unhappy, to deflect the rage we feel against them for their gifts, their fame. We can only stand the idea that van Gogh, or Virginia Woolf, say, was a genius and we're not, if we keep reminding ourselves that they were miserable most of the time. Psychotic even."

"You may be right," Polly said, employing the all-purpose phrase suggested to her for such moments by Jeanne. In her own mouth it sounded thin and phony, but Lennie seemed not to notice.

"And it's not only artists and writers. It's the same with all celebrities. We want to hear how beautiful and brilliant and rich and successful such people are; but we also want to hear what terrible childhoods they had and how they've been wretchedly poor or ill, or alcoholic, or frustrated in love. There's always going to be a residue of envy though, even so, unless the celebrity comes to a bad end. So what we really want is for them to kill themselves, or get themselves murdered, or die horribly of drink or drugs or cancer. Then our envy and hatred are satisfied, and our love can be pure."

"Maybe," Polly said, silently rejecting his theory. She didn't envy or hate Lorin Jones; she loved and admired her. Maybe that's the way it is for people like you, she thought. "But that's not what my book's going to be like," she added aloud.

"No? What will it be like, then, Polly?" Lennie leaned across the table, fixing his bright dark eyes on hers, and giving her a penetrating smile. "I know," he said, grinning. "It's going to be a no-holds-barred indictment of the patriarchal system. Isn't that right?"

Polly's immediate impulse was to tell Lennie to go to hell and walk out. But she checked herself; she had to get on with him, because among other things he held the copyright on Lorin Jones's work. He knows it, too, she thought furiously.

Seeing from her face that his guess was correct, Lennie grinned more broadly. "Lolly as an unrecognized genius destroyed by the male establishment, that's the idea, isn't it?"

"And what if it's true?" Polly burst out. "But I suppose

you wouldn't see it that way, would you?" she added more coolly, trying to match his infuriatingly detached tone.

"I don't know how I see it," Lennie replied after a pause. "All I know is, nothing's that simple."

Since Polly could hardly object to this truism, she did not reply. For a few moments the tape recorder whispered on, preserving the dissonances of dishes clattering, blurred voices, and Manhattan traffic.

"Listen, Polly," Lennie began again, speaking now without irony, and smiling at her with a patronizing intimacy that had no basis in their relationship. "I've known you awhile now; let me give you some advice. Forget the idea of writing a biography of my sister. You've got her paintings, that's all you need to make a good book. Besides, if you go on the way you're going, you could find out things about Laura you don't want to know."

You mean I could find out things you don't want me to know, Polly thought. She made a meaningless noise — the gas escaping from the pressure of holding down this and other angry speeches.

"Think about it." Lennie looked directly into her eyes and put a sinewy brown hand, furred with dark hair, on hers. "All right?"

Polly snatched her hand away. "All right, I'll think about it," she said, internally vowing not to.

But during the long ride home on the bus, Polly did think about it; or rather, she thought about Lennie Zimmern. How dared he tell her what to write? How dared he try to come on to her? And not for the first time, either. On more than one occasion in the past she had caught Lennie giving her this same calculated, intense, half-erotic look — a look that said, *How about it?*

What made it more infuriating was that Leonard Zimmern was exactly the sort of egotistic, willful man that Polly once used to get involved with. And though she had never given him the least encouragement, it was as if he somehow knew this, and could plug into her neurosis whenever he wanted to.

For it was a neurosis, Polly knew that now; and one with its roots in her earliest childhood. If you could really learn from experience, she would have learned to distrust this type years ago, by observing her father, who was totally undependable. He was now on his third wife, Polly's mother having been the first.

It might have been better, Polly sometimes thought, if her father had just walked out of her life for good when she was four; she would probably have adjusted to that more easily. But instead, for the next five years, Carl Alter kept turning up — though never reliably — to take his daughter out for the day. And Polly's mother, Bea, always made her go with him. She had read somewhere that almost any father was better than none, and she believed then — and still believed — almost everything she read if the author was a man and was called Doctor.

How often Polly had mutinied, as if she knew instinctively how hurtful the experience would be! How she had balked and protested when her father appeared at the front door of their row house! Even after she'd heard the bell she would sulk in her room, deliberately not changing into the "nice clean dress" laid out on the bed. Her mother would call again and again, her voice growing shriller and more anxious; finally she would come upstairs to pull off Polly's T-shirt and jeans, drag a brush through her matted brown curls, and cram her unwilling body into the freshly ironed nice dress, pleading in whispers with her daughter to be reasonable, to cooperate.

Usually, Polly would clumsily let herself be got ready. But sometimes, without knowing it was coming, she would have one of her temper tantrums. She would feel her face getting hot, and then suddenly her head would be full of big noisy black horseflies like the ones at her grandparents' farm, buzzing and stinging, and she would hear herself shout: "I won't go, I won't!" and before she knew it she would be screaming and kicking the floor. Even today those flies were still in her head somewhere, Polly knew, and sometimes they rose and swarmed.

When Polly was finally ready, Bea would give her a little shove out the door, and she would stump down the faded, fuzzy-striped stair carpet, looking as cross and ugly as she knew how. Which was fairly cross and ugly, for even when she was a child Polly's small stubborn chin, straight dark brows, and high coloring lent themselves well to angry moods.

As she followed her father along the gritty sidewalk, scuffing her patent-leather Mary Janes on purpose against the frost-heaved blocks of cement, Polly wouldn't even look at him. She would make her way as slowly as possible toward his stupid beat-up old car, a prewar Ford coupe that the previous owner had daubed a streaked chalky yellow with housepaint; it was known as The Yellow Peril. Her father used the back seat as a combined wastebasket and laundry basket, and it was always littered with empty beer cans, squashed cellophane and silver-paper packets of Camels, old newspapers, and grimy shirts and towels and socks.

Polly would ignore the smile and flourish with which Carl Alter held open the door of The Yellow Peril for her. She wanted to hurt him, she knew that now: to punish him for being such a crummy father, for ruining her whole day, for not coming to see her sooner, for leaving her in the first place. Okay, she might have to go with him, because of what Bea Alter referred to as "the legal agreement." If she didn't, Polly half believed back then, both she and her mother could be arrested and sent to jail. But she wasn't going to like anything her father might show her or tell her or give her. So there.

What followed, every time, was an elaborate process of wooing. Never since those days had Polly been courted with such skill, charm, invention, and indulgent patience — the art had probably died out, and just as well. Her father never made any comment on her flushed face or bad temper. He rattled on as they drove away, telling jokes and stories, whistling or singing:

> Over the white and drifting snow
> A ghostly voice came calling:
> "Where are you going to, Polly-O?
> Where are you going this morning?"

He never seemed to notice that she didn't answer, or that she was sitting in an angry bundle with her arms tight to her sides, as far away from him as possible on the ripped yellow-straw seat covers that always scratched her legs.

"Hey, Polly-O, look at that crazy red dog running round in circles ... that funny sign on the truck over there," Carl Alter would call out as The Yellow Peril, its exhausted exhaust system coughing and roaring, jolted its way down Mamaroneck Avenue. Or, "Knock-knock —" and after a stubborn silence from his daughter, supplying her line, "Who's there? ... Victor." Polly would squinch her eyes shut; she would set her jaw so as not to ask "Victor who?" She would vow not to give in.

But in the end she never could keep it up. Her father always knew so many funny new jokes; he thought of such surprising things to do. She would resist him as long as she could, but it was no use: a giggle would escape her at the punchline of a shaggy-dog story; or without meaning to she would find herself running beside him when he chased the pigeons in front of the courthouse, calling, "Come on, Polly-O! If you catch one, they'll let you keep it." What a stupid thing for a grown-up to do, she thought a few years later; how dumb he must have looked, that tall rumpled awkward man, running after a pigeon through the dry fallen leaves and waving his long arms around, and Polly-O stumbling after him, probably looking really dumb, too. Nobody can catch a bird. So why did he shout for everyone to hear, "That's it, Polly-O! You almost had him that time!"

But then he praised whatever she did, no matter how silly it was. At Rye Beach, when she bit off the end of her waffle-pattern cone and started sucking the strawberry ice cream out through the hole, the way her mother couldn't stand, and made as awful a noise as she could on purpose, her father didn't mind. He just said, "Hey, that looks like fun. How do you do it?" And then he proved such a slow learner, so uproariously inept and messy, that Polly had to burst out laughing. It was years before it occurred to her that he must have been playing dumb on purpose to amuse her.

Her father took her to all kinds of weird places, often on jobs he was working at the moment. He wrote detective stories, and someday, he explained to Polly, he was going to be rich and famous, but right now he had to get by the best he could, and do whatever he could to keep body and soul together. Would they separate otherwise? Polly couldn't help asking. "Well, sure; they might." Polly knew he was kidding, but she couldn't help imagining the soul part of her father drifting up into the air over Westchester and floating off sideways. It would look just like him, she imagined, with the same lumpy face and big brown eyes and untidy black hair, only sort of smoky and transparent like the ghosts in Saturday-morning movies.

Carl Alter took Polly to a junior high school where he was a substitute teacher, and to the offices of a magazine in Mount Vernon that printed pictures of naked ladies, and to the back part of the New Rochelle library, where worn books were rebound and there was a smell of glue and dust. When he was driving a taxi in White Plains he let her ride in the front seat with him. For a while he was working for the Fuller Brush Company, and drove around back streets selling brooms and mops and hairbrushes to ladies in three-decker wooden houses with pictures of Jesus over the sofa. Her father talked to them in an eager, grateful voice, not like his real one. They called him "young man," and gave Polly things to eat and drink she wasn't allowed at home: fig newtons, and powdery pastel Nabisco wafers, and iced tea with wet gray sugar in the bottom of the glass. Carl Alter didn't have Mommie's rules about nourishing food, or about not talking to strangers or telling them personal things. ("Yep, ma'am, this big girl is my daughter, would you believe it? She just won a prize for the best Memorial Day poster in her class.")

By the end of the afternoon Polly would be wholly lost. She would climb back into The Yellow Peril, slide across the broken straw stubble, and lean against her father as he drove back along Mamaroneck Avenue, feeling how large and solid and warm he was underneath the old cord jacket with the shiny leather patches on the elbows. When he spoke, she would turn up to him a face lit with the wide amazed smile that had always been her — and his — best feature.

But as they sat in their favorite booth in the coffee shop on Main Street, with a cherry Coke for Polly and a beer for Carl Alter, he would begin to shift about on the bench, to turn and look around the room. If he saw people he knew he would call and wave at them to come over. And even if he didn't, he'd stop hearing what Polly was telling him. Soon, too soon, he would scoop his change from the wet wooden tabletop and tell her to drink up; he would say that her mother would be wondering where the hell she'd got to.

On the ride home her father would be almost silent, or whistling in a thin, tuneless way. He would gun the engine and stutter through yellow lights, as if he couldn't wait to get there and be rid of Polly. When he stopped the car at the house he sometimes wouldn't even go around to open the door for her — he would just reach across and yank on the pitted chrome handle. "So long, Polly-O, see you next week, same time," he would say, but often that was a lie.

Once she had had some therapy, of course, Polly realized that she had still been in love with her father all those years, and furious at him for abandoning her, for forcing her to grow up in a family she didn't belong in. She told herself that it was the chase, the effort of wooing, perhaps even the novelty of being refused, that had engaged Carl Alter's attention. When he knew himself secure in his daughter's love he became restive, in fact bored with her. Because that was how men were. They'd do anything to persuade you into caring for them, trusting them, giving up your independence, taking on what they used to call — not that most of them would dare use the phrase nowadays — "the feminine role." And then once you were really caught, once you'd cut your options and were helpless and dependent, economically or emotionally or both, they disengaged as fast as they could.

With Elsa's help Polly had slowly moved toward forgiving her father, at least intellectually, for the way he had behaved when she was a child. She had taught herself to remember that he wasn't much more than a child himself — only twenty-two when she was born, an embarrassing six months after the hurried shotgun wedding of two college students who hardly knew each other. Polly was barely a year old when Carl Alter was drafted into the army, and it was two years after that before he came home to stay. Many young guys in his position, she had to admit, would have decided to forget that they had ever had a daughter.

But Polly still couldn't forgive her father for the way he had behaved later on, after her mother married Bob Milner and they moved to Rochester. She couldn't forgive him for not writing more often, or for coming to see her only twice a year, and sometimes not even that. Carl Alter was living in Boston then, but it wasn't that far, she used to think, opening the atlas and running her finger across green Massachusetts and pink New York State. It wasn't as if she were in Texas, or Alaska.

After a while Polly had decided she didn't care whether her father came to Rochester or not. He was an embarrassment, anyhow, with his broken promises, his unsteady jobs, his unpressed clothes and his battered old cars (The Yellow Peril had died, but it was succeeded by vehicles of the same genus, The Black Death and The White Whale). She decided she was really glad when he went to work on a small-town newspaper in California, across a whole checkerboard of colored states, because she wouldn't have to bother with him at all anymore.

By the time she reached high school Polly had realized

that Carl Alter not only seldom came to see her, he never sent any money for her support. It used to make her furious that her mother wasn't angry about this.

"I don't see why you want me to write to him," she had complained once. "I don't see why you can even stand him, after the way he's treated us."

"Oh, well," Bea Milner said, with her characteristic smiling sigh. "It's not his fault, you know. Carl never had any money; probably never will."

"It's his fault that he married you and then deserted you," Polly insisted.

"Oh no, darling. You mustn't think that way. It was nobody's fault. We were both so young, and we didn't think about the future. Things happen, that's all."

Which was typical of how her mother's mind worked, Polly thought as the bus ground its way through Columbus Circle. Bea Milner was a classic example of the unliberated woman. Men, and what men wanted, always had priority with her. When Bob Milner proposed to her she probably didn't even ask herself what it would mean to her daughter, or mind that it would be the end of her own career. And, like the virtuous heroines of Victorian literature, she would not bear a grudge, especially against a man; she was infuriatingly forgiving. A college junior gets a freshman pregnant, so that she has to drop out of school to be married, and then he leaves her, and all the effort and expense of the next twenty years fall on her, and that's just how Things Happen.

For years Polly thought she had learned everything she needed to know from her mother's mistakes. So, even though what she wanted in high school was to be a painter, she took care to finish college and then take a degree in art history: she wasn't going to end up a glorified secretary like Bea. And when she began to go out with boys, she was careful not to catch a baby.

But, having forgotten her painful early attachment, Polly was condemned to repeat it. Over and over again she became involved with unreliable men. Usually they were Jewish, and often they had something to do with art or literature, like Carl Alter. Or, of course, like Leonard Zimmern.

At home everything was as she had left it that morning: bed unmade, dishes in the sink, yesterday's *Times* on the sitting-room floor, and a general look of dust and emptiness.

The apartment was also empty in more than the psychological sense; and this was Polly's own fault, the result of one of her fits of bad temper. During that awful spring a year ago Jim had asked if it would be okay for him to ship his desk to Colorado, and Polly had shouted that as far as she was concerned he could have anything in the place he wanted. Jim must have known she'd spoken rashly, but he had taken her at her word. Saying that he hoped she would soon follow, he decamped to Denver with nearly half their furniture, plus one of the two signed Rauschenberg lithographs and the little Frankenthaler that had been their wedding present to each other. After he had gone, the apartment looked like someone who had been in an accident: its walls were scarred with lines of dust where bookcases and bureaus had stood, and further up by tender pale rectangles with a blackened nail hole in the center of each, like skin where bandages have been ripped off over a half-healed puncture wound.

Even now, the rooms were half bare. Polly had read recently that after a divorce the man's standard of living goes up by an average of seventy percent, while the woman's is reduced by half. It hadn't been that drastic for her; but even with Stevie's child support she hadn't been able to replace most of the kidnapped objects, and she'd let the housekeeper go this summer when she left her job. As long as she had Stevie, she didn't really care about the stuff, but now —

"I want my pictures and furniture back," she cried aloud. "I want my son back, damn it."

Talking to herself. Well, they said that was what happened when you lived alone: you became eccentric. Polly had also noticed that her mood swings were wider: she was up one day, down the next, as if she were on a roller coaster, with the same sense of giddiness and danger.

Stevie had been gone only two weeks, but already she was miserably sick of living alone. And this was just the start. For the next three months she would be wandering in a funk around this big empty apartment without even the Museum to go to. Nothing moved here now unless she moved it; nobody spoke unless Polly spoke to herself, or turned on the radio to fill the rooms with the lively voices of totally deaf people. When she talked back to them, even shouted at some idiotic ad man or cheered some commentator on "All Things Considered," they didn't answer; it was as if she didn't exist. Of course, Polly wasn't crazy: she knew they couldn't hear her, but all the same it gave her a bad, slightly insane feeling, as if she had disappeared.

Now that Stevie was gone, nothing happened day after day except the interviews for her book; at least, nothing serious or interesting to think about. Sometimes Lorin Jones's life seemed realer to her than her own.

If somebody else, anybody else, were living here, Polly thought, it wouldn't be so bad. And, almost in the same moment, she thought of someone who needed a place to live: Jeanne. Early this summer Jeanne's former apartment building had gone condo, and she'd had to move. At the moment she was camped out in a Queens sublet: two tiny low-ceilinged basement rooms whose honking radiators, flaking walls, and invasions of bugs she often mentioned with a sigh.

Jeanne kept looking at other apartments, but the housing shortage, even outside of Manhattan, was awful and getting worse: so far, anything she could afford on her tiny academic salary had been even more objectionable than where she was now.

Why shouldn't Jeanne stay here while Stevie was away, at least until she found a place of her own? They would be company for each other, and it would save them both money — and without Polly's child-support payments that would really make a difference. Besides, it made no sense for them to clean two apartments and cook two sets of solitary meals; that was pure waste of time, especially for Jeanne, who was a gourmet cook. It was a great idea, and there was no argument against it that Polly could think of, except — and here she scowled and let the frying pan she had been scouring slide back under the dishwater suds — what people might think.

Since Jim left, Polly hadn't had any serious relationship; Stevie had been the only important person in her life. If Jeanne moved in with her now, some of her friends would assume that they were sexually involved, and that Polly had become a lesbian too — after all, she'd talked enough about how she might be through with men for good. She had even said sometimes that she wished she were gay, because lesbian couples seemed to behave more decently than heterosexual ones.

And what would they think in Colorado? It wouldn't occur to Stevie to wonder if his mother was a lesbian, but it would probably occur to Jim, who knew Jeanne and didn't care for her. Jim would confide his suspicions to his new wife, a woman Polly had never met but naturally detested. *Yeah, maybe you're right,* this detestable woman would say. *I wouldn't be surprised; from what you tell me, Polly was always a man-hater.*

Well, the hell with them all, Polly told herself, scrubbing the frying pan again with noisy vigor. She wasn't going to begin arranging her life again in terms of Jim's opinions, or anyone else's.

PROFESSOR MARY ANN FENN,

University of Connecticut

It was such a long time ago. I'd almost forgotten about her, really. Then — it was an odd, odd experience, painful in a way. I was in New York for a professional meeting last winter, as I told you in my letter. And I went to that show of yours, "Three American Women." I was busy, but I made a point of going, because I was interested. I believe that women artists have new things to say to all of us. Important things.

Well, I was walking around the galleries, and I got to Lorin Jones's pictures. I thought they were attractive. Unusual. The colors were interesting, subtle. But I saw them as abstractions, and I've never cared much for abstract art.

Then I read the title of that picture: *Princess Elinore of the White Meadows.* Well, it gave me a shock. In elementary school, when I was eight or nine, I and my best friend made up fairy-tale identities for ourselves: I was Princess Miranda of the Larch Mountains, because I lived in Larchmont, and she was Princess Elinore of the White Meadows. I thought, could it be? I mean, either this Lorin Jones was my friend Lolly Zimmern, or it was a fantastic coincidence.

Well, I stepped back and looked at the picture for clues, and suddenly I saw that the pale green splotches of paint at the bottom could be meant for grass, and the sprinkling of white and yellow dots over them could be daisies. Then the bigger gray splotches higher up might be clouds. And the jumble of sticks and blots and veils of color in the middle was really a lot like the way a tree would look if you were up in it, and the wind was blowing hard. Or it could have been a fairy-tale castle. And that was right, because we used to climb trees and make believe they were castles.

Yes, or sometimes sailing ships. I'd forgotten about all that, but there in the gallery — it was like the uneven pavement in Proust, you know — it all came back to me, from — my lord, it must be fifty years ago. The hot nearly white summer sky, and how it felt to hold on to the rough speckled branches of the apple tree, and the little hard shiny green apples, like sourballs. And I remembered how the wind would toss us around, only we pretended it was ocean waves. And the clouds going by would be fish. All kinds of fish, whales, and schools of porpoises, and mackerel. Yes, especially mackerel, because there was a picture of a mackerel sky in our science book at school.

I had to be sure, so I practically ran downstairs — I didn't even wait for the elevator — and bought a catalogue. And there it was: Lorin Jones, born in nineteen-twenty-six in White Plains, New York. It had to be her. Well, I thought that was wonderful, and I began to plan how I'd write her a note, and tell her I'd seen her pictures. I'd ask the Museum to forward it, and we'd meet again after fifty years.

Then I read on down the page: where Lolly had gone to school, and the shows she'd had, and I turned the page over, and read a list of the collections her work was in. And then I saw: Died in nineteen-sixty-nine, in Key West, Florida. I just started crying, right there in the lobby of the Museum. I had to go and sit down on the bench by the door. I was so upset that I hadn't known what had happened to her, and I hadn't ever tried to find her again. I hadn't done anything.

Yes, we were best friends for a couple of years. But then in fifth grade Lolly's parents suddenly took her out of Westwind School. She just disappeared one day.

I don't know why. My mother said years afterward that something happened that fall at the Parents' Day picnic, after we'd gone home. Something went wrong. She didn't know what exactly, but she'd heard Lolly had been badly frightened by something. Or someone.

Some sexual thing, she implied. But I'm not sure that was it really. My mother liked to imagine almost everything as sexual.

Oh yes, everybody called her Lolly back then. That's how I always think of her now. Lolly Zimmern, ten years old. She's up in the apple tree, seeing everything you can see in that painting, pushing the branches apart and looking out between the leaves. With her dark wavy hair tangled and blowing, and her white thin face.

3

"Could I help you?" A slight, colorless young man, who looked in need of help himself, drifted across the half-lit Apollo Gallery to where Polly Alter and her rubberized poncho stood dripping rain onto the polished parquet floor.

"I have an appointment with Jacky Herbert. At ten." Polly checked her watch, holding out her wet wrist so that he could see, if he cared to look, that it was already five minutes past the hour.

"I'm sorry; I don't think Mr. Herbert's come in yet."

"I suppose I'll have to wait, then," she said, not trying to disguise her annoyance. She turned her back on him and wandered toward the front of the gallery, where a sodden gray October light pressed against the streaming glass of the picture window, giving the scene outside the look of an aquarium. Swollen, bug-eyed metal fish crowded and honked for positions on Madison Avenue, and umbrellas bobbed and dodged like multicolored marine plants.

Polly was cross not only at Jacky Herbert but — and more seriously — at herself. After her uncomfortable and unfinished interview with Paolo Carducci, the owner of the Apollo Gallery, she had put off calling for another appointment. She might never interview Carducci again now, because he had had a stroke which had left him, according to report, half-paralyzed and almost speechless. With a frail man in his late seventies, she should have known better than to lose either her temper or a single day. She would have to make do now with Jacky, the acting director of the gallery, who had only begun to work there just before Lorin Jones's final show.

Becoming more and more bored and angry, she turned

from the window to inspect an uninteresting collection of formalist still lifes. Outwardly the Apollo Gallery, once one of the most successful in New York, looked much as it did when Polly first visited it twenty years ago. It still kept its premises above an expensive antique shop in the East Seventies, and served coffee from its mammoth, convoluted espresso machine. But in the last two decades the gallery had gradually yielded its dominant position. More aggressive dealers had taken over entire floors of Fifty-seventh Street skyscrapers, or moved into Soho warehouses with enough wall and floor space to house the largest and most aggressive works. The Apollo continued to show what, comparatively, could almost be described as easel painting. It still represented many established artists, and had loyal and wealthy customers; but it was no longer on the cutting edge of American art.

"Polly!" Jacky Herbert called. He circled the reception desk and moved toward her with his characteristic tiptoe gait, which gave the effect of speed without its usual results. "So lovely to see you." Jacky was, as always, elegantly dressed: his suit and shirt and tie, in shades of glossy pale gray, fit as smoothly as sealskin. Also, he looked quite dry; either he had been here all along, or he had taken a taxi to the gallery instead of standing in the downpour waiting for a bus like Polly. "How have you been?" He bent and rubbed a soft shaved cheek smelling of lime toilet water against hers, and made goldfish kissing sounds in the air.

"Fine, thanks." Polly did not make a kissing sound; she despised this mode of greeting; besides, Jacky had made her wait nearly fifteen minutes for no good reason. "How about you?"

"Oh, getting along." Jacky gestured dismissively. He was a bulky man with grayed yellow hair, plump white ringed hands, shrewd flat gray eyes, and the handsome ruined profile of a Roman empress. In his youth he was said to have been a great beauty. Gossip attributed his remarkable collection of modern art to his early powers of seduction, and perhaps even of barter. Whatever the truth of this story, Jacky now lived an almost blameless life with a retired concert pianist named Tommy.

"And how is Mr. Carducci doing?"

Jacky made a tsk sound and shook his head slowly.

"Do they think he's going to recover?"

"The doctor won't say." Jacky's large pale face quivered. "I expect he doesn't know himself. But I have to admit Paolo looked rather dreadful when I saw him day before yesterday."

"That's too bad," Polly said, without feeling.

"We can always hope, that's what I tell myself. Well now." He forced a smile. "How about a tiny cup of coffee?"

"Okay. That'd be nice."

"Marvelous," Jacky said sadly, meaninglessly. He waved one flipper for her to follow him into the back room.

"Here, let me," he added as Polly began to struggle out of her poncho. "Goodness, it's absolutely sopping." He gave the rectangle of rubberized canvas a shake that seemed to express disapproval of more than its condition. "Now I'm going to hang this up right by the radiator, so it'll be lovely and dry when you leave. And why don't you give me that wet scarf, too?"

"Okay; thanks." She handed over a sodden red-and-black rag; Jacky hung it carefully, yet with an indefinable air of distaste, over a collating frame.

"Now shall we go into my office, where we won't be disturbed?... Good. Alan!" he called to the colorless young man. "Two cups of espresso, please. And no calls, please, for the next hour, unless it's a serious buyer.

"So, how is it going?" he said, shutting the door and pulling forward an Eames chair for Polly. He leaned toward her over the desk, smiling with his large white perfectly capped teeth.

"Oh, pretty well." Polly didn't smile; Jacky's fussy concern for her comfort, as if she were a possible client, hadn't mollified her, but made her more suspicious. What was he going to try to sell her?

"I'm so pleased. You know, Paolo said before his

stroke — Well, I think he was surprised, rather, that you hadn't come to see him again. He wondered if you were making any progress. And he said that perhaps we should try to interest some writer with more experience." Jacky flapped his hands deprecatingly. "But I said no, it has to be someone who hasn't got so many other interests. Someone who can take the time to interview everyone: go to Wellfleet to see Garrett and down to the Keys to talk to that awful Hugh Cameron. And I'm convinced it should be a woman, too. Polly is the right person. That's what I told him." Jacky smiled. "Oh, that's lovely, Alan." He took the "tiny cup of coffee," which in his big pale hand looked literally tiny.

"Well, thanks," Polly said grudgingly. Why was Jacky telling her this? To flatter her and convince her that he was on her side? To make her feel nervous and dependent on him? Or both?

"Sugar?"

"Yes, please." Polly held out her cup, then lifted the steaming espresso to her mouth and swallowed uneasily. Since Jacky Herbert was a man, she automatically distrusted him. He was also, of course, an art dealer, and — like most museum people — she was professionally suspicious of dealers. She knew that Jacky was currently engaged in gathering as many Lorin Jones canvases as he could find, with a view to selling them at large prices eighteen months from now when Polly's book appeared — indeed, he made no secret of this.

On the other hand Jacky (unlike Paolo Carducci) had always been lavish with praise of Jones's work. More than once he had castigated himself in Polly's hearing for not doing anything sooner about her paintings.

Also, like many people in the New York art world, Jacky was gay, and Polly didn't usually distrust gay men. It was clear that some of them, like Jacky, would have preferred to have been born women if they'd been given the choice. Besides, she sympathized with them because, like her, they were so often attracted to the wrong type of guy.

"You've been interviewing Lennie Zimmern, I hear,"

Jacky remarked after his assistant had left. "Hard work, I should imagine." He made a wry face.

"Well; yes, rather. He doesn't approve of personal biography."

"He wouldn't." Jacky giggled. "Wouldn't want his own written, I'd imagine. And whom else have you seen? Did you talk to what's-her-name, Marcia, the father's widow?"

"I saw her briefly. I didn't learn a hell of a lot, though. You know Lorin Jones never lived with her, and they obviously weren't close. I'm not sure I'll bother to see her again."

"I think you might, you know." Jacky leaned forward.

"I don't know. A friend of mine who works for *Time* says you should always go back for a second interview if you can. And bring a present, so they'll feel obligated."

"That sounds like good advice," Jacky agreed. "I expect Marcia could tell you a lot, if she wanted to."

"Maybe. There was something I meant to ask you about her, anyhow. Why aren't there any of Lorin Jones's pictures in her apartment? I mean, I already knew she didn't have any, because we asked at the time of the show; but don't you think that's a little odd?"

"I don't know that I do," Jacky said. "I remember Marcia telling me that after her husband died Lorin came over and packed up all the paintings she had stored there, and shipped them down to Florida. Except of course *Who Is Coming?*"

"Yes, I remember." Lorin Jones's paintings tended to have mysterious, equivocal titles; one of Polly's most difficult tasks would be to discover their meanings, if any.

"Of course that's in the Palca Collection now; Paolo sold it for Marcia after Dan Zimmern died. It was Lorin's wedding present to them, you know."

"She never told me that." The truth and nothing but the truth, Polly thought, but not the whole truth. "I'm surprised she wanted to sell it, considering."

"I expect she had to. I doubt that her husband left her

anything to speak of. Money never stuck to his fingers, from what I've heard."

"I wish I could have met Lorin Jones's father. You knew him, didn't you?" Polly bent to open her wet briefcase and take out her tape recorder. "Hang on a minute while I start this thing, if you don't mind."

Jacky visibly hesitated, then smiled rapidly. "No, go ahead. You've already promised to let me edit the transcript, remember? In writing." He giggled to take the edge off this caution. "If I'm indiscreet I can cut it out later, right?"

"Yeah, right," Polly agreed.

"Well, let's see then; what were you asking? Dan Zimmern. I met him three or four times, that's all, when Lorin had her last show here in sixty-four. He was at the opening, shaking everyone's hand as if he were the artist himself, very proud. And then he came back afterward several times. He'd always bring friends, and talk up Lorin's work; what a famous painter she was going to be. He'd tell them they should buy one of her pictures, as an investment. I think a couple of people actually did. But he never stayed long. One minute he'd be all over the place, the next thing you knew he was gone."

Yes, Polly thought; but at least he was there. Carl Alter had never made it to her first and only one-woman show, in Rochester during her senior year of college. "What was he like?"

"Oh, a big, good-looking old fellow; full of life. Smart too, probably, but he didn't know beans about art. A macho type. He was on his third wife, and well over seventy, but still looking around, eyeing the girls at the opening."

"Really." Carl Alter too was on his third wife, his daughter thought.

"Oh, Polly. Before we go on, I must show you something." Jacky levered himself up and opened a cupboard. "Look. This just came in, from that very sweet woman in Miami I was telling you about last week. She bought it in some little nothing gallery in Key West in nineteen-sixty-

five, and she's finally decided she wants to sell it." He lifted
a sheet of tissue paper. "You can see, it's a watercolor sketch
for one of the Florida paintings that was in your show,
Empty Bay Blues. Beautiful, isn't it?"

"Oh, yes." Lorin Jones's most characteristic work hovered in a no-man's-land — a woman's land, perhaps, Polly
thought — between representation, abstraction, and surre-
alism. Even in her least readable paintings, like this one,
shapes that might be birds, fish, flowers, faces, or figures
quivered and clustered. In reviews of "Three American
Women," the artists she was most often compared with
were Larry Rivers and Odilon Redon. The large oil *Empty
Bay Blues* merely suggested layers of shore, sea, sky, and
cloud. But here, between the flow and slide of paint in the
lower third of the watercolor, was something that might be
either a lizard or a drowned woman.

"The light on the sea isn't as ultramarine as in the oil,
you see; more a kind of translucent mauve. Wonderful,
really." Jacky's face expressed a genuine if mercenary ado-
ration. "Paolo doesn't care for the late paintings, but I think
he's very very wrong."

"*Empty Bay Blues* —That was one of the paintings you
refused to show here, wasn't it?"

"Please!" Jacky's voice rose at least an octave. "It wasn't
me, I was a mere underling back then. . . . But you mustn't
blame Paolo either, dear."

"No?" Polly asked, trying not to sound skeptical, but
failing.

"Really. You mustn't put it into your book that the
Apollo behaved badly to Lorin Jones, because it simply isn't
so. Paolo carried her for years when she wasn't earning
anything to speak of."

Polly said nothing. I'll put into my book what I goddamn want to put in, she thought.

"I guess I'd better tell you how it all was, so you'll
understand. Off the record, of course." Jacky glanced at her
tape machine.

"All right," Polly agreed, affecting not to notice the direction of his gaze.

"I've never said anything about this to anyone before, by the way."

"Mm." I'll bet, she thought, for Jacky was known to some people in the New York art world as The American Broadcasting Company.

"You've got to realize. Paolo did everything he reasonably could for Lorin, because he recognized from the start that she had real talent. But the trouble that girl gave him!" Jacky shook his large Roman head slowly.

"How do you mean, trouble?"

"Well." He lowered his voice, but at the same time, fortunately, leaned forward, ensuring that the sound level on the tape would be preserved. "Between us, Lorin Jones was very very difficult to deal with."

"Oh?"

"Terribly hard even to talk to, for one thing."

"She was extremely shy," Polly protested. "Everyone knows that."

"Oh, granted. But you see, it was almost impossible to negotiate with her. Sometimes she wouldn't answer Paolo's letters for literally weeks. Or at all. In the end, he usually had to appeal to Garrett, and then Garrett would have to manage everything."

"So you didn't see much of her here," Polly prompted.

"Not usually. Most young artists, you know how it is, they like to drop in every so often, or phone, just to remind you that they exist and are hoping for a sale. But not Lorin, ever, Paolo said. And she detested talking on the telephone. I had to call her once about something, and she whispered so low I could hardly hear her."

You call that "difficult," Polly thought crossly, but did not say. She was beginning to realize that Paolo's illness might be to her advantage; that she might learn from Jacky what she would never have learned from his boss.

"But then, when she had a show, it was another story

entirely. You absolutely couldn't keep her out of the gallery. She had opinions about everything: what the announcement should look like, how the pictures should be hung, who should be invited to the opening."

And why the hell not, Polly thought. "Really." In spite of her effort, her tone was chilly.

"Let me assure you, no one values the artist's prerogatives more than Paolo does," Jacky hastened to say. "Still, there are limits. And Lorin caused him endless trouble, even the very very first time she was included in a group exhibition here. Most people her age would have been wild with joy to have two paintings in a gallery like this. But there was no sign of gratitude from Lorin, Paolo said. Or ingratitude either, one has to admit; she hardly spoke to him when she was here. All the complaints came through her husband. 'My wife doesn't think this painting really looks right next to hers' — that sort of thing."

"And would Paolo move the other painting, then?"

"Well, yes — very possibly. Of course, Garrett Jones was a very very important critic; maybe *the* most important back then. Naturally Paolo didn't want to quarrel with him. They were friends, professionally speaking — still are, of course. You know how it is. But just between us, the Joneses drove him quite to distraction. 'All right, she paints not badly,' he'd say to me. 'But there are other good young artists who don't play the neurotic unapproachable prima donna.' "

"You don't think that maybe —"

"What?"

"Well, I just wondered. I mean, suppose it was Garrett Jones who had all those complaints, really, only he put them off on his wife."

"I shouldn't think so." Jacky frowned. "I mean, you've met Garrett; he's a fairly reasonable man, for a critic. Some people think he has an exaggerated opinion of himself, but then, why shouldn't he? He's been right about the New York art scene time and time again."

Or he's forced his views on the New York art scene time and time again, Polly thought.

"And Lorin ... well ... I mean, we all know that most artists are a bit peculiar. You have to expect that, aren't I right?"

"I suppose so," Polly said, realizing that as far as Jacky knew she was not now and never had been an artist.

"Well, Lorin was very very peculiar. And after a while, even her husband couldn't cope with her."

"Really," Polly said as neutrally as she could manage.

"The main problem was, she simply wouldn't let go of her paintings. She'd agree to have work ready for a show, and Garrett would promise to make sure that she met the deadline, and then nothing would appear. Over and over, it'd be like that. You see, she never thought a canvas was finished."

"I expect that often happens," Polly said, recalling her own experience.

"Well, not that often. Occasionally. But it was much much worse with Lorin. Even when her pictures were up on the walls she couldn't let them alone. The day after her first one-woman show here, Paolo told me, he came back from lunch, and a little still life next to the elevator was gone. He thought at first that'd it'd been stolen, naturally. But it turned out that Lorin had taken it herself; she'd decided it wasn't right yet. The assistant Paolo had then had tried to reason with her, but it simply wasn't any use. She just wrenched the picture off the wall and carried it away. She never brought it back, either. But of course it was still listed in the printed brochure, and for three weeks Paolo had to answer questions about it. You can imagine how trying that was."

"Um-hm," Polly murmured, attempting to sound sympathetic. What came to her mind, though, was a red-and-gray semi-Pollock canvas in her own show, back in Rochester. As soon as she saw it at the opening, she'd wished she'd never let it out of the house. If only she'd had the courage to take the miserable thing away the next day! What Jacky had said earlier, though he probably meant it only as flattery, was true: she was the right, the only person to do this book. The more she found out, the surer she was of her instinctive understanding of what Lorin Jones must have felt and thought.

"Well, Paolo was determined *that* would never happen again, and it didn't. I expect Garrett spoke to her firmly. Anyhow, for a while she was more reasonable. But then she left him, and things really got out of hand."

"Um-hm?"

"The real trouble began with her sixty-four show, the last one. It was over a year late to start with, because Lorin couldn't make up her mind that the work was ready, as usual, and Garrett wasn't around to make her see reason. Then, just after the opening, I came in one morning, and there was Lorin Jones over by the window, with a dirty Bloomingdale's carrier bag on the floor beside her, scrubbing one of the biggest canvases with a rag soaked in turpentine, and scraping at it with a palette knife."

"Really."

"I was horrified, I can tell you." Jacky giggled. "What made it worse, I'd only met her once or twice at that point, and at first I didn't recognize her, the way she was got up — in a dirty old black sweater and her hair all over the place. I assumed I had some crazy bag lady on my hands. I thought Paolo was going to kill me first and fire me afterward."

"So what happened?"

"Well, naturally I rushed over and asked what the hell she thought she was doing. At first she wouldn't even answer. I was actually getting ready to call the police. Finally she said, 'I'm working on my painting.' As soon as I heard that whispery little voice I realized it was Lorin. I didn't even try to reason with her, I simply dashed back to the office and telephoned Paolo, and then I called her in to the phone. But he didn't make a dent on her. Well, there wasn't much he could do, really. It was still legally Lorin's painting. Luckily, she didn't ruin it; we sold it the next week."

"Why the hell should she have ruined it?" Polly nearly shouted.

"Well, it's possible," Jacky answered huffily. "I mean,

there is such a thing as overworking, or don't you agree?"

"I suppose so," she admitted, cursing herself for her outburst. Against her will, she saw the stack of muddy overworked canvases that was at this moment leaning sideways in a disused tub in the former maid's bathroom of her apartment on Central Park West. "So that's why the Apollo decided not to give Lorin Jones another show," she said, trying to make this sound reasonable.

"No no no. What finished things here was much more serious than that. Lorin's possessiveness about her work, you see, it just got worse and worse. It was pathological, I really think, poor girl. She began to think of her paintings as literally part of her, you see, and she couldn't bear to be separated from them."

"I imagine most artists feel something akin to that, in principle," Polly said — though as a matter of fact she had often wished some supernatural force would suck her old canvases out of the tub and cause them to vanish forever.

"Oh, yes; in principle. But what that meant in practice, for Lorin Jones, what it came to mean, rather, was that she wouldn't sell her work. It was all right if the buyer was a museum, or a friend, so that she could visit the painting whenever she liked. But otherwise —" Jacky sighed. "What really drove Paolo round the bend was the business of the Provincetown triptych."

"You mean *Birth, Copulation, and Death,* from the Skelly Collection?" Polly knew the painting well — it had been featured in color in the catalogue of "Three American Women" and reproduced on a postcard; certainly it was one of Jones's most important works.

"That's right. Only if it hadn't been for Paolo, it wouldn't ever have *been* in the Skelly Collection. God knows what would have happened to it." He sighed. "You see, the Skellys decided to buy *Birth, Copulation, and Death* the second week of the sixty-four show, and Paolo was really happy for Lorin. He thought she'd be grateful, naturally, to have her work in a famous collection like that. But instead she threw a fit. She'd met the Skellys at her opening, and she'd hated them. She said they never looked at the paintings, all they did was walk around the rooms kissing their friends and talking about money. They were awful people, she said, and she wasn't going to let them have anything of hers. When Paolo told her it was too late for that she went perfectly white with fury. I think if she could have she'd have taken the canvases off the wall then and there and walked out with them. But they were far too large for that, thank God."

"How upsetting."

"Wasn't it?" Jacky agreed, mistaking her meaning — which was probably just as well. "And you have to understand, Paolo was very patient with Lorin. He did everything he reasonably could; more, actually. He positively bent over backward."

"Really." In her mind, Polly saw the small, spidery figure of Paolo Carducci, with his shock of crimped gray hair, bent over backward.

"He called Bill Skelly, and asked very tactfully if they were quite quite sure they wanted the Jones triptych; he said that if not, he'd be glad to forget the whole thing."

"But they wouldn't let him, I assume."

"Bill said nothing doing. Well, actually he got rather enraged. He suspected Paolo had had an offer he liked better, maybe from some museum, and his back was up, naturally. There was a lot of bad feeling between them for a while."

"Really."

"That wasn't the worst, though. Because, you see, Lorin didn't give up even then. Instead she did something quite mad: she phoned Grace Skelly, and in her whispery little voice she offered to buy the triptych back, dealer's commission and all. And when Gracie asked why, Lorin told her. You can visualize the reaction."

"I suppose so." Polly imagined Mrs. Skelly, a handsome, expensively dressed, loud-voiced woman who attended most of the private openings at the Museum, hearing that in

Lorin Jones's opinion she was unfit to own one of her paintings.

"Well, after that Paolo literally didn't dare hang Lorin's work. I begged him to reconsider; I told him she was an utterly marvelous painter, and he should make allowances. That's what I said, though my heart was absolutely in my mouth, because I'd only been working there a few months, you see."

"And did he listen to you?"

"Alas, no. He simply wouldn't have anything to do with Lorin anymore. He came right out and told her he couldn't take the risk."

"Why didn't she go to another gallery, then?"

"Well, you know." Jacky laughed and cleared his throat apologetically. "Word gets about. And Gracie and Bill — they're lovely people, really, but they don't like to be pushed around or called names by artists; they're not used to it. They never hung the triptych, and they wouldn't put it up for sale either. Kept it in the vault twenty years, till you borrowed it for your show. And probably Bill Skelly bad-mouthed Lorin a bit around town. Quite naturally. Nobody insults his wife and gets away with it."

"So that's how it was."

"That's about it. But you mustn't put any of this in your book, promise. It'd be fatal. I don't know why I told you, anyhow."

You told me because you are a notorious gossip, Polly thought.

"Promise, now. On your honor as a biographer." Jacky giggled.

"All right," she said.

As Polly stood damp and swaying on the Madison Avenue bus, she didn't yet regret this promise. Jacky's tale wasn't flattering to Lorin Jones; it even, as he suggested, cast doubt on her sanity. After all, throughout history works of art had been bought, and even commissioned, by collectors whose manners and morals left much to be desired: think of the Borgias, or J. Paul Getty. It was just one of the facts of life. Sooner or later these people died, and the work they had privately hoarded was placed on public view. To demand that only the wholly virtuous and refined be allowed to buy paintings would be like screening members of a theater audience for previous convictions.

Besides, there was nothing so awful about the Skellys. They were important collectors, and trustees of her Museum. They were famous for being interested in new young artists, and willing to take financial risks in support of their enthusiasms; they lent their extensive holdings freely and donated generously. It was not their fault that they had loud voices and a high opinion of themselves.

As for the Skellys' failure to hang *Birth, Copulation, and Death,* there was no proof that this came from vindictiveness. Most major collectors owned far more art than they could display at any one time. Though they might buy a lot of new work, they preferred to show currently well-known artists. Probably the reason the Skellys didn't hang Jones's picture for twenty years was at first that she wasn't famous, and then that she was dead and more or less forgotten.

Anyhow, there was no guarantee that Jacky's tale was true, Polly thought as she waited in the steady rain for the Eighty-sixth Street crosstown. Jacky wanted her to think well of Paolo Carducci and the Apollo Gallery, to regard them as sympathetic to artists. He was quite capable of making up a hostile story about Lorin Jones out of innocent bits of material, like a homemade terrorist bomb. Maybe Jones did once say that she'd rather have her paintings in a museum — who wouldn't? Maybe she didn't care for the Skellys personally — why should she?

But whether the story was true or not, it was true that for twenty years Bill and Grace Skelly had shut one of Lorin Jones's most important works away from view. If they had done it from fashionable prejudice, it was forgivable if regrettable. But what if Jacky was telling the truth? What if they had done it out of revenge, because Lorin hadn't played along, hadn't treated them with the grateful eagerness they expected, that Polly had often seen them expecting — and receiving — from artists?

As the bus crossed the wet park at Eighty-sixth Street, Polly had a vision. She saw, as Lorin Jones must have seen, a collection of dark air-conditioned vaults, storerooms, attics, and basements all over the Northeast. In each, one or more of Jones's paintings was imprisoned, shut away from light and air and from anyone who might admire and love it. She saw Lorin Jones, a slight pale figure in black, pounding on the doors of these temperature- and humidity-controlled dungeons, begging for the release of her imprisoned work. Against her, holding the doors shut, were ranged a mass of dealers, curators, collectors, and critics; in Polly's mind they took on the evil, grinning faces of grotesques from an Ensor painting.

This vision upset Polly, almost made her sick to her stomach — or maybe that was just the jolting of the bus. She mustn't be unreasonable, she told herself; mustn't become paranoid. That was what her colleagues at work would say; that's what she would have said herself a few weeks ago.

But were her colleagues right, or was it that, away from her job, and from the deals and arrangements and assumptions of the New York art world, she was beginning to see it clearly for the first time?

That was what Jeanne, with her suspicion of all established "patriarchal" institutions, would probably have said. Jeanne took it for granted that these institutions were corrupt and to be avoided, though it was sometimes necessary to work with them until alternative decentralized, egalitarian, woman-centered structures had been established. Every second Tuesday evening she and some of her friends met in an apartment on First Avenue to discuss this and other political issues; as yet, Polly hadn't joined them, though she had been invited.

Jeanne had moved into Stevie's room three weeks ago, bringing with her a quantity of possessions surprising for someone who had lived in so many different cities and apartments. Polly had had to stack most of Stevie's things in the spare room. But apart from this it had been a joy having her here. Jeanne was easygoing, well organized, sympathetic, and fair-minded; she was a lively conversationalist and an inspired cook. When Polly was alone she mostly opened frozen so-called gourmet dinners that, like airplane food, looked all right but tasted like reconstituted mashed potatoes, and she was always out of clean towels or butter or light bulbs, having to run down to the laundry room or out to the supermarket at awkward times.

Jeanne saw to it that they never needed anything; she brought flowers and books and chocolates into the house; she set her flourishing houseplants on the windowsills and added her large collection of classical tapes to Polly's. If Polly wanted to work, Jeanne was quiet and unobtrusive; but she was always ready to go shopping or to a film or a gallery after work and on weekends, when her girlfriend's suspicious, abusive husband was home.

Polly and Jeanne were so much together that Jeanne's friend Ida had recently nicknamed them the Gingham Dog and the Calico Cat, after the characters in Eugene Field's poem for children.

> The gingham dog and the calico cat
> Side by side on the table sat . . .

The reference was also to their taste in clothes: Polly wore a lot of checks and plaids, while Jeanne favored delicate, old-fashioned prints. When Polly looked the poem up she discovered that the characters fought like cats and dogs, and for a few days she worried about this, wondering if Ida had intuited some potential conflict. But so far she and Jeanne had never even disagreed seriously.

Polly's worry about What People Would Think had also faded. All Jeanne's friends knew she was in love with a woman in Brooklyn Heights, and Polly had taken care to tell Jim the same. His reaction had been, as usual, muted and neutral: "Oh, mmh."

The only problem with having Jeanne in the apartment was her girlfriend, Betsy. Polly didn't exactly dislike Betsy, but on the other hand she had nothing much to say to her. She was a bony, heavily freckled young woman (twenty-seven) with flyaway strawberry blonde hair and a hesitant, nervous manner. She was, Polly supposed, vaguely pretty; tall and leggy, with a miniature beaked nose like a little white parrot, and a swollen pink mouth that was always slightly open, as if she had started to speak and then stopped herself; something she often did. Her favorite painter was Salvador Dalí, and she didn't see the point of abstract art: the colors were kind of nice sometimes, she admitted, but it wasn't awfully interesting or complex really, was it?

Because of Betsy's husband's growing suspicions (he had found an unequivocally affectionate but unsigned note from Jeanne, and thought his wife was seeing another man), she and Jeanne had begun meeting in Manhattan. Usually they came to the apartment during the day when Polly was out; but last night Betsy had stayed over for the first time, telling her husband the literal but deceptive truth: that she was spending the night with a girlfriend. ("Oh yes, Betsy's here," Polly had had to tell him when he phoned to check up. "Sure, just a moment, I'll call her.")

Of course Polly wanted Jeanne to be happy, but it had made her uncomfortable that Jeanne and Betsy were being happy in Stevie's room and in Stevie's bunk bed. Most of the time she managed not to imagine what they did together. Probably not much, she thought usually: there was something silly and pointless about the idea of two soft female bodies rubbing up against each other. But last night, though she tried not to, she couldn't help listening and wondering what exactly Jeanne and Betsy were doing and whether they were doing it in the upper bunk or the lower one. In the lower bed there would be the problem of whoever was on top hitting her head — but maybe women only lay side by side, because otherwise how. . . . Up above, there would be the danger of falling out. She lay awake for some time waiting for a thud, a scream, a thump.

On the whole Polly hoped they had used the upper bed, where nobody ever slept except now and then one of Stevie's pals. That was stupid, because what difference could it make to Stevie, who would never know that Betsy had been here, anyway? Probably, Polly realized unwillingly, she was envious, because it had been over a year since she'd made love to anyone except, without much enthusiasm, herself.

When Polly got home from her interview with Jacky Herbert she was even wetter than she had been at the gallery, and chilled through. Jeanne took one look at her friend and insisted on her taking a hot shower at once.

"Well. All right," Polly said. It was so long since anyone had been there to meet her and show any sort of solicitude that she still received it almost ungraciously.

"And I'll make you a nice cup of cocoa."

"You don't have to do that." Polly struggled out of her poncho.

"I know I don't have to." Jeanne smiled. "But I want to." She headed for the kitchen.

"Has Betsy gone?" Polly called, pulling off her sopping loafers.

"Mm." Jeanne gave a long breathy sigh. "I'll tell you about it after you're warmed up."

"Not too sweet for you, is it?" Jeanne asked half an hour later.

"No, just right." Polly sighed with satisfaction. She had finished her shower and now sat in old jeans and a favorite lumberjack shirt at the kitchen table, drinking cocoa spiced with cinnamon and topped with cream, and eating Jeanne's homemade Scottish shortbread. "So is everything going well with Betsy?"

"I guess so." Jeanne sighed again. "She says she's going to tell her husband this week that we're in love."

"Oh, that's good." Jeanne did not reply. "Isn't it?"

"It's good if Betsy really does it. She promised she was

going to speak to him once before, you know. But it didn't happen."

"Maybe she's afraid of him," Polly suggested, remembering Betsy's husband's tense, edgy voice on the phone.

"That's what I think. But Betsy says not. She says she really did plan to tell him on Tuesday, but he came home with a terrible cold, and she hadn't got the heart to do it. Apparently his colds always last at least a week." Jeanne smiled joylessly and poured herself more cocoa, slopping it into the saucer in an uncharacteristically careless way.

"That's too bad," Polly agreed. "Still, I suppose it shows that Betsy's a very considerate person."

"It shows she's very considerate of him." Jeanne stirred her own cocoa crossly. "But there are three people involved here, right?"

"I see what you mean. Only, you know, I think she does love you."

"Yes. I think she does." Jeanne smiled again, but now very differently, in a sensual, reminiscent way that made Polly look away. "I know it's going to be all right eventually; I just get impatient."

"Well, sure."

"I know, really, that soon we'll be together every night." Jeanne nodded, agreeing with herself.

"Every night, here?" Polly tried to make this question casual.

"Oh, no; in Brooklyn Heights. As soon as that creep is out of the house, of course I'll move in."

"Of course," Polly echoed. But what she thought was: No more intimate conversations; no more homemade cocoa or shortbread. A chord of rejection and loss twanged in her, and the selfish wish that Betsy wouldn't be able to get her husband out of the house until Stevie came home. "Well, I hope it's really soon," she lied, ashamed of herself.

GRACE SKELLY,

art collector

Of course, as everyone knows, we were the first major collectors to buy Lorin's work. At the time almost no one who counted in the art world had ever heard of her. Everything was New York School, right? That's all most people would even look at.

No, I've never gone along with the crowd. I like to study a piece of art and judge it for myself. If I can relate to it emotionally and aesthetically, I don't give a damn what anyone else says. I play my hunches, and it's weird, but they almost always turn out to be right. Take graffiti art, a few years ago everyone was saying . . .

Oh, yeah, when I saw Lorin's paintings, they hit me like a bomb. That was at her last big show at the Apollo, when was it?

Nineteen-sixty-four, really? That long ago. Of course I was very young then, just a child bride really. But somehow I had an eye already.

Well, you know how it is at big openings. There was a crowd, and a lot to drink, and nobody was paying much attention to what was on the walls. I wouldn't be surprised if I was about the only person there who really looked at the work. But when I saw those marvelous paintings, I just knew I had to have one of them. And pretty soon I decided it would have to be the big triptych. It was an important piece, I just knew it. After I and Bill got back to the penthouse, it kept coming into my mind, the way a tune from a show you've just seen does sometimes, right? It was like a kind of obsession.

Well, the kinetic energy there, and the, uh, interplay of values. There was a physical tension between the three canvases, too, a kind of almost sensual vibration. You know what I'm talking about, you know the work. *Birth, Copulation, and Death*. Well, that says it all, right?

I told Bill the next morning, Honey, I can't get that damn painting out of my mind. It's really got something. I made him go back to the gallery with me. And when I pointed out all the exciting visual things that were going on in Lorin's work, he saw them too. He has a real instinct, you know, though he's not as quick on the uptake as I am sometimes. Last summer when we were in Rome . . .

Well, you know Lorin was living in Florida by that time, so Bill and I didn't see as much of her as we would have liked. But we got on together great, from the word go. She was such a sensitive, sympathetic person.

Yeah, I know she was shy, with strangers and people she didn't trust. There are a lot of assholes and climbers in the art world, I'm sorry to say. But it's the goddamn truth. But when Lorin was with people she knew appreciated her, and understood the complex things she was trying to do in her painting, she opened right up.

Oh, yeah, that's true, she hated to be separated from her work. Her paintings meant so much to her, they were almost like her children, I used to think. But of course she knew she was always welcome to come out to our place in Southampton to see *Birth, Copulation, and Death* again whenever she liked. We're used to having artists around, we know how to take good care of them. Jackson Pollock . . .

Well, no, actually she never visited us. It's a hell of a long way from the Keys. And she was so passionately involved in her work down there by that time, I guess she just couldn't bring herself to leave. She was always such an intense, dedicated person. It's tragic that she had to die so young, isn't it?

But at least she died knowing her most important picture was in good hands. I mean, it's a central work, right? Not only in Lorin's career, but in terms of American painting in the sixties, as a whole. It looks ahead to the seventies, too, of course. And even beyond. Because Lorin was way ahead of her time. Everyone knows that now, but Bill and I saw it from the start.

Oh yeah, sure, we told Lorin what we thought. Plenty of times. Artists need encouragement from people who count; they're like kids, in a way. And I think knowing how we felt about her and her painting was a real help to her, in those last hard years. I'm sure of it.

4

"How's it going?" Jeanne, who had come in late last night from a meeting and slept even later, padded into the sitting room in her long rose-flowered chintz bathrobe.

"Oh, I don't know," Polly sighed. She had been up since seven, awakened as usual by the clatter and noisy cooing of the bedraggled pigeons that nested under the cornice of the building. She had gone for her usual run around the reservoir, made coffee, and sat down to transcribe last week's interviews. "The more people I see, the more confusing it gets. It's like they're not even talking about the same woman."

"But there must be some you feel you can trust," Jeanne suggested, yawning a little.

"I suppose so. Sometimes I think everyone I interview is lying to me."

"Well, they probably are, one way or another," Jeanne said comfortably, padding into the kitchen area. She refilled the kettle and set it on to boil. "Have you had breakfast yet?"

"I drank some coffee."

"That's not breakfast. I'll make us something nice." She began to open cupboards. "You know you should never try to work on an empty stomach."

"Jacky Herbert said that Lorin hated the Skellys and didn't want to sell them her painting. There was a big brouhaha over it. And now Grace Skelly says they were close friends."

"Uh-huh."

"So which one do I believe?"

"Heavens, I don't know. Neither, probably."

"But suppose you had to decide?" Polly turned around from her typewriter to look at Jeanne.

"I guess I'd go with Mrs. Skelly. At least she's a woman. And according to you Jacky Herbert is a dreadful gossip." Jeanne, unlike Polly, had no sympathy with male homosexuals. She regarded them as, if possible, worse than so-called normal men, because they were more cut off from the sensitizing and civilizing influence of women.

"Oh, he's not so bad," Polly said. "He was sympathetic to Lorin all along, you know, but he couldn't persuade his boss to go on showing her work."

"That's what he says now." Jeanne smiled. "You're such a soft touch, Polly. You went to see Jacky Herbert full of perfectly natural suspicions, and you came home sorry for him. It sounds as if he completely snowed you."

Polly didn't want to be sidetracked into another discussion of whether she was in danger of being "seduced" by the men she had to interview. "My instinct is, Jacky's telling me more of the truth," she said. "But where's the proof? Mrs. Skelly sounded so sincere, and she gave me a great tea, smoked-salmon sandwiches and the most amazing brandied fruitcake. But somehow I didn't believe a word she said."

"If you know what you think already, why ask me?" Jeanne said teasingly, spooning home-ground coffee into a paper filter.

"I don't know, though. I've been worrying about it all morning."

"I can see that." Jeanne smiled. "But you really mustn't let yourself become obsessive about this project." She scuffed across the kitchen in the runover black ballet slippers she still wore in tribute to early ambitions as a dancer. Even now she continually took up and dropped classes in aerobics, "dancercise," "expressive movement," and yoga. "It's only a book, after all."

"I'm not obsessive; it's just that I want it to be absolutely first-rate," Polly said.

"And I'm sure it will be." Jeanne sifted instant oatmeal into a pan of boiling water. "Now, what do you plan to do today? I've got to occupy myself somehow, or I'll just sit and brood about what's happening in that house in Brooklyn Heights."

"Today's the day, then?"

"That's right." Jeanne laughed nervously. Betsy's show-down with her husband had already been put off twice, first because of his bad cold, and then because of a crisis at the computer company where he worked. The idea had come to Polly that Betsy was stalling, but she hadn't said this to Jeanne. "I promised not to call, but I'm meeting her for supper at six; it should be all over by then."

"That's good."

"Anyhow, don't wait up for me." Jeanne smiled as if in anticipation, then frowned slightly. "At least I hope it will be all over. Of course I know Betsy hasn't any more feeling for that creep, apart from a sort of distant pity. But I still can't bear the idea that she's living in the same house with him. I'm a very jealous person, you know," she added rather proudly.

"Really?" Polly asked, doubting this.

"I've been that way since I was tiny," Jeanne continued from the stove, where the kettle was boiling. "More coffee?"

"Okay, sure."

"I remember in fourth grade I was in love with a little girl named Eileen," Jeanne went on. "She had maple-brown hair, just as shiny as if it had been varnished, and huge golden-green eyes. The awful thing was, Eileen didn't love me. She liked me all right, but I just wasn't important to her, and I knew it. I was in agony."

"So what happened?"

"Well, I got her to agree that we should be best friends; I begged and insisted. But I was still jealous. I knew that if I had to stay home sick for two days Eileen would let someone else be her best friend; all they'd have to do was ask." Jeanne put two bowls of oatmeal with cream and raisins on the table and sat down opposite Polly. "We used to play this game at recess, out behind the school," she said. "We'd join hands in a circle, and one girl would stand in the center, and the rest of us would dance around her, and we would sing:

> Sally, Sally Waters,
> Sitting in a saucer,
> Rise, Sally, rise.
> Bow to the east,
> Bow to the west,
> Kiss the one you love the best."

Jeanne's voice rose in the tune, thin but pure. "Then the girl in the center would choose someone else to be It next. Of course I always chose Eileen. You were supposed to kiss them on the cheek, but I'd get as close to her mouth as I dared, even partly on it, pretending it was sort of a mistake. When anyone else picked Eileen I'd watch them furiously. If I thought they gave her a real kiss, I wanted to kill them. I imagined doing it in different ways; or sometimes I imagined a truck running over them in the parochial school driveway, and their blood being squeezed out over the blacktop, like an oil slick."

"Really?" Polly said, adding brown sugar to her oatmeal. "Kids' imaginations are violent, aren't they?"

"I didn't know what it all meant then. I couldn't have explained that I was in love. That's one of the dreadful things about being a child: you feel everything just as strongly, but you don't have a name for it."

"I know what you mean," Polly said. "It can be awful." What she saw was not a playground, but a booth in a coffee shop in Mamaroneck, and her father's face turned away from her toward friends who had just joined them.

"You always understand." Jeanne smiled, then sighed. "Well, anyhow. I thought after breakfast we might walk across the park, it seems to be a nice morning. And I told Ida and Cathy we might stop in. Then of course there's that new film in the Women Directors series downtown at two. What do you think?"

"You go, if you like," Polly said. "I have to transcribe two more interviews." She stood up.

"Not on Sunday, surely?"

"I do, though. I've got to review them before I go to Wellfleet tomorrow; they could be important." Polly sat down at her desk and turned on the tape. "There are a lot of assholes and climbers in the art world," it said in a self-assertive female voice, hardly proving Polly's point.

"But it's only ten thirty. You have all the time in the world."

"Nobody has all the time in the world," Polly said stubbornly. She swung her chair around and typed the sentence they had just heard.

"Good heavens. You know that's simply a manner of speaking. What's the matter with you today?"

"Nothing's the matter with me," Polly protested, wondering why she was so out of humor. "I'm concerned about my book, that's all." She heard how pompous this sounded, and added: "I'll tell you what. You go and see Ida and Cathy this morning, and I'll meet you all afterward at the film."

"Don't you want to see Ida and Cathy?" Jeanne asked.

"Sure I do," Polly said, though in fact she was sometimes uncomfortable when she was with Jeanne's friends and noticed that everyone else present was gay. "I just haven't got the time today."

"But they invited you, too. If you don't come, they'll think it's, well, rather strange."

"They'll think I'm working, that's all."

"Well, maybe." Jeanne's mild, caressing manner had begun to fray slightly. "But they'll think you're working, you know, on purpose. They're already not sure you really like them."

"I like them all right," Polly said; in fact she cared less for Ida and Cathy than for Jeanne's other friends.

"They feel you as a rather hostile presence, you know. Ida especially."

"Why should they feel that, for God's sake?" Polly shoved the typewriter back and set her elbows square on the desk. "I've always been perfectly nice to them. I'm not a hostile presence."

"I know. But that's how they feel."

Polly almost groaned. "If they think I'm hostile, they should be glad I'm not coming."

"Yes, but if you came, they wouldn't —"

"Anyhow, the question is academic," Polly interrupted, remembering too late that Jeanne was an academic. "I'm not leaving this room till I get these interviews typed. I keep having this fantasy of Lorin Jones, how she's waiting for me to start writing."

"Really?" Now Jeanne smiled indulgently; she was in favor of all sorts of visionary experience.

"Yes. I imagine her standing somewhere up to her knees in moving gray and white clouds, like one of her own pictures, with all her long dark hair blowing around, looking down at me, wondering why I'm not getting on with it faster. Sometimes she gives me a little wave."

"Really," Jeanne said again, but this time her expression was more thoughtful. "You know what I think?" she added. "I think you *are* becoming just a bit obsessed. I think you're falling in love with your subject." She smiled.

Polly turned and looked up at Jeanne. She ought to be joking, of course, but maybe she wasn't. "You think I'm in love with a woman who died in nineteen-sixty-nine?"

"I'm uneasy about your feeling for her, that's all. It just, well, doesn't seem absolutely healthy to me. All you think about lately is Lorin Jones."

"I'm writing a book about her, for God's sake," Polly explained, trying to keep her voice calm and not succeeding.

"I know that," Jeanne said, with a sigh of resignation. "And I know you want to get those interviews typed. You don't have to come to Ida and Cathy's with me unless you like."

You're damn right I don't, Polly thought, but did not say.

"They'll have to understand that I'm living with a workaholic, that's all." Jeanne laughed gaily. "I'll tell them you'll phone as soon as you're finished, all right?"

*　　*　　*

Alone in the apartment, Polly continued typing for ten minutes, then stopped to reheat her coffee. For the first time she felt the disadvantages of having become Jeanne's roommate. She didn't like being blamed for not wanting to visit Ida and Cathy, who weren't really her friends, and would probably be happier if she didn't come, so they could analyze her character the way they always did with people who weren't there. They talked in a kind of catty way, even in a bitchy way —

Polly scowled, catching herself in a lapse of language. Jeanne, among others, had often pointed out how unfair it was that when women were compared to animals it was always unfavorably: *catty, bitch, cow, henpecked*. While for men the comparison was usually positive: *gay dog, strong as a bull, cock of the walk*.

She turned on the tape recorder again and typed another page, then stopped, thinking of Jeanne again. She didn't like being called a workaholic, even affectionately. She didn't like being given permission not to see people she didn't want to see. It was, yes, as if she were a child, with a managing, overprotective mother.

Of course, when she really was a child, Polly never had an overprotective mother. Bea was only twenty when her daughter was born, and she'd had trouble enough protecting herself. She looked out for Polly the way an older sister or a baby-sitter might have done, without anxiety, encouraging her to become independent as fast as possible. Later, when Polly's half brothers came along, Bea had showed impulses toward overprotection, but her husband frustrated them; he didn't want his sons "made into sissies."

According to Elsa, Polly's former shrink, any close relationship between women could revive one's first and profoundest attachment, to one's mother. Physically, of course, Jeanne was nothing like Polly's mother — Bea Milner was much smaller, for one thing. But to a child all grown women are large. And psychologically there were similarities: Jeanne, like Bea, was soft and feminine in manner, and given to gently chiding Polly for her impulsiveness, hot temper, and lack of tact. Elsa's view had been that Polly needed Jeanne to play this role because she hadn't had enough "good mothering" as a child, and that Jeanne needed to play it because she was a highly maternal woman without children.

But I'm not a child anymore, Polly thought. I don't want mothering. Anyhow, I'm four years older than Jeanne, the whole idea is stupid. She poured her coffee and added less sugar than usual.

Again she started typing and stopped. Something else Jeanne had said was bothering her; what?

Yes. Jeanne had accused her of being in love with Lorin Jones. That was ridiculous, realistically. But if love meant admiring someone, thinking about her all the time, speculating about the tiniest details of her life, wanting to know everything she'd ever done, talking about her to everyone —

Yes, and staring at her photograph, imagining impossible scenarios in which they might meet. . . . In the latest one, it turned out that Lorin Jones wasn't really dead; it was someone else who had died in Key West, and Lorin had been living and painting on a tiny island off Cape Cod for fifteen years. Polly would somehow discover this when she went to Wellfleet (of course, Garrett Jones and his wife wouldn't know it themselves).

She would hire a motorboat to take her to the island, and land on a tiny pebble beach just as the sun was setting over the water. She would walk up a narrow sandy path through scrub oak and juniper, and there would be an old gray shingled house half-concealed by blackberry brambles. The door to the big studio in back would be open. Inside a tall slim woman in her late fifties, still beautiful, though her long dark hair was streaked with gray, would be standing at an easel. At first she would be distressed that she'd been discovered, but Polly would reassure her: she would look into Lorin's fringed dark eyes and promise never to reveal her secret.

Soap-opera stuff, Polly thought, giving an angry shake of her head. But she had to admit it suggested that there might be something in what Jeanne had said. It hadn't occurred to Polly before that she might be in love with Lorin Jones, not only because she was dead, but because she was a woman; but naturally it had occurred to Jeanne.

In Jeanne's view, love and sympathy between women was natural and beautiful; it was heterosexual relationships that made trouble. It couldn't help being that way, she said, because women and men were emotionally incompatible, and even sexually incompatible except in the most mechanistic sense. The male's natural instinct was for a quick, anonymous squirt of seed; the female's for a long, tender cherishing. That was why she and Betsy were so peaceful and happy together.

It was probably true, Polly thought, that when people were of different sexes it was harder for them not to misunderstand and hurt each other. I've had many more women friends than men. And felt more comfortable with them, and trusted them more.

Except for Stevie. And at this thought, a familiar desolation and anxiety rolled over Polly like a cold smelly mist. She still missed her son awfully. She called him every week, but that almost made it worse. Usually the connection to Denver was good, and her son's voice so loud that he could have been in his room at home, talking on the toy telephone he'd got for his eighth birthday and strung along the hallway of the apartment.

What agreeable conversations they used to have, Polly on the kitchen stool, and Stevie lying on the bunk bed in his room, pretending to be in the jungle, or on a space station. "I'll tell you a secret," he used to whisper sometimes; and Polly would learn something he hadn't been able to say to her face. "It was me that ate the rest of the mint chip ice cream, but I'm sorry." "This is Captain Mercury 5000 calling. I don't like Miss MacGregor at all, and none of the other kids do either." Sometimes he would say, "Tell me a secret, Mommy."

Now the distance was real, but they didn't really talk.
— Stevie?

— Hi, Mom.

— How are you, pal?

— I'm okay.

— And how's everything in Denver? How are you liking your school?

— It's all right.

— Did you get your allergy shots this week?

— Uh-huh.

— And how were they? Did they hurt?

— They were okay. You know.

— So what's happening out there?

— Nothing much. I got a new video game, it's called Space Lords.

— Space Lords?

— Yeah, it's really keen, Mom. It's got seven skill levels. There's this computer-generated monster, see . . .

In these conversations, almost the only time Stevie became expansive was in describing his latest acquisitions: video games, hiking shoes, tapes, classic comics, a battery-operated pencil sharpener, an elaborate backpack with a frame, a sleeping bag, a new sort of tennis racket. His life seemed to Polly to be filling up with these things; she imagined him in the spare bedroom of Jim's house in Denver (which she'd never seen) surrounded by more and more objects. Objects, most often, that she couldn't have afforded to buy for Stevie and that he would have no use for in New York.

The idea of all these objects made Polly so angry that last week she had asked to speak to Jim and protested, complaining that he was spoiling Stevie and buying his affection. Jim had replied in the calm infuriating voice that she knew so well, the voice of someone dealing with a totally irrational person. Everyone in Stevie's school had these things, he explained; all the kids played tennis and went hiking and camped out. If Stevie didn't have the right equipment he couldn't join in his friends' activities; he'd be a kind of outcast.

What Stevie said most often on the phone was "Don't worry, Mom. I'm having an okay time." Naturally this made Polly worry. Maybe it meant that he was unhappy but wasn't telling her because he didn't want to hurt Jim's feelings; maybe it meant that he was happy but didn't want to hurt hers. If he was unhappy enough — or happy enough — he might return to New York psychologically damaged, or alternatively he might want to stay in Denver forever. And there was no way of knowing for sure until he got home.

— *But you're not telling me anything, pal!* Polly often wanted to scream at him over the phone. Only she knew she mustn't do that; it could turn Stevie off totally.

Polly had tried to talk about these worries to Jeanne, who was very sympathetic but not reassuring. Yes, maybe Stevie wasn't communicating his real feelings, she had said. Of course that must make Polly feel bad. But that was how boys were once they began to mature — it was hard, but she'd probably have to get used to it.

Polly was at the kitchen counter that evening eating a slice of Jeanne's lighter-than-air confetti angel food cake and idly paging through the *New York Times* travel section when she heard her friend come home from her meeting with Betsy. She knew something was wrong at once, because it was still so early, and then because for the first time in their acquaintance Jeanne looked completely disarranged, almost distracted. Her bouncy blonde hair hung in uncombed shreds, and her pale blue down coat was buttoned wrong.

"Would you like supper?" Polly asked. "There's some tomato soup on the stove."

"I couldn't eat anything." Jeanne started to walk about the kitchen aimlessly.

"What's the matter, is something the matter?"

"Yes, it is." Jeanne opened a cupboard door and slammed it shut. "She didn't tell him."

"Betsy still didn't tell her husband about you?"

"That's right." Jeanne tried without energy or success to unbutton her puffy coat.

"Oh hell. I'm sorry." Polly got up and went to put her

arms around her friend. Because of the coat, it felt like embracing a half-inflated balloon.

"I can't stand it, I just can't!" Inside the balloon, Jeanne collapsed onto Polly, weeping. "It's so unfair."

"Yeah. . . . There, there."

"She says she can't bear to hurt him. So I said, 'I suppose you think it's all right to hurt me,' and she said, 'No, but you're stronger than he is." Jeanne gave a choked sob.

"There, there," Polly repeated, feeling helpless and indignant.

"She swears she's going to tell him soon, but this wasn't the right moment. So I said, 'When is the right moment?' " Jeanne stood back on her own feet shakily, and wiped her wet powder-streaked face with the side of her hand, not improving its appearance.

"And what did Betsy say?"

"She said she just didn't know. I think that's a lot of C-R-A-P. I think she's never going to tell him." Jeanne tried again to unfasten her coat, but her hands were still shaking. "It was awful, Polly — I got so upset — I threw my plate on the floor, everybody was looking at me —" She choked on a sob. "Veal parmigiana."

"What?"

"That was what I was eating. It went all over the restaurant floor." Jeanne gave a miserable laugh. "It was so stupid and embarrassing, destroying innocent crockery."

"I guess you have to, sometimes," Polly said.

"No. It was awful; I was awful." Jeanne finally succeeded in taking off her coat, and let it slump to the floor, something Polly had never seen her do. "The thing is, as long as Betsy's husband doesn't know what our relationship is, I'm in a completely false position."

"Mm," Polly agreed.

"I think he must know." Jeanne bent to retrieve the coat, and dropped it on a stool from which it at once slid off. "Unconsciously, at least. Only he won't admit it to himself." She began to wander around the room again. "But maybe he's too stupid. At least he knows Betsy doesn't love him anymore. If she ever did." She fell into a chair and looked around distractedly. "Is there any coffee left?"

"Sure." Polly turned on the flame under the pot.

"I think maybe he knows, or suspects anyhow. Because whenever I come over he sulks and slams things around, and shouts for Betsy to hurry up and make lunch or something."

"He sounds like a pig." Polly set the coffee in front of her friend, together with a carton of the heavy cream she preferred.

"He is. A complete pig." Jeanne nodded miserably. "She's afraid of him, that's what it is," she added, dumping in sugar. "She says not, but I know she must be. After all, he's already hit her once."

"Betsy's husband hit her?"

"Yes. He struck her in the face with a plastic flyswatter. He said afterward it was a mistake, he meant to swat a fly. I know those sorts of mistakes. My brother used to make them all the time." Jeanne lifted her mug. "Thanks. That tastes good."

"I'll start another pot," Polly said.

"I told Betsy, I can't go on like this. I can't. I mean as long as she doesn't acknowledge me, I feel as if I'm some kind of dirty secret in her life. I told her that. I said, 'Betsy, my darling, I can't go on with this relationship any longer unless it's out in the open.' "

"And what did Betsy say?"

"She started crying, and said she just didn't know what to do." Jeanne sighed heavily and was silent.

"So what's going to happen?" Polly said finally.

"I don't know. But I told Betsy I'm not going to see her again until she tells him the truth. I can't stand it, that's all there is to be said."

As it turned out, though, that was not all. For nearly an hour Jeanne sat sipping cup after cup of coffee with cream and picking at the angel food cake and weeping a bit from time to time, while she rehearsed the history of her affair with Betsy, and drew parallels between it and other affairs in her past. This was not the first time, Polly learned, that she had been hurt or betrayed. Jeanne then broadened her scope to relate events of a similar sort that had happened to friends and acquaintances.

Eventually she yawned, sighed, thanked Polly for listening, and dragged herself off down the hall to bed. Polly sat on in front of the unread Sunday *Times*. What she mainly felt, besides a painful sympathy for Jeanne, was a wistful disillusion. If even two women couldn't be happy together, what good was it all?

Maybe, if you had to be in love, with all the problems and craziness that involved, it was better to be in love with someone who was dead. A dead person couldn't do you any harm emotionally; she or he couldn't criticize you or betray you or leave you. And you couldn't do her any harm either, so there was no guilt.

As Polly lay in bed, slipping toward sleep, there was a soft knock at the door.

"It's me," Jeanne's voice said. "Can I come in?"

"Sure." Polly reached for the bedside lamp.

"I can't sleep," Jeanne whispered. She sat down on the end of the double bed and wrapped her ruffled pink flannel nightgown around her feet. "I keep thinking about Betsy. Just thinking the same things, over and over."

"I know how it is. After Jim left, I had insomnia for weeks. Hey, I think I have some Valium put away somewhere."

"I already took one." Jeanne let out a long thin exhausted puff of wind. "It's that room, you know. Especially that bunk bed. I keep thinking of how she was there with me. It's like it was haunted."

"Yes."

"Listen, could I sleep here, just for tonight? I promise I won't toss around or have nightmares; the Valium should start to work pretty soon."

"Well — sure."

"Thanks. You're a real pal." Jeanne gave her a grateful

hug; then she shuffled around to the far side of the double bed and got in. She turned her back to Polly and dragged the covers completely up over her head. Polly wondered how she could breathe.

True to her vow, Jeanne was unconscious in five minutes. She did not jerk or thrash about, but lay quietly, giving out only a regular soft slur of breath and a steady animal heat. It was Polly, now, who turned and shifted her position. Over a year had passed since she had shared her bed with anyone, and she was acutely conscious of the new slope of the mattress; of the heavy, warm sleeping shape a foot away, and of its sex.

Well, here she was in bed with a woman, and what did she feel? Restless and uneasy; and not exactly excited, but keyed up, tense. Maybe what she wanted was for Jeanne to turn over, and put her arms around her, and hug her again.

But Jeanne was deep in a drugged sleep, and besides she was physically and emotionally exhausted by her scene with Betsy. And did Polly really want to do with Jeanne what Jeanne did with Betsy? What was that, anyhow?

These questions, and others related to them, kept Polly awake for over an hour, and when she finally dozed off it was into an uneasy slumber broken by bad dreams. In the last one she was shopping in the local A&P, only she was naked. She was searching the shelves for something to cover herself with, and finally she found a green plastic trash bag, and she pulled the bag over her head, and it only came down to her waist, and it was very hot and sticky, and she couldn't move her arms, and she was trying to move them, to scream, to tear a hole in the bag, and she was naked and there were a lot of women in the aisles looking at her, and she gave a series of stifled desperate cries and woke in the middle of the bed, with Jeanne's arms around her from behind.

"It's all right, Polly," Jeanne was saying to her gently. "It's all right, it's just a nightmare."

"I thought —" Polly gasped as if she had been running. She turned over toward Jeanne, still trembling a little, and panting for air.

Jeanne, misunderstanding, gathered her closer. "It's all right," she crooned. "Do you want to tell me about it?"

In the dark, Polly shook her head vigorously. "No." Then, since this sounded ungracious, she added, "But thanks. I'm glad you were here."

"Me, too," Jeanne said. "I don't know what I would have done tonight without you. All the way back from Brooklyn on that awful subway, I felt I wanted to die. I almost hoped some crazy delinquent with a gun would get on." She hugged Polly, holding her close but not tight. It wasn't like what she was used to, it was more like being hugged by Stevie when he was little, or her mother; warm and fond and safe. Polly, with a half sigh, let herself relax into the warmth and softness.

"I'm glad he didn't," she said.

They lay quiet. The green numbers of the digital clock flipped on the nightstand: 4:23 A.M.

"It's true about sleep being the balm of hurt minds," Jeanne murmured. "I mean, I'm still perfectly miserable about Betsy, but I don't want to die anymore." She laughed a little sadly.

"That's good."

4:26 A.M. 4:27 A.M.

"I feel so much better," Jeanne said, moving one hand to stroke the thick curls at the back of Polly's neck above the pajama jacket. "If you want it, I'd like to make you feel better, too."

Maybe I do want it, Polly thought. If I don't try, I'll never know. "All right," she said uneasily. She swiveled farther toward Jeanne, and put her arms around Jeanne's flannel nightgown.

"Polly, dear," Jeanne whispered, and kissed her: a long, gentle, deepening kiss.

Gratefully, awkwardly, Polly reached up to touch Jeanne's fine long hair, so unlike her own; and then the warm yielding flesh of her neck under the flannel ruffle.

"Oh, that's nice," her friend said. Her kisses were soft now, fluttering. "Oh, yes. Do that again."

SARA SACHS VOGELER,
artist and illustrator

Yes, we were good friends for a while.

It was in about nineteen-sixty, sixty-one, when I was study-ing at Cooper Union, and Laura was still living in New York. I guess some people already knew who she was, but I'd never heard of her, though of course I'd heard of her husband. We met at the Modern: a guy I knew from school was working there, selling tickets; he introduced us. But he just said: "Laura Jones" — I didn't connect it.

We got on pretty well from the start. There was a new show of drawings, and we went around it together. It turned out we liked most of the same things. Then we had tea in the members' lounge; it was the first time I'd ever been up there.

Yes, of course Laura was nearly ten years older than me, but I didn't realize it then. She had on the kind of clothes she always wore, paint-streaked jeans and sneakers and an old black turtleneck sweater. And no makeup, and a mass of long dark hair. She looked like a student too.

No, she didn't seem especially shy.

I don't know. Maybe she felt comfortable with me because I was young and kind of awkward. I was just a skinny kid from the Bronx, and I didn't have any social manner.

We used to meet about once a week. We'd walk around the Village, go to galleries, have a sandwich and a malted, sketch in the park, that kind of thing.

I don't know. We talked about painting, the work we'd seen, new techniques, you know. I remember Laura'd just discovered Piero della Francesca, and she wanted to try doing frescoes in egg tempera. I got interested too, and we went around to art stores and tried to find out about that.

No, it turned out to be too complicated, and awfully expensive.

Sure, we talked about other things: films, and books. And I guess I told her some of the trouble I was having at home, the way my parents were always after me to study something useful like bookkeeping, because they were afraid I wouldn't get married.

No, I don't think she ever gave me any advice. But she was a good listener, you know.

How do you mean, strange?

I don't know, maybe. I mean most artists are kind of strange, compared to other people, don't you think? I guess I'm a little strange myself, at least that's what my husband tells me.

Well, for instance, there were a lot of ordinary things Laura didn't like, hated really, and I didn't like them either.

A whole heap of things. I can't remember most of them now: TV, and pay telephones, and Léger and Stuart Davis, and wobbly Jell-O salad with fruit in it, and men in brown felt hats, and watches with metal bands. . . . We had a word for all of them: we called them "creepos."

Well, what happened was, she came to Cooper Union to look at a painting I was doing. A couple of people saw her there, and afterward they mentioned that she was married to Garrett Jones and had shown at the Apollo and been written up in *Art News*.

She hadn't said anything about any of it to me. She'd told me she was married, but she didn't say to who. I got the idea that he was an older man, and pretty well off, but she didn't want to talk about him. I thought maybe it wasn't going too well.

Yes, it made me feel a little funny. I didn't understand why Laura'd never even told me she had a gallery. Now I see it differently: I think maybe her success embarrassed her. Maybe she thought she didn't deserve it, kind of. I mean, she must have known she deserved it, but maybe she thought she wouldn't have had it so soon without her husband's help.

She didn't say much about my work, not that I remember now. There was one drawing of a mouse that she liked, but that was just kind of a joke. I'd done it for my niece's birthday. Most of my painting was abstract then, big canvases. It's funny, though; I never thought of it before, but about ten years later, after I had kids myself, I went back to drawing animals for them, and that started a whole new direction in my art. My last show . . .

Yes, we went to her place a couple of times, when Garrett Jones wasn't there, and she showed me some of the small semiabstract flower canvases she was doing then, the ones everybody compares to Redon now.

They about knocked me over. I knew then she was way ahead of me.

I don't know if Laura had other friends near her own age. I never met any. The important artists of her generation, people like Rauschenberg and Johns and Rivers and Frankenthaler, I don't think she saw anything of them. What she met in New York was the middle-aged established painters, and then the dealers, the collectors, the critics. And the hangers-on, the creepos. At least, that's the idea I got from her.

Yes, I tried inviting her to have lunch with some of us after class a couple of times, but it didn't work out. Laura kind of froze up, and my friends thought she was snooty. The thing is, she was serious about painting, and she was really good, but none of them wanted to admit it. All they could see was that she was married to Garrett Jones, and he was promoting her. Afterward they said things like "Sure, I could show at the Apollo too, if I was sleeping with him."

Not really. I only met him once, at a happening. You remember happenings?

This one was in a swimming pool at a New York health club. It was a good location for something like that, a big empty underground space, all Art Deco tiles and weird acoustics. There was a mixed audience: students, artists, musicians, and some collectors and café society types, because word was starting to get around. I was there with a couple of people from school, sitting on the tiles at the edge of the pool and waiting for things to start, and I saw Laura come in with this middle-aged man, that I knew had to be her husband. Anyhow, my friends recognized him. Laura stopped in front of us, and said hello, and sort of introduced us. She was got up like I'd never seen her before, very glamorous, in a long black skirt and an antique fringed silk shawl and silver chandelier earrings.

I was kind of nervous. I mean, Garrett Jones was incredibly powerful in the art world then, and I knew that to my friends he was the uptown establishment: the enemy, you know. And besides he was old enough to be my father.

Well, they just said hello, mostly, and went on past us and sat in some folding chairs that were reserved for important people, I guess. And the happening started. While it was going on I looked over a couple of times to see how they were liking it. Laura seemed interested, I saw her smiling, but it was obvious that her husband was disgusted. And then in the middle of everything, when they brought in buckets of fish and started throwing them at the audience and splashing us with water, Garrett Jones walked out, sort of pulling Laura behind him.

I guess I felt bad that she went along with him. I kind of looked up to her, and I wanted her to stand up for herself, you know? The next time we met, I didn't know what to say to her about it, so I didn't say anything, and neither did she.

Well, not much. After that we sort of drifted apart. For one thing, Laura was in New York less and less. Garrett Jones kept dragging her off to Cape Cod, and she'd be gone for months. We used to mail each other postcards, mostly of pictures we liked. And when I got married she sent me this drawing I showed you, of me being carried away over New York by a big bird. Because of Dave's last name, you know.

I wrote to her when our first child was born, but I didn't hear anything back. Then much later I found out she'd died down there in Florida, at about the same time. She probably never even got my letter.

I was really broken up, even though I hadn't seen her for years. Every time I thought about her I started crying. Well, I was expecting again; I think that always makes you emotional. When the baby came and it was a girl we called it Laura, sort of after her. I always liked the name anyhow.

No. I wish we could afford one, but her prices are so high now, and with four kids to put through college . . .

What I think is, marrying Garrett Jones, it didn't do Laura's painting any good in the long run. It cut her off from the artists she should have known, and made them, well, kind of despise her. This was when pop art was coming in, and he was really stupid about it, he called it vulgar and self-serving. He couldn't see beyond his own heroes, people like Rothko and Motherwell and Kline. Of course later on he went for color-field and hard-edge abstraction in a big way, but by that time Laura and he were separated.

The thing is, if it hadn't been for Jones, Laura's painting might have developed differently, been more contemporary. He kind of surrounded her and cut her off. She was really good, but her work was completely out of the mainstream, almost irrelevant to what was happening here in New York in the sixties.

Yes, I guess I do hold it against him. Even now.

5

With an uneasy lurch and dip of its wings, the commuter plane swerved south toward Provincetown over a flat ocean like oily crumpled metal. Polly, who was one of only three passengers, caught her breath hard. Maybe we're going to crash, she thought. I'll never write my book, or see Stevie again, or Jeanne. It didn't seem possible: only a few hours ago, in her traveling clothes, she had sat on the bed in which her friend — her lover? — lay asleep in a swirl of blankets and sheets and pink ruffled and flowered flannel nightgown, like a warm, untidy rose.

"I'm leaving for the airport now," Polly told her softly, hoping she would wake.

"Mm?" Jeanne opened one pale-lashed hazel eye.

"I'm going to Wellfleet to see Garrett Jones."

"Oh, right."

"So long then." Polly bent over Jeanne, who turned her head and gave her a soft sleepy kiss.

"Come home soon," she murmured.

Come home to what? Polly wondered now. Had Jeanne's kiss been romantic or only friendly? Was the odd, awkward, lovely thing that had happened last night the beginning of something serious, or was it just an incident? Polly didn't know, and if she died now, she never would know.

Again the tiny plane hiccuped, tilted sharply, and righted itself. Polly could feel the contents of her stomach (weak sugary iced coffee and a soggy airport-cafeteria cheese sandwich) rise and contemplate departing by the nearest exit. She imagined being sick in the middle of the air; then as the toy plane listed sideways again she imagined herself drowning, trapped inside its tinny body — or would she die of the impact first, even over water? Fear and hatred of Garrett Jones made her clench her hands on her seatbelt. What the hell did he mean, telling her that Cape Air was perfectly safe? Probably he wanted her to arrive in Provincetown in a state of nervous confusion, so she wouldn't ever really get it together to question him. Or maybe he hoped she'd crash on the way to Provincetown, and never arrive at all. She should have followed her original plan: rented a car and driven down from Boston. That would have taken longer and cost more, but when she got to Wellfleet she would have been well and alive.

Apart from recommending this awful flight, Garrett Jones had done nothing in the years Polly had known him to earn her distrust. At the time of "Three American Women" he was, she had to admit, unfailingly courteous and cooperative. He had sent several of his former wife's paintings to the Museum, and provided information on the whereabouts of others; in a few crucial cases he had persuaded reluctant collectors to lend items for the show. Later on he wrote a brief, graceful appreciation of Lorin's work for the catalogue. This essay, however, did not mention that Garrett and his wife had ever been divorced or even separated. "I don't think that's really relevant," he had explained smoothly when Polly queried the matter on his proofs.

When Polly told Jones she was thinking of writing a book about Lorin he was graciously enthusiastic. He recommended her for the fellowship, and offered to supply photographs, letters, and the names and addresses of people she might like to interview. Now he and his present wife had invited her to visit them in Wellfleet before they closed the house for the winter and returned to New York, so that Polly could see where Lorin Jones had once lived and worked.

But in spite of Garrett Jones's cooperation and good manners, Polly didn't trust him as far as she could throw him. Which, since he was a tall, heavy, elderly man who must have weighed at least fifty pounds more than she, was not very far. Probably, Polly thought, she couldn't even push him any great distance. But she was going to have to push him, psychologically at least.

She didn't kid herself: the next twenty-four hours were going to be a battle. Probably Garrett Jones would do all he could to present himself in the most favorable light possible, and to conceal any evidence of the damage he had done to Lorin and of how unhappy she must have been in Wellfleet. Polly had to prevent him getting away with this — to cut through his sophisticated platitudes. The patience and tact Jeanne had always recommended would only go so far. Judging by what had happened when she had lunch with Jones in New York, they would only result in his telling her a lot of innocuous anecdotes with an air of courteous self-satisfaction. Eventually she'd have to push and shove, to confront him directly.

There was no point in trying to be too nice, either, because when Polly's book came out, in about eighteen months, Garrett Jones would stop speaking to her anyhow. If she was really lucky he might be dead by then, seeing that he was seventy-three now. Otherwise she would be in trouble, because though Jones didn't have as much power in the art world as he once had, he was still formidable. If he wanted to, he could probably do her serious professional harm. But that was a risk Polly'd decided she had to take.

Swerving sickeningly, the toy plane bounced down onto the end of Cape Cod and stuttered to a stop between stands of dusty-looking scrub oaks. In Central Park October still blazed with color: here the landscape was stripped and ashy, ready for winter.

Shaky, half-nauseated, but relieved to be alive, Polly climbed out into a strong crosswind and gulped cold salty air. As she lugged her duffel bag toward the toy terminal, she thought at first that Garrett Jones hadn't come to meet her. Then she recognized him, disguised as an old sea captain in jeans and windbreaker and visored cap.

"Hello there, Polly! Grand to see you!" he shouted as

she got within range. Before she could recoil he had put both hands on her shoulders and kissed her wetly on the cheek. Furious, she raised the arm that gripped her canvas bag and wiped her face with the back of her wrist.

"Is this all your equipment?"

"This is it."

"Traveling light, eh? I admire that in a woman. Here, let me." Not waiting for a reply, Garrett Jones wrenched her bag out of her hand and, in spite of his years, started toward the parking lot with a lively, almost rolling seaman's gait.

"Well, and how have you been?" he called jovially, turning a bronzed, weather-beaten countenance toward Polly as she scrambled to catch up.

"Fine, thanks."

"Did you have a comfortable flight?" He grinned, to her mind evilly.

"Fine, thanks," repeated Polly, determined not to show any weakness or fear. She felt caught off-balance, like some Amazon commander who has entered the field well prepared for war on land and is suddenly obliged to fight a naval battle. Until this afternoon she had never seen Garrett Jones in anything but a business suit; she had thought of him as an essentially urban, indoor type, someone who would be ill at ease in the country — to her advantage. In manner he had always been rather formal, addressing her as Miss Alter. Now he was affecting to be another person with another, more intimate, relationship to her. No doubt he was doing this to unsettle and confuse her.

With a grin, or possibly a grimace, Garrett Jones slung Polly's small but heavy bag into the back of an ancient green Volvo wagon, slammed the tailgate, and went around to unlock the passenger door. Polly detested having doors opened for her. She believed that the gesture, harmless as it seemed, was hostile: it was meant silently to establish that she was weaker than Garrett Jones and to put her under an obligation to him. But she suppressed her protest — it was bad tactics to start hostilities too soon.

"So what would you like to do first?" Jones asked as he

climbed in beside her. "I wish I could take you out for a sail, it's a hell of a fine day for it, but my boat's already in dock for the winter. I could try to borrow one from our neighbors, if you'd like."

Polly scowled. To go sailing with Garrett Jones in this windy, stormy weather would just give him a chance to finish what Cape Air had begun: that was, to make her sick and helpless; maybe even to nearly drown her. "Oh no thanks, Mr. Jones, don't bother."

"Garrett, please." He put his hand on Polly's arm and smiled into her eyes in a false fatherly way. "And I hope I may call you Polly."

"All right," she said ungraciously, thinking that this was the sort of question it was almost impossible to answer in the negative.

"Grand. Well, if you don't fancy sailing, the other notion I had was, I might drive around a little, show you some of the locations between here and Wellfleet that Laura used in her paintings."

"Yes, I'd like that," Polly said.

"Right, then." Garrett gunned the engine and pulled out onto the road, swinging the wheel around as if he were navigating a sailing ship, and headed up into the dunes at top speed. Polly wondered if he was trying to terrify her with his driving, but since he too was at risk she decided not to worry about it.

"Now." He stopped the Volvo at the top of a grassy rise. "Here's where Laura made the sketches for *Deposition*. About the same time of year as this, it must have been. Like to get out, probably you could see it better."

"Okay."

Garrett Jones started around to open the door for Polly; but she wasn't having any more of that, thanks, and by the time he got there she had scrambled out and slammed it behind her. Score one for me, she thought. She leaned against the side of the car with the low sun and the hard wind in her face, squinting at the sweep of sandy hills, the twisted beach pines like giant bonsai, the flattened silvery crescent of ocean. It was clearer to her than ever that *Deposition* — the largest of the three abstracts Garrett Jones had lent to the Museum show — was in fact a landscape.

Lorin Jones stood here painting this scene, she thought. At this time of year, maybe even this same hour of the afternoon, with the light coming low and from the left. I stand in her footsteps, am joined to her now by space and time. And also separated from her forever. A wave of loss and longing drowned Polly, as if the sea, the scrub, and the sand were dissolving and blowing over her in a fine haze of damp, gritty tears.

"You remember that picture, *Deposition,*" Garrett said, leaning against the car beside her.

"Naturally," Polly replied irritably, jolted out of her mood.

"You'll recognize that hollow in the dunes, then, and the shack over there with the purplish roof. Might have thought it would've fallen down by now, but these old Cape buildings are tough."

I'm old, but I'm tough, Polly heard him say; *don't think you're going to put anything over on me.* It occurred to her that his phony old-salt costume had the same message. It also said: *I am at ease here, in control; Cape Cod belongs to me.*

"I'd like to get a photograph of this view, if you don't mind."

"Good idea." He moved aside, allowing her to open the door for herself this time.

"*Deposition,*" she said as she returned the camera to her tote bag. "Tell me, do you happen to know what it means — why she gave her painting that name?"

"No idea." Garrett Jones grinned. "You know, Laura always had trouble with titles. When she got stuck, she would shut her eyes and open some book. Just the way my Aunt Mabel used to consult her Bible for spiritual guidance. Only with Laura it was usually Webster's Dictionary: she'd open it and put her finger on a word, or maybe a couple of words, and that would be it. I figure this was one of those times. It needn't mean anything."

"It seems pretty appropriate to me," Polly contradicted, quoting from her notes: " 'Deposition: A statement under oath, taken down in writing to be used in court in place of the production of the witness.' Isn't that what a painting is, too? Or should be?"

"Uh, yes, perhaps." Garrett Jones gave her a surprised, shrewd look. Score another for me, Polly thought. In her mind she ran over her list of Lorin Jones paintings, wondering which had been named at random from a dictionary. *Pigeon Hawk. Carbon Dioxide. Goatfish. Perispheres. Go.* Yeah, maybe. But not *Though They Know the War Is Over, They Continue to Fight.*

"Of course, one could read that title in other ways," Garrett added, recovering. "You could think of a 'deposition' as simply something that is set down, deposited. Or as referring to the time of year the painting was done, the end of summer. It could mean a kind of abdication of nature's power, as in 'The king was deposed.' Isn't that so?"

"Mm," Polly conceded.

"We'll never know what it meant to Laura, though."

"I suppose not." You'll never know, anyhow, she thought silently.

By the time the car turned onto Marsh Road in Wellfleet, Polly had seen four presumed sites of Lorin Jones's paintings — none of them as obvious as the first, since during the years Lorin lived on the Cape her work had become steadily more abstract — and had photographed them all. Her digestive system had returned to normal, more or less, and her mood was greatly improved. Not only the places Garrett Jones had pointed out, but everything she looked at seemed to bring her closer to her subject: the clear cool light, the spare oriental shapes of dune and pine and reeds, the muted colors, the greenish black calligraphy of the bare trees. She was possessed by a kind of euphoric déjà vu: at every other bend of the road she saw something magically familiar.

"Fine view, isn't it?" Lorin's former husband roared

against the wind as they passed a sweep of grassy marshland faded to buff and divided by a shimmer of choppy bay. "Ah, I should tell you. Abigail is awfully sorry, but she can't join us this evening. She has a crisis over some article about houseplants."

"Oh, that's too bad," Polly replied vaguely and insincerely, not turning her eyes from the landscape. She had nothing against Abigail Jones, a pretty, faded woman of about fifty who was a freelance women's-magazine writer, with little to say for herself and nothing to say about Lorin Jones. But if Polly had to confront Abigail's husband, it would be a lot easier and more pleasant if she weren't around.

"So seeing as how I'm not much of a cook, I thought we might go out for dinner. There's a pretty good seafood place in Eastham that's still open this time of year. How does that sound to you?"

"Oh, fine," Polly said, thinking that it might also be strategically to her advantage to face Jones on neutral ground.

"Good. Well, thar she blows." With a crunch of sand and gravel, he turned into a driveway between browned lilac bushes.

In spite of the implication of this announcement, Garrett Jones's house, once also Lorin's, was in no sense a whale. It was larger than Polly had expected from the photographs, and instead of standing in open fields was surrounded by carefully tended shrubbery.

Inside, the place seemed to have little to do with either art or Lorin Jones. There were a few good small contemporary pictures, including one of Lorin's that had been in Polly's show, but the rooms in which they hung were unnaturally neat and overdecorated in conventional Early American Colonial style, presumably by Abigail Jones, for they looked exactly like one of her color features in *Homes and Gardens*.

"The sitting room ... the dining room ... the study ... our bedroom." Garrett Jones led Polly through the downstairs.

"Very nice," she felt constrained to say. "It's not at all what I expected, though."

"Well, of course it was very different when Laura lived here. The house was damn near falling apart when I bought it back in nineteen-forty-nine, and there was no garden then, just long meadow grass right up to the walls. And of course the new extension wasn't built. We didn't even have electricity for the first few years. Abigail's done wonders. . . . Now let's go upstairs, and I'll show you Laura's studio." He led the way, rather slowly and heavily, up the steep, narrow staircase.

"Here we are. Rather small for a studio, but it's the only place in the house with unobstructed north light. Nothing much left from Laura's time, I'm afraid. This is Robbie's room now, our younger son, but he's away at Choate, of course. Sorry about the mess."

By Polly's standards, the mess was minimal. This room at least looked as if a human being lived in it; there was a reassuring clutter and shabbiness about the shelves of books and airplane models and shells and sports equipment, the posters of yachts and tennis stars tacked to the sloping wall beside the long dormer window. As if drawn by a magnetic force, Polly crossed the floor, pushed aside a gray corduroy curtain, and gazed out through the faintly green, bubbled old panes of glass, toward the misty sea.

"You recognize the view?" Garrett Jones's voice sounded close behind her. "Laura painted it over and over again, of course. It's in *Pigeon Hawk* and *Strata* and a number of her other pictures."

"I recognize it," Polly said, moving aside.

"She made a lot of sketches from these upstairs windows. I still have a few of them; I'll show you later. If you'll come out here in the hall, for instance, you can see —"

Reluctantly, Polly followed Garrett Jones and allowed him to demonstrate the scenes of various paintings, meanwhile wishing that he would go away so that she could be alone with them.

"And now let me show you where you'll be bunking."

Garrett tossed Polly's bag onto a double four-poster in a painfully tidy guest bedroom full of antique prints and spool tables and hooked rugs. "Here you are. If you want to wash up, it's right across the way." He pointed with the full extent of his arm, like a captain indicating something on the horizon. "Oh, incidentally, I've put out a few more old photos I found. They're here on the desk."

"Thank you."

"I figured you might like, say, half an hour to have a bit of a rest and change for dinner. Then we could take off about six, all right?"

"All right, sure," she echoed, looking down at her cord slacks, plaid shirt, and Shaker-knit sweater, thinking that she'd be damned if she was going to tart herself up to go to a Cape Cod restaurant with Garrett Jones.

As soon as he had descended the stairs Polly went into the bathroom, lifted the pink-terrycloth-covered lid of the toilet — wouldn't you know? — and sat down, less confident than before. She had realized that by driving her about, carrying her bag, and putting her up overnight, Garrett had set up the invisible expectation that she would behave like a polite houseguest. He had, in a word, set her up. Well, she would just have to forget about good manners.

As she crossed the hall, Polly felt the magnetic force again, pulling her toward Lorin's studio and its window. Again she stared out, over the fading ochre and gray and blue horizontal stripes of lawn, scrubland, marsh, sea, and cloud-streaked sky that, like several of Lorin's paintings from this period, resembled geological strata. In some of them the rocks seemed to have been sliced vertically, as sometimes happens in nature. But here, too, out the window, was the same dark slash bisecting slipped layers of beautiful pale color: the tall gray trunk of a dead elm.

Lorin Jones didn't hate this place, as her friend Sally Vogeler had implied, Polly thought; she loved it. Here in this house, deep in this pale light-washed landscape, she knew it was so.

Lorin stood here, where I am standing, she thought. She

saw what I see; she felt what I feel as I move down through the geological layers of her life. Joyful, apprehensive, confused; moved by the beauty of this place, oppressed by the heavy presence downstairs of Garrett Jones.

Suddenly Polly shivered, as if in a draft: she had the conviction that Lorin Jones, who had so often stood by this window, was here now behind her. It wasn't a totally new idea: she had felt the presence of Lorin's spirit before, but only inwardly, metaphorically. Now the sensation was realer and stronger. As she turned around she almost saw Lorin's wavery ghost in the shadows: the tangled dark hair, the wide sleepwalker's eyes. She blinked; the image faded into shapes of furniture and patterns of wallpaper, and was gone.

A soapy wave of longing washed over her. "Lorin." She whispered the name half-aloud. "Lorin . . . I'm here."

Downstairs somewhere a door slammed. Polly started and, not wanting to meet Garrett Jones again yet, retreated.

Back in the guestroom she took up the snapshots he'd left for her. Three of them, blurred and light-struck, showed groups of people in outdated sports clothes. With some difficulty she managed to pick out Lorin Jones, but could recognize no one else. The last photo, larger and clearer, was of a small sailboat. Lorin stood in the cockpit, holding on to the mast and partly obscured by the sail; she wore an open white shirt over a dark bathing suit. On deck, nearer to the camera and in sharper focus, a man in brief bathing trunks was grinning into the sun. He was robust, handsome, blond — the sort of man women were instantly attracted to, the sort that Polly herself would have been attracted to before she knew better. Could it be Hugh Cameron, for whom Lorin had left her husband?

No, of course not. It was — she recognized him now — Garrett Jones himself, maybe thirty years ago. Polly felt queasy, as if she had just seen a film run backward at top speed. Still, this photograph explained something she hadn't understood, which was why Lorin had ever married Garrett.

Now she could pick out Garrett Jones in the other

photographs, too: by his height, the breadth of his shoulders and chest, and the swatch of fair hair that flopped into his eyes in all four snapshots. Even today, she realized, it was there; Garrett hadn't gone bald, and the same unruly lock, now grayed almost to white, still fell across his brow. He was still, for his age, a good-looking man.

Why did Garrett want her to see these photos, in which her subject was mainly an indistinct blur? Obviously, because he wanted her to know and write that when Lorin Jones married him he was a fine physical specimen; that they were, as Jacky Herbert had put it, a handsome couple.

And would she write that? Well, yes, because it seemed to be the truth; and because it explained the marriage. Lorin Jones was a genius, but she was also a woman. Why shouldn't she, like Polly, have made at least one serious mistake in a rush of passion?

"No salad dressing for me, please."

"Oh, that's right." Garrett gave a little apologetic chuckle. "I should have remembered," he added, falsely implying to the waiter that Polly was his close friend or relative, though in fact they'd only lunched together once before. And probably the waiter believed him, Polly realized with irritation, because they didn't look unalike, both being blunt-featured and stocky.

For nearly an hour, on the drive to Eastham and then in this expensive restaurant, Polly had followed Jeanne's advice and behaved with careful politeness. She had put up with a second alteration in Garrett Jones's appearance and manner, from scruffy old salt to country-club yachtsman (navy blazer, checked shirt, paisley scarf), and made no comment on his erratic driving. She had allowed him to overrule her proposal that they split the bill. ("Impossible. I couldn't even consider it. No, this is my pleasure.")

She had also listened to a series of anecdotes about famous painters he had known, without pointing out that she'd already heard several of them. She was used now to the way people who were being interviewed tended to drift into unrelated tales of their own lives; but Garrett was really carrying it to an extreme.

To calm herself, Polly took another gulp of the pricey white wine Garrett had insisted on ordering and had already drunk nearly half of. He had also chosen the most expensive item on the menu, broiled lobster. If she'd known he was paying she would have ordered that too, instead of baked cod.

Polly couldn't explain to the waiter that she wasn't related to or a close friend of Garrett Jones, but she could demonstrate it. Without making any effort to be discreet, she hauled her tape recorder out of her tote bag and set it on the red-and-white-checked tablecloth. That would show him that this was a professional interview.

"Is that your tape machine?" Garrett asked as soon as they were alone.

"That's right."

"Hmf. Do you really want to use it now, at dinner?"

Obviously I want to use it, Polly thought angrily, or I wouldn't have brought it out. But she merely said: "I thought it might be a while till our food comes. And there's so much you've told me already, about art and artists, that I really wish I'd recorded. I don't want to miss any more." Jeanne would be proud of me, she thought, not sure she was proud of herself.

"Yes, but —"

"Besides, you were just starting to talk about Bennington College, where you first met Lorin. How did that happen?" She pressed RECORD.

"I don't recall exactly," Garrett said, after a pause in which Polly could see him wondering whether to refuse to go on.

"But she was in one of your classes, wasn't she?"

"Er, yes." Garrett took another swig of wine and capitulated. "The Tradition of the Modern, my big lecture course. But it was considerably later that we really got acquainted. In Laura's last year."

"Oh, yes?"

"I'd seen her in my class, of course. But it was her paintings I really noticed first, in the student show at the end of her junior year. I was very much struck by them: they were so strong, so original, not like most undergraduate work. And then when I connected the name with the face I was surprised again."

"Why surprised?"

"Well, Laura was so slight, so shy, so ethereal-looking. Not at all what I would have expected from her work. It was amazing to me that such a quiet, beautiful girl could paint like that."

Yes, Polly thought. Because you expect gifted women to be noisy, ugly Amazons. "And then you began seeing each other?"

"No. Not then. School ended, and she went home. But I have to admit I thought about her all that summer. In the fall, we met again at the faculty show and talked a little, and then Laura came to my office to look at a book on iconography that wasn't in the library. I realized then that she wasn't just very talented, she was intelligent and articulate — once you could hear what she said in that whispery little voice. And those are qualities you don't always find in gifted artists. As you must have discovered." Garrett grinned.

"I know what you mean," said Polly, who had had her troubles with stupid silent artists: last year there had been a male sculptor whose "statement" for the catalogue was almost illiterate.

"And at the same time, you see, she seemed — how shall I put it? — lost in this world. She was a virgin, of course. But beyond that, she was the sort of girl — well, you'd almost be afraid to let her cross the street, she was so dreamy, so innocent, so vulnerable. So aware of her natural surroundings as a painter, and so oblivious to them in every other way. More Meursault?"

"Not just yet, thanks," Polly said. Garrett's tongue

seemed to be loosening; maybe it was to her advantage that he should drink most of the wine. "So you thought of marrying her already," she murmured.

"Not then, no. I didn't even realize at first that we were falling in love." He paused, turning the glass in his heavy red hand.

"You didn't know at first," she prompted.

"No." There was another and even longer pause, broken only by the thin whirring sound of the tape recorder. She tried again:

"But then —"

Garrett remained silent, gazing past Polly. You loved Lorin too, she thought with a reluctant sympathy, and you lost her.

Yes, she added to herself, hardening her heart, and how did you lose her? "Still, eventually you knew you were in love, and then you decided to get married," she suggested.

"No." With an appearance of effort, Garrett turned his gaze back toward Polly. "I didn't think that far ahead. We were just consumed by it, consuming each other — I don't think young people feel that strongly now."

Young people? Polly thought. Yes, Lorin was young; but you were thirty-five.

"These yuppies one sees everywhere today, they're so rational and calculating. They don't love impulsively, romantically, without thinking of tomorrow."

"No," Polly agreed, wondering if in Garrett Jones's mind she was a rational, calculating yuppie.

"But that's how it was with us. It wasn't till late in the spring that it occurred to me that Laura would graduate soon and I might never see her again."

"Mm."

"It was after a lecture on French cathedrals. One of those freak warm nights you sometimes get in May, with sudden thunderstorms, and we all had to make a dash for it to get to the building where the reception was. Most of us had raincoats or umbrellas, but when Laura arrived she was sopping wet and barefoot, carrying her sandals, in trailing damp gauzy clothes that stuck to her body.

"I tried to get her to go back to her room and change; so did several other people. She was shivering with cold, but she refused. She claimed she'd dry off soon, but naturally she didn't. Finally she was persuaded to leave. I can still see how she looked walking away across the wet grass, through the oblongs of light from the windows. So slight and pale, with her long dark hair dripping down her back like some kind of exotic weed. There was something elfin and unworldly about her, almost not human." Garrett stared past Polly, into the past.

Yes, she thought, the scene vivid in her mind. Then, with a little shock: he feels what I feel; we are longing for the same person.

"What was I saying?" Garrett asked finally.

"You realized you might not see Lorin again," Polly prompted.

"That's right. I'd never said anything about the future, you know, and neither had she. But I knew she was planning to go to New York to study that fall. And that troubled me, too: the idea of Laura alone in the city, in the zoo the Art Students League was back then. She wouldn't have enough time to paint, either; her father was willing to pay her tuition for a year, but he thought she should get a part-time job to help cover her living expenses. And I knew how easily she could be exploited by people in New York — By dealers. And by men too. I couldn't let that happen."

"So you decided to marry her," Polly said.

Garrett shook his head. "I decided to ask her to marry me; I had no idea she'd agree. Almost no hope. She seemed so young, so beautiful, so gifted and free —"

Again Polly felt an unwanted rush of sympathy. She beat it back down, focusing on the word *free,* recalling the facts of the case.

"I see." She took a breath, determined to have the truth

out of him. "But you were married already, weren't you?" she added, watching Garrett's face.

"Er, yes." He blinked his bloodshot blue eyes in their net of creases. "Yes, I was, as a matter of fact. And does that shock you?"

"No, not much," Polly admitted, forced onto the defensive.

"Times have changed." Garrett sighed. "You young people, nothing much shocks you, right?"

"Well, not that sort of thing," Polly said, unwilling to be classed either as Puritanical or as totally immoral.

"People were shocked then. Very. Some of them wanted to have me fired." Garrett sighed again, then shook his head. "But that's all ancient history. You probably weren't even born then." He smiled kindly but a little condescendingly at Polly.

"Besides, you know," he continued, "my marriage was really over by then." He leaned forward across the table, gazing at her persuasively. "It was one of those impulsive, misguided wartime things. We'd hardly known each other, but I was about to go overseas with the navy —"

"Mh," Polly muttered. Impulsive; misguided. That's what my father probably said, she thought, when people asked why he left my mother.

"It was a mistake from the start. We weren't ever any good for each other. Except physically." His voice sank to a reminiscent murmur on the last words. Probably the tape would not pick them up, but Polly heard them.

"With Laura it was so different," Garrett resumed, clearing his throat. "The more I saw of her, the deeper in love we were. And then she needed me, not like Roz. I knew I could protect her, help her. She was so obviously gifted, and I had friends in New York, dealers and museum people, who would look at her work seriously if I asked them to. I knew she wouldn't ever show it to them herself. She was terrified of strangers, you know."

"Mm," Polly admitted.

"So I knew that without me she wouldn't have a chance.

She might never be recognized as a painter — you know what the scene is in Manhattan — or at least, not for years. The problem was, my job was in Vermont, and Laura needed to study in New York: she'd already learned all she could at Bennington. I didn't know what to do." Garrett shook his head; the swatch of thick gray-white hair flopped into his eyes, just as in the old photographs.

"So then —"

"So then I was offered a place as regular art critic on a New York paper. It seemed like fate.... Oh, thank you." The waiter had returned with their dinner. Polly turned off her tape recorder and moved it from the table to her lap.

"Ah. The lobster is excellent," Garrett announced presently. "Let me give you a taste."

"All right," she agreed. "And maybe you'd like some of my cod."

"Thank you."

Polly transferred a hunk of fish and some wedges of tomato and pepper to Garrett's plate, and looked up to see him poking a fork dripping with pink meat and melted butter at her face, as if she were a small child. There was a struggle between indignation and guile, which the latter won: she didn't want to antagonize her subject yet.

"Nice, isn't it?"

"Very nice," agreed Polly, who had swallowed the lobster with some difficulty.

"Do have some more."

"No, thank you. . . . You knew Lorin Jones's father," she remarked, trying for a casual tone while discreetly turning her machine on again. "What was he like?"

"Dan Zimmern? He was a tough old dog." Garrett Jones grinned and mashed sour cream and chives into his baked potato. Either because he no longer knew he was being taped, or because the wine had gone to his head, his manner had loosened considerably. "Wore out three wives. When I met him he was nearly sixty, but he was still damned handsome, almost like an old-time movie star. He was a charmer. Even the last few weeks of his life, when he was in the hospital most of the time, he fluttered the nurses' hearts."

"Is that so." My father could end up like that, Polly thought. Though he didn't look like a film star, and wasn't conventionally handsome, you could call him a charmer. She felt another surge of empathy with Lorin Jones.

"Of course he was a complete philistine where contemporary art was concerned," Garrett continued between bites. "Didn't understand in the least what his daughter was up to. Though once she started to have some success he became very proud, went to all her shows."

"Yes, I've heard that."

"Dan wasn't dumb, though. I remember something he said to me once. Or quoted, maybe: 'In the absence of happiness, pleasure and power are the best the world has to offer.' "

"Pleasure and power?"

"In that order." Garrett laughed. "And it was clear he had an appetite for both. All you had to do was watch him eat, or hear him talk about his job. . . . When I first met him I thought he was a coarse cynical old, uh, fellow." Garrett swallowed; had he been going to say "Jew"? "I was sorry for Laura, having a father like that."

"How did they get on together?"

"Pretty well, considering. Dan was a warm-hearted guy; he really cared a lot for Laura, though he had no idea what went on in her head. I think she loved him too, in her way. And after a while, I began to appreciate him myself. I'm sorry now I never got to know him better."

Because you've grown to be like him, Polly thought, watching Garrett crack open a lobster claw and spear the meat into his handsome, ruddy old face. Once you were young and in love, but now you prefer power and pleasure. You've worn out two, maybe three wives.

"Have some more wine."

"Oh no thanks."

"Come on. You might as well, it'll go to waste otherwise. I've got to quit drinking now, because I'm driving home."

"Well. All right." Polly allowed Garrett to fill her glass.

"Not a bad Meursault. I remember the first time I tasted this wine, in France; in nineteen-thirty-seven it must have been, when I went to see the cave paintings in Lascaux with . . ."

Before she could stop him, he was off on another round of name-dropping anecdote. She reached under her napkin and turned off the tape recorder.

6

Garrett Jones continued talking through the rest of dinner and on the drive home — and was, Polly had to admit
sometimes interesting or amusing. She herself said almost
nothing; the unwelcome feeling had come over her that she
was not behaving very well. Of course, under his courtly
manner Garrett was an old-fashioned male chauvinist, who
had probably made Lorin Jones's life unhappy in many
ways. But he had given up a good deal of his valuable —
and, at his age, limited — time to Polly and her project; he
had bought her an expensive seafood dinner, and answered
all her questions. Worse still, he appeared to like and trust
her.

"So what?" said the impatient voice of Jeanne in her
head. "All's fair in war, remember?"

Polly tried to remember this, but it wasn't easy. As they
turned into the driveway she had a strong stupid impulse to
warn Garrett, to confess that she intended to betray and
expose him as soon as she discovered anything to betray or
expose.

But maybe there wasn't anything much to discover, and
so it would be all right, she thought as they entered the
house. "Nonsense," said Jeanne's voice. "All he's given you
so far is a lot of self-serving lies about how much he loved
Lorin and helped her career. For Christ's sake, don't let him
snow you. Just keep smiling, push him a little harder, and
you'll get what you came for."

Well, maybe, Polly said silently to Jeanne; except now
his wife will be listening. You mustn't expect too much.

But as it turned out, Abigail wouldn't be listening. "I
guess your wife's gone to bed already," Polly remarked as

Garrett switched on a green-shaded tole lamp in the sitting room.

"My wife?" For a moment Garrett, who had been describing Venice in the 1950s, seemed not to know which wife she was referring to. "Oh, Abigail. Oh no, she's in New York. She had some crisis about an article, didn't I tell you?"

"You mentioned it, but I thought —" For the first time, it occurred to Polly that she was alone at night in the middle of nowhere with an old man she had thought of for months as an enemy. On the other hand, what harm could Garrett do her?

"She was sorry she couldn't be here, but I assured her we'd manage. I can cook breakfast, at least." Garrett gave a forced-sounding laugh. "Well, make yourself comfortable while I light the fire." He moved an overpolished brass screen aside, stooped heavily before the hearth, and struck a match on the bricks.

"'There we are," he murmured with satisfaction as the pale flames rolled up. "And how about a little Courvoisier?"

"Well . . . all right."

"To your book," Garrett proposed presently, leaning toward Polly from the other end of the fat chintz-covered sofa to clink balloon glasses.

"Thank you." Unused to brandy, she gulped; the fumes swirled up her nose, prompting a half-suppressed sneeze. "Could I ask you a few more questions?"

"Of course, anything you like. But no tape recorders, please. They always remind me of Watergate." He laughed and leaned back; broad, ruddy-complexioned, confident.

And so they should, maybe, Polly thought. "All right." She took out a notebook, then set her open bag down behind the arm of the sofa, and turned on the machine inside, feeling guilty but determined. I have to do this, she excused herself silently; I have to be accurate.

"When I had lunch with you and your wife in New York, you said that Lorin's parents weren't much alike," she began, opening the notebook and trying to read her list of questions in the fluttering firelight.

"That's putting it mildly." Garrett laughed again. "I've sometimes wondered if that was why Lorin was so high-strung. It's always been my theory, you know, that when parents are very different temperamentally their children are in trouble, because they're composed of discordant elements. There's a kind of genetic static produced."

"It could be." Is that what happened with me? Polly wondered: half conscientious practical mother, half erratic emotional father? "And how did Lorin's parents get on together?"

"Oh, well enough, I think. Celia was devoted to her husband. And Dan loved her, in his own way. He never really appreciated what he had, though. Didn't really see much difference between Celia and that noisy peroxide blonde he married after she died, with her fake Matisse prints, you know, what's-her-name."

"Marcia."

"That's right. You've met her?"

"I interviewed her."

"Well, then you know." Garrett grinned confidentially. "You didn't care for Marcia Zimmern?"

"Christ, no!" The brandy was beginning to loosen his tongue. "Did you?"

"Not very much," Polly admitted, similarly affected.

"I couldn't stand the woman. And of course it was far worse for Laura. She never got over her father's marrying someone like that less than a year after Celia died. Never forgave him, really."

And why should she? Polly thought. "Tell me, though. In what way was Celia Zimmern unlike her husband?"

"In every way. They were completely different types. For one thing, I don't think Celia gave a damn for either pleasure or power. Couldn't focus on them; that wasn't where her interests lay." Garrett considered, rotating his glass. "What mattered to her was her family, Laura and Dan. And after that art, books, music, nature."

"Mm."

"I'm sure it was from Celia that Laura got her sensitivity

to the natural world. And her love of paintings — Celia started taking her to galleries and museums almost as soon as she could walk. Her shyness, too; but in Laura it was exaggerated, into an almost pathological fear of unfamiliar people and situations."

"Pathological?" Polly frowned.

"Well, yes. I think it was. It was almost impossible, for instance, to persuade Laura to meet people in the art world who could help her. I kept explaining that once someone came to know her and like her, they'd be more apt to look at her paintings seriously. She'd always say, 'What if they get to know me and hate me?' "

"I see," said Polly, though to her this seemed a sensible question.

"I just couldn't convince her, no matter how important the occasion." Garrett shook his head. "Shy and stubborn: it was an exhausting combination. The stubbornness she got from her father, along with his energy; her mother was always gentle and yielding. And Laura had his looks, of course. Celia was pretty too — beautiful, but in a much more subtle way. You didn't notice at first how lovely she was. Some people never realized it."

"I know, I've seen pictures," said Polly, not wanting to be classed with these ignorant people.

"She was a wonderful woman." Garrett sighed. "Y'know, I was out there with Laura one day, the spring after we were married, and Celia was showing me around the garden. She was a very gifted gardener. Not professionally, of course, like Abigail: the place was always untidy, in process, and she didn't go in for nursery plants, except for roses."

"Roses," Polly repeated.

"Yes; Celia had wonderful old roses. Some varieties I've never seen before or since. But mainly she liked wildflowers. She used to go out into the woods and fields with a basket and dig up clumps of weeds. Her beds were full of trillium and wild hyacinth and narcissus and different sorts of long grasses."

"Mm."

"Well, you know, I looked at her, that damp spring day, as she knelt there with the trowel in her hand, transplanting a clump of white violets, and the idea came to me that it was Celia I should have married, not Laura. She was only six or seven years older than me — if she'd been a few years younger she would have been perfect. She had a first-rate mind, but she wasn't pushy or argumentative like most educated women."

"Really," said Polly, wondering if this classic antifeminist statement was being taped. "So you think Celia would have suited you better than her daughter."

"In many ways, yes. For one thing, she was a genuine intellectual. She could talk intelligently about anything: art, aesthetics, psychology, philosophy, literature. . . . Compared to her, Laura was only a beautiful, willful child." Garrett shook his head slowly. "But of course one always falls most passionately in love with children — or with the child in the other person. Isn't that so?"

"I guess it can happen," said Polly, who had never had this experience. She dropped her hand over the arm of the sofa to make sure her bag was open and the tape recorder exposed. "And did you ever tell Celia Zimmern how you felt about her?"

"No; how could I? But I think she knew. I'm sure she could sense that there was a sympathy between us. There's a kind of vibration one feels sometimes in the presence of a really sensitive woman. I've experienced it often. In Paris, just after the war . . ."

Before Polly could head him off, Garrett sailed into another sea of anecdote, this time romantic rather than professional in nature. Now, however, he didn't drop names, but rather held them just out of reach ("A very beautiful woman, and a gifted poetess — you've read her work, I'm sure, she's in all the anthologies . . . ," etc.). As he reminisced, leaning back easily into the flowered cushions, with his fire-sparked brandy glass in one hand and the other arm resting along the top of the sofa, the creases in his face were softened by the rosy light and his blunt, handsome features warmed and enlivened. For the first time he strongly resembled his old photographs.

"You've had a lot of experiences," Polly said when Garrett paused to refill their glasses, hoping to change the subject. "But I wanted to ask —"

"Yes, it's been a fascinating life," he interrupted. "I've thought sometimes of writing my memoirs. I certainly have enough material. My publisher's suggested it, too." He gave a sigh. "But I don't know. It means so damned much work, going through all my old letters and papers, writing to people I've lost track of completely, getting all the names and dates and places right."

He sighed again, then grinned at Polly, his pale blue eyes sparkling. "Of course, if I could find an assistant — a collaborator, I should say. Somebody who knew the art world, and had a gift for research. That might help get me started, don't you think?"

"Sure, why not?"

"It would have to be someone young and energetic, of course. Someone like you —" Garrett leaned over and put his strong knobbed hand on Polly's, patting it in a fatherly manner. "I think we could work together, y'know? Believe there's a sympathy between us already. A natural understanding."

"Thank you," Polly said, smiling nervously; more than ever, she felt herself to be in bad faith.

"So how about it?" Garrett asked. "Like to help me?"

"It'd be an interesting project," she temporized, wondering if he could be serious. "But when I finish my book next year I've got to go back to work, or I'll starve." She gave an awkward light laugh and eased her hand from under Garrett's.

"Don't worry about that," he assured her; his hand now rested on Polly's tan cord slacks. "If I agreed to take on the project I'd get a fairly decent advance from my publisher. And I don't see why we couldn't manage a nice little grant for you." He gave her thigh a friendly squeeze. "I say 'little,' but it'd be a good deal more than you earn now, I can assure you."

"The Museum would never hold my job for me that long," Polly said, moving her leg away, but unobtrusively. It was late at night, and Garrett was half-addled; she didn't feel all that sober herself.

"Sure they would; I'd see to it. You know your boss is a good friend of mine." He grinned again, then stooped to poke up the fire, stirring smoke into the room. "Think about it, all right?"

"All right," Polly agreed, wondering if she should. A year — two years, it might well be — working for and with Garrett Jones, what would that be like? A week ago, even a few hours ago, she wouldn't have considered it. But now the idea seemed vaguely possible. She no longer feared or distrusted Garrett — she almost liked him. And after all, he had known everyone in the art world for the last fifty years; his book could be really interesting.

"Good." He smiled and closed his eyes.

Polly yawned, realizing how tired she was, then gathered her resources; she mustn't let Garrett fall asleep yet. "Tell me a little more about the time you and Lorin spent here," she said. "Were you usually in Wellfleet all summer?"

Garrett opened his eyes and shook his head as if to clear it: his gray forelock flopped. "Aw, no. Not me. I was reviewing regularly for the paper then. Had to be in New York for openings right through June. And even when there wasn't anything on in town there'd be shows in other parts of the country. I was on a train or a plane half the time."

"So Lorin was here more than you were?"

"Oh, yes. Much more. You see, already back then she was turning against New York, all that scene. Even before I had the house insulated and the furnace put in, she started coming up in May and staying on later and later into October. It was crazy, because it can get damn cold this time of year. The wind used to really howl through the walls."

"How did she manage, then?"

"Wasn't easy. She'd try to keep warm by turning on the

kitchen stove and painting in there, or dragging an old electric heater around from room to room after her. You should've seen my electric bills. And even then, she sometimes had to wear gloves to work."

"Really." Polly saw it in her mind: the bare trees tossing outside the studio window; Lorin in paint-spattered jeans and sweater and black leather gloves, standing between her easel and the dull orange glow of an old-fashioned coil heater.

"Then, once we had the furnace, she started coming up here all year round."

"For weekends, you mean?"

"More than that. Weeks at a time. Didn't matter what was going on in New York, after a while. Some friend could be having an opening, or I might have bought tickets for a play, but Laura would just take off. Eventually she got to dislike the city so much she spent most of the year here."

"All by herself?"

"Well, yes. Usually. Of course I came up when I could ..." Garrett blinked, whether from guilt or grief or mere sleepiness Polly could not guess. "I didn't come as often as I should've. I know that now." He nodded his large, handsome old head slowly. "But it was an awful long trip when you couldn't afford the plane, and I had so damn much traveling to do already."

"Lorin didn't go with you on your trips?"

"Not after the first year or so. There were a couple of disastrous times ... I would've liked to have her along, though; it was lonely for me on the road."

"It must have been lonely for her here, too," Polly said, struggling with another impulse toward sympathy.

"She didn't seem to feel it. People didn't mean that much to Laura, you know. ... Even I didn't mean all that much to her, as it turned out." His voice had become shaky.

"How do you know that?"

"A man always knows, if he's not a fool. And so does a woman, I think." Garrett gave Polly a meaningful look. "Right?"

"I suppose so," Polly admitted. I was a fool then, she thought, taking another gulp of brandy. Both of us were fools, trusting people to whom in the end we didn't mean all that much. "Still, she married you," she said, trying to console him. "She must have cared once."

"Oh, I admit that." His smile was wry. "But if she'd continued to care, she would've stayed in New York with me. Isn't that right?"

"I suppose so." Polly remembered her husband's betrayal and felt another rush of sympathy for Garrett. "But did you ever say you needed her — did you tell her that?"

"Hell, sure I did. I explained to Laura a hundred times that I had to be in the city for my job, and I wanted her with me. It was like talking to a blank canvas. Sometimes she seemed to be listening, but she didn't really hear."

Exactly, Polly thought, recalling scenes from her own past.

"So do you think it was a mistake, your marriage?" she asked.

Garrett did not answer at once; he gave a long, heavy sigh and refilled his glass. "Sometimes I think both my first two marriages were mistakes," he said at last. "I couldn't make either of my wives happy, and they couldn't make me happy. They couldn't give me what I needed."

"And what was that?" Polly asked. "I mean, for instance."

"Well. For instance, I wanted children very much. But my first wife couldn't have a baby, and Laura wouldn't."

"She didn't want children?"

"No. I think she was afraid of it, the whole process, you know." Garrett shook his head slowly. "Now I'm what our pediatrician calls an elderly father." He smiled wryly. "But as far as I'm concerned, that's better than never being a father at all, you know? People without kids, they don't really care what happens to the world after they're gone, unless they're saints. They're only interested in their own lives, isn't that right?"

"I know what you mean," Polly said.

"Of course you understand; you have children." Garrett swayed toward Polly and put his hand on hers again. This time she did not remove it.

"I have a son," she said, wondering where Stevie was at this moment and what he was doing.

"Yes, you told me." Garrett gazed past Polly's shoulder into the dim cream-flowered wallpaper. Then, slowly, he turned to her again, first smiling, then staring. "You know something," he said suddenly in a different, stronger voice. "You kind of remind me of her. Laura."

"Really?" Polly gasped as if the smoldering logs had exploded into a burning blaze of fireworks.

"I don't know why." He shook his head. "You don't look much like her. There's something, though. Maybe it's the voice."

"You think I sound like her?" Polly said, listening to the words as they issued from her lips in Lorin's ghostly tones. She had never heard Lorin speak, and never would; as far as she knew, Lorin's voice was never recorded.

"Mm, yes, a little."

Polly stared at Lorin Jones's husband. Suppose it was true — who had a better right to say so? And after all, hadn't Polly suspected this all along? Hadn't she noted the overlapping of their lives, marveled that both were only children, and Jewish; that they shared a county, a city, a profession? And even, almost, a name; Polly remembered her shiver of recognition when she heard that in childhood Lorin was known as Lolly.

Here, in Lorin's old haunts, they had drawn even closer together. All day she had walked in Lorin's footsteps; and sometimes, surely, Lorin's ghost had walked beside her.

"This was her home; this was the place she loved," Polly announced, sure of it now.

"That's right." Garrett sighed. "That's why, when I realized she was determined to spend most of the year here, I began doing everything I could to find a teaching job nearby, so I could be with her more of the time."

"But you didn't find one."

"No; I found one, eventually. Only it was too late. I came dashing up here to tell her about it, she was gone. Hadn't even left me a note."

"That's hard," Polly exclaimed.

"It about killed me, at the time. If you want to know." Garrett nodded slowly twice. "You see, I'd had no idea. . . . Laura'd never complained, never said anything. Only, more and more, she started avoiding me. And she wouldn't talk to me about her work any longer. I guess I should have known; but she was always such a solitary person, and it came on so gradually. That last year or so —" He stared into the middle distance. "I knew she'd hit some kind of a serious block, but she wouldn't let me help her, or make any suggestions about her painting. Finally, she wouldn't even show me what she was working on. After dinner she'd go up to her studio and shut herself in. If I knocked on the door she wouldn't answer. Sometimes she'd stay in there for hours, till it was past midnight or later, and I gave up waiting for her and went to bed."

"I'm sorry," Polly said; yet she seemed to know intuitively why Lorin Jones had wanted to escape from Garrett and his intrusive sympathy. Over the centuries, always, the artist has had to flee the critic. And yet, how awful for both of them! She imagined the long silent evenings in this house; Lorin shut in her studio, staring at an empty canvas; Garrett pacing the other rooms.

"I never thought . . . I should have given her more space, maybe. Or I should've tried harder to talk to her. Christ knows she was unhappy. Must have been. She must have hated her life here. Hated me too, probably till she died."

No, that didn't sound right, Polly thought. "Not necessarily," she said, forgetting the rule that an interviewer must not offer contrary opinions.

"You think not?" Garrett stared at her tipsily, as if she knew the answer.

"Did she ever say she hated you?"

Garrett shook his head. "Just said, when I finally had a letter from her — wasn't a letter, really: only a couple of lines on half a piece of drawing-paper — just said, she had to go away. Said she was sorry."

"She didn't hate you," Polly declared, transported, possessed. She didn't need to ask any more questions; she knew everything about Lorin Jones: how long and in what distress she had stared at that piece of drawing-paper; how hard it had been for her to write those few words.

And she knew, too, how Lorin must have felt the day she left Wellfleet forever. She raised her eyes and imagined looking around this room for the last time, unable to speak all her regret, all her resolve. Then, struck by his silence, she glanced back at Garrett. His eyes were closed again; his broad chest under the checked shirt rose and fell in a slow rhythm.

"Well, guess I'd better be going to bed," she said, reaching over the arm of the sofa to turn off her tape recorder. "Been a long day."

Garrett's pale blue eyes blinked open. "Tired, are you, child?"

"Mm. Rather." Polly began to get up; a wave of dizziness came over her. The brandy, she thought, sitting down again on the edge of the sofa.

"Wait a sec. Don't go yet. I want to say —" Garrett put his hand on hers again in what no longer seemed a paternal manner. "Having you here, talking to you. It means a lot to me." His voice was thick with emotion.

"I'm glad I could come," she replied almost at random, listening still to her own — or Lorin's? — voice.

"Y'know I can't speak to Abigail about Laura. She still gets jealous."

"Mm." Well, she might, Polly thought. Abigail is just an ordinary woman, and Lorin was unique, beautiful, a genius —

"Having you here — it's as if she'd come back to me in a way, y'know?"

"I know," Polly said, feeling the blaze of consciousness again.

"You're a good girl. Do a good book, I bet." Garrett squeezed her hand again. "Give me a goodnight kiss."

She hesitated. But after all, why not? "All right." She aimed for the red, mottled surface of his cheek, but Garrett turned his head at the last moment and landed a warm and definitely sensual smack directly on her mouth, at the same time pulling her against him.

For a moment Polly let it happen; she felt and gave warmth and pleasure. It had been over a year since she'd given any man more than a peck on the cheek. Then, recollecting who and where she was, she pushed Garrett away and stood up fast; the room spun.

"Aw. Don't go yet."

"Got to," Polly insisted through a dizzy blur. "I'm really tired. Uh, well, thanks for everything. See you later."

"Pleasant dreams," Garrett called, raising himself with an attempt at courtesy, then falling back among the cushions. He gave her a woozy wave and smile, and closed his eyes.

Polly listened as she made ready for bed, but there was no sound from below. Probably Garrett Jones had passed out on the sofa. She felt drunk and confused, angry at herself, angry at and sorry for him. She remembered Jeanne's warnings, her own cautions to herself. For Christ's sake, she was here as a researcher, she was supposed to be cool, impartial, detached. To sympathize with Garrett, to see him as in some ways a tragic figure, that was forgivable. But to kiss him was muddling, unprofessional, unseemly.

Brushing her teeth over the bathroom sink, where Lorin Jones must so many times have stood to brush her own teeth, Polly emitted a cross, confused gargling sound, and spat.

Never mind, Lorin said suddenly in her head. *It was I who kissed him, not you.*

Yes, Polly thought. That's how it was. She lifted her eyes to the mirror, and saw there a kind of double image. In the dim backlight she seemed paler, her hair darker, her eyes enlarged and shadowed, as if Lorin's last photo had been superimposed on the reflection of her face.

You're drunk, she told herself. It's only because you're wearing a dark sweater, and haven't had your hair cut since August. She snapped on the fluorescent tube above the glass; the resemblance vanished. Again she was stocky, round-faced, short-haired. But it had been there, for a moment.

As Polly climbed dizzily into bed, she realized that her distrust and fear of Garrett Jones were gone. She felt instead only what Lorin's ghost must feel: pity and affection for her handsome, self-centered, insensitive husband, now a famous elderly man who — too late — blamed himself bitterly and longed for his child bride. Yes; but now, through Polly's intercession, Garrett knew that Lorin had cared for him; she had kissed and forgiven him.

"Is that right?" she asked aloud in the dark. "Is that what you wanted?"

There was no answer. But as she sank into an alcoholic drowse, Polly's final sensation was that Lorin approved and was there; that the whisper of the bare trees outside the window was her whisper, the cold breath of the wind against the clapboards her breath.

7

At first Polly thought she was having another nightmare. There was a heavy weight on her, a smothering heat and constriction.

"Wha! Help!" she choked out, and half woke in the half-dark to an unfamiliar room where someone much larger than Jeanne was lying on top of her, nuzzling at her neck.

"Darling. Don' be afraid." The weight and the moist searching kisses, smelling of drink, continued. It was, it must be, Garrett Jones.

"No! Get the hell off me!" she shouted, shoving the resistant bulk aside with all her strength. She struggled upright, fumbling for the mock-kerosene lamp, then finding it and switching it on.

"Polly, my sweet." It was Garrett; he was sitting heavily on the double bed beside her. He had changed his clothes again and was wearing white silk pajamas and a red damask robe with satin lapels, like someone in a thirties comedy of high life.

"Please, go away."

"I startled you, little one; f'give me." He reached to pat her arm, but missed. "Were you 'sleep already? I'm sorry I took so long to come to you; must've dozed off."

"Wha'd'you mean? I didn't— "

"You look so lovely, all warm and tousled." Garrett swayed toward Polly, feeling for her breast with one heavy red hand. She batted it away and slid to the other side of the mattress.

"What a charming costume. Always have thought men's pajamas were awfully sexy on a girl."

"Listen, Garrett, goddamn it," Polly was almost shouting again. "I don't want to make out with you."

"I thought you 'ere waiting for me." Now his tone was hurt and aggrieved. "I thought, surely —"

"Well, I wasn't." Reminding herself that her host was drunk, Polly tried to speak quietly and with authority. "Please, get out of my room now, okay?"

"What's the matter, darling? You were so sweet all evening." He smiled boozily and began to edge across the rumpled sheets and ruffled eyelet pillows toward her. "Be a little kind to me now."

Taking advantage of his slowness, Polly scrambled out of the bed on the far side. She circled a chintz-cushioned rocker, banging her toe; dashed out across the hall, and into the opposite room.

"My dear girl, what's the matter? Where are you?"

Polly did not answer. Breathing hard in the dark, she slammed the door and fumbled for, found, and shot the bolt.

"Polly, my dear."

She patted the wallpaper, feeling unsuccessfully for a light switch. On the other side of the wall she could hear Garrett shuffling about in the hall, banging doors open.

"Polly, darling. Where are you?"

"Go back to bed!" she called.

"Darling, please." Garrett was outside her door now, rattling its handle. Polly moved over the cold floorboards in the dark, knocking against what sounded like a standing lamp. She groped about, clutched its cold twisted metal stem, righted it, and turned it on. The room that once had been Lorin's studio glowed into view.

"Please! Let me in."

What the hell was she supposed to do now? Polly thought. She sat down on a quilted bedspread patterned with Western ranch brands, then got up again and pulled the spread back. The bed was unmade, but there were several blankets. She could spend the rest of the night here if she had to.

"Polly?"

Don't answer, Polly told herself. She crawled into Garrett's son's bed on top of the mattress pad.

"Polly, dear!" The door rattled violently.

She dragged the blankets and spread up over herself, blurring Garrett's cries.

"Lolly!"

Polly raised her head. Had she really heard that?

"Darling, please!" He was almost sobbing.

I'll never get back to sleep now, she thought. Maybe I should let him in. Maybe it would prove to him that Lorin had forgiven him, because he thinks I'm her. She pushed back the blankets and half sat up.

"Lorin?" she whispered. "Is that what you want?" She shoved the covers aside and stood on the flat braided coils of the bedside rug.

"Darling! Just wanna kiss you goo'night."

Polly took a step forward, and felt the chill of the polished floorboards under her bare feet. But I'm not your darling, she thought. I'm not Lorin: for one thing, she loved you, and I don't. She got back into bed again; dragged up the covers.

"Please, dearest. Lemme in."

I'm sorry, Polly said in her mind, not to Garrett but to his wife's ghost. *I can't do it. Do you understand?* But there was no answer. She was alone in the dark in a house on Cape Cod, and a drunken randy old man was trying to get into her room and her bed.

"Hello in there . . . hello?" he cried finally and feebly. There was a silence; then the sound of steps going away. A heavy confused noise, as if Garrett had stumbled and half fallen. A door closing; silence.

Well, Jeanne warned me, Polly thought, turning over under the scratchy blankets. She remembered her friend's body, so light and soft and fresh, comparing it to Garrett Jones's coarse, inert bulk. I didn't listen to her, she thought, and now look what's happened. Among other things, I've probably made a permanent enemy; men don't like to be turned down sexually.

"Lorin, help me," she whispered. "You got me into this."

But the wind outside, that was once so clearly Lorin's breath, had subsided. This room, where she had spent so many long hours, felt cold, dark, and empty of her spirit.

"Lorin?"

Though there was no further sign, Polly lay awake for a long time, listening.

"Oh, good morning." Garrett Jones hardly glanced around from the stove; his tone was constrained, unfriendly. In the hard morning light both he and his expensive country clothes looked older and more worn.

"G'morning," Polly answered warily.

"Sleep well?" He did not quite look at her.

"Yes, thanks," she lied.

"Coffee?"

"Yes, thanks." Polly sat down, wishing she could leave at once. Probably Garrett was wishing the same thing; but there was no plane out of Provincetown until her noon flight.

As Garrett put a mug of coffee and a plate of dry, burned-looking toast before her, they exchanged an uneasy glance.

"Sorry about last night," he said, stiffly and not very apologetically. "Seems like we both had too much to drink, got our signals crossed."

"That's okay," Polly mumbled. In the glare of day, it was all too clear that Garrett had never shared her exalted view of last night's events; he had no idea that she had been acting as Lorin's proxy, loving and pardoning him — or not pardoning him — in Lorin's name.

"I could've sworn you were giving me the go-ahead."

"Well, I wasn't." She took a gulp of lukewarm, bitter coffee.

"Or maybe you changed your mind."

"No, I never —" Polly's voice faded; not only did she not want to discuss it, she felt partly to blame for what had happened.

"I think you changed your mind." Her discomfort seemed to encourage Garrett; he gave her a narrow smile. "What happened? Tell me, I'm interested. Was it my age?"

"No, uh," she stuttered, taken aback.

"Maybe you think I can't please a woman anymore, but you're wrong, you know. I'm still competent."

"I didn't —" Polly flushed. "I just don't want to get involved with you, that's all."

"Well, you were certainly giving off different signals last evening." He laughed in a meaning way.

"I was not." Polly felt herself becoming furious as well as nervous and guilty. "I suppose you think any woman you take out to dinner wants to go to bed with you."

"No-o." But Garrett half smiled; it was clear that he did think this.

"Anyhow, you're married."

"Oh well, yes." He dismissed this smoothly, waving a piece of unburned toast smoothed with marmalade. "I'm married. And Abigail's a wonderful woman, of course. Very beautiful." He looked hard at Polly, clearly communicating the idea that she was not beautiful. "And tremendously steady and kind." This, too, was said pointedly.

"I'm sure she is," Polly agreed coolly, trying to control her hurt and fury.

"I have to admit it, though, she's not exciting; not like Laura. Never was, really." Garrett's tone was almost confidential now, though not pleasant. "And now. . . . Well, Abby's fifty this year. And you know, with most women, after fifty there's not much juice in them. They kind of dry up, like grapes left on the vine." He grinned and shook his heavy, handsome head, as if both enjoying and deploring the sexual double standard. "How old are you, Polly, by the way?"

"I'm thirty-nine, if it's any of your business," Polly said furiously.

"Really? I thought you were younger." It was clear that this was not a compliment. More likely, Garrett was excusing himself for having put so much effort into trying to seduce her. He gave her a hard, cool glance, and added, "I should've known. Young women today, they don't make a fuss about a man's being married, in my experience. They're free romantic spirits; they make love to anyone they fancy." He smiled in a reminiscent way. "And any time."

"Well, I don't," Polly said with force.

"No, quite." Now his look conveyed that she was middle-aged and inhibited; perhaps also that she didn't get that many opportunities.

"As a matter of fact, if you want to know, I'm a lesbian," Polly said, speaking these words aloud for the first time in her life.

"Really?" Garrett blinked.

"That's right."

"Ah." He smiled broadly, easily, for the first time that morning. "Well. Excuse me. If I'd known —" He sat down at the highly polished Early American table opposite her. "You should have told me that last night, really," he added pleasantly, leaning forward. "Now, shouldn't you?"

"I suppose so," Polly admitted.

"I realize it's not the easiest thing to say." Garrett's whole manner had changed; it was open and friendly. "But it would have avoided a lot of trouble. I wouldn't have made a fool of myself, or given you such a fright." He laughed. "And, by the way, I want to assure you of my discretion. I won't say anything to anyone."

"That's all right. I mean, thanks," Polly added grudgingly, wondering whether she should believe him. But what difference did it make anyhow? She *was* a lesbian, since the night before last.

"That's not much of a breakfast," Garrett remarked, looking at her plate, on which the burned toast remained. "Let me make you some bacon and eggs."

"Uh —"

"Come on." He smiled. It was clear that his self-esteem and goodwill had been completely restored.

"No thanks." Polly still felt cross and embarrassed. She cast around in her mind for something hurtful to say that would not be discounted as coming from a lesbian.

"Well, then, if you've finished breakfast," Garrett interrupted her search, "I'd like to take you out to the barn, show you some of Laura's work that's still here."

"I — all right," Polly agreed, shelving her impulse in the service of a higher good.

"Now I don't want you to get too excited," Garrett cautioned over his shoulder as Polly followed him along a path beaten through long faded grass that matched his gray-blond hair. "Laura took almost all her finished work with her when she ran out on me. She couldn't bear to be separated from any of it, maybe you've heard that."

"Yes, I have."

"I think myself it was because she remained a child in so many ways. Her paintings were, what do the psychologists call it, a kind of security blanket for her. Well, here we are." Garrett shoved open the weather-beaten sliding door of the barn. He had resumed his windbreaker and peaked captain's cap, and his aspect was again nautical and jaunty. "I keep Laura's drawings in this old fridge. You should get yourself one, y'know. It's as good as a safe if there's a fire."

From the rusted chrome shelves of the refrigerator Garrett removed a worn black portfolio tied with tapes and two manila folders. "Here, you can see." He opened one of the folders and began to turn over sheets of paper. "It's mostly just notes, unfinished sketches, that sort of thing. Just what Laura left behind when —"

He did not finish the sentence, but Polly was not listening anyhow. Her attention was fixed on the drawings: some of them quick sketches, others detailed impressions of a shed, a skeleton leaf, a sleeping cat. They were executed in pencil and pen, a few lit with white or brown chalk, others with streaks of blue or sea-green wash. Realistic as most of them were, there was an oddness, a characteristic attenuation Polly recognized instantly.

"I tell you what," Garrett said. "Let's take everything into the house where it's warm."

"Okay, sure." Polly had not noticed the temperature; now she realized that a damp, freezing wind was blowing through the barn.

How can this be happening? she thought as she followed Lorin's husband back through the long beaten-down grass. How can I deserve it, when I didn't do what Lorin wanted last night? But maybe she *had* done exactly what Lorin had wanted, or at least what she had done: shut her husband out of her room, out of her life.

Inside, Garrett Jones cleared the dining-room table of its brass candlesticks and careful display of waxy-looking autumn fruit, and reopened the folders. There was more there than Polly had ever imagined or hoped for — not only drawings, but notes, bills, postcard reproductions of paintings —

"Oh, wow," she exclaimed as he leafed through the contents. "I didn't know you had all this stuff. You never said — nobody told me —"

"No one was interested, really. Not till you appeared." Garrett smiled and turned over a half sheet of paper, across which was scrawled a shopping list in Lorin's faint, spiky hand:

> *zinc white*
> *toothpaste*
> *grapefruit juice*
> *narcissus bulbs*

"You kept everything," she murmured.

"I wrote and offered to send it all on to Laura, once she was settled," Garrett defended himself, though Polly hadn't meant it that way. "She never answered my letters. Or the lawyer's. I used to wonder sometimes if that fellow tore them up."

"Fellow?"

"That bastard Cameron. You've heard of him, I imagine."

"Oh, yeah."

"Met him?"

"Not yet. I'm hoping to interview him when I go down to Key West next month, though."

"Yes? Well, good luck." Garrett's tone implied that she would need it.

"Tell me about him," Polly said, shifting her attention with difficulty from the drawings.

"About Hugh Cameron?" He almost sneered the name. "Well, I only met him a couple of times, and I didn't pay him much attention. I didn't imagine that he'd ever be of any importance to me, naturally." Garrett shook his head. "He was just one of the usual crowd of rather scruffy young people at the Provincetown Arts Center that year. He wasn't even a painter; he was a poet. Or rather, he called himself a poet, because he'd had a few nothing poems in the kind of magazines nobody reads."

"I see." Polly made a mental note to look up these poems.

"The truth was, he had the artist's temperament without any talent to speak of. That's not uncommon, you know. And all right, it's a tragedy. But if you find yourself in that position, you've got to cut your losses, the way I did. If you don't, pretty soon you're just a pathetic phony."

Polly looked at Garrett. You wanted to be a painter yourself once too, she thought.

"Anyhow." Garrett cleared his throat. "The Arts Center not only houses would-be artists and writers during the off-season, they have readings, mount exhibitions. I was a member of their board at the time, and when I was on the Cape Laura and I usually went to their openings. That was how we met Hugh Cameron, sometime in October, as near as I can remember."

"I see. And then?"

"And then nothing, as far as I was concerned." Garrett shrugged. "I saw him again at another opening in April; I remember because Laura was talking to him for a while, I couldn't imagine why. By then his time in Provincetown was almost up. They throw the fellows out on May first, you see, and rent the studios to tourists. He had no job, no money, no place to go from there.

"The way I read it, sometime that spring he probably took a hard look at Laura. He already knew she was a successful painter, and he guessed she had a little money — more than a little by his standards, probably, because from the start I let Laura put everything she made from her painting into her own bank account. She didn't use it except to buy art supplies; I gave her an allowance for her clothes and housekeeping, and I paid for everything else.

"So I figure Cameron decided it'd be convenient for him to fall in love with Laura, and feed her a lot of hogwash about the integrity of the artist, and the destructiveness of the critic, and the need for truly sensitive people to abandon the conventional world and live for each other and their art. He tried to justify himself with that kind of talk afterward, to anyone who would listen.

"If he'd been a painter Laura would have seen through him in ten minutes. Hell, her mother, Celia, if she'd been alive, she would have seen through him in five, because she knew something about poetry. And so did Laura's brother, Lennie — he could spot a loser like Hugh at twenty paces. But Laura didn't have their ear."

"So she left here with him at the end of April?"

"Yes. On May Day." Garrett smiled wryly. "Cameron made a lot of that later, apparently. It was the sort of cheap symbolism he liked."

"And you had no idea this was going to happen."

"Not a clue. As I said, Lorin didn't leave a note, so at first I wasn't concerned. I was driving down from Providence, and I hadn't said exactly when I'd be coming. When she wasn't here, I figured she'd gone out sketching, or maybe even up to Boston overnight on the ferry; she did that sometimes. I searched all around the place, and walked down to the inlet, because she used to go there a lot to paint. After it got dark I phoned some of our friends, but nobody'd seen her or knew anything. Then I looked in the closet, and most of her clothes seemed to be there, so I started to think about car crashes, and the weirdos who could be lurking about on the beaches or in the pine woods."

Over twenty years later, Polly heard in Garrett's voice an echo of the panic of that evening. "So what did you do?"

"Well, I was kind of wandering around the house, calling up different people and pretending to them that nothing was wrong. I went into Lorin's studio to look for a phone number. Before I hadn't noticed anything out of the way, but now I realized that most of her equipment was gone."

"You knew then that she'd left you?"

"No, not really. It could have just been a painting excursion. I knew the next day. I discovered then that she'd cleared out not only her own bank account, but also the joint account we kept here. Nearly six thousand dollars, it was, because I'd just put the money in for a new roof."

"Oh, hell," Polly murmured, wondering how she would ever justify this.

"I don't want you to blame Laura too much," Garrett said, registering her tone. "I figure it was probably Cameron's idea. Laura didn't have any understanding of money, or any sense about it. She would have lived by barter if she could have."

"So you knew, or at least you suspected, that Lorin had gone off with Cameron," she suggested.

"Christ, no. He didn't even cross my mind."

"Then you had no idea he'd fallen in love with her," Polly said, putting it this way in an attempt at tact.

"No. If you want to call it that. All I know is, he had a Scotsman's instinct for where the money was. As long as Laura had funds he stuck to her like rubber cement. When the cash was used up, and her paintings weren't selling anymore, he just peeled off."

"Yes, I heard — I mean, Jacky Herbert said Cameron wasn't around when Lorin was dying."

"No. He was up in Maine. The goddamn creep." Garrett's voice roughened. "Let's forget about him; it's all ancient history now. Here. Take a look at this." He pulled the old black portfolio toward him and, with some difficulty, untied its frayed and faded tapes.

Inside there were only a few sheets of paper: three or four large drawings with pencil notations about color, evidently preliminary sketches for paintings. Underneath them, covered with a sheet of creased tissue that Garrett lifted off carefully, was a big gouache of what might have been an explosion of fireworks, or a lake in the woods in autumn, the whole scene speckled and shimmering with red and orange and gold, almost pointillist.

"Oh!" Polly cried. "I've never seen — I didn't know —"

"It's not finished, of course."

"Really?" It was true, there was a large irregular white area in one lower corner, streaked with a vague wash of ochre; but patches of nearly blank canvas were not uncommon in Jones's work.

"Well. Maybe it's finished, in a way. Maybe that's how Laura wanted it."

"It's beautiful." She stared for a long moment at the painting; and then up at Garrett accusingly. "You never mentioned — This could have been in the show."

"Yes, I suppose so. But — Well, I suppose I didn't want it there. That little pond — You can see it's a pond?"

"Yes."

"Well, it's over in the woods in Truro. Laura and I used to go there sometimes together, the first autumn we were here. I don't like to look at it much now."

"I see." It's where they made love, Polly thought. This brilliant storm of light and color was the memorial of, the transubstantiation of, an erotic encounter.

She stared at Garrett, but his face was averted toward the window. "You could sell it," she suggested, feeling as she spoke that this was crass. "I'm sure the Apollo Gallery —"

"I don't want to sell this picture, damn it." Garrett's tone was rough. "I tell you what," he added more gently. "Why don't you take it?"

"Me?" Polly's voice rose.

"Yes, you."

"Oh, I couldn't do that."

"Why not?"

"Well, I mean, for God's sake. It's too valuable."

"I don't need money," Garrett said almost angrily. "I'd like you to have it. That is, if I could be sure you wouldn't hang it anywhere I'd ever have to see it again, or sell it to some damned collector or museum, at least until I'm gone. I don't want to come across it unexpectedly somewhere, you know what I mean?"

"Yes; I understand."

"Good." Garrett cleared his throat. "Now, about this other material. I expect you'd like to have copies of some of the drawings."

"I'd like a copy of everything, really," Polly said eagerly. "Of course, I'll pay —"

"Don't worry about it. There's a fairly good Xerox place in P'town. I can go there after I take you to the plane. Or, if we left a little early" (he checked his watch) "they might be able to copy the stuff before your flight."

"That'd be fantastic," Polly said. It came into her mind that Garrett was being generous and helpful. "You know, I'm amazed that you would go to all this trouble for my book. I mean, I really appreciate it."

"Thank you." Garrett smiled. "But why should you be amazed?"

"I just meant — uh, well, I meant," Polly stuttered. "Some men might bear a grudge, I mean about last night."

"That'd be foolish, considering the circumstances." Garrett laughed. "Actually, you know," he added very casually, "sometimes women who love other women are surprised to find they can also enjoy men — or rather, they can enjoy a man who understands what they prefer physically." He gave her what was surely a meaning look. "I remember when I was living in the Village, back in the thirties —"

"I'm not like that," Polly interrupted. She had heard

before of men who prided themselves on their ability to, as they put it, "convert" homosexual women.

"Ah. Pity." Garrett smiled briefly, and pulled Lorin's gouache toward him along the table. Carefully, he lowered the protective covering over it.

The proposed gift was a bribe, Polly thought. I have just refused the implied bargain, and so it's been withdrawn. She felt angry but relieved, for now Garrett was no longer decent and generous. He was exposed instead as a dirty old man who wanted to buy sex with his dead wife's painting — even worse, with a painting of the place where he and she had once made love. Crass, horrible, disgusting.

Yet as the colors dimmed under the worn tissue, Polly felt a stabbing pang of loss. She thought that she would probably never in her life see this picture again, and almost wished that she had accepted Garrett's implied bargain.

"Well, maybe we should pack up," he said with a wheeze. He moved the drawings onto the table, lifted the shrouded painting, and replaced it in the old black portfolio. Slowly he retied the tapes; then he held the portfolio out toward Polly. "Right. Here you are."

Startled, she took a step back. "I can't," she exclaimed, abashed by her own thoughts. "I don't deserve —"

"Of course you do." Garrett grinned at her. "You don't know how glad I am that someone's finally writing the truth about Laura. And how especially glad I am that it's someone like you." He looked at Polly with an expression at first warmly friendly, then uncertain. "Or maybe you don't really care for this picture."

"Oh, no!" she cried. "It's wonderful."

"Well, then."

Still Polly hesitated. But a soft reverberation in her ear, Lorin Jones's voice, or her own voice — and, after all, hadn't Garrett said they were the same? — seemed to whisper: *Take it; I want you to have it.* Slowly, she held out her arms.

JANET BELLE SMITH,

short-story writer

Oh yes, I remember Laurie Zimmern from college. Of course, she was only at Smith for one year, my sophomore year. Then she transferred to Bennington, which was really a much better place for her. She was a strange girl, young woman, I suppose you'd say now. Even for Bennington, where it was more fashionable to be strange then; I believe it still is.

I don't recall how we got to be friends. I think perhaps it was because of a book of Beardsley drawings that I'd bought, and Laurie asked if she could borrow it. I remember thinking at the time that she was like a Beardsley drawing herself, all long smooth curves of black and white. She was very striking then, beautiful really, very slim, with white skin and those great dark eyes, and masses of dark hair. She wore it in a long bob with thick bangs, like some ancient Egyptian princess. It looked odd back then, when most everyone had short bouncy curls.

If your hair didn't curl naturally? Well, you got a permanent wave.

Her clothes were very odd too, by our standards. I remember the first evening of my sophomore year, going down to dinner in the dorm. There were the new freshmen in their candy-striped or madras-check dresses, or flowered skirts and blouses with Peter Pan collars, like what all the rest of us were wearing. And there was Laurie, in a long flounced red gypsy skirt and a ratty black scoop-neck cotton jersey. I felt sorry for her, but I thought she'd soon notice that her clothes were all wrong and do something about them. Only she didn't. Then for a while I thought she must be on scholarship, and couldn't afford to buy anything new. Well, you know, I was awfully conventional then. It was the way I'd been brought up.

But it turned out that Laurie wasn't poor: her parents were quite well off. She wore those sorts of clothes because she wanted to. Most of them she found in secondhand shops — of course, this was long before that became fashionable. I used to shudder sometimes at what she'd bring back from the Salvation Army. To tell you the truth, I still feel that way. I'd never buy anything used; one has no idea where it's been or what odd diseases its owner might have had.

Oh, no, she went to real stores sometimes. We even went shopping together once. I remember it because Laurie did this really strange thing.

It was in New York, over spring vacation, and she took me to Klein's on Union Square. I'd never been there before, and I was appalled by the crowds, all those people pushing and shoving. And there were these awful warnings against shoplifting posted up everywhere: a crude drawing of a woman with staring eyes looking through bars, and underneath it said in both English and Spanish, in great black capital letters: DISHONESTY MEANS PRISON — DO NOT BRING DISGRACE ON YOUR FAMILY. I felt as if I were surrounded by thieves; I clutched onto my handbag like mad the whole time I was there.

But Laurie loved it. She found this dress on a rack — it was quite nice, black cotton with a square neck trimmed in black cotton lace. And she liked it so much that she said she thought she'd buy two. I assumed she was joking, but she explained that then she'd never have to bother about what to wear, because one of the dresses would always be clean.

Oh yes, she bought them both. And she actually did wear them when we got back to college, every single day that the weather was warm enough, for at least a month.

Yes, that seems rather enterprising, if eccentric, now; but by our rules at the time it was really shocking, almost crazy. You were supposed to put together a different outfit every day, repeating yourself as seldom as possible. When you wore a dress again you'd be careful to have new accessories, a different belt or scarf, you know. Even today . . .

No, I think probably I was the only person at Smith who got to know Laurie at all well. You see, she didn't really fit in, and of course she was very shy, too, and she said such odd things. Some people thought she was a hopeless neurotic; others just felt she was rather standoffish and affected. Most of my friends couldn't see why I wanted to have anything to do with her. But I found her fascinating, really, especially at first. She was awfully well read for a freshman, for one thing. And I knew she was amazingly gifted.

I always thought it was a shame Laurie went into abstract art, because she could draw so beautifully. I still have some sketches she made of me and a pot of English ivy. But there certainly was something strange about her, and she wasn't putting it on. I suppose it might have been better if she had been, in a way.

I didn't mind Laurie's being strange at first. I didn't pay any attention to what my other friends said, until one evening toward the end of the year. I was writing a paper on Hawthorne, and Laurie knocked on my door and asked me to come and see what she'd done to her room. Because she was a freshman, she had one of the smallest rooms on the corridor, but she'd gradually decorated it so that somehow it looked much bigger, and not like a college dorm at all. There were a lot of little mirrors, and an Indian print spread on her bed, and heaps of embroidered pillows in bright colors, scarlet and crimson and plum, that you'd think wouldn't go together, but they did. On the floor she had one of those big fuzzy-edged pale Indian rugs with a design of a tree full of peculiar birds. And she had strange posters, and lots of leafy tropical plants —

No, you have to realize, this was back in the nineteen-forties, those things weren't clichés yet, they were original — weird maybe, but exciting. Laurie was way ahead of the fashion, you know. Because what most of us had in our rooms then were African violets and chintz armchairs and the Oriental throw rug from one of the spare bedrooms back home; and the girls who weren't so well off had Bates Piping Rock bedspreads and curtains.

So naturally I was interested, and I followed Laurie down the corridor to see what she'd done now. She opened her door, shoved it back as far as it would go, which wasn't very far, because there was something wedged up against it inside. I squeezed in after her, and she put on the light.

Well, it was upsetting. Everything had been turned backward or upside down. Laurie had tacked all her posters to the walls wrong side out, and shoved the furniture around, so that the chest of drawers and the desk couldn't be opened: they were slap up against the walls, and you could see the raw unpainted wood in back. Her lamp was still on the desk, but it was upside down, balancing on its white pleated shade, with the brass base sticking up. The chairs all faced the walls, too, and the rug was upside down on the floor.

The worst thing was the bed. Heaven knows how she'd managed that, because our college furniture was solid oak, and very heavy. It looked quite dreadful, lying on its back with its square legs in the air, each one ending in a kind of metal claw caster, and the ribs of its slats were exposed, like something that had been killed. And the plants were awful too. All the pots on their sides and some of them upside down, spilling out dirt and leaves. It frightened me, really.

Well, I stood and looked at it. And Laurie looked at me, and gave me this little smile, and said, "Isn't it nice?" I thought she was kidding, and I wanted to play along, so I said, "Oh, yes. But where will you sleep?" "I don't know," she said. "Maybe I won't sleep for a while."

Yes, she did leave it that way, but only for a few days. Then I think the maids — we had maids then, you know — complained that they couldn't get in to clean, and our house-mother made her put everything back.

I didn't know what to think. If I'd been more sophisticated I probably would have wondered if she'd been smoking marijuana or something. I guess mostly I was amazed by the whole thing, and frightened, like I said. It was as if Laurie were saying, My life here is upside down, inside out, and backwards. She seemed so serious, and I couldn't be sure it was a joke.

No, really, I don't think that it was, quite.

Yes, it made a difference. I had to realize that Laurie wasn't quite normal. And by the end of the spring term, when exams came, she'd gotten very strange. Of course, a lot of girls did become tense then, and do odd things; another friend of mine used to sit up all night studying in the bathtub — without water, of course — because it was so uncomfortable there she couldn't go to sleep. But with Laurie it was worse, somehow. She didn't eat properly, and in the end she sat through one exam, biology I think it was, without writing a single word.

It turned out that all she'd done for three hours was to pull out her eyebrows very slowly, hair by hair. I saw her afterward, and the strange thing was, she didn't seem at all upset, and she didn't look too bad either.

A bit like one of those fifteenth-century European portraits, a Memling perhaps. Odd, but rather elegant. You know it was fashionable in those days for ladies to pluck out their eyebrows completely.

I did see her once or twice over the next summer. We met in New York and had lunch and went to some galleries. I was glad to see her again. But we didn't really keep up with each other after that.

Well, for one thing she'd acquired this rather crazy hatred of Smith College. She said it had a malevolent philistine atmosphere; and she wanted me to leave too, before I was poisoned by it. But of course I couldn't leave Smith; I didn't want to, anyhow. And then Laurie transferred to Bennington and made new friends; and that was it, really. We lost track of each other. I'm sorry about it now. I've never known anyone else like her.

No. Well, I did try to write about her, several times, but it never worked. Of course, the story would have been partly about my reaction to Laurie, but still. . . . She always came out quite unbelievable, or simply weird, which wasn't the point at all. I think that often happens when one tries to portray exceptional people. And if one excuses it by explaining within the story that the character is a genius, or is going to be famous, well, it's rather like special pleading, isn't it? It doesn't convince. I think that in fiction, at least my own particular kind of fiction . . .

8

On a cloudy, snow-soiled afternoon a week before Thanksgiving, Polly Alter strode into her sitting room with wet feet, damp windblown hair, and a heavy flat brown-paper package, which she placed carefully on the sofa. She peeled off her sodden coat and boots and flung them into the hall closet. Then she cut open the parcel and drew out Lorin Jones's gouache of the pond in Truro, now professionally matted and framed. She cleared the sitting-room mantel, removing some battered brass candlesticks and Jeanne's pots of trailing begonias, and set the painting in their place. Finally she stepped back and stood square before it, hoping for a kind of miracle.

Since she'd gotten back from the Cape, Polly had been having serious trouble with her project. What she couldn't get over, or around, or out from under, was that Lorin Jones had been immature and self-destructive and mean enough to leave her relatively decent husband without warning for a low-grade opportunist, stopping only to clean out their joint bank account. The more Polly thought about this the worse she liked it. Before she and Jim separated they had discussed the move for months, and they had split their assets fairly and equally. According to Garrett, the theft — you couldn't call it anything else — had been Hugh Cameron's idea; but that only meant that Lorin was weak and suggestible as well as sneaky.

The immediate problem was, how was Polly going to handle this episode in the biography? Was she going to be equally sneaky and leave it out? Or was she going to expose her subject as a deeply flawed personality?

Though Polly still loved Lorin Jones, she no longer

admired her unreservedly. And the magical sense of identity with Lorin was gone. The visit to Wellfleet, the transcendent experience of being in Lorin's landscape and home, the hovering presence of Lorin's spirit, appeared to her now as a kind of false, fleeting enchantment; or in more prosaic psychological terms, a temporary delusion.

To believe oneself haunted by Lorin Jones, possessed by her ghost — that was getting in too deep even for a biographer; maybe especially for a biographer. But now Polly floundered in muddy shallows, where every day she felt Lorin drifting farther away from her, dissolving further into a damp, lifeless collection of facts, a clutter of other people's faulty memories and prejudiced opinions. To make anything out of this lumpish amorphous mass — this pond-spawn — seemed a more and more difficult task. She no longer had any clear idea of who Lorin Jones had been, or what Lorin had thought or felt. Sometimes she was so baffled and depressed that she considered taking Lennie Zimmern's advice: give up the idea of a biography and just do a study of the work, a modestly expanded version of the "Three American Women" catalogue.

The trouble was, she didn't even feel sure about the work any longer. When she held her off-color slides up to the light, or stared at the uninspiring gray-and-white reproductions, she felt nothing; she could think of nothing new to say. Some days she plodded on only because she didn't know how she'd explain it to her colleagues at the Museum and to the Foundation if she quit. Maybe the Foundation would want its money back.

The interviews she'd done lately had been mostly upsetting or useless. According to the last one, when Lorin Jones was in college she was almost a textbook schizophrenic. Assuming that wasn't true — and there was no way of proving this — either Janet Belle Smith (who was, after all, a professional writer of fiction) had been making up stories, or else Lorin Jones had put on a crazy act for Ms. Smith out of some perverse sense of humor.

Jeanne had tried to help Polly through this period of

doubt and anxiety, but she was still in a funk herself over her breakup with Betsy, and nothing she said seemed to help. The truth was, Jeanne didn't really approve of Polly's project, because she didn't approve of individual biography as a genre. As a Marxist-feminist historian, she believed that it was counterproductive to write about atypical persons — so-called heroes and leaders. She preferred to analyze statistics, or investigate the lives of ordinary citizens. In her view, Polly had succumbed to the biographical fallacy — the old-fashioned patriarchal idea of history as "the lives of great men." To extend this interest to "the lives of great women" was to play by male rules.

"Why not write my life?" Jeanne had joked last week, not for the first time. "Historically and sociologically speaking it's just as significant as Lorin Jones's. And you'd have a lot easier time collecting the data." She laughed a little bitterly, perhaps with reference to the many times she had gone over the sad history of her affair with Betsy.

"That's true, for sure," Polly had said, also laughing. But she knew Jeanne wasn't wholly kidding: like most of the people Polly had been interviewing, she really wanted Polly to pay attention to her and write about her instead of about Lorin Jones. Again, a sense of blocked communication and restless impatience washed over her.

Now, though, standing before the newly framed picture, Polly felt almost hopeful. The fireplace was cold and bare; it hadn't worked since they'd moved in. But even in the gray indirect light that was all this room ever got, Lorin's painting flickered and flamed rusty gold, fumous ochre, and steely blue. The flecks of color that suggested falling and swirling leaves seemed to tremble and flutter; those that suggested ripples on the surface of water shook and quivered. The canvas was alive with the dissolution and transformation of autumn, and with Lorin Jones's passionate love for paint and for the physical world. Yes, Polly thought. This was the real thing: a work of genius. But what did it reveal about the woman who had created it?

She gazed until her eyes watered and the colors swam;

until she felt herself standing in a storm of paint, no closer to an answer. Finally, dizzied, she turned away. She set Jeanne's begonias on a windowsill and carried the candlesticks into the kitchen.

"Oh, for God's sake!" she cried as she looked around. When she'd left that morning the room had been clean; now there were dirty dishes in the sink and crumbs on the table; the milk, eggs, bread, and jam had been left out, and the saucer of margarine was a viscid yellow pool with a dead fly in it. Before her quarrel with Betsy, Jeanne wouldn't have left even an empty cup on the table; but depression had turned her slothful and scattered. "We broke up, that's the phrase I use when people ask me," she had said the other day. "But you know, for me it's literal; I still feel as if I'd been smashed into pieces." Polly's anxiety about her book, meanwhile, had made her hyperactive and impatient; no wonder they weren't getting on as well as before.

Of course part of the trouble was sex. Since she returned from Wellfleet she and Jeanne had tried three times more to love and comfort each other, and it hadn't quite worked. Polly felt loved but not satisfied, and Jeanne, it was clear, hadn't really been comforted.

What Jeanne liked, it had turned out — or at least what she seemed to want and need now — was to kiss and cuddle and gently caress, to drift warmly and slowly toward and then away from a state of arousal without orgasm. No, she didn't miss it, she had told Polly. The idea of a violent spasm rather revolted her, as a matter of fact; she'd often thought that it was mostly something men, with their more brutish and animal sexuality, had recently tried to foist on women. After all, for centuries nobody had ever talked about a female climax.

The trouble was, it wasn't like that for Polly. At the beginning of each encounter she sighed and marveled at Jeanne's silky rose-flushed skin, at her delicate, subtle strokes and fluttering, nibbling kisses. "Oh, that's so lovely," she would murmur, returning them with interest. "It's you that's lovely," Jeanne would whisper, raising her pale loose curls from Polly's thigh. But later on, when Polly started to really let go: to shout, to grip, to pant and thrash about, Jeanne would become still and draw back, looking at her friend with embarrassed concern, as if she were having some kind of fit.

For Jeanne too, it was clear, their encounters were not really satisfactory. There is a folk belief that men are melancholy after coitus; Polly hadn't usually found this true; but Jeanne was always a little sad and silent afterward, though she tried to hide it. Polly would say, "Are you all right?" and Jeanne would answer, "Sure, I'm fine." She was thinking about Betsy again, Polly suspected; but when asked about this Jeanne denied it.

The worst thing really, Polly thought, was that communication between them had begun to break down. For years, when they were just intimate friends, she and Jeanne had been able to tell each other everything. Now that they were intimate in another sense, they'd started concealing their thoughts and feelings from each other. Polly couldn't tell anybody what was on her mind; she couldn't even confide in her best friend, because Jeanne was her best friend, and if she knew how lonely and frustrated Polly sometimes felt after they had made love she would be hurt and miserable.

What Polly hoped was that once Jeanne had got over that stupid Betsy — who definitely didn't deserve her — she would become more active and enthusiastic in bed, and happier afterward; not to mention more use around the house. If she didn't, Polly didn't know how long she could stand it.

Jeanne could have picked up before she left for the university, she growled to herself as she stood in the kitchen revolving these uncomfortable ideas. She knows how I hate mess. But if I mention it she'll be cross and hurt. She'll claim that she overslept and was late for work, or that she was restless and had an awful night — though she was snoring like a big tabby cat when I left.

But these thoughts were petty, unworthy of a true friend, let alone a lover. Polly shoved them aside. She cleaned up the kitchen — it only took a few minutes, after all — and dumped an ashtray full of Jeanne's cigarette butts into the trash. Jeanne was supposed to be quitting smoking again, or at least cutting down, but as usual she was cheating. Finally she carried Jeanne's scuffed ballet slippers back down the hall.

As she entered what had been Stevie's room, Polly remembered with a flutter of joy that she would be seeing her son in less than a week. She was flying to Rochester next Wednesday, and Stevie would get in from Denver soon after. They'd have Thanksgiving at her mother's as usual, and then fly back to New York together on Friday.

Jeanne would be away then: she was spending the weekend with Ida and Cathy, who were making Thanksgiving dinner for a dozen women. She had invited Polly to join them, but even if Polly hadn't been going to her mother's she would have hesitated. She ought not to hesitate; she ought to get used to, even welcome, the company of other gay women. The trouble was that though she liked most of Jeanne's friends, Ida and Cathy always made her uncomfortable. Whenever she went there she felt that they (especially Ida) were watching her for signs of prejudice and wrong thinking.

Before Jeanne left, though, Polly had to have a serious conversation with her. Right now, Stevie's room was full of Jeanne's clothes, her books, her posters, her tapes and cassette player; her typewriter and her students' papers covered Stevie's desk. Sometime in the next week all this stuff had to be moved out. Polly could wait and hope that Jeanne would find the energy to take care of it; but probably in the end she'd have to do the job herself.

"Hi." Slowly, Jeanne shut the apartment door behind her and put on the bolt and chain, something Polly usually forgot, and Jeanne mentioned. But now she said nothing; silently, Polly resolved not to say anything about the mess in the kitchen.

"Hi there."

"How's everything?" Jeanne set down a bag of groceries on the sofa and dropped beside them with the same sort of inert gravity.

"Not too bad." Polly turned around from the desk and raised her eyes to the mantelpiece, but Jeanne did not follow her gaze. "I brought Lorin's painting home today."

"Oh, yes?" Jeanne briefly turned her head.

"I think the framer did a pretty good job, don't you? I was afraid that chrome strip might be too wide, but I've decided it's really all right. And it's great over the fireplace."

"Yes. Nice," Jeanne murmured.

"I don't know how you can say that." Polly smiled. "You've hardly glanced at the picture."

"I don't have to. I looked at the thing for hours when you brought it back from Cape Cod."

Though it irritated Polly to hear Lorin's painting called "the thing," she suppressed this. "You know, it makes a big difference to me to have something of hers here. It's weird, but it makes me feel maybe I can do the book after all."

"That's nice," Jeanne said in the voice of one who was weary of Polly's doubts.

"I was thinking, whatever you want to say about Garrett Jones, I've got to be grateful to him for this."

"Not too grateful, I hope." Jeanne stood wearily and began to unwind a long filmy white wool scarf.

"What do you mean?"

"Well." Jeanne was taking off her coat now. "I mean, you wouldn't want it to interfere with what you write."

"How could it interfere with what I write?" Polly asked, beginning to bristle. "It's just the opposite — it's going to be a help, an inspiration, I hope, for God's sake."

Jeanne sighed. "I didn't mean the picture. I just don't want you to forget why Jones gave it to you, that's all. Would you like a cup of Red Zinger?"

"No thanks." Polly sat for a moment frowning at the shimmer and glow of paint, fading now with the daylight; then she followed Jeanne into the kitchen. "What did you mean by that? Why do you think Garrett gave me Lorin's painting?"

"Well, isn't it obvious? If the thing is worth as much as you say, it surely must have been intended as a bribe. Jones must have thought that after that you couldn't possibly say anything nasty about him in your book."

"I don't think — It wasn't, not for a moment —" Polly began to sputter. "Garrett gave me the picture because he's glad I'm writing about Lorin, and anyhow he didn't want to look at that landscape. It upsets him, I told you why —" She tried to ignore Jeanne's skeptical smile. "Anyhow, I'm not going to say anything nasty about him."

"Oh, really?"

"I'll tell the truth, that's all."

Jeanne laughed for the first time, and Polly realized her meaning had been mistaken. In fact, she wasn't planning to write anything unpleasant about Garrett Jones, because she no longer blamed him for Lorin's problems with the New York art world. No doubt he did leave his wife alone too much, and fail to understand her. But can any man, let alone a critic, really understand a gifted woman? And he supported her professionally and financially; he loved her, in his way, and allowed her a fair amount of independence.

"That's the spirit," Jeanne said, still giggling softly.

"I haven't got anything against Garrett Jones," Polly insisted. "He's been very decent to me, considering everything."

"Oh, come on. What has he done for you, when you get right down to it?" The kettle had begun to boil, and Jeanne's temper was evidently also on the simmer. "He's given you a dirty old half-finished picture —"

"It's not dirty." Polly flushed; it was true that there was a crease and streak of dust down one edge of the paper; but now that it had been framed the damage was scarcely visible.

"— and he's tried to con you into ghostwriting his ridiculous self-important memoirs."

"Well, he didn't succeed." Polly was getting angry her-

self. They had had this conversation before, though in po-
liter and vaguer language. "Anyhow, he thought he was
doing me a favor. New York is full of art history graduates
who would jump at the chance."

"Uh-huh." Jeanne poured boiling water into an antique
Japanese teapot, a gift from Betsy in happier days. "You're
kind of a pushover, you know, Polly," she added. "All any
man has to do is be a little polite and you're convinced he's
a nice person."

Polly didn't answer, though the retort sprang to mind
that giving someone a painting worth several thousand dollars was not just being a little polite.

"I'm surprised he didn't try to seduce you into the
bargain," Jeanne continued. "He's supposed to consider
himself God's gift to women." Polly did not respond. "Or
maybe he did?" she suggested.

"Of course not," she declared, adding an outright lie to
an earlier lie of omission. If Jeanne heard the whole story
she would expect Polly to forswear speaking to Garrett
Jones again, which would be professionally very inconvenient, and she would probably blame her for not having
slapped his face. Polly imagined herself slapping the face of
Garrett Jones, a sleepy, half-tipsy, romantically foolish elderly man; the idea was unattractive. "But I think he liked
me, that's partly why he gave me the picture."

"I expect it was because you'd already softened him up so
well. You'd sweet-talked him, the way I told you, and won
his confidence." Jeanne smiled, silently taking the credit.

"Mm," Polly murmured a little distractedly. It had just
occurred to her that what had happened that night in Wellfleet might also be credited to Jeanne's account. Because of
her Machiavellian advice, her talk about staying cool and
pretending to agree with whomever she was interviewing,
all that first day Polly had acted falsely, suppressing her
opinions, playing the passive, admiring female. No wonder
Garrett had assumed that she admired him, that she would
want to help write his memoirs; that she would welcome his
wet kisses. She sighed aloud.

"You sound exhausted," Jeanne said.

"Yeah, I'm a little tired." She yawned; she had slept only about six hours the night before.

"Why don't you take a break?" Jeanne set her teacup in the sink. "You were up so early, you must be worn out."

"I could use a nap, maybe," Polly admitted.

"That's a good idea." Jeanne, in her turn, gave a little yawn and sigh. "I think I'll join you; my students were exhausting today. And maybe we might tumble about a bit first," she added, smiling, alluding to one of the couplets about the Gingham Dog and the Calico Cat that had now taken on a private erotic meaning for them:

> ... The gingham dog and the calico cat
> Wallowed this way and tumbled that ...

"Okay." Polly only half smiled. Jeanne's comments about Garrett had rubbed her pelt the wrong way.

Half an hour later they lay entwined in a rumple of tan plaid sheets. Jeanne had fallen into a doze; but Polly was not at all sleepy, for some reason — hell, for the good reason that she was not satisfied.

As they made love, Polly had suggested that Jeanne help her out a bit more vigorously. Jeanne had agreed at once; but soon her gestures became mechanical. Then her hand faltered and forgot its stroke; she lay back and began to purr, "Mm, that's nice. Yes, lovely," rising to a low crescendo of pleasure and gratitude. "Oh, wonderful," she sighed finally. "Thank you, darling." Then, sleepy and sated, she sank into a trance.

Polly raised herself on one elbow and stared at her friend: her pale-lashed eyes, her fine tousled hair: her plump, satiny skin; her large soft white breasts and her small pink half-open mouth, from which an audible breath, too slight to be called a snore, issued rhythmically. Unlike Polly, Jeanne had an enviable ability to doze anytime and anywhere.

It was natural to drift off after sex anyhow; when Polly

was fully satisfied she too wanted to float away. Most women felt that. Men too: Jim Meyer sometimes — Polly stopped in mid-memory, annoyed that she should even think of Jim at a time like this.

Of course, ever since he left she had been troubled with occasional heterosexual fantasies; but since she'd been to bed with Jeanne they'd been perversely more frequent. Maybe it was because she was aroused and not satisfied that she kept thinking about what sex used to be like. Even in the act of love with Jeanne, she would recall in vivid color some moment in her past, or even from her recent visit to Wellfleet.

Why did she keep remembering that embarrassing evening, that awkward, undesired embrace? She wasn't interested in Garrett Jones, that sad, pretentious old man. She hadn't liked kissing him, didn't want to kiss him again. What haunted her was what he reminded her of: the sensation of a man's body pressed against hers, the flat, heavy hardness; the willingness to take charge, conveyed not in words but through gestures and murmurs of pleasure.

It would be so much better if she could really love Jeanne, or some other woman. And maybe she could, Polly thought; she loved Lorin Jones, after all. But she couldn't love Jeanne in the way she loved Lorin. Among other things, Jeanne wasn't a genius.

On the other hand, she was alive and here. And she was warm, affectionate, loyal. She loved Polly; she was thoughtful and kind, bringing her flowers and baking her sponge cakes. It's true that the flowers, usually bought in subway stalls, never lasted very long, and that lately the cakes tended to be lopsided or sink in the middle. But the impulse was fresh and whole.

Maybe it was all Polly's fault; maybe she was basically a cold, guarded person, incapable of real warmth or intimacy even with another woman. Maybe that was why Jeanne was still depressed, untidy, touchy, and preoccupied. She sighed and flopped face down beside her friend, trying in vain to sleep.

*   *   *

"Hey." Jeanne yawned, slowly opened her eyes, and raised herself on one elbow, gazing at Polly. "It's no good really, is it?" she said after a moment.

"What?"

"I mean, it isn't working. You're still all tensed up."

"I — yeah. I guess it's just the way I am."

"It's not only you." Jeanne reached down to stroke Polly's forehead, smoothing back her crisp untidy curls. "It's not right for me either. The problem is, I really love you as a friend, but you're not my type." She sighed.

"What?" Polly turned on her side.

"If you were, I would never have agreed to come and live here back in September; it would've been just too painful."

Startled, Polly half sat up, looking at her lover. "You mean you're not attracted to me?" she said, her mouth remaining open in surprise.

"Well, no. Not really." Jeanne smiled apologetically, and shook her head. "The thing is, I mostly always go for thin confused young redheads or strawberry blondes, like Betsy. You're much too sensible and grown-up for me."

And too old and too fat, Polly thought, wanting to laugh miserably.

Jeanne must have noticed some change or spasm in her friend's features, for she hastened to add, "I don't mean you're not awfully pretty, Polly dear. I'm sure there's lots of women who would be interested in you. Ida said to me once —"

"Then why did you suggest —" Polly cried, sitting up to face her friend, repelled by the idea of having been discussed in this way with Ida.

"Well, I suppose because I was so miserable and frustrated. And so were you. But it really wasn't a good idea, you know. You've been wonderfully nice to me. The trouble is, I'm still horribly in love with Betsy, even though I realize I'll probably never see her again. But anything else feels as if I was being unfaithful to her."

"I see." Polly still wanted to laugh or cry; the whole thing seemed to her like a bad joke.

"Anyhow, darling, you're not really all that attracted to me either." Jeanne smiled.

"I am, but — At least —" Polly gave a long nervous sigh. "I just have a different idea of what it's like to make love, I suppose. But I thought you —"

"I know." Now Jeanne laughed out loud, lightly and a little sadly. "We were both being polite to each other."

"I guess so."

"I tell you what. Let's get out of bed and go to a really silly movie. Something with wild animals in it, or aliens from outer space."

"Okay. I'll find the *Times* and see what's on uptown." Polly stood up.

"You know what, though," she added, turning back in the doorway. "If you're really still in love with Betsy, maybe you should call her. I mean, it could be that's what she's waiting for."

"Maybe," Jeanne said, her expression darkening. "Or maybe not." She picked up the pillow on which she had lain and thumped it meditatively. "All right. I'll think about it."

KENNETH FOSTER,

painter

Yes, I checked my records: Laurie Zimmern was in my second-year painting class in the spring of nineteen-forty-five, at Bennington.

I recall her perfectly. My legs may be shaky, but my mind is quite clear. Besides, I always remember my gifted students.

There weren't so many as you might think. If I had one or two out of a class of twenty I counted myself lucky.

No, you don't know right away. It's not as easy as that. You see, it's not just ability that makes for success. If you teach for as long as I did, you realize that in any year a few of your students may have real talent, and a few may have real ambition: the passionate drive to be an artist. In my second-year class at Bennington most of them usually didn't have either, not so as one could notice.

They were nice enough girls. Several of them went on to marry well, and collect paintings fairly intelligently, because people like me and Garrett Jones had taught them a little something. But they weren't artists.

Yes, talent *and* drive; to make it in the art world you need lots of both. If you only have the one, it's a tragedy. I've known so many young people who wanted desperately to be painters. They'd have done anything for that, given up anything, worked night and day for years, but they simply hadn't sufficient gift. You could see that their entire lives would be a misery.

Oh yes, I've tried to tell them, especially at the beginning. It doesn't do any good; all that happens is that they class you as an evil life-destroying philistine. They add you to the list of the people who killed John Keats and let van Gogh die penniless, and so forth.

And then sometimes, what's almost worse, you get the ones who have the talent but not the drive. They let their parents or their wives or their husbands talk them out of trying to become serious painters, because it's not safe or respectable. They go to law school instead or into business or just have babies. The hours of my life I've wasted talking to those students! It's awful to contemplate.

No, with Laurie Zimmern it was different. She had the ability: a wonderful, very subtle, color sense, and her drawing was exquisite. And she wanted to paint tremendously; I think that was almost all she ever wanted. But the world outside of the studio terrified her.

Well, for instance, I remember the reception for the Bennington student show at the end of that term. There was quite a crowd. Everybody in the department was there, naturally, and a fair number of relatives and friends and townspeople. It was the first time Laurie'd ever exhibited, and she was so frightened she literally couldn't speak.

Yes, she did gain a little more confidence over the next year or so. But I didn't think she'd ever have enough to make it. Only, you see, she was smart. She wanted to be a famous painter, and she wanted it fast. And she was intelligent enough to know what she was like, and that she desperately needed somebody to promote her work and stand between her and the world.

Well, that year, her junior year, she had three paintings in the student show, and it was clear to anyone who had any sense that they were by far the best of the lot. Garrett wanted to meet the artist, so I introduced them. I still blame myself for that, rather, though of course how could I have known? Anyhow, they met. Laurie saw her chance, and she took it.

Single-minded. You can say that again. She certainly didn't let anything stand in her way. Or anyone. His wife meant less to her than an old paint rag. You know he was married then, I assume.

And I suppose you also know that he was married to my present wife.

Oh yes, he was.

No, if you want to know, that doesn't surprise me at all. Garrett never mentions it now, but he and Roz were married for seven years. When he got the appointment at Bennington she gave up a first-rate job in New York to go with him, and took one in the dean's office at half the salary.

Oh yes, I knew them well. Until Laurie Zimmern appeared on the scene we were good friends, the three of us, we did everything together.

I loved them both. They were fine-looking people, big and fair and full of energy. And extremely happy together. Roz had such warmth and wit and high spirits, she was always ready for anything, and Garrett was brilliant. I was only a few years younger, but I looked up to him intellectually: he knew so much, and his artistic taste and judgment were always impeccable.

Well, you see, another thing I've learned over the years is that some men, even brilliant men, are hopelessly weak where women are concerned. And of course there's a certain sort of woman who can sense this, and use it to her own advantage.

I don't think it had anything whatsoever to do with love, at least not on her side. If you want to know my opinion, the only things Laurie Zimmern ever loved were herself and painting, in that order.

Oh, I suppose she was beautiful. Well, she would have had to be, to interest Garrett, and she would have had to be gifted.

Yes, it's true people often say that. And I can't deny there's a similarity, especially in her early paintings. But even then Laurie's work always had a kind of mystical, surrealist side to it that mine never had — that I never wanted it to have, either.

No. It wasn't a matter of influence; it was something more basic, I think: a similar way of seeing the world. Of course I did teach her some technical things. And I suggested the names of a few past artists whose work she might look at. That's really all you can do for someone like that. It's ironic, you know: it's not the best students one can actually teach, it's those who are merely clever and talented.

Very good. And if she hadn't gone off the deep end and run away with that ridiculous young man — if she'd lived — I think she would be recognized now as one of the most important painters of her generation. Yes, absolutely.

I don't see any contradiction. Genius has nothing to do with character; some of the greatest artists have been saints, and others have been bastards.

Oh yes. We see a good deal of Garrett and Abigail. At first Roz didn't even want to hear his name, and one couldn't blame her. But after Laurie left him and he remarried it was easier. We both like Abigail very much. Besides, it's a long time ago now. And Roz is such a wonderful, generous woman: she doesn't bear a grudge. As she says, an elephant never forgets, but who wants to be an elephant?

Of course, it will never be quite the same, but what ever is in this life? The four of us get on very well. Last summer we went on one of those Swan cruises together. We toured the Greek islands, and I did quite a lot of watercolors.

Yes, it was a great success. If my legs hold up we're going to try one to the hill towns of northern Italy this coming spring.

9

On the night before Thanksgiving, in her stepfather's house in Rochester, Polly lay in bed in the attic room that had been hers since the age of nine. The steep slope of the ceiling and its freckled, flaking whitewash were as familiar to her as her own skin, now also beginning to freckle and flake. Her childhood books were still on the shelves behind the door, her old posters — Monet and the Beatles — still on the walls. The burnt-sienna homespun curtains that she had hemmed herself were sun-faded, but they caught on the handle of the casement window in the same old way.

Her attic was still, Polly thought, the only really attractive room in the house. The others were comfortable enough, but wholly unaesthetic; there was no vulgarity or pretension in their decoration — only utter lack of taste. In the sitting room forest-green upholstery clashed with olive-green carpeting and sea-green brocade curtains, all of the most durable quality; Early American furniture contended with heirloom Victorian and Danish Modern. The pictures and ornaments had been chosen solely for their symbolic value: family photographs, footstools covered in tapestry roses by Polly's mother, ashtrays and a magazine rack made by her half brother in school, and an embarrassing sub-Degas pastel of a ballet dancer that had won her a prize in seventh grade. Even worse were the souvenirs of Bea and Bob's vacations: tourist-shop watercolors of Provincetown and Paris, a gilt papier-mâché tray from Rome, a Royal Wedding plate from London, and a huge hideous prickly-pear cactus from New Mexico. (When she was eleven Polly, having heard that alcohol was a sure if slow poison, had tried to kill this monstrous plant by pouring sherry into its pot, and the following month gin. The cleaning lady had been accused of tippling, but the cactus had thrived, and continued even now to thrive.)

As Polly used to complain rudely and hopelessly when she was a teenager, the house didn't have to look this way. It was large, well designed in the style of the 1920s, and built to last. An English professor just around the corner on Crossman Terrace whose children Polly had gone to school with had an almost identical house; but it was beautiful inside as well as comfortable, full of elegant furniture and pictures and leafy green plants arranged with thought and care.

But it wasn't only for aesthetic reasons that Polly always felt uncomfortable in Rochester. The house reminded her, still, of what her life there had been like. Walking into it was like walking into a thin fog, a damp miasma of ancient anger and depression.

The move to Rochester had been great for her mother, she saw that now; it was what Bea had always wanted, a stable marriage to a reliable man who had progressed steadily if not brilliantly from physics graduate student to full professor. After what she'd been through it must have been great to have a big comfortable house near the park and two sons who were born at respectable intervals and had Bob's placid temperament and his talent for math and science.

But in this happy family Polly was an outsider. She hated math; she had bad moods and screamed and wept and threw things. She was too old for her new family — ten and thirteen years older than her half brothers. She didn't match her mother and Bob and the boys, with their straight hair and neutral light-brown coloring. She didn't even have the same name as they did; a girl in her class once asked if she was adopted. Often people who came to the house for parties didn't know who she was. "You must be the baby-sitter," a woman in a shiny red dress with beads on it said to her once in the kitchen.

Her mother did try to get Polly to baby-sit, but usually

she wouldn't, because her little brothers always ganged up on her as soon as their parents were out of the house, and wouldn't mind what she said. They were stupid, spoiled little kids, she thought then; now they only seemed totally dull and conventional.

Lorin Jones also had a half brother she didn't particularly get on with as a child, Polly recalled, feeling a faint echo of her old shiver of identification. Only it was worse for me, she thought: I had two of them.

When Polly was fourteen Bob Milner won a prize for a textbook on physics, and a reporter from the *Times-Union* came to interview him. Polly was at a friend's house that afternoon, only two blocks away, but nobody called her to come home and be in the photo of Professor Milner and his family, or even mentioned her in the article. Bob said he was sorry about it afterward, when it was too late. "That's okay," Polly told him. "I'm not related to you anyhow."

Her mother was different: Polly felt related to her, though she couldn't understand why she liked Bob and the boys so much — didn't she see how boring they all were? Bea at least wasn't boring; she sometimes made surprisingly shrewd, even witty comments on people and events. But she was hopelessly unliberated and unambitious. She was still grateful to Bob Milner for marrying her and taking her to a dreary city like Rochester; she still couldn't get over how nice he was compared to most men.

And the infuriating thing was that Bob *was* nice. He had always tried to do the right thing by Polly, she had to admit that. He paid to send her through college and graduate school; he never favored her half brothers over her when it came to presents or music lessons or trips. Of course, one reason he was so nice was that he'd always had everything his own way at home; Bea saw to that.

For instance, Bob Milner had been allowed to name his sons Albert and Hans after the two physicists he most admired; Bea had no input in the selection, any more than she'd had in the selection of Polly's name — her father's grandmother had also been called Paula. Once, when she was in college, Polly had asked her mother if she'd minded having her husbands choose the names of all her children. At first Bea had seemed not to know what Polly was talking about; then she smiled and rested her hands on the old treadle sewing machine at which she was piecing an ill-designed patchwork quilt. "No, it never occurred to me," she said, shifting the folds of material. "But I don't think names are all that important, do you?"

"I think they're very, very important," Polly had replied; at the time, she had been thinking of changing her name to Stephanie for no good reason that she could remember now.

Except maybe that was why I wanted to call my kid Stephen, she thought. I wanted him to be the kind of person I thought a Stephen or a Stephanie was then, probably because of *Portrait of the Artist as a Young Man*: independent and artistic and brave.

And what kind of person was Stevie now? Polly sighed. At the moment, she had no idea.

It had been a real dismal scene, as he would have put it, ever since he got to Rochester. She was stunned when she saw him loping along the airport corridor toward her, looking inches taller in his new cowboy boots, and transformed outwardly into a Western preppie. His unruly brown hair (so like her own, and before always about the same length) had been cropped and tamed, and he wore an unfamiliar red ski parka covered with zippers and flaps and strips of Velcro.

"Oh, Stevie, baby!"

"Hi, Mom."

Not only was his greeting constrained, for the first time in his life Stevie seemed to suffer rather than return Polly's hug and kiss. On the way to her mother's house he suffered rather than answered her questions. He hardly looked at her, but kept staring at the backs of Polly's half brother Alby and Alby's new wife, Carolee, in the front seat. Maybe her son was abashed by Carolee's presence, though strangers had never made him shy before: on the way to La Guardia in

August he'd had an animated conversation with the cabbie about tornadoes.

At home it was no better. Polly had been looking forward to this moment for months, but she was unable to break through Stevie's reserve. At her suggestion he sat in the kitchen while she made the walnut cake he had always liked; he cracked nuts for it and licked the bowl, but his conversation was a series of monosyllables and platitudes. "Yeah ... No ... Sure, I'm all right ... Dad's all right ... School's all right ... No problem," he kept saying. Her beloved child, whose lively volubility had always been her joy, had become a polite, inarticulate stranger.

At dinner, though, he fell into the familiar noisy, banal style of conversation at the Milners', dominated as usual by the men. He and Bob and Bob's sons compared computer games and sci-fi films; they traded stories of mountain climbing and white-water canoeing, while Bea and Carolee provided a cheering section. Afterward Stevie helped the men wash up and then followed Alby and Hans into the study to play poker. It was always that way in this house: you practically never had a private conversation. She might as well resign herself to it; after all, tomorrow she and Stevie would be leaving for New York, and she'd have him to herself for two days.

She certainly hadn't had him to herself yet, Polly thought the following evening, clearing the table while her mother scraped and rinsed the plates, as they had done in this same kitchen every Thanksgiving since Polly was nine. Bea Milner had a new dishwasher now, and leaves had been added to the dining table as the family grew, but otherwise everything was almost eerily the same as it had been thirty years ago. Presumably, some of Bea's dreary forget-me-not china must have broken and her flowered linen dishtowels worn out from time to time, but they had been replaced with similar china and towels.

Meanwhile, Bob and his sons and Stevie were watching football on TV, just as they did every year, and Polly and her mother were cleaning up, even though they had also cooked dinner. The men usually pitched in after meals, but on Thanksgiving they were always exempt. Polly had resigned herself to this; it was something else that riled her now: the fact that Alby's wife, Carolee, was in there watching football with the men.

"I don't see why Carolee doesn't have to help us," she complained, covering a Pyrex dish of cranberry sauce with plastic wrap. "After all, she's not a guest anymore, she's part of the family now, isn't she?"

"Mm, yes," Bea agreed placidly. She was a small, sturdy, rather pretty woman with tinted and waved light-brown hair and a more lined, less defined version of Polly's features. Her large round eyes were pale rather than dark, and there was something neat and birdlike about her movements. "But you know, dear, she's a tremendous football fan. I think she gets just as excited by a game as Alby or Hans, don't you?"

"I guess so," Polly agreed; she could hardly do otherwise, when her sister-in-law's cheerleader shouts could be heard all the way to the kitchen. They were even louder in the dining room when she went back for a load of dessert plates. As she stacked them she thought how apt her roles and Bea's were. She brought her mother complaints and irritations, like soiled dishes, and Bea, with her mild wash of resignation and explanation, patiently sluiced the mess away. Even though she saw through the process, it still made Polly feel calmer.

"I do really feel Carolee is one of the family now, you know," her mother said as Polly returned.

"Oh, yeah," Polly replied; in her opinion Carolee, who was a scientist and a jock, was all too much like a Milner.

"I think she's going to be good for Alby. Of course, she's not as brilliant as he is; but she's an awfully nice girl, don't you think?" Bea helped herself to a couple of grapes from one of the plates Polly had just brought in; her eating habits were also birdlike.

"She's nice enough," Polly agreed. "But she's not very interesting."

"Well, maybe not." Bea sighed as she scoured the sticky dish that had held sweet potatoes. "But I don't think that really matters so much. You know, Polly, when you're young you always want people to be interesting. Then later on you find out it's much more important for them to be serious and decent. I've noticed that at work."

"Oh?" For the last eight years, Bea had been an assistant dean — a glorified secretary, really — in the university summer-school program.

"Whenever we get an application that says a student is 'interesting,' and not much else, I always put a little *W* next to his or her name now. For Watch out." Bea giggled suddenly. Since she usually didn't drink, the glass or two of sherry she allowed herself on holidays always made her a little blurry.

"How is your job going, by the way?" Polly asked, realizing that in the clamor of family news Bea had volunteered none of her own.

"Oh, very well. Of course, this is our quiet season, we're only just getting the catalogue together."

"So things are all right with you," Polly said; it was hardly a question, for Bea was chronically contented.

"Oh, yes. I have everything I want." She hesitated, holding an ugly Corning Ware serving dish under the tap; the warm water, splashing on its edge, sent up a kind of transparent fan. "I'd like for you to be happier, that's all."

"I'm fine," Polly said.

"I worry about you sometimes, you know."

"Oh?" Polly said, surprised; it was unlike her mother to worry about anything.

"Mm. You see, when I married Bob, I thought it would be the best possible thing for you, to grow up in a pleasant place like Rochester. In a normal family. But I wonder sometimes if maybe after we moved here I didn't pay you enough attention. I was always thinking about the boys:

Alby's asthma, and the trouble Hans used to have with reading. But you were so sensible, so articulate, so talented; I knew you'd always be all right. At least, I thought you'd always be all right." She wiped back a stray lock of hair with one wet reddened hand.

"I am all right, really," Polly assured her. For years she had wanted to hear her mother admit that she might have done something wrong. But now that this was happening it made her embarrassed and uncomfortable, as if the kitchen were tilting and sliding into the cellar.

"You weren't really unhappy, growing up here, were you?" Bea dropped the dishcloth into the sink and turned to look at her daughter.

"It was okay. It was fine," Polly lied.

"I was so sorry it didn't work out for you with Jim. But I expect you'll find another nice man soon." Bea put a handful of spoons into the dishwasher, giving Polly a quick little smile that was also a question.

"Mh," Polly said. No, I'm not going to find a nice man soon, she thought, because there aren't any "nice men" in New York. What I'm looking for now, probably, is a nice woman.

I might as well tell her the truth, she decided, staring past Bea at the new kitchen wallpaper, which had a clumsy pattern of spice tins in avocado, orange, and brown. (Why would any graphic artist have wanted to design such a drearily hideous wallpaper, or any shop have ordered it?) She'll be upset, Polly thought, but so what? It was always so hard to get a rise out of her mother; why shouldn't she be upset for once? "I'm not sure I will," she said. "Uh, you know my friend Jeanne, that you met in New York last year, the one that's sharing my apartment now."

"Mm." Her mother nibbled absently at the end of a leftover breadstick.

"Well, she's a lesbian. And I think I might be one, too."

"Oh, Polly." Bea dropped her breadstick into the dish-water. "Really?"

"I'm not sure. But I might."

"Well, dear, if that's what you want," Polly's mother said finally. She wrapped some celery in a piece of plastic. "I mean, your friend Jeanne seemed like a very nice girl."

"Yes, but she's not, I mean, we're not —" Polly stuttered.

But Bea wasn't listening; she was gazing past her daughter with an odd faraway smile. "You know, when I was in high school, I had this *tremendous* crush on the captain of the girl's tennis team."

"Really?"

"Oh, yes." Bea giggled again; she was certainly tipsy. "She was so tall and athletic; she reminded me of your father, in a way. Well, I suppose I should say he reminded me of her when I met him, because of course that was years later."

"You mean, are you telling me, you and this girl were lovers?" Polly stared at her mother across a counter of marbled avocado vinyl.

"Oh, no. Well, not exactly, anyhow," Bea said, smiling and fitting a plate into the dishwasher. "I mean, I positively adored her, but we didn't *do* anything, of course. Well, not anything *serious,* you know." She giggled.

"I thought you'd be shocked," Polly said, a little shocked herself.

"No, dear. It's not like men, after all, is it? With those awful bars they go to, and the dreadful diseases they get. If it was Hans, say, of course I'd be very worried for him. But it's different for us. There's a woman in my office now, she and her friend have been together for eighteen years, and they're the nicest quietest people you'd ever want to meet, except they do have rather an awful Abyssinian."

"An Abyssinian?" Polly, confused by everything her mother had said in the last few minutes, saw a dark-skinned butler — or cook, maybe? — in a turban.

"A cat, you know." Bea giggled. "But I think really it would be better not to say anything about it to Jim," she added. "I mean, not until you're sure. He likes people to be consistent. And if it turns out not to be so after all, he'll think you don't know your own mind."

Polly stared at her mother again; never in her life had she heard her suggest that anything should be kept from Jim. "Okay," she agreed, wondering if she knew her own mind, or anyone's.

"And the same for Stevie, don't you think?" Bea added two cups to the dishwasher.

"I wasn't planning to say anything to Stevie, not yet," Polly agreed. "I thought I'd wait until he moves back home."

"Much better. Well, I think that's all the plates we can fit in on this load." Bea poured the detergent dispenser full of grainy pink-and-white powder from a box named Comet, closed the door, and pushed ON.

When Polly, with Stevie behind her, unlocked the door to her apartment on the afternoon of the day after Thanksgiving, she expected to find it as she had left it: empty, cold (she had turned down the thermostat), dark, and untidy. Instead it was full of warmth and light and flowers. An explosion of ice-pink long-stemmed roses crowned the desk; another even larger one of gladioli spread green-and-white moth wings above the coffee table.

She stood dazed; then there were steps in the hall and Jeanne came running in.

"Oh, Polly!" she cried, almost laughing. "The most wonderful thing has happened, Betsy's left her husband!"

"That's great," Polly said, jerking her head to warn Jeanne that her son was there.

"Oh hello, Stevie." Her friend's voice dropped an octave and lost volume.

"Hi," Stevie replied with an equal lack of enthusiasm.

"Well, anyhow." Jeanne took a breath. "I've moved my things into your spare room. I thought I'd stay here tonight and tomorrow, it's so horribly crowded at Ida's. People are sleeping all over the floor, and you can simply never get into the bathroom." She smiled uneasily. "If it's okay with you, that is."

"Sure, it's okay," Polly repeated; what else could she say?

"What was that all about?" Stevie inquired audibly as he followed his mother down the hall.

"Nothing. Just somebody Jeanne knows, who's been having trouble with her marriage." Polly swallowed, distressed to hear herself lying — fudging, at least — to her son.

As soon as Stevie had left to visit a friend she got the details. Jeanne had phoned Betsy the night before Thanksgiving, with dramatic results. "I'm so grateful to you," she cried, hugging Polly again. "Really, if you hadn't suggested it, I might never have called her."

At the other end of the line, Betsy had wept with relief. "I thought it was too late; I thought you never wanted to see me again," she had sobbed happily. Then she had packed her bags, called a taxi, and come straight to Jeanne. While Polly was in Rochester they had had a joyous reunion in Polly's bed.

"I knew it would be all right," Jeanne said, smiling. "I mean, I knew you'd got Stevie's room all ready for him, and I didn't want to mess it up. Of course I changed the sheets again for you. Oh Polly, it was so lovely." Jeanne held out her arms as if to embrace the whole world; her cheeks were flushed pink with retrospective pleasure. "You don't mind?"

"Nh." Polly shook her head, irritated to discover that she did mind. "Of course not. So where's Betsy now?"

"She's at her parents' house up in New Canaan, till Monday. She was supposed to have gone there for Thanksgiving, with the husband, but she called to say she was sick. She's going to tell them everything now."

"Uh-huh," Polly said. "So she'll be staying there for a while?"

"Oh no; just for this weekend. It's much too far to commute to the college, and of course we want to be together. We'll share her place in Brooklyn Heights as soon as that creep leaves." Jeanne leaned over the gladioli, pinching off a half-dead bloom.

"He's going to move out, then?"

"Oh yes. He'll have to, because Betsy owns half the

apartment; it was bought partly with her parents' money. But I thought that until then she could stay here."

"He-yere?" Polly couldn't prevent a break of dismay in the middle of the word.

"Just for a little while. After Stevie leaves, of course. I thought what we might do is move the bunk bed into your room, maybe take it apart into twin beds, that'd be more convenient for you. And then move the double into Stevie's room for us." She smiled brightly. "That would be so much nicer."

"Well," Polly said. "I don't know."

"Naturally Betsy would help with the expenses, so we'd all be saving money."

"Mm," Polly said, thinking that her friend hadn't said "share." But then, why should she? From Jeanne's point of view, Polly was almost rich. Jeanne was scraping by on a mingy academic salary, and Betsy, who taught freshman composition part-time on a one-year contract, was even harder up.

All the same, Polly felt cross and beleaguered, like a child whose parents were arranging her life behind her back. She didn't want Betsy in her apartment, and she wanted to sleep in her own bed. But to say so would sound selfish and grudging. And after all, it would only be for a few weeks, probably. It couldn't be more, because Stevie would be home for good before Christmas. "That's true," she admitted.

"Oh, wonderful. Thank you, dear." Jeanne, who had been shifting uneasily along the sofa, bounced up to give Polly another quick hug. "I want to apologize to you, too," she added. "I know I've been awful to live with ever since I broke up with Betsy."

"You haven't, really."

"Oh, yes, I have, Polly. I've been frightfully moody and distracted, and not much help around the house either. And you've been an angel to put up with me. But I'll make it up to you now; we both will. Oh, I'm so happy. I'm going to call Betsy right now."

* * *

"I'd like to ask you something," Polly said after Jeanne had murmured a final series of childish endearments into the phone. "When Stevie gets home, could you give us some time alone to talk?"

"Oh, sure. Is something the matter?"

"No; I just didn't get much chance to see him in Rochester. My family was all over the place, you know what they're like. So if you could stay out of the way for an hour or so —"

"How do you mean, out of the way?" Jeanne said, her voice rising slightly. "Do you want me to go out and walk around the block for an hour? Because I can't go into the park now, you know; it's nearly dark out already."

"No, of course not," said Polly. "But if you'd just, I don't know, go and work in my bedroom while I make dinner?"

"All right," Jeanne agreed. "Just let me know when I can come out, okay?"

But in fact Jeanne didn't stay in the bedroom. Instead, after Stevie returned, she wandered around the apartment like a cat whose territory had been invaded — though maintaining a considerate silence. *Don't worry, I'm not going to interrupt your conversation,* her manner seemed to say. *But you can't fault me for going to the bathroom or looking for the* Times.

Whether it was because of Jeanne's hovering presence or not, Polly was unable to break through Stevie's reserve, though he'd been fairly voluble on the plane and in the taxi from La Guardia, talking about what he wanted to do in New York and the kids he planned to see. Over supper he was still unnaturally quiet and polite; and whenever something almost like a conversation got going, it soon died away. Maybe because it was clear that though Jeanne was really trying, she found his subjects — skiing in Colorado, *Star Trek,* Halley's Comet — deeply uninteresting. If it was going to be like this, Polly thought, she might as well have stayed in Rochester, surrounded by relatives. It might even have been better; if Stevie didn't talk to her there she wouldn't have noticed so much.

But was it really Jeanne's fault, or had her son in fact become an alien? Because after the dishes were done, he spent the rest of the evening on the telephone and in front of the TV. ("Mom, do you mind? I don't want to miss 'Miami Vice.' ")

"Well, how was it?" Jeanne asked when he was in bed. "Did you have a good talk with Stevie?"

"Not yet, really." Polly sighed. "We're still sort of awkward with each other, you know."

"Yes, I noticed that."

"He's not in Colorado now, but he still seems almost that far away. And he's developed such awfully good manners."

"He certainly eats much less sloppily," Jeanne agreed.

"I don't mean just his table manners. It's, like, his whole attitude. He's so cool and polite, it almost scares me. I just don't know." She paused, waiting for Jeanne to ask, "Don't know what?"

"I mean," she continued, "I guess I should expect it to take a while for him to feel at home again, but hell —" Again Polly waited, and again her friend did not speak. "Of course, at that age three months is a big chunk of your life; it's like a year or so for you or me." No comment. "I realize I've just got to hang in there, give him time. But right now I hardly recognize him as my own kid."

"Polly, dear. Stevie's fourteen now. He's not your kid anymore. He's growing up, turning into a man." Jeanne pronounced the noun with distaste; "Turning into a monkey," she might as well have said.

"I suppose so."

"I know it's hard for you to face facts sometimes." Her friend's voice was kinder now, soft and soothing. "But you've simply got to reconcile yourself to losing him eventually."

It was Polly's turn now not to answer. I don't reconcile myself, I won't! she thought. And it isn't hard for me to face facts, either. She opened her mouth to say this, then shut it, remembering how thin the walls were; if she and Jeanne raised their voices in an argument Stevie might hear it. "Maybe," she muttered finally. "Well, I'm getting sleepy. Goodnight."

She stamped crossly down the hall to her room, and then lay awake for a long time, wondering as she thrashed and turned whether Jeanne was right. Was her Stevie, the one she knew and loved, gone for good? Or was he only hidden under a laconic new manner and expensive Western clothes?

Polly had just finished making a late breakfast for her son the next morning and gone into the bathroom when she heard a smash of china and a shout of "Oh, fuck it!" from the kitchen.

She dropped the *Times,* pulled up her jeans, and hurried down the hall, arriving in time to hear Jeanne wail: "Oh, no! Not Betsy's darling Japanese teapot!"

"I'm sorry — I didn't mean to —" Stevie had backed away from Jeanne's misery and fury into a corner; his mouth was open, his elbows raised defensively.

"Oh, hell. Maybe we can mend —" Polly began.

"Don't be stupid! Can't you see it's hopeless?" Jeanne stooped to the floor, then rose with a bony white fragment of china in each hand and an expression of deep bereavement. "Oh, she'll be so sad!"

"Hey, I'm sorry. But I didn't touch the thing, honest," Stevie protested. "I just opened the cupboard door, and it fell off the counter. Whydja have to leave it like that?"

"I left Betsy's teapot exactly where I always leave it; where it belongs." Jeanne was in control again; her tone was cool. "Anyone who had eyes in their head would have seen it —"

Stevie's look of guilty dismay shifted toward exasperation. "Listen, I said I was sorry already, for shit's sake." Jeanne flinched at the obscenity, but made no other reply. "Whadda you want me to do? You want me to buy you a new one? Okay, I will."

"I'm afraid you won't be able to do that," Jeanne said with a tight smile. "It was an antique; it belonged to Betsy's grandmother."

Half an hour later Polly squatted on the kitchen floor, wiping the worn marbled vinyl with a wet wadded paper towel. She was mopping up the last of the cinnamon rose tea, and also the last tiny sharp shards of Japanese china. From this position she heard the front door close, signaling that Jeanne had gone out to buy a new teapot. ("No, thanks, I'd rather do it myself. You wouldn't know what to look for.")

Now there were steps in the hall; Stevie slumped in the kitchen doorway.

"Aw, Mom," he said. "You don't hafta do that. I already cleaned up the mess."

"I know you did, pal." Polly sank back onto her haunches and smiled up at him. "I just want to be sure nobody comes in here in the middle of the night and starts screaming around because they've cut their foot. This china is really sharp." She shook her head; she already had a slash on one knee.

"I guess she'd make a hell of a fuss." He grinned.

Though this wasn't what Polly had meant, she let it pass. She was so happy to have the real Stevie back, talking to her in his real voice. He had even, she noticed, changed into one of his old shirts, a red checked flannel that they had bought on a trip to Macy's last winter, now too short in the sleeves.

"Hey, Mom," he said, opening the refrigerator. "Can I have some of that cake, or were you saving it?"

"Sure you can have it, if you're hungry." She got to her feet. "Have anything you want."

"Great." He vanished behind the refrigerator door, emerging with the remainder of Jeanne's apricot torte in one hand and a bottle of tonic in the other. "There's never much to eat at Dad's house."

"That's too bad." Polly could not help grinning.

"Yeah, that Debbie, she's always on a diet."

"That's too bad," she repeated with equal insincerity.

"Hey," Stevie said, chewing. "You're not still pissed at me about this morning?"

"I never was pissed at you. It was an accident, that's all. Only you've got to watch your language with Jeanne, okay, pal? Curse words freak her out. You know some people are like that."

"Yeah. I know. Listen, Mom," he added, swallowing.

"Mm?"

"How come Jeanne is staying here? Doesn't she have anyplace else to live?"

"Well, not right now. She's looking for an apartment." Polly's smile faded. "And she couldn't go home for Thanksgiving, because she doesn't have any real family." (Not strictly true; Jeanne had a father and brother in Portsmouth, New Hampshire, but she despised and feared them.) "Do you really mind it that she's here?"

"I dunno." Stevie shrugged. "I guess not. I mean, I know she's company for you when I'm away. I just don't see why you like her so much, that's all."

"We're really good friends," Polly said firmly. "She was awfully kind to me last month when I had the flu. And you've got to admit she's a great cook. Wait till you taste the chocolate mousse she's making for us tonight — you still like chocolate, don't you?"

"Yeah, sure," Stevie said, but without eagerness, and in his former constrained manner.

"I know Jeanne's a little —" Polly's voice seemed to freeze up. "Anyhow, I'm sure once you get to know her better you'll like her."

"I don't hafta like her, Mom." Stevie took a swig of tonic directly from the bottle; if Jeanne were to see this, she would be revolted. "You don't like all my friends."

"I do too," Polly protested.

"You don't like Billy all that much."

"Well." Polly grinned. "I guess maybe I don't. But it's nothing personal, it's just that he's such a computer freak; he never has anything to say to grown-ups."

"Anyhow, Jeanne doesn't like me either, so who cares?" Stevie shrugged and opened the refrigerator again.

I care, Polly wanted to say, but the words would not leave her mouth. "What makes you think that?"

"I d'know." Stevie paused, looking at his mother over the open door of the fridge, his heavy eyebrows drawn into a puzzled frown. "It's just— The way she keeps watching me. I feel like she's kind of got it in for me; she wants me to fuck up. Like this morning. I figure she sort of left her dumb old teapot out on purpose, to see if maybe I would break it."

"Oh, Stevie," Polly exclaimed. "Jeanne wouldn't do anything like that." But her son, who was eating cranberry sauce with his fingers, did not reply.

An hour later, after Stevie had left, Jeanne returned carrying a plastic bag marked Pottery Barn.

"Did you find a teapot?" Polly looked around from her notes.

"Well. I found a kind of teapot." Jeanne halfheartedly unwrapped a plain white pot. "It'll have to do for a while."

"How much was it? I'll pay you now."

"No rush, dear. It was nothing, only about twelve dollars."

"That's not nothing." Polly stood up and began to look for her handbag.

"Please, don't bother. I tell you what. Someday when I have time I'll go over to Bloomie's, and if I find a pretty one you can buy me that." Jeanne's smile was open and charming, her tone casual, but what Polly thought was that her friend was still furious.

"All right," she agreed, for after all fair was fair. But what an awful lot of fuss about a "dumb old teapot"!

Not that that was so unusual. Jeanne always overvalued objects; she could go into raptures over some battered mir-

ror frame or motheaten fringed shawl in a shop window on
Columbus Avenue. The high point of her trip to England
two years ago, to hear her tell it, had been the Victoria and
Albert Museum, and during her occupation Stevie's room
had become a gallery of frayed silk and bubbled glass and
chipped marquetry.

Jeanne cares for things more than she does for people,
Polly thought. But then for most of her life Jeanne hadn't
had anyone of her own to care for. Her mother had died
when she was ten, her father and brother were coarse
heavy-drinking French-Canadian paternalist types, and she
had no children. Polly looked at her friend again, but now
with pity.

"Where's Stevie, is he in my room?" Jeanne asked.

His room, you mean, Polly thought, but forbore to say.
"No, he's gone visiting."

"Ah." Jeanne sank onto the sofa with a sigh, lit a cigarette, and picked up *Vogue,* which she occasionally bought
herself as a treat the way she bought bags of chocolate-
covered cherries. "You know," she said casually over the
magazine a few moments later, "it's Stevie who should pay
for Betsy's teapot, not you."

"And *you* know Stevie won't have twelve dollars." Polly
almost laughed; it was characteristic of her son, as of her
father — whom, she realized, he was also beginning to resemble physically — that he couldn't save money. But
Jeanne didn't smile.

"I expect he has twelve dollars somewhere, in a savings
account or whatever. Or at least he has an allowance."

"You really think Stevie should pay you out of his
allowance? But he only gets two dollars a week. Even if he
gave you half of that, it'd take him a long time."

"Well, why shouldn't it?" Jeanne smiled. "He might
learn something that way."

"Learn something?"

"Yes, learn to be a little more careful of other people's
property. If that's possible." She laughed lightly.

"Well, maybe he could pay part of it," Polly said, struggling with her own irritation. "But I don't really think — It was just an accident, after all." She looked at her friend for confirmation, but instead there was silence. "I mean, it's not as if Stevie meant to break the teapot."

"I'm not so sure about that." Jeanne turned a page of *Vogue* with a scissoring sound.

"Oh, of course he didn't." Polly shook her head, smiling. "You —" She stopped. You're both being ridiculously paranoid, she had been about to say, he thinks you left it out deliberately. But that could lead to real trouble.

"I realize Stevie's your innocent child. Or rather, he was. But he's growing up now, and you've got to grow up a little too."

"You mean, you really believe —" Her voice rose.

"I wouldn't be surprised if he did it on purpose." Jeanne's manner was affable. "Accidentally-on-purpose, at least. I mean, heavens, it was in plain sight on the counter. Nobody could have missed it, not even a man, unless they'd wanted to."

"Well, Stevie could. And hell, I know he's growing up. But that's why it happened; he's growing so fast now he's gotten clumsy. He doesn't know how large he is, so he bangs into things, knocks things over. Most adolescent boys are that way."

"Yes, that's the usual excuse, isn't it?" Suddenly Jeanne's tone had become bitter and uneven. "That's the way it is in this world: men are taught as children that once they start getting larger and stronger they can smash up things and people carelessly. They can go on doing it all their lives, really, and they'll be excused and forgiven; they won't have to pay. It's the women who will always pay, in the end. The way my mother did."

"I didn't mean —"

"But you see, you didn't say, 'All adolescents smash things up.' Nobody ever says that. Girls are growing fast too at that age, but nobody makes those excuses for them. If they break something they're punished. They have to learn to control themselves and respect other people's property. Isn't that true, now?" She folded her round, rosy arms against a lavender jacquard sweater.

"Well, yes, I suppose. But I think you're being unfair to Stevie," Polly said stubbornly. "And he felt it too. He thinks you don't like him, you know. And maybe he's right."

Jeanne got up and came over to her; she crouched down by the desk until her face was on a level with Polly's. "Don't say that," she said; her voice was soft, trembly. "I love Stevie, because he's your child. It's just that I worry about what's happening to him, what happens to all males in this society. I mean, look at him now. He's lived with you all his life; then he goes to stay with his father for a couple of months, and he comes back completely changed."

"I don't think he's changed all that much. Underneath —"

"Of course, the process isn't complete yet. He's only fourteen. I know it's hard." She put one hand on Polly's arm and gazed at her with round pale eyes in which tears seemed to brim. "I'm very sorry for you — for both of you. But you mustn't think I dislike him. Please."

Jeanne's voice was gentler than ever, her posture suppliant, yet Polly felt as if her friend's hand were a heavy weight pressing on her. "All right, I don't," she finally had to say.

MRS. MARCIA ZIMMERN,

widow of Lorin Jones's father

Aw no, I'm glad you came round again, and not just 'cause of the cookies from Fraser-Morris, either. It was sweet of you to remember. I adore them, but it's hard for me to get across the park in this wet weather, with my bad leg. Take a couple yourself, come on.

Don't be silly, you don't need to lose any weight.

That's right. And how about a little drink to go with it? I always think you need a pickup, a heavy wet day like this, when it starts to get dark so early. Gin and orange is what I usually have...

Oh yeah, I've been thinking about Laurie, trying to remember for your book. One thing that came to me was, how she used to love artichokes. It was kind of a joke around here, that if they were in the stores I had to have them when she came to dinner. And I had to make real hollandaise sauce, she didn't like the kind in a bottle.

Nah, I don't care for them myself; they don't agree with my stomach, too acid. But Laurie just loved them. She'd always eat hers slow, while the rest of us were waiting to get on with the meal, and she'd arrange the leaves on her plate in different kinds of artistic patterns, like a fan or a water lily. Or like a fish, sometimes, with scales, you know.

No, nothing new came to me about her paintings.

Oh yeah, sure, she gave us a picture when we got married. And I sold it after Dan was gone, Mr. Herbert's right.

No ma'am, it wasn't that at all. I decided I didn't want it, that's why.

Don't apologize: anybody might think it was for the money. And I won't deny it was a relief to have a little extra cash at the time. Did you know, after a death they freeze all your bank accounts?

Yeah, the joint ones too, that's the worst. I tell all my married friends: it don't matter how much you love your husband, get yourself a separate account . . .

But listen, I don't want you to write in your book that Dan didn't provide for me properly. I've got no complaints. We enjoyed it while we could, that was his philosophy. We had great times together: we went to Europe and Mexico and Israel and South America. I rode on a camel in Egypt and I saw the river covered with white long-legged birds thick as Jones Beach on Labor Day. Live in the present; I believe that. I had a wonderful life with Dan, I don't regret anything.

No, the reason I sold that painting of Laurie's was, I didn't care for it.

Well, I can't say exactly why. It just wasn't the kind of thing I like. I don't want you to get the wrong idea, I love modern art. You see those prints over the sideboard?

Yeah, and did you know, when Henry Matisse made them, he had got such bad arthritis he couldn't paint, but he didn't give up, he went right on cutting out pieces of colored paper, I admire that.

Then of course there's the Chagall etching in the hall that I showed you last time. It's very valuable, my son says. But I'd never sell that picture; it always reminds me of my grandmother from Poland, my father's mother. The stories she told. It makes me weepy when I think how she never got to come to America till her eyes were fogged up with cataracts and she was too old to see anything . . .

What I didn't like about Laurie's painting? Well, the colors, for one thing. I never liked that kind of colors, those dreary

browns and grays and misty violets. But what really bothered me, if you want to know, was — can I sweeten your
drink?

Have another cookie, anyhow ...

Yeah, okay, Laurie's painting. *Who Is Coming?* she called it.
Well you've seen the picture, you remember how there's all
these wispy bug kind of things floating in it? And then
there's a much bigger one, sort of coming down out of the
air on the left-hand side, a moth it could be. Or a woman in
a lavender chiffon nightgown, maybe, very thin, with wispy
pale brown hair, or it could be feelers, what d'you call them?

Antennae, yeah, that's it.

Okay, maybe it's an "abstraction," but that's how it always
looked to me. And I figure Laurie meant it that way too.
Who Is Coming? Well, it wasn't Laurie, because her hair was
long and dark, nearly black, and it sure as hell wasn't me. So
who was it that was coming?

I'll tell you who: it was Laurie's mother, Celia. And that's
why she gave it to us, because she wanted Dan to be reminded all the time of his dead wife, and she wanted me to
be reminded, too. Haunted, you could say. She wanted me
to have to look at Celia every damn time I walked into this
room.

Nuh-uh, I certainly didn't say anything to Dan. If he didn't
get the idea himself, I wasn't going to put it into his head.
What I did was, I suggested we should move the painting
into the study. I told Dan I thought it was lovely, but it
didn't match my color scheme: the gold carpet and upholstery and these red and blue accents that I chose to harmonize with my Matisse prints, they wiped Laurie's picture
right out, I said.

Nah, I didn't get anywhere. Dan thought it'd hurt Laurie's
feelings if we even just moved her painting from over the
fireplace, where she'd hung it, into the corner there. But he

loved me, he wanted me to be happy, so he offered to have the whole room redecorated to harmonize with Laurie's picture.

God, no. That was all I needed, to have my beautiful apartment done over in Celia Zimmern's favorite sad wishy-washy colors.

There was nothing I could do about it. I just made up my mind not to see the picture. I trained myself not to look in that direction, and most of the time I didn't, for sixteen years.

Yeah, that's why I got rid of it, soon as I decently could after Dan was gone. Rod, that's my son, he said to me the other day, "You should of held on to that picture, Ma, I bet it's worth a lot now." But I don't have any regrets. I wasn't going to have that dead-moth woman coming in over my mantel a day longer than I could help.

Maybe. My sister said, if you want to look at it from a religious point of view, Celia's won: she's got him back now. Not that I believe any of that stuff. Anyways, if there is an afterlife, there's so many females fighting over Dan that a sad little bug like her wouldn't have a chance.

Don't get me wrong, I never had anything against Celia Zimmern. She was a nice enough woman, from what I hear; I only met her once. And everybody knows she was smart. She was a real highbrow, reading heavy books all the time. I think she made Dan feel kind of a clod, not that she probably meant to. But she was awfully kind of dim and washed out and ineffective. She sure wasn't the right woman for him.

Pretty, yeah, I'll give you pretty, but in marriage pretty isn't everything. I'll tell you what my mother said. She said, "What for did Dan want to marry a shiksa in the first place? You know what you get with a shiksa? Wonderbread. No taste, no nourishment." And then Celia was sick so often, those last couple years, she wasn't much use to anyone.

Oh, yeah, of course he was fond of her. When she was sick he got her the best doctors, he did all anybody could do. But every time he had to go to the hospital to see her it just about broke him up. He always said to me, "Marcia, when I go, I want to go fast." After his heart attack, the doctor told him, take it easy, Mr. Zimmern, no exertion, no alcohol, no tobacco, no steak eggs butter, I don't know what all, a nap every day, you could live for years. He tried it for a week, maybe two, then he said the hell with it. He said he might as well be dead already as live like that.

Yeah. He was gone in six months. But I figure it was what he wanted. He couldn't have stood to waste away slow like Celia did.

No, I didn't dislike her, I was sorry for her, really. It was her daughter I couldn't stand.

Well, for instance. Most normal kids would be happy if their father found someone he could make a good life with, instead of moping around alone the rest of his days in that big sad empty White Plains house. Dan's son, Lennie, he was always decent to me, not that we had much in common, but he used to come to dinner sometimes, and bring a bottle of wine, and we'd have a good laugh. . . . But Laurie — or "Lorin" like you keep saying — and that's another thing, that fancy name she picked out for herself. Affected, I always thought. Dan never could get used to it, he went on calling her Laurie, so I did the same. But I know she resented it. When she phoned it'd always be "This is Lorin here," and I'd say, "Just a moment, Laurie, I'll get your father." Here, let's have a little more gin. Come on, what's the harm? We're both grown women.

How did she treat me? Well, she hated me from the word go, really, that's what I always felt. For one thing, she thought I was too young —

I was about forty, and Dan was going on sixty-five, but so what? He had more energy and nerve than most men half his age. If he came into a room, it was like a two-hundred-watt bulb went on, right up to the end. When he was in the hospital, dying, even then, he was so . . . excuse me.

I didn't mean to get weepy. It's just that — I mean, I loved my first husband, he was a nice boy, but he didn't know from nothing compared to Dan. Dan was the best thing that ever happened to me. You know, a widow with two kids, she doesn't get many offers, not that kind anyhow. Sure, a lot of men were willing to take me out, give me a good time. But marriage, forget it. When Dan asked me I didn't stop to think, how soon will I be a widow again? You've got to bet on your instincts, isn't that right?

Anyhow, that's what I always say. But Laurie couldn't see it. She thought I was marrying him for his money, probably, not that he had all that much. And besides that, she thought I wasn't educated enough. And then it was her opinion that we didn't wait long enough after her mother was gone, and she blamed me for that.

Well, it was nearly seven months, most people would have said that was enough, specially since Celia had been in and out of the hospital for so long. But not Laurie. . . . Besides, if you want to know the truth, she thought he was too chummy with me before Celia died.

Okay, suppose it was true? Dan was a healthy, good-looking man, and Celia hadn't been a real wife to him for a long time, if you know what I mean. But his daughter couldn't accept the facts of life. She was jealous, like a spoiled little girl. Only she wasn't a kid anymore; she was nearly thirty. She was awful to me.

She treated me like a wicked stepmother, that's what I always thought, as if I was persecuting her or something.

It wasn't anything definite she did. But for instance, if you want to know, most of the time she wouldn't even speak to me, not really. Okay, she was shy, but so what? After you know somebody a few years, you should get over shyness. But it was always the same: every time we saw her, almost every remark she addressed to her father. It was like I wasn't in the room, only now and then she'd give me this sneaky Cinderella look.

No, Dan couldn't see it. He was such a sweet guy, he always believed the best of anyone close to him, you know, and she was his baby daughter.

Oh, she knew what she was doing. Yeah, she knew, all right. I'm sorry to have to say this to you, seeing as how you've got to write a whole book about her, but Laurie Zimmern wasn't a nice person.

10

A cold dull day in early December; an opening at the Museum. Polly was there, huddled on a sticky black leather bench in a back hallway near the telephone booth. She appeared to be waiting to make a call, but in fact she was hiding out.

She should never have come here, she thought; she should have gone straight home after her appointment at the endodontist's. But she hadn't wanted to admit that besides hurting her and frightening her and insulting her and giving her a first-class headache, Dr. Bebb had ruined her whole afternoon. It was bad enough that he had insisted on calling her "Paula" and told her that she probably ground her teeth at night, but he had also had the nerve to compare his work to hers.

"Marge Dunn tells me you're an author," Dr. Bebb had remarked as she lay tilted back nearly ninety degrees in his padded vinyl chair, staring up at a fizzing fluorescent light fixture and at his monstrously enlarged pale fat fingers, bulbous nose, and thick spectacles.

"Weh, noh exac-uh," she replied, gagging as he began to pack her jaw with lumps of cotton.

"But you're doing research for a book, right?"

"Euh," Polly agreed, feeling betrayed by Marge, her regular dentist — who seldom hurt her even a little, and then always with advance warning and most apologetically.

"A novel, is it?"

"Euh-euh."

"Nonfiction," Dr. Bebb deduced, his pale enlarged face stretching even farther in a self-congratulatory smile.

"Euh."

"Hard work?" He blew an airgun into Polly's mouth. "Kinda like being a detective, I bet."

What was this, an interrogation? Polly thought. She declined to make a noise for either yes or no.

"I said, kinda like detective work, your research, is it?" Dr. Bebb repeated, pausing with the electric drill in his fat hand.

"Euh," Polly agreed, realizing that the sooner she answered, the sooner all this would be over.

Dr. Bebb smiled his fat smile. "Hold real still now," he ordered, and lowered the drill. A loud, unpleasant vibration filled Polly's head, and a jarring, buzzing pressure.

"Rinse, please," he said finally. "You know, Paula, I sometimes think what I do here is kinda like investigative research," he added, poking fat sausage fingers and a steel probe into her mouth. "Following a tooth to its roots. You never can tell ahead of time what direction a root will take, did you know that?" He moved the probe, producing a twang of high-level pain.

"Euh!"

"Sorry," Dr. Bebb said unfeelingly. "So I figure we have something in common, right?" He paused again, instrument in hand, but Polly refused even to mumble a reply. We have nothing in common, you fat bastard, she thought.

Oh yes you do, a voice in her head replied. Haven't you been probing for the diseased roots of Lorin Jones's life? And aren't you planning to fill them up with cement and cover the whole thing with a shiny white deceptive surface?

She should never have gone to Dr. Bebb, Polly thought as she sat by the phone booth. Or rather, she should have walked out five minutes after they met, because she knew by then what he was like. You might think that in a city the size of New York there would be a competent female endodontist, but Marge knew of none. She always sent her patients to Dr. Bebb. "He's a good man," she had insisted. "Howie" — her husband, a dental surgeon — "thinks the world of him."

Well, maybe he'd fooled Marge and her husband, but he

didn't fool Polly. His specialty wasn't ordinary repair work, but a combination of the murderous and the mortuary. She had recognized him as a natural enemy at once, but her natural animal reaction to threat — fight or flight — had been blocked by reluctance to appear cowardly and neurotic, and by Marge's remark that if Polly didn't have root canal work soon she would lose two upper molars, and eventually the ones below as well. So instead of hitting Dr. Bebb with her Peruvian tote bag, or climbing out of the dental chair and fleeing his office, she had stayed and let him kill her tooth and embalm it with cement, and give her a splitting headache.

But then, almost everything that had happened in the last week or so had given her a headache. The first one, minor but nagging, began on the Monday after Thanksgiving during Polly's interview with Lorin Jones's stepmother, who had portrayed Lorin as self-centered and spiteful. She had also related a story that, if repeated in the biography, would do Lorin's reputation nothing but harm. Polly would just have to forget it, as she would have to forget a lot of the other stuff she'd heard lately; lies, all of it, probably.

Polly's second and worse headache dated from the following day, when Betsy had moved into the apartment. It was great to have Jeanne in good spirits again, overflowing with affection, and turning out a remarkably inventive series of casseroles and fancy pastries.

Polly ought to be grateful to Betsy for having caused this transformation, but instead she was already sick of her. Unlike Jeanne, who taught full-time and had constant meetings of her department and a range of other scholarly and feminist associations and committees, Betsy was free most of the day. She had to be at the college only two mornings a week; otherwise she was always at home, and always occupying the bathroom: taking long strawberry and apricot bubble baths that left fuzzy red or orange rings in the tub, washing her clothes, or shampooing her fine crimped strawberry-blonde hair, which when wet took on the color of damp sawdust. The rest of the time she was wired up to a Walkman and soft-rock or romantic-classical tapes. Often, presumably unconsciously, she would hum or sing aloud in accompaniment to them. "Yeh-yeh, a-yeh yeh," Polly could hear her warbling tunelessly as she highlighted in yellow Magic Marker the books and articles recommended by Jeanne, or wrote in her journal or ironed a blouse. Not until late in the afternoon, when Jeanne came home, did Betsy unplug herself.

Also, unlike Polly and Jeanne, Betsy was congenitally untidy. As she wandered about the apartment she left a trail of objects: shoes, sweaters, handbag, comb, bobby pins, coffee cups, spectacles (her pale blue eyes were nearsighted), magazines, and loose pages of the newspaper. As a result, she was always drifting (or, without her glasses, stumbling) from room to room looking for whatever she'd mislaid. "Darling, you've simply got to pick up as you go, so you won't keep losing things," Jeanne often said to her; but she spoke as one might to a spoiled yet beloved child.

Sensing that she was unwelcome, Betsy had tried hard to win Polly's favor. For instance, she constantly offered to make lunch for her. Her specialty was tiny tasteless low-calorie open sandwiches: slices of avocado and pimiento arranged around a quartered hard-boiled egg on triangles of toast; or mashed water-pack tuna garnished with olives and watercress on Ry-Krisp. If she had depended on Betsy to feed her, Polly would have starved.

Betsy also volunteered to wash Polly's sheets and towels in the basement laundry room, and to go to the grocery and the dry cleaner's; she never left the apartment without asking if there was "something, anything" she could do. "Yeah, sure," Polly often felt like saying. "You could move out."

Polly knew she was making Betsy feel unwanted, and that she was probably doing it out of jealousy, because she missed having Jeanne to herself. She even missed sleeping with her; not only or perhaps even mainly in the sexual sense, but in every other sense.

It had been awfully pleasant to share her bed with Jeanne. She didn't churn about the way Jim used to do, roiling up the bedclothes and protruding his hard elbows and knees into Polly's territory. Everything about her was soft, easy, enfolding. After the light was out they would lie warmly and loosely together, sorting out the news of the day. And if Polly woke with a start later on, her heart pounding, her muscles tensed — as she sometimes did — she had only to turn toward her friend. Without rousing, Jeanne would put out her arms and gather Polly to her, drawing her gently down into a slower rhythm of breath, into a deeper and sweeter sleep.

But now all this was over. It was Betsy who shared the warmth and softness and intimacy; Betsy who monopolized Jeanne's attention and sympathy — which she needed because, Jeanne said, she was so young and helpless.

And so demanding. In the evenings, after Betsy had done the dishes (not very well most of the time), she would come to sit by Jeanne on the sofa and give her a greedy, childish hug. After it, she would never quite let go. Instead, as they chatted, she would continue to lean against Jeanne and squeeze her hand or her arm. At intervals she would rub up against her like an overgrown puppy, and kiss and caress her, not minding that Polly was in the room; maybe even enjoying it.

What Polly should do, of course, was to find someone she could kiss and caress; but the more time passed the less likely that seemed. She was finished with men, and the women she'd met through Jeanne either weren't available or didn't attract her. Maybe, Polly thought miserably, she would never make love to anyone again. For the rest of her life, nobody but dentists and gynecologists would ever touch the inside of her mouth or of anything else of hers. Instead of having sexual experiences, she would lie helpless in medical offices, with her feet in metal stirrups or a paper bib tied around her neck.

Polly sighed, almost groaned. As soon as she could gather her strength she was going to shove her way back through the mob in the gallery, which ought to be thinning out soon. She was going to go home, take a lot of Actifed,

and climb into her bed. Or rather, she thought with irritation, into Stevie's bed, because hers was now in Stevie's
room with Jeanne and Betsy.

In a couple of weeks, of course, Jeanne and Betsy would
be gone and Stevie would be home. Home for good, she
wanted to say; but even that wasn't certain now. Last night
while she was on the phone to him in Denver, he had
mentioned that his father thought it might be a smart idea
for him to stay on in Colorado through next June, so he
wouldn't have to switch schools in the middle of the year.
"And how do you feel about that?" Polly had asked, making
a serious effort not to scream.

"I d'know," Stevie said in a polite fade-away voice.

"Well, think about it, okay?" she shouted into the receiver.

"Okay," Stevie had replied, sounding thousands of miles
off; as he was.

"Let me talk to your father, please," Polly said, the
horseflies of rage already beginning to swarm and seethe in
her head; and when Jim came on the phone she could not
prevent herself from shouting at him. As usual, he remained
disgustingly reasonable and calm. Yes, he had mentioned
the possibility, he admitted. But he thought that they should
let Stevie decide for himself; that would be the best and
fairest thing. The best, maybe, Polly thought furiously; but
how could it be the fairest, when Jim was there on the spot,
always ready with his sensible arguments, his expensive
bribes, his — in her mother's phrase — "normal family
life."

Right now, maybe, Stevie was deciding to stay in Denver forever, and she was hiding in a museum hallway with
a bad headache and an incipient throbbing pain in her jaw.

Almost as soon as she had arrived she'd realized that she
never should have come. She'd thought it might distract her
and cheer her up to see old friends; instead, it had made her
feel worse. Everyone she knew seemed overdressed, slightly
unreal, and peculiarly solicitous; they asked how she was
with an air of expecting bad news. Also, as she might have

foreseen, many of them wanted to know how her biography of Lorin Jones was coming along. "Oh, all right, thanks," she had to lie over and over again.

Then she ran into an old acquaintance who'd heard that Polly was on leave and assumed she was "getting back to" her painting. "Oh no, I gave all that up years ago," Polly had to say. "I'm doing a book on ... " et cetera.

"You've given up painting? Oh, dear. But why?"

Polly hadn't tried to explain it. Instead, she had excused herself to go and hide in the washroom, like some embarrassed teenager.

There, in front of the sinks, she had a lowering but enlightening vision. She glanced into the mirror and realized that the novocaine Dr. Bebb had shot into her jaw had not only left half her face numb, it had paralyzed the muscles on one side, giving her a look of lopsided frozen misery. No wonder so many of her friends had inquired about her health and spirits. She had no way of knowing how long the paralysis would last; but there wasn't any point in waiting around to find out. As soon as the crowd diminished a bit she'd take off.

From where she sat now Polly could see a section of the main exhibition area, a lofty, smoky, spotlit space crowded with multicolored bodies and objects. Again, as at the Apollo Gallery two months ago, she felt as if she were gazing into an aquarium: this time a huge one packed with marine life, with every sort of fish and crustacean and aquatic plant: a crowd of fluttering, many-hued fins and fronds, glittering scales, and waving claws and feelers — everything covered with a smoky froth of stale bubbles. None of these creatures were looking at the pictures and sculpture; rather, they were crawling and swimming around them like crabs and fish circulating unaware among rare corals and sunken treasure.

"Darling." Jacky Herbert was swimming toward her now, his considerable stomach straining a shiny pale gray satin waistcoat quilted in scales. "I was so hoping I'd see you here."

"Hi there."

"How are you?" Jacky bent down to goggle at her. "Heavens, what's happened to your face?"

"I've just been to the dentist. Root canal work."

"Ooh, horrid. I had that last year, I know exactly how hateful it is. You poor thing." He subsided onto the bench beside her. "But I'm going to cheer you up. I have such marvelous news: I've discovered two new little Jones watercolors we didn't even know existed."

"Oh, great." Polly tried to sound enthusiastic, wondering why she had to try. Maybe she was going into a clinical depression.

"You must come down to the Apollo very very soon, so I can show you the photos. I'm sure you'll want slides. They're from about fifty-seven, fifty-eight, my favorite period almost. Though I do adore those strange late paintings too; if only there were more of them! . . . How is the book coming, anyhow?"

"Oh, all right."

"I hear you saw Grace Skelly." Jacky sucked air like a fish.

"Yeah. She told me how close she and Lorin Jones were, and how awfully happy Lorin was that the Skellys had bought *Birth, Copulation, and Death*."

"Well, what did you expect?" His voice bubbled with suppressed mirth. "You don't imagine Grace wants to go down in history as someone an artist couldn't stand to have owning one of her paintings? You didn't contradict her, I hope."

"Well, no. But I'm certainly not going to publish her version."

"That's too bad." Jacky giggled outright. "You could do yourself some good that way, you know. Grace would be very very grateful; and one thing you have to say for the Skellys, they pay their debts."

"But her story's a complete fabrication. You told me so yourself."

"So what? Nobody else is going to know that. And besides, who can be sure my story was true either? I'd certainly deny it if anyone asked me." He giggled again, puffing his cheeks up with air and shaking his head solemnly. Then his expression changed. "I hope you're not for a single moment considering publishing what I told you," he added in an offhand manner, gazing away from Polly.

"Why not?" she asked. She wasn't fooled by the tone; she knew that Jacky always seemed most lively and intense when he was relaying unimportant gossip; when he adopted a careless, uninterested style he was deadly serious.

"Surely you're joking." Jacky almost yawned, but he also turned and looked hard at her.

"Why should I be joking?"

"Because if you did print what I told you, darling," he drawled, "the Skellys would never buy another picture from me, or lend anything to the Museum as long as you worked here; and Bill would probably sue you for libel."

"You really think he'd do that?"

"I'd say it was a very very strong possibility. And it wouldn't be the first time; you remember that *Art Today* case. Of course it was settled out of court finally. Ten thousand and costs to the plaintiff. In nineteen-seventy-two dollars."

"That's not fair."

"Life's not fair. Don't be naive, Polly." Jacky sighed. "But let's talk about something pleasanter. I understand you hit it off very very well with Kenneth Foster."

"Yes, he was quite helpful. He told me a lot about Lorin's early work, and what she was like in college. He admires her as a painter; well of course you know that. But he didn't care much for her as a person, apparently. He preferred Garrett." Polly kept her voice neutral, though what she had thought during the interview was: A thirty-five-year-old professor seduces a twenty-year-old student, and leaves his wife for her, and Kenneth Foster blames the student; that's really taking male bonding pretty far.

"Ah." Jacky did not comment further.

"One thing he said that amazed me was that he had married Garrett's first wife after the divorce. And now they're all good friends, he claims. I found that hard to believe."

"Oh yes. It's quite true."

"Most people I've spoken to don't even know Garrett had a first wife."

"Yes, well." Jacky made his fishy moue. "I'm not surprised he didn't mention it. Garrett prefers to forget whatever doesn't fit his image, don't we all. If someone does happen to hear about that marriage, his line is that it was just one of those brief impulsive wartime things. But in fact he and Roz were together for six, seven years."

"What's she really like, Mrs. Foster? I only met her once, at some opening."

"Oh, quite nice. Of course she's had rather a hard life; she's not kept her looks too well."

"Was she pretty once?" Polly asked this doubtfully; she remembered Roz Foster as overweight and raddled-looking.

"Oh, very. I think painters' wives always are, don't you? At least to start with. Yards of red hair, and a lovely creamy skin. Garrett always went for the beauties too, even though he wasn't a painter. He thought he deserved them. The way Paolo put it once, Garrett thought he was God's gift to women, and he wanted to play Santa Claus." Jacky giggled.

Polly laughed too, but uneasily; it crossed her headache to wonder if Garrett Jones had given Jacky or someone Jacky knew a skewed version of her visit to Wellfleet.

"Lorin wasn't the first student Garrett had fooled around with, of course," Jacky went on. "But she was the first one he really fell for, and he got careless."

"And so his first wife found out?"

"Eventually. And Roz was miserable. She really loved him, from what I hear. She couldn't eat or sleep, she started to drink too much, smashed up the car, threatened to kill herself. Garrett was at his wit's end; he was seriously scared. He didn't want a suicide on his conscience; who would?"

"So then?"

"Well. What finally happened was that Kenneth Foster took Roz off his hands, so he could marry Lorin, and Garrett made Kenneth famous. He's like the Skellys: he pays his debts." Jacky giggled.

"You really mean —" Polly looked at the art dealer with something between doubt and disgust.

"Please, don't get me wrong." Jacky waved his flippers. "I'm not trying to say that Foster isn't a marvelous painter. But without Garrett he might not have the sort of international reputation, or command the prices, that he does now. And has for years, of course. Anyhow, that's all ancient history. And really the marriage has been surprisingly successful. There was a sticky patch at one time, but Roz has been in AA for twenty years now, and they're a very very devoted couple today." Jacky blew out a sigh. "None of your concern, thank heavens. I mean," he drawled, "nothing you'd ever want to put in your book."

"No," she agreed.

"That's just as well. Anyhow, you must be nearly ready to start writing now."

"Yes; pretty soon," Polly said. "I have an interview upstate to do first, and then I'm going down to Key West to look for Hugh Cameron."

"You think he's still there?"

"I know he's there. At least he was three months ago. He hasn't answered my last letter, but it hasn't been returned either, so I figure he's still around." Polly didn't mention that Hugh Cameron's only response so far had been one line scrawled in felt-tipped pen across the bottom of her original inquiry: *Sorry — haven't time to answer your questions.* "Anyhow, I want to see the place, look at the house where Lorin lived, try to talk to people who might have known her."

"Ah. Of course." Jacky took a gulp of the smoky gallery air and let it out with a slow wheeze. "You know, while you're down there —" he added in a studiedly lazy voice that at once alerted Polly.

"Yes?"

"You might poke about a bit; see if you can spot any more paintings."

"Oh, I will."

"It would be especially nice if you turned up one or two of the late graffiti ones. There's a lot of interest in those, you know."

"I know," Polly agreed. Lorin Jones's final Key West paintings were remarkable for their inclusion of words or sometimes whole phrases in the manner of Dine or Kitaj. The two that had been included in "Three American Women" had attracted much attention.

"If you manage to get into Cameron's place you might see something," Jacky suggested.

"Well, I'll look. But didn't Lennie take everything away after Lorin died?"

"Ye-es. Supposedly. But it wasn't all that much, if you think about it. I've asked myself sometimes, why do we have so few Joneses between sixty-four and sixty-nine? Far far fewer, for example, than in the previous five years. And then there are the two large canvases that didn't sell at her last show. They seem to have vanished completely. Of course it's always possible that she destroyed them afterward, or painted them over."

"But you think Cameron might still have them."

"I've always thought it was very very likely. From what I've heard, it would be like him to have forgotten to give Lennie one or two things. Perhaps out of carelessness, perhaps out of sentimentality. Or perhaps just out of natural orneriness; who can say?"

"Maybe it was greed," Polly suggested. "He could have wanted the money."

"No." Jacky shook his large head slowly. "Not that, probably, because the paintings weren't worth much at the time. And then maybe Lennie didn't look too hard either. Nobody's going to knock himself out over pictures that'd sell for maybe a few hundred, even if you could find a buyer. Which you most likely couldn't, back then."

"No," Polly agreed.

"But now everybody wants a Lorin Jones; they're worth twenty, twenty-five thousand, and rising. It's a whole different kettle of fish. If you own one you've got to think about insurance, burglar alarms, restorers, the lot. You sell it, you can buy a year's worth of dope, a sports car, a trip to Spain, whatever an individual of Cameron's type wants."

"You think Cameron might have some pictures he'd like to sell now?"

"It's a possibility. Of course it'd be rather a dilemma for him. Legally he doesn't own anything of Lorin's, because they were never married and she died without a will. Everything belongs to Lennie. So if Cameron wanted to sell anything he'd have to do it under the table."

"That wouldn't be so easy," Polly protested. Most collectors she knew of bought art partly for the pleasure of showing it off, and partly as an investment. They hated a dubious title: it meant lying to people who came to the house; and could be really embarrassing if they decided to sell the painting later or give it to a museum for a tax write-off. The first question then would certainly be, What was the provenance?

"No. If Cameron means to sell he's got to find someone who wants a cut-rate Jones and is willing to keep it permanently under wraps. And I don't think he — or anyone, probably — could do that. For that kind of deal you have to have a really important work on offer — a Johns or a Rothko or something of the sort. But that's where you might have an advantage."

"Me?" Polly frowned; her headache felt worse.

"You, darling." Jacky yawned. "I couldn't approach Cameron, because I'm known to be a reputable dealer. But you could hint to him that you might be interested in buying a Lorin Jones, if he happened to have one lying around."

"No thanks." Polly spoke with force and ill-suppressed indignation. "I'm not interested in getting mixed up in that kind of deal. Anyhow, I haven't got the money."

"Of course not," Jacky said smoothly; he leaned over and patted her arm. "But it would be a good way of finding out if Cameron does have anything, wouldn't it?" He smiled fishily. "And maybe getting it back."

"Well, yeah, but I don't know —"

"You see, if you found one of Lorin's paintings in Cameron's possession, Lennie and I could go to my lawyer, and find out what could be done. Possibly just threatening him with a lawsuit would be enough."

"Suppose it wasn't?"

"Well, we could actually sue. And then there's always the police. I imagine he wouldn't want that." Jacky giggled. "Anyhow, if you should run into anything, I'd be grateful if you'd let me know as soon as possible. You can phone the gallery collect any time. Leave a message on the machine if I'm not there. . . . Oh, Doris, darling! Marvelous to see you. Looking so very very well!"

Jacky rose to his feet and kissed the smoky air beside the cheek of one of Polly's former colleagues. She excused herself from their conversation as soon as possible and went into the telephone booth, now fortunately empty.

To give verisimilitude to her excuse, she lifted the receiver and called her own number. The blurred but unpleasant underwater buzz of the dial tone filled her ear, and then an empty ringing; Jeanne and Betsy, she knew, were out. As she listened she gazed through the greeny-brown tinted glass, picking out Jacky and her other acquaintances among the swarming, swimming crowd in the gallery. It looked even worse to her now; a tank of lies, deals, subterfuges, and deceits; of slippery aquatic creatures, of things drowned and rotting.

She stared at the strips and shapes of brilliant color floating above the crowd; works of talent, even perhaps of genius. What were they doing here, sunk halfway into this slimy aquarium? she thought. And what was she doing here?

But then, that's what Lorin Jones must have asked herself. The New York art world Polly saw now was the one Lorin must have seen: a vision of an underwater hell that drove her first to Wellfleet and then even farther, to Key West. Leaving a trail that Polly must, whatever she felt about it, follow.

*   *   *

The apartment was empty when Polly got back. On the kitchen counter was a note from Jeanne suggesting that she join them at a dish-to-pass Affirmative Action benefit in the Village, and instructions on warming up the supper she'd left in case Polly didn't feel up to another party.

Wearily, gratefully, she turned on the oven and began to open her mail, which consisted entirely of bills and circulars. There was also a large, badly wrapped parcel for Stevie, sent by her father from San Diego; HAPPY BIRTHDAY FROM GRANDDAD was scrawled in red felt-tipped marker above the address, and HANDLE WITH GREAT CARE PLEASE, FRIENDS below it. In spite of this appeal, or maybe because of it, the package had come apart at one end, exposing part of an inner wrapping paper printed with pink and yellow teddy bears.

Polly scowled as she looked at it, then sighed. This parcel was in every way typical of Carl Alter. The soiled and refolded brown paper, the coarse hairy tightly knotted string, the incongruous inner wrapping, the appeal to the kindness of strangers, the public expression of private sentiments; and most of all the fact that it was five weeks late. When she was a child, her father's gifts always arrived after the occasion or never, and it was the same now with his grandson.

And what the hell was she going to do with the thing? It was too late to mail it to Denver; it would have to wait till Stevie got home. And meanwhile she would have to write her father and explain what had happened. Or maybe it would be quicker to call; she hadn't spoken to him in a couple of months anyhow. Not that they ever had much to say to each other. Polly didn't care what articles he had published lately in *California Living* and the local newspaper or how his high blood pressure and his current wife's orchids were doing; he didn't care what was happening to her, he never had. But every few months they went through the motions.

So, after she had eaten Jeanne's veal-and-mushroom

casserole (first-rate, as usual) and homemade noodles and green beans, and washed up, and made herself a cup of coffee, Polly dialed San Diego.

"Yeah," her father said after they had exchanged the usual superficial news. "I know when Stevie's birthday is, sure I do." (Uh-huh, Polly thought.) "I just wasn't able to find the kind of binoculars I wanted to send him right away, see."

"Binoculars," she repeated, thinking that considering the way the package looked they were probably broken; and then that as usual her father's present was not only late but inappropriate. There was no use for binoculars in New York except to spy into neighbors' windows, and she certainly didn't want Stevie to start that. Yes, but in Colorado they'd be welcome, she remembered miserably. "I tell you what," she said. "I'll put on a new card, and give them to him at Christmas."

"Nah, nah," Carl Alter objected. Polly could see him shaking his head once or twice fast, the way he did. "I don't want Stevie to have to wait any longer. You give them to him now, okay?"

"I can't do that," Polly said with irritation. "He's in Denver now."

"In Denver? Oh, yeah. Right."

"He's been there since September," Polly said, positive that her father hadn't bothered to listen to her before, or more likely hadn't bothered to remember. She would have thought he was losing his memory, except that he'd always been like that.

"Well. You must miss him."

"Very much," Polly said crossly.

"He's coming home for Christmas, though, hum?"

"Yeah. But I don't know, he may go back to Colorado again for the spring term."

"Ah. Well, that's too bad," Carl Alter said without concern or emphasis. "But you can visit him, that'll make it all right."

What a stupid, callous thing to say, Polly thought,

feeling the familiar angry buzz in her chest. She should fly to Denver, stay in a motel, and have a couple of restaurant meals with Stevie, and that would make it "all right."

"That's what you ought to do," her father continued. "Go to Colorado and visit him. Yep. You do that."

"Oh, is that so!" Polly cried, losing her temper. "Well, I'm surprised you should say that, considering you practically never visited me after I moved to Rochester."

There was a moment of silence on the cross-country phone line. "That was different," Carl Alter said finally. "You never wanted to see me."

"I did, too," Polly insisted; she was damned if she was going to let him get away with this.

"Aw, come on. Back in Mamaroneck, whenever I came to take you out for the day, you used to have a tantrum. Your mother told me so. She practically had to force you to come with me."

"But that wasn't — I didn't —" Polly stuttered furiously, and fell silent, not trusting herself to speak without swearing.

"Never mind, Polly-O. I understand how it was. But you and Stevie, that's different. Right?"

"I guess so," Polly said flatly. Goddamn it, of course it was different. She loved Stevie; until this fall they hadn't ever been separated. But what was the use of saying this to someone like Carl Alter? What was the use of shouting at him?

"So if he's in Denver, you go see him, okay?"

"Okay," Polly said flatly.

"And I tell you what else you do. You find out what Stevie wants for Christmas, and I'll send it to him."

"I don't see the point of that," Polly said, again fighting for control. "You won't remember anyhow."

"I will so; I promise. What the hell —"

"It'll be the same as it was with me," Polly cried furiously. "You were always promising! Two years running, you promised to buy me an Etch A Sketch."

"An Etch A Sketch?" Carl Alter repeated at the other end of the United States.

"It was a kind of screen with dials, you could draw pictures with it, and I kept asking you— Oh, never mind," she added, ashamed now of her outburst. "I'll ask Stevie what he wants, but you know it's probably too late for the Christmas mails already."

"I tell you what. Maybe I'll send him a check, he can pick out something himself."

"Yeah, that's a good idea," Polly said wearily, thinking that of course it would never happen; less angry now with her father — because what was the use? — than she was with herself for having blown up at him after all these years. "You do that," she added.

DANIELLE ZIMMERN KOTELCHUK,

former sister-in-law of Lorin Jones

Hey, Polly, before you start, I want to apologize for never getting down to New York. See, what happens is, I plan to go, every so often; but somehow I never make it. When you live on a farm, even a part-time one, there's always just too much to do on weekends: there's the garden, and the horses have to be fed and exercised, and the dog's about to have puppies, it's one damn thing after another. That's one reason.

I guess the other is, I've gotten to hate the place. And of course Bernie never liked it. But it's weird, a city girl like me. Though I still love Paris: I go there every summer for a couple of weeks if I can. But I realized the other day, literally all I've seen of New York in nearly three years is Kennedy Airport.

Okay, you want to hear about Laurie. I've been thinking what I could tell you that'd be useful. There ought to be something; I knew her for nearly twenty years. But I never felt I knew her all that well, or that we had much to say to each other.

No, I don't mean I didn't like her. I liked her well enough, but she just wasn't on my wavelength.

Well, for example. I'm pretty much up front, always have been, and Laurie was the elusive, silent, secretive type. When I first met her, I thought she was a kind of Rima, a bird girl — did you ever read *Green Mansions*? Those immense eyes, and all that untidy dark hair. Her husband treated her that way, as if she were some fragile woodland creature, too delicate for this world.

I don't know. Probably she realized it was part of the deal, if you look like that.

Well, you must have noticed that thin women attract a different kind of man than plump ones do. If you're under-weight you get older men, fatherly guys, who like to think of women as frail and helpless. They want to protect you and shield you from the world.

Right. Whereas if you're overweight you draw the opposite type. Whatever their age, what they basically are is little boys who want to be taken care of. If you're really built like a house, guys like that take one look at you and cry "Mommy!"

I think it's harder to be too thin. Especially if you're small, too; then you get the aggressive macho types, who like to refer to their wives as "the little woman." And if you're really unlucky you can attract the kind of man who's look-ing for someone vulnerable, so he can hurt her or even destroy her.

No. In my opinion, most of the time it's not luck; it's a choice. I tell my women's studies students, what they're doing when they order that double fudge sundae, or shove it away, is choosing the kind of man they want, the role they want to play in a relationship.

Yeah, I think Laurie was doing that too, probably uncon-sciously. But Garrett certainly fit the pattern. He was always running after her with a sweater. And when the family got together, he was the one who did all the talking, and told us what a great artist she was going to be. Later on, when she began to get a reputation, he'd boast about her most recent success.

I think she was very embarrassed by it. When Garrett started quoting her latest review, or telling us what impor-tant collector had just bought one of her paintings, she always looked kind of miserable to me.

Oh, sure, I think she was very gifted. Nobody doubts that now, do they?

Yes, when I was married to Lennie we had a couple of her paintings. But he took them when we split. I got the kids and the house and most of the furniture, it was a fair deal. Lennie was never mean, not about money anyhow.

No, I don't miss them that much. I prefer more content in art. I know it's totally unfashionable, but what I really go for is nineteenth-century French realism: Courbet, Manet. Delacroix and Géricault even. Of course that's my period. I like a lot of color and action.

We didn't see them all that often. Lennie's father enjoyed having his family around on holidays, so he'd make an effort to get us all together. But he and Marcia were traveling abroad a lot of the time.

Yes, we saw more of Laurie the first couple of years we were married, before her mother died. We used to stay at Lennie's father's house in White Plains whenever we came down to New York. Lennie didn't get on too well with Dan, but he liked Celia, even though she was his stepmother. But she was less like a classic stepmother than anyone I ever met.

She was a really nice woman. I didn't pay any attention to her at first, she was so pale and dim and self-effacing. She looked a lot like Laurie, but she didn't have her striking black-and-white coloring or her energy. When you walked into a room full of family, Laurie and Dan were the first people you noticed, and Celia was about the last.

Well, Lennie'd told me she was awfully intelligent, and when I finally started to talk to her, I found out he was right. Celia'd read just about everything, even in my field. All of Proust and Colette and Camus, for instance, and mostly in French. Balzac, though she didn't appreciate him. Gross, he seemed to her — "earthbound" was her term — and greedy, and too interested in money. But that's *la condition humaine,* like he said, right?

About all she ever did was read, and work in the garden a little. I never saw her cook or sew or clean or anything like that. Of course they had a live-in housekeeper, and Celia was already ill when I met her.

You couldn't tell, except that she always seemed tired.

I think she knew she didn't have much time left. She always used to ask me what'd been published in Paris lately that was interesting; and when I recommended something she'd call Scribner's bookstore in New York and order it sent that day, first-class. I thought that was kind of silly and extravagant back then, but afterward I realized she'd been afraid she might miss something otherwise.

The infuriating thing is, the kind of cancer she had is curable now, it has only about a ten percent fatality rate. If she'd been born twenty years later she'd probably be alive today, and maybe she'd have accomplished something too, because she had such a remarkable mind.

I figure that Celia knew everything, really. Only she couldn't do anything about it, at least it seemed like that to her.

For instance, she saw that Lennie and I were going to have a rough ride together, but that we'd both survive it one way or the other. And I'm sure she knew Lennie's father was sleeping with some woman from his office, who turned out to be Marcia. And she knew Dan couldn't stand her being ill.

He despised weakness, you see. Lennie inherited that from him. Except the kind of weakness Lennie despises isn't so much physical or moral as intellectual. He can't stand stupidity, even in kids, and you know all kids are stupid sometimes. I remember once his shouting at Roo, "Why must you be so childish?" But the thing was, she *was* a child, she was only about four then.

Yes. I never thought about it before, but I think Laurie despised weakness, too.

All kinds. But with her it was her own weakness as well as other people's — probably more than other people's.

No. She had a lot more drive and will than her mother, but she didn't have her father's stamina. Celia said to me once, "I wish Laurie were a little bit more like you, a little tougher."

No, after Dan married Marcia we didn't see them so much. We'd always go to New York for Thanksgiving, though, and Laurie and Garrett would usually be there.

It wasn't very comfortable. Lennie didn't get on with his dad, like I said, and Laurie couldn't stand Marcia.

Well, she can be pretty hard to take, but she's got a good heart. She still sends my kids presents on their birthdays, even though they're grown up. Ridiculous presents, mostly. My youngest, who's in the Peace Corps in Africa, got a five-pound box of Whitman's Sampler chocolates from her last February, because she used to like them as a little kid. Of course it was congealed into a kind of chocolate soup by the time it arrived, but you have to appreciate the impulse.

Yes, every year till Laurie left Garrett. And we went to stay with them a couple of times on the Cape.

It was all right. The main trouble was, pretty soon we had two small kids, and they didn't have any. Roo was always knocking something valuable over; and our Celia was a baby, and you know how babies cry, just for exercise sometimes.

Yes, I met Hugh Cameron a couple of times, not on the Cape, but later, before he and Laurie settled in Florida.

He was a child, that's what I thought. And was going to be one permanently, you could see that even then. One of those innocents who make trouble wherever they go. Men like that, they ought to glow in the dark, as a warning to women.

Yes. They were like children, both of them, playing hooky from real life.

No. She made me awfully impatient sometimes, but I knew that in a way it wasn't her fault. She was brought up wrong. Her mother was wonderful in her way, and Dan was all right too, but he was the original macho man. He liked sports and parties and excitement and bossing women around. But he was generous, and he was really fond of our kids; they still miss him.

The thing was, they were your typical patriarchal couple: Dan ran everything, and Celia just drifted around him. So naturally Laurie grew up assuming that men would take care of her. When she finally tried to stand on her own feet and take care of herself, it was too late. That's what I think.

Yes; something did happen to her as a kid. When she was about ten, I think. It was at a Parents' Day picnic at the country day school she went to. Laurie sort of wandered away and got lost, and when they finally found her she was hiding all crouched down in a corner of a little wooden playhouse in the nursery-school yard, without any panties.

She hadn't been raped or anything, I know that. The family doctor said so. But she'd been just about scared out of her wits.

Nobody ever found out what happened exactly. Laurie wouldn't say; she would hardly talk for weeks. There was a terrific uproar, and her parents took her out of that school and sent her somewhere else.

It was bad for all of them. One problem was, everybody in the family blamed themselves for not watching Laurie more carefully. The one who blamed himself worst was my ex-husband. His dad had told him to go and find his sister, but he didn't want to be bothered, so instead he just climbed up the fire escape behind the school and read an Ellery Queen mystery.

No; I don't believe that people are ruined by one bad childhood experience. I mean, everybody's got something they can blame their whole life on if they want to. I got knocked down and stepped on, they can say, and I'm just going to lie here in the mud for sixty years so everybody can see how badly I was hurt. I think you choose your own life. Events happen to you, sure, but it's up to you to decide what they mean.

Well, if you're really haunted by something, I think you should go to a good shrink, get it out of your system.

No, Laurie never did, not that I know of. It wasn't her kind of thing. But of course that was a choice too.

11

In the mauve afterglow of a warm December sunset, Polly Alter stood by the registration desk of a women-only guest house in Key West, dizzy with heat and travel fatigue. This morning in New York everything had been gray and gritty, like a bad mezzotint. She'd woken with such a sick, heavy cold that she called to cancel her flight, but all she could get on the phone was the busy signal. Giving up, she dragged herself and her duffel bag out to the terminal. There, aching and snuffling, she shuffled onto a plane and was blown through the stratosphere from black-and-white to technicolor. Five hours later she climbed out into a steamy, glowing tropical afternoon with coconut palms and blue-green ocean, exactly like a cheap travel poster.

It wasn't only the scenery that was unreal. Most of the people she'd seen, beginning with the taxi driver, were weird. They moved and spoke in slow motion, as if something were a little wrong with the projector. Lee, the manageress of Artemis Lodge, was so slowed down she seemed drugged. It had taken her five minutes to find Polly's reservation, and now she couldn't find the key to Polly's room.

"I know it's here somewhere. I just can't locate it right this moment, is all," Lee drawled, smiling lazily. She was a sturdy, darkly tanned, handsome woman, a middle-aged version of one of Gauguin's Polynesian beauties. She had a bush of shoulder-length black hair streaked with stone gray, a leathery skin flushed to hot magenta on her broad cheekbones, and knobbed bare brown feet.

While Polly waited, Lee shifted papers and slid drawers open and shut. She kept breaking off her search to answer the phone, to find a stamp for another guest, to offer Polly passion-fruit juice and nacho crackers (Polly declined, feeling her stomach rise), and to assure her that if she couldn't get into the room tonight she'd be real comfortable on the porch swing.

Polly slumped against the desk with her duffel bag and her stuffed-up nose and her headache, listening to the irritating tinkle of the colored-glass wind chimes as they swayed in the sultry evening breeze. Maybe she should just get the hell out of here now and find a motel.

As Lee set down her sweating purple glass of passion-fruit juice and began to search again through sliding heaps of papers, Polly asked herself if maybe Ida, who had never liked her, had deliberately sent her to a dump full of crazies.

"Listen," she said. "It's getting late; maybe I'd better go look for a motel."

"Hell no, you can't do that." Lee laughed almost nervously. "Ida'd kill me if I let any friend of hers go to a motel."

"I'm not really a friend of Ida's," Polly protested. "I mean, I don't know her that well, she just recommended —"

"Eureka!" Grinning broadly with triumph, showing strong white irregular Polynesian teeth, Lee held up a key. "I knew it was here somewhere."

The first thing Polly did, after dumping her luggage on a garish orange batik bedspread and going out for a hamburger, was to call Hugh Cameron. She stood in a telephone booth at the front of the coffee shop watching a procession of tourists and weirdos pass along Duval Street, and trying over in her mind the speech she had rehearsed. ("This is Paula Alter from New York, you remember I wrote to you about Lorin Jones. I know you said you were busy, but I've come all the way to Key West to talk to you, it's really important, so . . . please . . . if you could . . .")

As she listened to the ring, she imagined Cameron slowly, impatiently getting up from his chair, crossing the floor. . . . He was a difficult, rude person, everyone in New

York said so. He might shout at her or curse her — tell her to get lost, to fuck off.

The steady burring of the phone, at first menacing, gradually became mechanical. Either Hugh Cameron wasn't home, or he wasn't answering. Ill, exhausted, she slumped against the side of the booth. She wished she had never come here; she wished she had never heard of Key West, or of Lorin Jones. She was tired of chasing this elusive contradictory woman around the East Coast, tired of trying to sort through the lies and half lies of her former associates. Ultimately, it was Lorin's fault that she was here in this steamy miserable place instead of home in bed.

Really, everything that had gone wrong for her over the last few months was because of Lorin Jones. If she hadn't had to travel around doing interviews, she would never have agreed to Stevie's spending the fall term with his father. Jeanne wouldn't have moved in, so there would have been no awkward sexual encounter between them, and Betsy might never even have set foot in the apartment.

And it was Lorin's fault, ultimately, that Polly was probably going to lose her son. Stevie still hadn't definitely decided that he wanted to return to Denver after Christmas, but Jim said he seemed to be "leaning in that direction." It was a typical Jim cliché, but Polly couldn't help but imagine it literally; she saw Stevie standing just east of Denver, on some high snowy mountain road, leaning toward the city as if in a hard wind.

Also, when Jim last called, he had informed Polly that he had some "very good news": his new wife was expecting a baby. When she heard this Polly felt a surge of irrational rage that made it impossible for her to congratulate him. How dare Jim have any other child than Stevie? This was followed by an even stronger rush of furious envy. I could have a baby, too, she thought, I'm not forty yet; but I never will. Probably I will spend the rest of my life completely alone.

Polly's nose was running again; her head ached worse. She hung up, paid for the half-eaten hamburger, and staggered back to her room. There she peeled off her once-crisp shirt and slacks, now sweaty and limp. She brushed her teeth with disgustingly lukewarm water that refused to run cold, climbed into the low, creaking rattan platform bed, and more or less passed out.

She woke late the next morning, hot and sweaty in a heavy splash of orange sun from the window whose blind she had forgotten to draw last night — hot and sweaty, too, from the receding clutch of, yes, a wet dream. Well, no wonder; she'd been celibate for weeks, and before Jeanne for nearly a year. Now she was in a place where the very air, blowing from the fishing piers and the tidal flats, smelled of sex. The dream had had a shore and fish in it too, and — she remembered with irritation — a man. She lunged out of bed and went in search of a shower, preferably a cold one.

But as she stood in the cool flood of water Polly noticed something else: her flu was gone. For some goddamn reason, she felt perfectly well. Okay. What she had to do now was finish her research, go back to New York, write the book, and be done with it; through with Lorin Jones forever. She scoured herself dry with a coarse striped beach towel, and put on her Banana Republic jumpsuit, which seemed right for an explorer in dubious tropical territory.

Downstairs, after a late breakfast (sweet, pulpy fresh-squeezed orange juice, decaffeinated tea, and muesli), she tried Cameron's number again from the guest-house phone, while Lee, who had insisted on hearing all about the project, openly listened. When he didn't answer, Lee was optimistic.

"Aw, don't worry. Probably the old guy was out last night; and he could be at work now. What's his job?"

"I don't know. He was teaching at some college in the Midwest about ten years ago, but nobody seems to know which one. But I figure he must have retired by now, since he's back in Key West."

"Well, still. He could be buying groceries at Fausto's or anywhere. Why don't you forget about your research for a while, go out and enjoy yourself? Have a swim; see something of the island."

"I haven't got time for anything like that, I'm afraid," Polly said tightly.

"What's the hurry, hon?" Lee gave her a wide friendly, maybe even more than friendly, grin. "You can stay here as long as you like; I'll put you on the weekly rate. And it's a really pretty day out, you should take advantage of it. There's supposed to be a storm on the way."

"A storm?"

"Yeah, it was on the TV this morning — not those newsroom idiots in Miami, but our local radar station, so it could be true. You wait half an hour, I'll come with you." She leaned so far over the cluttered bamboo desk toward Polly that her low-cut oversize tangerine muumuu gaped, revealing full brown breasts with enlarged mushroom-colored nipples. Her flesh had the heavy, inert luster that Gauguin admired, and Polly didn't.

She hesitated only a moment before declining. It was the first offer, or hint of an offer, that'd come her way since the fiasco with Jeanne. But even if she'd found Lee attractive there was something about her, just as there was about Key West, that put Polly off: something loose and lazily over-heated. Besides, even if she stayed longer on this loose, overheated island she had no time to waste: she had to check out all seventeen art galleries in the Yellow Pages, visit the Bureau of Vital Statistics and the library, and keep trying Hugh Cameron's phone number.

Some hours later Polly stood in yet another gallery where nobody had ever heard of Lorin Jones, going through the pretense of looking at the exhibit. The paintings were still lifes mostly, large acrylics thick with muddy reds and oranges, ugly derivatives of the recently fashionable new realism.

God, she thought, standing in front of a soupy over-worked portrait of a television set and a dirty potted philodendron, I could paint as well as that. Better. What a farce it all was: a no-talent artist like this could get himself shows, grants, prizes, dealers, reviews, sales to museums and collectors (all described in the glossy brochure the gallery owner had pressed upon her). So why the hell had Polly ever quit?

Moving away from the pictures, she stared out the plate-glass window. A cloud had slid over the sun, changing everything. Like a stage set after the lights have been turned off, Key West had lost its meretricious charm; it looked faded, tacky, makeshift.

I should have kept on with my painting, she thought. Then maybe I wouldn't be trying to write a book about somebody I never knew, can't know. Who wouldn't have liked me if I had known her, because she didn't like critics and dealers and museum people; everybody says that. She would have hated me, probably.

And I might have hated Lorin Jones if I'd known her, Polly thought, staring out at the loose-leaved unnatural trees, the peeling white frame houses, and the potholed street. I do hate her, in a way, because of all the trouble that's come into my life through her. And because she was a brilliant painter, and I'm not.

The whole thing was bitterly unfair. Why should someone self-centered and evasive and untrustworthy like Lorin have received this gift from the gods, instead of a warmhearted, straightforward, honest person like Polly Alter?

No sense in asking this. When thousands of people were starving and dying all over the world, a little divine slipup like giving Lorin Jones genius and enduring fame and Polly Alter nothing but unprofitable drudgery, and some old muddy canvases stored in a disused bathtub, didn't even signify.

But in a way it wasn't so much the gods' fault as Lorin's, Polly thought. When she was a child, an adolescent, her drawings and paintings had been warmly praised, just as Lorin's were; she too had won prizes and honors. In college, and for a few years afterward, she had hoped, even almost expected, to become an established American painter. She couldn't paint full-time, like Lorin, because she didn't have a rich, influential critic for a husband; she had to support herself. She didn't have an entrée to New York galleries, either. But she had struggled on, working and hoping, until it all went wrong.

And when had it all gone wrong? Polly knew exactly when. It had happened in Eastham, Massachusetts, on her honeymoon, at the moment when she came down to breakfast and saw Lorin Jones's landscape over the sideboard in the dining room of the inn, above two turned wooden candlesticks and a bowl of oranges. She had gazed and admired; she hadn't known yet, or hadn't admitted to herself what it meant: that someone else, Lorin Jones, had already done everything she'd ever wanted or hoped to do in painting.

But unconsciously she must have realized what had happened to her. Because it was from that moment that her hand had faltered, her work had begun to go bad, as she struggled not to imitate Jones, to avoid her choice of colors, her characteristic subjects, her handling of paint. Without lifting a finger, just by being born twenty years sooner, Lorin Jones had destroyed Polly Alter as a painter.

And Polly couldn't do anything about it. She couldn't paint anymore, and she couldn't even the score; she couldn't hurt Lorin Jones, because she was already dead. Instead, she had contracted to exalt her rival, to make her even more famous and admired.

Or — the possibility hissed in her ear like a snake — she could write her book to show that Lorin Jones, however gifted, was a cold, selfish, vengeful, secretive person, and a complete neurotic. She could suggest that there is a choice sometimes between being a good person and a good painter, and that Jones had chosen the darker path.

Leaving the gallery, Polly headed north and west across the island in the direction of the house where Lorin Jones had once lived. If she was really lucky, its owner would be home and willing to talk. If she was really unlucky, the building would have been torn down and replaced by a motel or a grocery.

The sun had come out again, and the sky was the color
of a gas flame, but nothing she passed seemed real. The
houses were too small and uniformly white, the sun too
large and glaringly luminous, and everything that grew
looked as stiff and unnatural as a Rousseau jungle: giant
scaly palms like vegetable alligators; scarlet-flowering de-
ciduous trees with enormous writhing roots and varnished
leaves and long snaky pale brown creepers hanging down
from above. Below them gardens burgeoned with unnatural
flowers: oversized pink shrimps, glossy magenta trumpets
with obscene red pistils, and foot-long crimson bottle-
brushes.

The fauna were just as exotic and unreal as the flora.
Huge speckled spiders swayed in six-foot webs between the
branches of the tropical trees; little pale gray lizards skit-
tered nervously along whitewashed fences, then suddenly
froze into bits of dried leaf. In one yard there were white
long-necked birds the size of turkeys; in another a tortoise-
shell cat as large as a terrier.

And then, even worse, there were the people. A bearded
bum with a foot-long iguana draped around his neck like
her grandmother's old fox fur; a woman walking two
long-haired dachshunds in plaid boxer shorts; a man in a
Karl Marx T-shirt and frayed canvas sandals getting out of
a white Cadillac. A half-naked youth waved to Polly from
an upstairs window; and in one of the flowering trees overhead a long-haired pirate in a red bandanna and gold earrings, pruning with a wicked-looking chainsaw, grinned
and shouted at her to look out below.

As she made her way across town, Polly kept an uneasy
watch for Hugh Cameron. She'd never seen a picture of
him, but whenever she passed a tall, fair, thin man in his
sixties ("pale and weedy" had been Garrett Jones's phrase),
she gave him a quick, suspicious stare. In front of the library
(which was of shrimp-pink stucco) she almost crossed the
street to ask the guy if he was Cameron, and only halted
because another elderly man came out of the building at the
same time and addressed her suspect as "Frank."

＊　　＊　　＊

The house Lorin had once rented was still standing. Like so many others on the island, it was a white frame cottage or bungalow — smaller than most, better cared for than some. Polly recognized the square pillars and the heavy shadowing overhang of the roof under which Lorin Jones had stood in her last known photograph.

In the side yard, behind a tall picket fence, two youngish men in Hawaiian shorts were sunning themselves on a deck. One had shielded his face with the *Wall Street Journal*; the other was reading *Christopher Street,* holding it horizontally over his head as a sunshade. Two gay yuppies, wouldn't you just know it, had taken over Lorin's old house.

While she stood and stared, the one reading glanced at her, then lowered his paper and sat up. "Excuse me, are you looking for someone?" he called.

"No." Polly hesitated. "Well, yes, sort of."

"Maybe we can help." He came to the gate and leaned over it, followed by his friend.

Yes, it was their house, they told her, speaking almost in unison, but they knew nothing of its history. They'd bought the place three years ago, from an old lady who was dead now. No, they'd never met her. All they knew was she'd lived up in Miami and rented the place out for years to a succession of low-life types. It was an absolute wreck, a real disaster area. But since then they'd done it over completely; the former tenants probably wouldn't have even recognized it.

"Oh. Well. Thank you," Polly kept saying, her spirits sinking lower with each revelation. She started to leave, but the yuppies wouldn't allow it; they insisted on taking her around first.

"Aw, no, it's no trouble. You've come all this way, for Christ's sake. Anyhow, we love to show the place off, don't we, Phil?"

"Right," Phil agreed. "Besides, we're grateful to you. It's kind of thrilling to find out that a famous painter once lived in our house."

"You know, it's fantastic luck that we were around when you came," his friend said, holding open the screen door. "Practically fate."

"Ron's right. See, most of the year we're up in the Catskills and the place is rented out. We just come down for vacation in December; that's the slow time in real estate."

Polly followed Phil and Ron through the anonymous-looking low white rooms with their straw matting, glass-topped bamboo tables, waxy-leaved tropical plants, and bland framed posters, like some up-market resort hotel. Lorin's spirit was wholly absent; nothing suggested that she ever could have lived or worked here.

Phil and Ron were unaware of Polly's disappointment. Euphorically they showed her all their improvements ("You like the bathroom? Well, if you could have seen it before we moved in you would have absolutely shuddered, wouldn't she, Ron?") and invited her to have lunch with them on the deck; they wanted to hear *all* about Lorin Jones.

"Thanks, but I don't think —"

"Oh no. You must, absolutely. It's all ready anyhow. I've got a nice estate-bottled New York white wine in the fridge, and fresh croissants from the French bakery. And Phil's made a great shrimp salad with sprouts and his special green sesame dressing. There's lots more than we ought to eat." Ron patted his perfectly flat stomach.

Polly opened her mouth to refuse politely. She didn't drink at lunch on principle, and she would obviously learn nothing more here. But something blurry and laissez-faire — the backwash of her cold, or the indolent sensual spirit of Key West — seemed to have gotten into her, and she found herself accepting instead.

Halfway through the meal, she was glad she had. While she was describing Lorin's early work, Ron suddenly put down his fork.

"Say, Phil," he exclaimed. "Maybe that's how the lizard got into the broom closet."

"Hey, right! Come on, we'll show you."

Polly followed them into the house. There, on the back

wall of the closet below a shelf, was an exquisite pencil drawing about two inches by three. From a few feet away it looked like a real lizard.

"It could be Lorin Jones's," she said, catching her breath. "Of course there's no way of being sure. But why would it be in the closet?"

"Maybe this was where she saw it," Ron said. "These lizards often come indoors."

"They come into the house?"

"Oh, yeah," Phil confirmed. "We see them all the time."

"Ugh." Polly looked around uneasily.

"They're useful, you know. They catch insects: flies, mosquitoes, you name it."

"You're suggesting that she did this from life," Polly said.

"I guess so. What do you think?"

"It could be," she repeated. For the first time in many weeks, Lorin's ghost was suddenly present to her, standing close beside her in the broom closet, drawing carefully on the whitewashed plaster with one thin pale hand. Drawing a self-portrait, Polly thought; a portrait of her own soul: thin, evasive, nervous, cold-blooded.

"You know, it's a relief to think an artist made this picture," Ron said. "We've always been a little leery of it, really."

"Leery?"

"We weren't really worried, of course—" Phil put in with a kind of laugh.

"Oh, yes, we were. You especially. You wanted to paint it over."

"Well, see, we thought it might be some kind of — you know, superstitious stuff."

"Voodoo," Ron supplied. "There's still a good bit of that here on the island, you know. Especially among the black population. Most of them are from the West Indies originally —"

"The Cubans, too," Phil said. "There's a waitress in the Fourth-of-July that I'm positive has the evil eye. And peculiar things do happen in the cemetery sometimes."

"Like what?"

"Oh, well. I don't know. You see funny moving lights at night. Or you hear noises — "

"It's probably all just foolishness," Ron interrupted. "You know how people like to talk."

"I suppose so," Polly said. She shook her head to clear it of foolishness. "Were there other pictures like this here when you bought the house?"

"No, nothing," Ron said. "But of course most of the rooms had probably been painted since your artist died. Maybe more than once, in all that time. I mean, how long was it, between her and us?"

"About twelve years," Polly admitted. She turned and scanned the walls. Under the glossy white paint, were there other larger, more beautiful, more disturbing drawings: reptiles, insects, birds, flowers, faces — ghostly visions, hidden from her now as so much about Lorin was hidden?

Polly walked slowly back toward the guest house in the increasing afternoon heat, feeling overfed, dazed, and disconnected, as if she were floating through a TV show with the color turned up too high. Maybe she was slightly drunk, or her cold was coming back. Or maybe she was suffering from climate shock; she had never been in the tropics before, or anywhere south of Washington, D.C. Maybe that was why everything looked so brilliant and nothing seemed real.

Probably I should go back to my room and try to sleep it off, Polly thought. Then I ought to go to the county courthouse and look for the records of Lorin Jones's death — from pneumonia, according to her brother. Before she came to Key West Polly had accepted the diagnosis without question, but now it seemed the most blatant of lies. How the hell could anyone get pneumonia in this climate, let alone die of it?

Partly to delay a possibly futile task, partly because the sun was so hard and bright, Polly turned off onto a shaded side street. Here she had to walk more slowly, for heavy-scented sprays of flowers hung down into her face, and the sidewalks had been crazily heaved and split by twisting reptilian roots.

She checked Lee's map again and saw that she wasn't far from Hugh Cameron's house. Maybe he'd be home now; maybe if she confronted him in person she'd have a chance of getting him to talk. She had to find him and interview him, because nobody else seemed to know what had happened to Lorin Jones after she left Wellfleet, how she got to Key West, what she did there, or how she died. If Polly couldn't talk to Cameron there would be a great awkward gap in her book, and she would look like an incompetent ass.

The house on Frances Street was another low white bungalow, unremarkable except for a particularly odd tropical tree covered with what looked like purple orchids. And for its location: it was directly across the street from the town cemetery. Also, Polly realized despondently, the house itself looked like a tomb: closed up, almost abandoned. The front windows were shuttered and there was a drift of dead leaves on the porch; the high wooden gate to the back yard was overhung with brambly bougainvillea, blossoming a glaring scarlet. Either Hugh Cameron was out of town, or he was a slob who didn't care what his place looked like.

Polly climbed the steps and rang the bell. No one came, and there was no sound from inside the house. Cursing her luck, wondering what the hell to do next, she walked slowly on down the street. In the heat of mid-afternoon it was silent and deserted. Presumably everyone was either at the beach or having a siesta. A sudden, demented impulse came over her, a desire to emulate them, to return to her room and the heated dreams of last night; or to doze half-naked on the hot sand, surrounded by the half-naked bodies of strangers. But it would be stupid and slothful to waste her time lying down either inside or out. She wasn't here on vacation, she was here to work. And what she should do now was go back to Hugh Cameron's house and leave him a note.

As she retraced her steps along Frances Street Polly noticed something moving at the far end of the next block, right by Cameron's place. Yes! the side gate was opening under the bougainvillea, and a man carrying an extension ladder was coming out. It was definitely not Cameron, though, but a tall blond guy about her own age in white painter's overalls, heading for a pickup truck by the curb. But if he'd been working on the house, this guy might know when Cameron would be back. Polly started to run toward him.

At the sound of her feet on the uneven sidewalk the man shoved the ladder into the truck and turned. From a distance of about thirty feet, he gave Polly first a glance of casual curiosity, then a grin of sexual appreciation; finally he held his arms out wide, mockingly, as if to catch her.

Polly stopped short at the opposite end of the block, abashed and angry. The painter grinned, shrugged, climbed into the cab, started the engine, and drove off.

Immobilized, Polly watched the vehicle turn the corner, displaying a legend on its side: REVIVALS CONSTRUCTION. The shiny aluminum ladder winked as it caught the sunlight, and the red rag tied to its end gave her an insulting little wave as it disappeared.

She continued to stand on the sidewalk, breathing hard, though she'd only gone a few yards — furious at both him and herself. Why hadn't she just run on past, ignoring the bastard? Or, more practically, why hadn't she walked up and spoken to him, asked where Cameron was? She'd lived in New York for years; she was used to being joshed and leered and whistled at by pig construction workers. If this guy imagined she was interested in him, running toward him, she could have turned on the chilly, scornful look that she always directed at those ignorant creeps.

It was this awful climate: the sun, the heat, the humidity: slowing her down, mixing her up. She set her jaw, checked the map again, and started at a steady New York pace for the center of town.

By half-past five Polly had called Hugh Cameron again three times unsuccessfully. She had refused Lee's iced herbal tea and homemade carob cookies. She had discovered that the county courthouse records office was closed for the afternoon, and she had visited two more art galleries and found out nothing. In one of them the walls were covered with overpriced schlock seascapes and posters, and nobody had ever heard of Lorin Jones. The young woman in the other, more sophisticated, gallery had no idea that Lorin Jones had ever lived in Key West.

This gallery was air-conditioned, and her conversation with its owner pleasant; but when Polly emerged onto Duval Street a new blast of depression and hot air engulfed her. Already the shadows of the buildings were lengthening; she had been in Key West for twenty-four hours and accomplished zilch. She had collected no useful information, and she couldn't reach the bastard she'd come to interview. All she had found was a tiny drawing whose authorship could never be proven. As Polly stood on the sidewalk trying to decide what to do next, tourists and hippies and freaks pushed past her, all headed in the same direction. They must be on their way to Mallory Dock, where according to Ron and Phil throngs gathered every evening to gawk at outdoor performers and the sunset over the Gulf of Mexico. Polly had no interest in either, but the flow of traffic and her own fatigue and lassitude pulled her along with the crowd. And maybe that wasn't such a bad thing. After all, sunset on Mallory Dock was an established local ritual, one that Lorin Jones must have known of — probably witnessed.

At the dock, a raised cement jetty on the far side of a large parking lot, the tourists were already thick. The pale, light-speckled sea was dotted with boats of all sizes from dinghy to trawler: sailboats plunged and turned, motor launches idled raucously, and in the middle distance a cream-sailed schooner rocked at anchor. Farther out, low gray-green mangrove islands floated on the horizon like vegetable whales.

A few members of the crowd sat on the low wall at the outer edge of the pier, gazing across the water. Others loitered at the stalls on the inland side, buying cheap shell jewelry, palm-frond hats, slices of red watermelon, bad watercolors, clumsy woven leatherwork, hand-painted T-shirts, and crumbly homemade cookies. But the press was greatest around the street performers: two clowns, one on a unicycle; a skinny contortionist; a huge sweating giant who juggled with flaming torches; a Caribbean steel band; and a pair of white-faced mimes accompanied by a performing poodle.

According to Ron and Phil many of the same acts came to Mallory Dock year after year. Could any of them have been here in Lorin Jones's time? Not likely; in the late sixties most of these people would have been toddlers; only the mimes looked even middle-aged.

Since it was possible that Lorin had once seen them, Polly edged into the crowd around the mimes. In spite of their strenuous antics they seemed to be suffering from the heat and humidity as she was, and perhaps from a similar depression. Their movements were dreamy, exhausted, and artificial — even arty; their costumes classical. They might have posed for Picasso in his blue or rose period, or for one of his imitators. The woman wore a faded rose tutu; her partner, wrinkled azure tights and a lozenge-patterned tunic. But their faces were painted like clowns' faces, and the man had on an orange fright wig and a red ball nose. Were they deliberately mocking the classic images of modern art, images that must float in the subconscious of at least some of the circling, gawking tourists?

As she watched, the scrawny poodle, which had been dyed a faded pink and wore a ruff and dunce cap, was encouraged to leap onto a high stool. The male clown then did a wobbly headstand, and the woman placed a tissue-paper-covered hoop between his uplifted feet. Then, with exaggerated moues and gestures, she urged the poodle to jump through the hoop. But each time it was about to do so, the clown pretended to lose his balance. He fell to the ground, miming consternation and embarrassment while the crowd laughed. Then, miming pain and woozy comic determination, he stood on his head again, and again the woman placed the hoop between his feet. Every time the man fell, the poodle hesitated and barked anxiously. Since its human companions remained silent, its harsh, excited yap was jarring.

Yeah, Polly thought. That's how it is. Men are unreliable and incompetent show-offs, playing to the public for sympathy when they fail. The woman encourages the poodle, who's obviously their child; but the man lets them both down. Right on. She shook her head to clear it and eased her way out of the crowd.

As the hazy sun slid toward the pale crumpled water, she headed back up the pier, idly scanning the stalls. Then, less idly, she halted near a table heaped with batik-print shirts that looked as if someone had thrown up on them in Technicolor. Behind it stood someone she thought she'd seen before: the workman with the ladder who'd been at Cameron's house earlier that afternoon. At least, this guy had the same golden tan, long narrow features, and streaked light hair. And, look, his faded green T-shirt, with the sleeves rolled to the muscled shoulders, was printed with the words REVIVALS CONSTRUCTION. Maybe her luck had turned; at least she'd been given another chance to find out where Cameron was.

She moved toward the stall, then stepped back, waiting for some customers to finish their purchase.

"Hey, lady!" Revivals Construction called to her. "Don't go away. I've got just the thing for you." Up close he looked more worn than he had at a distance: his tan was leathery and tattooed with lines, especially around the eyes, and his hair wasn't blond, but a bleached and faded brown.

Polly halted, prepared to give him a freezing look. But the guy's tone was anonymous; probably he didn't remember seeing her before. Very likely he routinely stared and whistled at any female that came within range. She moved forward again through the crowd.

"Thanks, honey." He counted out change for a customer and handed over a plastic sack, then turned back to Polly. "Here. This'll look real good on you." From the pile of

T-shirts he pulled out a rose-red one speckled in a white paint-drip design like an early Pollock.

"I don't know —" Actually the shirt wasn't half-bad. "How much is it?"

Revivals Construction gave her a sidelong smile. "For you, four dollars."

Polly studied the cloth for flaws. "The one you just sold was six-fifty."

"Yep. The uglier they are, the more they cost.... Sure it's washable." (This was to another customer.) "You can put it into the machine if you want. It's up to you."

"All right," Polly decided, digging into her tote bag.

"I saw you before this afternoon," she added as she paid. "Over on Frances Street."

"Yeah." He half smiled. "I saw you too."

"I wanted to ask you something," Polly persisted, a little discomfited.

"Sure.... They're all natural fabric, one hundred per-cent cotton, pure vegetable dyes, okay? ... All right, ask me."

"You were working on a house."

"I was ... What? Six fifty each, like the sign says, two for twelve." Three oversize teenagers in shorts had shoved their way through the crowd. "Extra-large, right over here.... Listen," he added to Polly. "This is a madhouse. Why don't you meet me for a drink after sunset? Say in half an hour.... Sure, we've got children's sizes, wait a sec. They're in a box underneath here somewhere.... Okay?"

"Okay," Polly agreed.

"Billie's on Front Street. Out back in the garden, it's quieter. You got that? ... Right. Here you are, don't grab, please: kiddie sizes two, four, six, eight. If you don't want that one, don't throw it at me, just put it back on the table, okay? Jesus ... So I'll see you later."

Around Polly as she turned to go there was a change in the crowd; a rise and focusing of sound, a movement away from the stalls and the performers toward the sea. Caught in a layer of smoky vapor, the sticky raspberry sun balanced on the shimmering horizon, then began to flatten and dissolve. There was a hush, then an increasing patter of applause; finally even a few cheers. Polly didn't join in. The ceremony seemed to her not, as Phil had put it, "kind of cute," but phony and self-indulgent. Even before the applause had slackened she had begun to make her way back through the crowd toward Duval Street.

12

The garden of Billie's bar was hedged and overhung by lush, loose-leaved tropical plants, and by strings of colored Christmas-tree bulbs just beginning to spark the lilac twilight. On a low platform under a shredding palm a man in a cowboy shirt was strumming a guitar and wailing a sad country-Western song into a microphone.

Polly chose one of the scabby white-painted metal tables near the shrubbery and far enough from the music to make conversation possible.

"Can I get you something?" a long-haired waitress asked, balancing her tray on her skinny hip.

"No, thanks. I'm waiting for someone." Polly was thirsty; but if she ordered before he came, Revivals Construction would think her either rude or an alcoholic or both.

Around her the tables were beginning to fill; it was nearly half-past six. Maybe Revivals Construction wasn't coming; maybe he'd decided he didn't want to see her again after all. Polly felt cross, restless, and — very irrationally, because why should she give a damn — rejected. She picked at the blistered white paint of the table, and stared at the laughing and drinking tourists around her.

"Hi!" Revivals called, waving from the entrance to the garden.

"Hi," Polly called back. As she watched him dodge, with considerable speed and grace, between the crowded tables, she admitted to herself that he was what most women would consider a very attractive man; tall, broad-shouldered and narrow-hipped, with a lot of light hair and a face almost cubist in its assemblage of elegant angles and planes.

"Sorry I'm late." He yanked out the chair next to hers, smiling unapologetically.

"That's all right," Polly said.

"Never again. I'm through with those damn T-shirts."

"You're quitting your business?"

"Huh? Oh, no. That's not my business; I was just minding the stall for a friend. This place okay by you?"

"Oh, sure." Polly sat back a little. It was clear from Revivals Construction's easy triangular smile and the way he had dragged his chair closer to hers across the gravel that he thought he'd picked her up — or, worse, that she'd picked him up. She could disabuse him of this idea, but then he might get huffy and uncooperative.

"Like the music?"

"Oh, sure," Polly repeated, though she hadn't been paying attention.

"That guy used to be a star up in Nashville."

"Really?"

"Had three record albums. He's damn good. But nobody here's even listening to him, if you notice." He shook his head. "Stupid bastards."

"That's too bad."

"Yeah. But that's tourists for you." Revivals Construction shrugged, then half smiled. "Present company excepted, of course." He set his elbow on the table and leaned toward Polly. His arm, bare almost to the shoulder under the rolled sleeve of his dark green T-shirt, was also cubist in design, its blocks of muscle and bone outlined in veined ridges. "So how'd you like the sunset?"

"Well." Polly hesitated, but there was no point in not saying what she thought. Revivals, thank God, wasn't somebody she had to interview, and had no connection with the New York art world or with Lorin Jones. "It really wasn't all that great, you know. I was surprised anybody applauded."

"Yes. But they always do. The tourists assume it's a show put on for their benefit."

"That's what I thought too," she said, surprised.

"They believe that the sun bows down before them. Literally." He grinned and touched her wrist. "So what're you drinking?"

"I guess I'll have a beer," Polly said, aware of an instinctive reaction in her arm and thinking that she'd better clarify the situation fast. "What I wanted to ask you —" she began.

"Just a sec." He waved to the waitress. "Two Millers. Okay?"

"Sure." But maybe what she ought to do was play along until she found out what the hell had happened to Hugh Cameron, who still didn't answer his phone.

"By the way, the name's Mac."

"I'm Polly," she responded, thinking that in her childhood first names had been a sign of intimacy. Now, when waiters and flight attendants introduced themselves as Jack and Jill, their meaning was reversed.

"Nice to meet you." Mac held out his hand. The strength and duration of his grip clearly suggested that he had, as Jeanne would put it, designs on her person. "So, how long are you in Key West for?"

"I'm not certain. Three or four days, maybe."

"Aw, too bad. I was hoping you were down for the whole season." He grinned meaningly.

"No." Polly smiled back almost against her will, feeling a once-familiar rush of consciousness. Five years ago she would have enjoyed sitting in a tropical garden, flirting with a good-looking guy; she knew better now.

"Having a good time so far?"

"So-so." Polly told the truth automatically, then realized that it sounded like a line; and that was how Mac responded to it:

"Maybe you haven't been to the right places. You like to dance?"

"Yes . . . no." She felt as if her feet were sinking into quicksand. "It depends."

"Depends on what?"

"Well —" Polly was rescued by the arrival of their beers.

"Thanks, Susie. . . . So, here's to your stay in the last resort."

"The last resort?"

"That's what we call it." He lifted his sloppily foaming glass and knocked it against hers. Polly heard herself laugh awkwardly. "So what've you seen up to now?"

"Nothing much. The ocean, a lot of art galleries. I mean, one resort town is much like the next, isn't it?"

"Not always." Mac grinned. "There's some special attractions here in Key West. Have you seen the pelicans yet?"

"Pelicans?"

"Yep. Big seabirds, they sit on the piers down by the docks, waiting to steal fish off the boats."

"How big?"

Mac paused and tilted his head. "Oh, four, five feet tall, some of them."

"Five feet tall?"

"You go down to Garrison Bight at the right time, you'll see them." He must be kidding, Polly thought, but she wasn't sure. Key West was weird enough to have birds like that. "Okay, what did you want to ask me?" The question was put almost mockingly; Mac clearly thought it had been just an excuse to meet him.

"I wanted to know —" Polly took a breath. "That house you were working on this afternoon —"

"Mm?" He sat back, smiling lazily. The colored bulbs in the bush beside him cast a hot red-and-blue half light on the flat weathered planes of his cheek and jaw.

"On Frances Street, near the cemetery." Polly plowed ahead. "You were there with a pickup truck."

"Right: I was cleaning out the gutters. They always get jammed up with leaves this time of year." He frowned, as if suspecting Polly for the first time of an ulterior, nonsexual motive, then smiled slowly. "You want something revived, maybe, or constructed?" His tone hovered equivocally between contractor and seducer.

"No, what I want —" Polly remembered to smile back.

"See, I was trying to find the man who lives there, Hugh Cameron —"

"Yeah?" Now Mac looked wary, displeased: the progress of his pickup had been interrupted.

"I came down here to Key West to interview him, actually." Polly leaned toward Mac, smiling, but his manner and tone remained cool.

"Oh, yes? What did you want to interview him for?"

"Well, it's for this book I'm writing. It's a biography of a painter he used to know. I've been phoning him ever since I got here Tuesday night, but nobody answers. I was wondering if he was out of town."

"Yes, he might be." Mac leaned back even farther now, and looked away.

"You haven't seen him lately?" she persisted, knowing as the words sounded out that this was a strategic mistake.

"What? No." Mac took a swig of beer, staring into the foam-crusted glass. "The house is rented out from this weekend, anyhow."

"Rented?"

"Oh, yeah. A lot of local people rent their places in the winter. A house like that, three bedrooms, a pool, you can get twenty-five hundred a month for it, easy." He still wasn't looking at her.

"Really?" Polly smiled hard, and tried to reestablish a friendly conversational tone. "I had no idea of that. No wonder there's so many yuppie types around."

Mac did not reply, only shifted in his chair and stared off sideways. She followed the direction of his gaze to three pretty girls at a table on the other side of the garden. He's caught on that I'm not interested in him, she thought, so he's turned off. She felt a researcher's anxiety — and a stupid, automatic pang of loss. "You think Mr. Cameron's left town already?"

"Could be." Mac shrugged.

"Do you have his new address?"

He shook his head slowly.

"But you must know how to get in touch with him," Polly persisted. "He has to pay you for cleaning his gutters, doesn't he, for instance?"

"I've been paid already." Mac surveyed the garden again, drained his beer, checked his watch. "Listen, I've got to go. Got to have dinner with some friends."

"Okay," Polly said in a falling tone of frustration and disappointment. Her bad luck had returned with a vengeance.

"Well." Mac stood up. "See you around." He produced a meaningless, empty smile.

"Thanks for the beer."

"No problem." Mac started to lope away; then he stopped and turned, looking hard at her. "Say." He took a step nearer, paused for what seemed to Polly a long while, then added, "How about you meeting me later on tonight? We could go dancing."

A reprieve, Polly thought. "Sure, why not?" she heard herself answer. It's not that I care anything for him, she told herself, but I've got to get that address.

"I could pick you up about nine. If you're not too fancy to ride in a truck." He grinned.

"Of course I'm not." Polly tried to make this casual rather than either indignant or suggestive.

"Okay then. Just say where."

Back at the guest house Lee, in a tropical-flowered red muumuu, set two plates of steamed fish on the table and refilled both their balloon wineglasses. She'd insisted on cooking supper, though she'd allowed Polly to contribute a bottle of Soave. "So now tell me all about your day," she said, smiling.

"Okay." Polly described her lunch with Ron and Phil, her frustrating visits to Cameron's house and to the galleries, and the sunset on Mallory Dock. She included Mac's aphorism on this ceremony (without attribution) but not her conversation with him at Billie's. It was bad enough to admit that she was seeing him again later that evening.

"You're going out with this guy you saw coming out of a house with a ladder?" Lee leaned forward; her black looped hair swung and her nearly black eyes sparkled with amusement.

"I've got to," Polly explained. "He's the only person I've met who has any connection with Hugh Cameron."

"So what's he like?"

"Oh, I don't know. About forty-five; not bad-looking," she said indifferently.

"Not bad-looking, huh?" Lee laughed suggestively.

"If you like that sort of thing," Polly said flatly.

Lee gave her a weighing look. "Well, have a good time, and stay out of dark alleys," she said finally, and stood to clear the plates away.

"Don't worry." Polly also started to rise, but Lee pushed her down with a warm brown hand.

"No, don't get up. I've got a rule, no guests in my kitchen."

Alone, Polly sat frowning at the hand-loomed tablecloth, displeased with herself. Because of her impatience, she had nearly messed up at Billie's. She should have let Mac think she was here on vacation, and later just casually asked him about Hugh Cameron. In fact, she should have followed Jeanne's advice on sweet-talking men, advice that had made her so uncomfortable when it referred to Jacky Herbert and Garrett Jones. But after all, Jacky was almost a friend, and Garrett was an important critic, someone she'd probably know professionally for years. Mac was just a local handyman; after she left Key West she'd never see him again.

Now, though, she had to spend a whole evening with him in some local dive. Well, it could be worth it. He must know how to reach Hugh Cameron, or at least be able to find out. And he might have other information too. If he'd worked for Cameron before, for instance, he could have been inside the old bastard's house and seen if he'd still got any of Lorin's paintings. Until Polly found out all Mac knew, she'd better go on pretending she was interested in him.

You are interested in him, a voice said inside her, not in her head but considerably lower down.

I am not, Polly said.

"Here you are." Lee returned bearing a rough-hewn wooden bowl heaped with brilliantly colored tropical fruit, and looking even more like a Gauguin painting. "I wish I could take you out myself, show you some of the town," she said. "There's a really good piano bar down on Duval Street. Trouble is, I have to stay in tonight, I've got guests driving from Miami, and God knows when they'll turn up."

She placed the bowl in the center of the table and, standing so close that her broad hip brushed Polly's shoulder, ran one sinewy brown hand through her curls. "You've got really nice hair, you know that?"

That was all she said, but Polly was as sure as if it were spelled out in the complicated hand-weave of the tablecloth that Lee was attracted to her and, having just heard that Polly didn't care for men, wanted to make something of it.

But since women were more subtle and tactful about these matters, if Polly didn't respond Lee would make no further approaches, or certainly no overt ones. Lee would never grab her, or blurt, "Hey, let's go to bed." No one would be embarrassed, and no one's feelings would be hurt. But it would be easy now for Polly, just by touching or complimenting Lee in return, to silently reply, *Yes, let's.*

"Are those real mangoes?" she asked instead.

"That's right." Lee smiled as easily as if nothing had happened or been decided. And maybe it hadn't, not yet. "Why don't you try one? I should warn you, though, they're kind of messy to eat."

"Wow," Polly said, gasping with surprise and also with relief as the door of the Sagebrush Lounge swung to behind her and Mac, shutting them into a warehouselike space hung with animal horns and antlers and vibrating with noisy air conditioning and amplified country-rock music. On their left was a crowded dance floor, on their right a long bar against which men in work clothes and cowboy gear were leaning. Mac's costume matched theirs; he had traded his Revivals Construction jersey for a blue Western-cut shirt with pearl snaps. Polly still wore her rumpled Banana Republic jumpsuit; she wasn't going to change as if for a date, especially not with Lee around.

"Didn't expect anything like this in Key West, huh?" Mac shouted against the music. Waving to two men at the bar, he led her to a table.

"You can say that again," Polly shouted back, taking another deep breath. The Sagebrush Lounge was on an ill-lit back street somewhere out near the airport, next to a swamp and across from a trailer camp. On the way there, though she had kept up a sort of conversation, most of her mind had been occupied by Lee's remark about dark alleys, and the possibility, increasing as Mac drove farther and farther from the center of town, that he would turn out to be a psychopathic rapist. Her instinct told her he wasn't; but how many women had been raped or even murdered because they trusted their stupid instincts?

"I figured you'd enjoy it, 'cause you appreciate country music," Mac said, or rather yelled. " 'Course, this is pretty mainstream stuff."

"Those guys over there, they look like cowboys."

"Yes, it's what they think, too."

"Of course there's no ranches in the Keys," Polly yelled, determined not to seem a fool.

"Well, not down here. They're further up, around Marathon."

"Really? You actually mean cattle ranches?"

"Yep. The Sea-Cow brand, it's famous in these parts."

"I don't believe you." Polly laughed.

"Okay." Mac smiled. "Have it your way. Like a beer?"

"I thought, maybe a white wine spritzer," Polly yelled, aware that she'd already had nearly half a bottle of Soave at the guest house.

"I wouldn't advise that here." Mac grinned. "Take it from me, only the beer's worth drinking; unless you go for the hard stuff."

"I'll stick to beer."

"What?"

"Beer," Polly screamed, thinking that in this clamor it wasn't going to be easy to bring up the subject of Hugh Cameron's present whereabouts.

"Right."

Almost before she could catch her breath a bottle had appeared before Mac and a bottle and glass before her; sexual stereotyping, evidently. She poured the beer, resolving to drink it as slowly as possible: she'd need to keep her head in case Mac did turn out to be a psychopathic rapist. Maybe what she should do right now was make some excuse to leave the table, call Lee, and tell her she was in the Sagebrush Lounge with Mac — Mac who?

"Say." Polly made an effort to breathe normally. "What's your name, besides Mac?"

"Huh?" Under the pounding beat of the music she heard a fractional hesitation, which she put down to Mac's reluctance to, as he would probably put it, get involved. "MacFlecknoe. Richard MacFlecknoe. Like the poet. But we're not related, far as I know. And you?"

"Polly Alter." The music had crashed to a romping halt, and her name sounded out abashingly loud. "Well, Paula really," she said, moderating her voice. "Only nobody I can stand ever calls me that."

"Then I'll make sure not to." Mac smiled slowly. "Hey. You know that guy you wanted to interview?"

"Hugh Cameron. Yes, of course."

"I found out he's in Italy for the winter."

"Italy?" It came out almost as a wail.

"Yep. In Florence. I've got the address for you, right here." He held out a scrap of folded paper.

"Oh, thanks." Polly tried to look grateful, but it wasn't easy. She had neither the time nor the money to follow Hugh Cameron to Italy, and even if she did there was no guarantee he'd agree to talk to her. All she could do now was get whatever information she could from Mac. Maybe he could give her the names of some of Cameron's friends in

Key West, people who, if she was lucky, had been here when Lorin Jones was alive.

"Like to dance?" The music had started again, just as loud but to a slower beat.

"All right," she agreed.

But as Mac led the way onto the floor, Polly realized that the other couples had stopped jigging and shaking *en face,* and were now clasped together in swaying pairs. Uneasily, she allowed him to put his arms around her, and placed her hand on his shoulder. It was years since she'd danced the two-step with anyone — by the time she got to college it was already out of fashion.

The tune was simple, soupy, a childlike whine of lost love spun over a slow pounding beat. Mac held her at a polite distance at first, but soon he began to gather her closer. Annoying, presumptuous, but it was easier to move in sync this way, swaying together, almost soothing. She only liked it because it had been so long since she'd held anyone. . . . But this was a man, and a complete stranger. She should pull back, so as not to give him any ideas.

But she didn't pull back. You can't afford to get him miffed, you've got to remember your research, she told herself, easing her arm farther along Mac's shoulder, feeling his muscles move under the cloth. First things first.

"That man whose address you gave me," she murmured. "Hugh Cameron."

"Mh." Mac looked down at her.

"D'you know him well?"

He swung her around, then spoke. "Not all that well, no."

"I understand he's a real basta—, I mean, kind of a difficult person."

"Oh yeah? He hasn't treated me too badly." Mac took a firmer grip on Polly, bending their joined hands behind her back and pulling her so close that the whole length of his body was pressed against hers.

Taking a long breath, trying not to notice this, Polly plowed on. "You've been working for him quite a while?"

"Huh?"

"Cameron, I mean."

"Mh."

She waited, but he said no more. But the beat of the lowbrow music continued, they moved smoothly together. Polly felt herself blurring, loosening, becoming sensually addled, as if she'd been soaking too long in a hot bath. She gave herself a hard mental shake and tried again, speaking now in a sleepy murmur that matched the music. "So have you been in Key West a long time?"

"Yeah, I guess you'd say so."

"Really — how long?"

"I d'know. Nineteen, twenty years, off and on."

"Then you could have met Lorin Jones yourself." Mac, swinging Polly deftly around, did not reply. "The artist I'm writing about."

"Mh?"

"Did you ever know her?"

"Nope." Mac was resting his head against Polly's now; as he spoke his hot breath fluttered her hair. "Can't say I did."

Bad luck again, Polly thought; but another part of her, which was sick to death of Lorin Jones, breathed *thank God*. What it wanted now, what it needed, was to forget Jones for a while, to stop questioning and prying, to move to the simple thump and twang of the country band and murmur almost meaningless remarks.

"I always liked this old tune."

"Yes, it's nice."

But she could not disguise from herself that all the time, under their slow, banal exchange, another far more lively conversation was going on. Mac's body and hers, like two good-looking oversexed morons, were speaking to each other; and she could hear clearly what they were saying, over and over again:

— *Hey, you want to?*

— *Aw, sure.*

— *When?*

—*Anytime*.

I don't do that anymore, she said to the moron that was her body; but it didn't hear her.

The band repeated the last chorus and went into a crescendo. Holding her close, Mac did an expert dip, and came up again as the song ended.

"I like the way you dance," he said, moving back but keeping one arm around her.

"Thanks." Polly didn't return the compliment. What she had to do now, she thought fuzzily as the music started up again, was get out of here before anything else could happen.

"Do you clog?"

"What?"

Mac gestured at the dance floor. Most of the couples had left, but those that remained were beginning to stamp and wheel and gallop around in tandem, like children playing horses.

"Oh, no."

"It's easier than it looks, y'know. I'll teach you sometime." He steered her back toward their table. "Like another beer?"

Polly nodded, then instantly regretted this. Well, you don't have to drink it, she told herself as he held up two fingers to the waitress.

"Hey, Polly." Mac leaned toward her and half shouted over the cantering dancers. "You married?"

Polly shook her head. "I was once."

"Yeah? So was I." He smiled. "Didn't work out, hm?"

"No."

"Me neither. It was a bust from the wedding night, only I got stubborn and stuck it out for three years."

"With me it was all right for a while, but then my husband insisted on moving to Denver."

"And what was wrong with Denver?"

"Nothing. Only I couldn't get a job there." Why am I telling him all this, Polly thought, listening to her own voice, which sounded like someone else's. Because he doesn't mat-

ter, that's why, she answered. They were confiding in each
other, yes, but only with the anonymous frankness of strangers who find themselves on the same bus or plane and know
they won't meet again.

"Uh-huh. Kids?"

"I've got a son, he's fourteen. But he's with his father
now, for this school term. Till Christmas."

"Rough, huh."

"Yes," Polly agreed, wondering how Mac knew this —
it must have been her tone of voice. "Yes, I really miss him."

"You're lucky, though. What I miss, it's the kids I never
had."

"You could still —"

Mac shook his head, looking away, then slowly turned
back. "I can't find the right woman," he seemed to say, but
since he didn't raise his voice this time it was hard to tell.
The music was louder, the couples stomped and tramped
faster; it made Polly dizzy to look at them. What she ought
to do, she ought to say she had to get back, as soon as he
finished his beer, because she wasn't going to drink hers —
Except, she noticed, she already had.

The band paused for breath, then started another slow
number, a wailing song about lost love.

"Let's dance," Mac said, rising.

This time Polly didn't try to make conversation. She
allowed herself to fall at once into a warm drifting blur, to
lean against Mac, move with him. Because it didn't matter,
as soon as the music ended she'd go home. But now —
now —

"Hey," Mac whispered presently, his mouth against her
face. "You know that place you're staying? That Artemis
Lodge."

"Mm."

"Artemis, you know who she was?"

"I think she was some kind of Greek goddess," Polly
said.

"Right. A jealous virgin. She turned her best friend into
a bear on account of she'd slept with Zeus."

"Really?"

"I'm not as illiterate as you might think."

"Mm." Polly recalled something Ron or Phil had said, that many of the permanent residents of Key West were middle-class dropouts, ex-hippies now managing restaurants or galleries, or running charter boats — or, why not, repairing houses for a living. "Nice people, most of them," Phil, or Ron, had declared.

"Anyhow," Mac said. "That place of yours. It's a lesbian guest house; at least that's what I hear."

Polly swallowed; then, damning herself for her hesitation, said, "Yes, I know. I'm a lesbian."

"Yeah?" Mac laughed. "You could have fooled me." He circled with the music, holding her even closer. It was clear that he didn't believe her; or if he did believe her, didn't care.

"So how's it going, your research?" he asked as they returned to the table.

"Oh, okay. Well, not all that great lately. Coming down here wasn't much use."

"Not much use, huh?" Mac said, with a grin. "Sorry to hear that."

"I didn't mean— It's just — " What is the matter with me, the beer, Polly thought. "I mean, I came all the way to Key West, and spent all that money, and now I can't locate Hugh Cameron or anybody who knew him or Lorin Jones, and I can't even get into his house."

"Get into the house? What good would that do, if he's not there?"

"I want to see if he still has any of Lorin Jones's paintings. The museum where I work put on a show a couple of years ago in New York, and I wrote to ask if he had anything we could borrow, but he never answered."

"Ah." Mac rotated his empty glass.

"Maybe you've noticed, if you've ever been in the house."

"Noticed what?"

"If there were any pictures. Oil paintings, they'd be, or maybe watercolors."

"Pictures." Mac appeared to be thinking. "I don't remember, really. I guess I never paid much attention. Like another beer?"

"Oh no, no thanks. I've got to get back." Polly looked at her watch. "The manager at the guest house said she was going to call the police if I wasn't home by twelve."

"She did?"

"She's afraid you might be a psychotic rapist," Polly heard herself say, or rather lie.

"She never even saw me," Mac protested.

"I know."

"She probably thinks all men are rapists." He laughed.

"I guess she might." Polly mentally kicked herself for playing along, for misquoting and misrepresenting Lee.

"Personally, I've always liked cooperation when I make love." Mac turned toward Polly. Something looked at her out of his eyes; she tried to look away, didn't quite make it. "Okay, shall we go?"

Abruptly the smoky, pulsing sensual blur of the Sagebrush Lounge was replaced by the warm, silent night outside. Polly felt a tense, twanging apprehension — or was it expectancy? — as Mac drove along a dark side street, taking her — where?

"So you're gay, huh?" he said abruptly. "Since when?"

"I've been living with a woman for two months," Polly told him, accurately but deceptively, and realizing that even this didn't sound like much. Or maybe it did, for Mac had just swung onto a broad, well-lit boulevard, edged on one side with movie theaters and drive-ins and motels, and on the other with a row of blowing palms and the dark choppy waters of the bay. "That is, I was living with her," she added, unwilling to suggest that she was two-timing someone.

"You mean you aren't anymore," he said, or asked.

"No, not exactly," she admitted.

"Ah." They had turned onto a street that Polly recognized as not far from Artemis Lodge. There seemed to be nothing more to say, so she said nothing. It's over, I'm safe;

I won't see him again, she thought, and was furious at herself for not being relieved.

"Listen, I've got an idea," Mac said as he pulled up outside the guest house. "What if I was to get — I mean, I think maybe I could get the key to Hugh Cameron's house, from the rental agent."

"Oh, could you?" Polly gasped.

"Sure. Well, probably. I could tell them I had to check the bathroom pipes or something. Then you could meet me there tomorrow after I finish work and look for those paintings."

"That'd be really great." In her enthusiasm, Polly put a hand on his arm. "If it's not too much trouble —"

"No. A pleasure." Mac covered her hand with his. "So I'll see you over there, say about four?"

"Great," Polly repeated. She started to slide away across the seat of the truck, but he didn't remove his hand; instead, he tightened his grip. "Well, hey, thanks for the drink."

"Hey, you're welcome." Mac turned full toward her. He kissed her hard but very briefly, releasing her before she had time to react. "See you at four tomorrow," he repeated as she scrambled down out of the cab.

The pickup truck roared off, and Polly, in what her mother would have called a State, stood on the porch of Artemis Lodge. The door was locked, and only one ruby-chambered electric lantern burned in the hall. Either Lee was out, or she'd already gone to bed. Polly let herself in and climbed the stairs to her room.

What are you so upset about? she asked herself. Your luck's turned. Tomorrow you're going to see Cameron's place, and who knows what you might find there? Pictures, drawings — letters and notes even, if Mac doesn't stop you —

Or, let's put it this way, another voice said. You're going to meet a man you hardly know in a town you hardly know, in an empty house, where there probably aren't any paintings anyhow, because probably that was just his way of getting you there, and doing what he wants to you.

And what you want, said another treacherous voice.

The room felt hot and close and crowded; Polly shoved up the sash of the window, but the breeze that blundered in, sticky with the odors of tropical flowers and auto exhaust and tidewrack, was even more insidious and oppressive. Sex, it whispered.

All right, you feel something, the first voice shrilled in Polly's ear as she paced the narrow strip of straw matting between the bed and the open window. But that's just because you haven't made it with anyone in nearly a month; naturally you're susceptible. It doesn't mean you have to fall into bed with whoever comes along, especially not with a man.

All right, you'll be alone with Mac. But if he makes what your mother would call an indecent suggestion, all you have to do is say no; he's not going to jump you. If you can't control yourself, if you have to sleep with someone, Polly told herself, it doesn't have to be Mac. There's Lee, for instance — a generous and warmhearted (if rather scatty) woman, who likes you and is right downstairs in the guest house.

Polly fixed the image of Lee in her mind; mentally she removed Lee's flowered muumuu and contemplated her low full leathery breasts, her thick waist, her sturdy brown Polynesian hips; her bushy black armpits, the probable black bush below. . . . But she felt less than nothing. Lee wasn't what she wanted; what she wanted —

It was her old ignorant desire for the Romantic Hero, recurring like some persistent tropical weed. Over the last two years this rank growth had been, she'd thought, thoroughly rooted up, and the earth where it once flourished raked hard, trampled down. But now, in the steamy, unnatural climate of Key West, the weed had sprouted again.

It was an addiction, really, like Jeanne's addiction to cigarettes. There ought to be an organization for it, Heterosexuals Anonymous, it could be called, and when the uncontrollable urge came over you, you'd telephone their hotline and some nice woman would talk to you till you felt better. Jeanne had said she'd been through everything, trying to stop smoking: group meetings and individual therapy and hypnosis and clove cigarettes and nicotine gum, changing to a brand she disliked, tapering off gradually, going cold turkey. Eventually she'd realized that she was becoming obsessed with smoking-or-not-smoking; and that this obsession was crowding out the whole rest of her life. She couldn't concentrate on anything else properly; she couldn't finish an article, or give a decent lecture, she couldn't enjoy seeing her friends or going to a film or having a good meal or sometimes even making love with Betsy, because she kept thinking about cigarettes. So finally she decided, the hell with the whole thing. It was a lot easier, Jeanne said, just to have a smoke when she wanted one and then forget about it.

Is that how Polly ought to treat her own addiction? Should she just sleep with Mac once — assuming that was what he had in mind — and get it out of her system? Right now, she not only found him attractive, she liked him. But probably it wasn't really affection she felt, just disguised sexual need, aggravated by the climate. And probably it was only a matter of time before he'd do or say some ugly chauvinist thing, and then she wouldn't have to care about him.

Besides, in a case like this it would be wrong to turn to Lee. You didn't use another woman like that, you had respect for her feelings, her integrity as a person — where had she heard that phrase recently? Yes, from Jeanne. If Jeanne were here now, though, she would tell Polly not to do what she was in great danger of doing.

Eleven thirty-five. Late, but Jeanne often stayed up late. And even if she'd gone to bed, this was a crisis, she wouldn't mind getting up. Unless of course she and Betsy — but then Polly remembered how, when she and Jeanne had slept in the same bed, Jeanne would always unplug the telephone before they "tumbled about a bit."

Polly tiptoed downstairs to the lobby, stopping at each creak of the staircase, shifting as much of her weight as she could to the worn mahogany bannister.

In the sleeping house, the ringing of the phone in the apartment on Central Park West sounded so loud that Polly expected Lee to appear at any moment, followed by several of her guests. All right, let them come. Help me, she would say to them and to Jeanne. If you don't, I'm going to do something irrational, something dangerous. But nobody answered the phone, and nobody came.

13

At a quarter to four the following afternoon Polly sat on the wide leaf-littered steps of Hugh Cameron's house, under heavy bulging clouds that had done nothing to lower the temperature. It seemed if anything warmer than yesterday; the light had a diffuse, oppressive purplish tint. Mac's not coming, she thought for the fourth or fifth time. You should be glad; now you can't do anything you'll be sorry for afterward. But she didn't feel glad; she felt ashamed and angrily disappointed, like a recovered alcoholic who'd tried to fall off the wagon in front of a package store that turned out to be shut.

If she could have reached Jeanne her resolution might have been strengthened; but Lee, who should have been on the same side, was no help. In spite of what some people might have taken as a sexual rejection, she had remained friendly and interested. "Had a good time last night?" she had asked at breakfast, and when Polly admitted that it hadn't been too bad, and that she was meeting Mac again today, Lee grinned knowingly. Probably she was a sexual alcoholic herself; probably most people in Key West slept with anybody they fancied who came along, regardless of their sex, occupation, age, marital status, or political party. Sure, go on, enjoy yourself, she had said to Polly, more or less; Polly had listened to her, and now look what had happened.

The whole trip to Key West had been a waste of time and money, a useless expense of spirit. Today, for instance, she had spent hours in the newspaper files at the county library without finding a single reference to Lorin Jones. She had also gone to the county courthouse and, after an interminable delay, seen a certificate that listed the cause of Lorin's death as "pneumonia." Lennie Zimmern had told her what he thought was the truth; but Polly still had doubts.

She stared across the cracked and tilted sidewalk and the potholed street at the cemetery opposite. Could Lorin Jones be buried there? And if so, how could Cameron stand to look out every day on the grave of the woman he'd deserted and allowed to die?

This Key West cemetery wasn't like the ones up north. There were no weeping willows, no pruned shrubbery, no clipped lawns and orderly, ranked tombstones. Instead, behind a padlocked iron gate and a cyclone fence topped with barbed wire (what for?) was a wide expanse of untidy open land crowded with funeral monuments. No, not monuments, Polly realized — tombs. Soapy white marble and rough gray stone packing cases lay scattered in the long faded grass, like the debris of a freight-train wreck. Some were crowned with statuary or elaborate scrolled carvings, and many with garish arrangements of plastic flowers: waxy crimson and orange roses, purple pansies, white lilies. Most unpleasant of all, under several of the nearest tombs the earth had shifted or buckled, so that they canted up into the air at a crazy, improper angle. You could almost imagine that the dead people inside, Lorin among them, were trying to get out, or had already gotten out. Maybe that was the reason for the barbed wire. Maybe they were there, invisible, all those evil spirits who, like Lorin Jones, had died violently or too soon, clinging to the cyclone fence with their thin dry lizard hands, clamoring for the lives they had lost.

Polly checked her thoughts, annoyed; such morbid fantasies weren't her style. They must be the result of Phil's and Ron's gossip yesterday about voodoo, or of something heavy and hot and abnormal in the climate. Besides, Lennie Zimmern had said that his sister's ashes had been scattered in the ocean off Key West; she wasn't even here.

All right, she would give Mac five more minutes, Polly decided; then she'd leave. There was probably nothing here anyhow. It had been more than fifteen years, after all, and Lennie'd been to the house on Aurelia Lane then and taken everything back to New York.

Two minutes. One minute. Okay, the hell with it. But as Polly started down the walk, the Revivals Construction pickup turned the corner.

"Sorry!" Mac called, parking on the wrong side of the street with a screech of brakes and leaping onto the curb. "Been waiting long?"

"It's okay." Late three times out of three, she thought; it must be a character trait. No point in complaining, though; she'd probably never see him again after today.

Mac gave her the warm, uneasy smile of someone who deserves and expects to be scolded. "Had a good day?"

"So-so." Polly shrugged.

"Sorry to hear that." He grinned; it was clear that he wasn't particularly sorry — or, to be fair, particularly glad. "Shall we go in?"

Behind its closed shutters and drawn bamboo blinds the interior of Hugh Cameron's house was silent, shadowy and almost cool. At first Polly could see nothing; then she began to make out, floating halfway between the floor and ceiling, a very large painting. It might be — it was, surely —

"That what you were looking for?" Mac asked.

"I — I think so," she said in a strangled, panting voice.

"Wait a second." There was the rattling sound of a blind being raised. A slotted golden light widened across the tiles; the huge canvas glowed out, white and umber and peach, patched with vermilion and scribbled with black writing. Yes: it had to be one of Lorin Jones's late graffiti paintings, but looser and more brilliant than any she'd ever seen. What might be an *M* or an *H* had been scrubbed in thick pale color down one side of the canvas, in the manner of a pastel Franz Kline; and a line of fine writing ran diagonally up from the opposite corner.

"Yes. It's Lorin's, it's got to be!"

"Really," Mac said indifferently.

"I don't understand it. Lorin Jones's brother was sup-

posed to have come here after she died and collected all her
work, and he never even mentioned this picture."

"Mh?"

"I don't see how he could have missed it."

"Maybe it wasn't in the house," Mac suggested, gazing
idly through a sliding glass door at a pool surrounded by
unnaturally white plastic furniture and unnaturally green
shrubs. He doesn't care, he's not interested, Polly thought.
And he's not interested in me either, not anymore. She
should feel relieved, but instead she felt hurt and miserable.

"You mean Cameron could have hidden it?" she said.

Mac shrugged, not turning around.

"You couldn't hide something like this; it's too big."

"Sure you could," he said. "Put it out back against the
fence, cover it with an old drop cloth or something."

"Maybe. I suppose that would have been like him, the
creep."

"What makes you think he's such a creep?" Mac strolled
back into the center of the room.

"Everybody says so. For one thing, he walked out on
Lorin Jones when she was dying. He didn't even try to help
her."

"That's what they say?"

"Mm."

"And that's what you're going to put in your book,
huh?"

"Yes, why not? I'm planning to tell the truth." Polly
turned back to the picture; holding her head sideways, she
tried to decipher the line of writing. "*What is . . . what is the
meaning,*" she read out. "It looks like *meaning,* or maybe it's
morning — of wind. What do you think?"

"Lemme look." Mac came up close behind her.
"*Memory,* I think," he said after a pause. "*What is the memory of wind under the sea?*"

"It sounds like verse. Lorin Jones's dealer, he thinks the
words in these late paintings mostly came from Hugh Cameron's poems."

"Could be," Mac said.

He's bored with me, he's waiting for me to leave, she thought. All right, forget about him. Concentrate on your job. "I'll have to check," she said. "The trouble is, I haven't tracked down much of Cameron's work, though I know —"

Polly started; Mac had just rested his hands on her shoulders. "— there were at least two volumes of poems, but I haven't —" She turned and opened her mouth to finish the sentence; he closed it with a long kiss.

I'm not ready for this, Polly thought, feeling herself sinking; I didn't expect — Her eyes focused on a wall of bookshelves behind his head. Cameron's books. And Cameron's poems must be here somewhere — "Wait," she whispered when Mac paused for breath. "Not now — not yet —"

"I know." Mac grinned. "You want to see the other picture."

"There's another one?"

"I think so. In there." He gestured with his head toward an open door.

The second room, which also opened onto the deck, was mainly occupied by a low queen-sized bed. Over it hung what was surely, even in the dim light from the shuttered window, Lorin Jones's lost painting, *Aftershocks.* Polly recognized it from the blurred black-and-white photo in the files of the Apollo Gallery, but only by the semiabstract seaweed shapes along the lower edge, for this painting had been terribly damaged. There was a raw, jagged-toothed hole in the center, as if something large and violent had burst through the canvas from behind.

"Oh, shit," she choked.

"What's the matter?"

"You can see." Polly was in better control of her voice now, but her head was still full of angry buzzing. "It's Lorin Jones's picture, the one that disappeared after her last show, but it's been all ripped up." By Hugh Cameron, of course. He was the sort of man who might destroy his lover's painting and hang the evidence of the crime over his own bed for nearly twenty years.

"Yeah?" Mac came closer. "Looks to me like it was done on purpose," he said.

"I suppose it was," Polly said tightly. "By that bastard who lives here."

"No, I meant by Lor— your artist. Look at the way the words are written."

It was true; a line of script, not present in Jacky's photograph, began in the upper left of the picture and continued below the hole, curving out and up toward the right. To make it out Polly had to lean forward over the platform bed — Mac must be farsighted.

"*You never saw it coming . . . till it was gone,*" she read slowly. "I don't know — I suppose it's possible she did it herself," she conceded, realizing as she spoke that if this were so the importance of the work hadn't been reduced; it might even have been enhanced. "But there's no way of proving that. I wonder —"

"Wonder about it later, okay?" Mac had moved much closer. He ran his hand slowly down her back; all the way down.

"No, wait. I have to —" Breathing hard, Polly took a step away.

"Come on." He pulled her to him. "That thing won't fly off."

No, it won't, she thought. But I will, my ticket is for the day after tomorrow. I've got to plan. What I need is evidence that the paintings are here. Photographs, I need color photographs. It's too late today, but I could rent a camera tomorrow, or borrow one — maybe from Lee? Then when I get back to New York —

But she couldn't think clearly now. Now she was in a bedroom in Key West with a man who was kissing the back of her neck. His mouth was hot, his tongue insinuating. She was leaning toward him, against him.

"Oh, Polly," Mac whispered, pulling her toward the bed.

Stop, wait, she told herself. But another part of her replied, Why not? It's what you want. And besides, it's what

Mac wants; even what he deserves for letting you into this house, helping you to find Lorin's paintings. She swayed and fell slowly onto the rough off-white cotton bedspread.

All right, go ahead, a voice said in her mind. But keep some control of yourself. All right, kiss him, it panted. All right, let him pull open your shirt and lick your breast. But for God's sake don't let yourself care about him, or you'll be hurt and betrayed again. Remember, you hardly know him; remember all the horrible social diseases they've invented lately.

But in spite of this good advice, it was Mac who first broke off; he raised himself on his elbows above Polly, then half sat up.

"Hey," he said softly. "Hold on a sec. I have to tell you something."

"Okay," she gasped. Realizing that she had one hand on the paint-spattered bulge in his jeans, she snatched it off as if she had been burned. Dizzy, full of heat, her heart pounding, she moved away from Mac. Herpes, she thought.

"It's —" He swallowed.

Well, go on, she thought, staring at him, more and more terrified. Gonorrhea, syphilis. Or those awful warts they had now, what was their name? "Yes?"

"I —"

Maybe even AIDS. After all, this was Key West.

"I — I've been living with this woman, up on Sugarloaf Key."

"Well?" Polly said. There was a pause. "And?"

"That's it. I just thought I ought to tell you."

"That's it?"

"Uh-huh."

"Okay." She laughed with relief.

"What's so funny?"

"Nothing. Only I thought you were going to tell me you had, you know, some awful infection."

"Nope." He grinned. "Far as I know, I'm clean. I've been with Varnie over two years, never did anything like this before." He looked at Polly. "You don't mind?"

"No. I mean, hell, I'm only here till Sunday morning. I don't care who you're living with."

"I'm glad to hear that," Mac said. Then, under his breath, what might have been "Or maybe I'm sorry."

"Huh?"

"Never mind." He rolled back toward her; with one warm, work-roughened hand, he pulled her Banana Republic safari shirt fully open. "Shhh."

Half an hour later the squares of the straw rug were littered with cast clothes, and their owners lay dizzy and entangled on the rumpled bedspread. Above them, Lorin Jones's lost painting floated, mysterious and — in spite of the gaping hole in its center — serene. If it hadn't been for you, Polly thought blurrily, slipping toward sleep, I wouldn't be here in Hugh Cameron's bed. I would never have known —

It was weird what she felt, even weirder than what had happened in Wellfleet, though in a way it was like that. It was as if she had magically become Lorin Jones, and the man who lay beside her, with his work-roughened hand loose on her breast and one leg across hers, was Hugh Cameron.

But of course that wasn't even right magically, because this had never been Lorin's house. It was only another backwash of all these months of immersion in Jones's history: a sign of her obsession, her confusion of her own life and Lorin's, Jeanne would have said.

Half-awake now, Polly unwound herself from Mac and raised herself on one elbow to look at him. Naked, he was a worn and flawed umber above the waist, but smoothly pale below to the ankles. His body, like his face, was long and spare, all steep planes, narrow ridges, and clearly outlined muscles.

Well, you did it, didn't you, she told herself, and waited to feel shame and embarrassment, but felt only pleasure, joy, and a rush of affection. I like him, it said: I don't want to leave Key West, I want to stay here with him. . . . She shook her head angrily: how stupid and greedy the body is, how careless of the good of its tenant!

She ought to be angry, though; if not at herself, then at the world. Why should it be arranged so badly? Why should it be so much better with a man she hardly knew than with a woman she loved?

A warm shudder of wind bent the branches outside and gushed into the bedroom. Mac stretched, yawned, opened his eyes, and smiled lazily at the ceiling. Then he turned toward Polly, and his expression changed.

"Oh, Christ," he whispered, and sat up.

"What's the matter?"

"Nothing." He smiled again, but briefly and uneasily. "That was lovely, lovely," he said, not looking at her.

Yes, Polly thought. Now he wishes he hadn't. That's how men are, remember? He wants to get away as soon as he can. She began to rise.

"Wait. Don't get up yet." Mac put out one hand to stop her. "You're so beautiful lying there." He stroked her near breast with one finger, as if it were a sculpture made of some rare, exotic material, then leaned over to kiss it.

"Shouldn't we —"

"Shh."

"Jesus, look at the time," Mac said after a considerable interval. "Maybe we should get some clothes on."

"All right," Polly agreed. This isn't his house, she suddenly remembered, it's a rental property. He's not supposed to be here, not like this. She imagined Hugh Cameron walking in; or, much more likely, the rental agent. Shameful for her; disastrous for Mac. Rapidly, she bent to retrieve her red cotton bra and panties from the floor.

"Listen, I've got to go back to the job, check with my crew," Mac said, dragging on his jeans. "But that shouldn't take long. How about supper?"

"All right," Polly heard herself agree, too eagerly.

"It's nearly five now. Say six o'clock?"

"Sure." But what about that woman Mac said he was

living with? she thought, tying her track shoes. The woman with whom, presumably, he had supper last night — and then lied to so that he could go with Polly to the Sagebrush Lounge. Well, it was none of her business.

None of your business? her guardian angel remarked, appearing suddenly in Polly's mind; she was a tall stern marble figure like a Greek statue, probably the Artemis of Artemis Lodge. *Where's your female solidarity, your sympathy with your own sex? You don't have to see him again tonight.*

It's just for a few hours, Polly explained. *Then she can have him back.*

"I'll drive you home now," Mac said, opening the door for her. "Then I can pick you up in about an hour at the guest house, okay?" He smiled as if sure of her answer.

"Well. . . . Okay," Polly said.

As dusk fell the low clouds thickened; flushed indigo and purpled gray, they billowed over the island like O'Keeffe's giant dark flowers. The wind that had started up that afternoon was blowing stronger.

"Yep, that storm the TV promised is on its way," Lee said, smiling, nodding. She had already congratulated Polly on the discovery of Lorin Jones's missing paintings, and promised to borrow a Polaroid camera for her. When Polly let on that she was going out again that night with Mac, Lee grinned knowingly. "That's right, honey," she said. "You can't work all the time, not in Key West."

"Well," Polly said. "This is work in a way; it's research. I'm hoping he'll tell me something about Hugh Cameron."

"I'll bet." Lee's wide flat Polynesian lips spread in another grin. "I'm sure you know what you're doing anyhow."

"Oh, I do, don't worry," Polly lied — because what the hell *was* she doing? What had she done already?

Well, one useful thing: she had called Jacky Herbert at the Apollo Gallery to report her discovery of the two lost paintings. After all, even if she hadn't found Hugh Cameron, this trip to Key West had been a kind of success.

In more ways than one, she thought now, looking sideways at Mac, who sat next to her at the outdoor bar of an oceanside restaurant called Louie's Back Yard. The wind, stronger here, shook the trees overhead, sending down a scatter of tiny leaves; it flung a succession of spotlit creamy green waves against the sea wall. Most of the other customers had retreated to a higher and more sheltered deck or gone inside.

"You want to try a piña colada?" Mac suggested. "It's the local specialty."

"Sure."

The bartender, a long-lashed Michael Jackson type, squirted syrups and shook them in a blender, then placed before Polly what looked like a tall vanilla milkshake, with its own pink paper umbrella. She sipped the sugary froth warily.

"Too sweet, maybe?"

"Well, kind of."

"Don't drink it then," Mac said. "Have something else."

"All right. I'll have a spritzer."

Mac waved and ordered. "Listen, I don't want you to give up on Key West. Tomorrow we'll go to the Full Moon Saloon; it's a kind of funky place, but they have good conch chowder and real Key Lime pie."

"You think I'm having supper with you tomorrow," Polly said, trying not to smile.

"What's the matter, can't you make it?"

"I'm not sure. I just wondered —"

"Yes?"

"What about that woman you told me you were living with?"

"That's my problem." Mac's voice went cool, then uneven. "Does it bother you?"

"Not really," she said, equally cool.

"Okay then." He stared out over the darkening, churning sea.

It might not bother me, but it bothers you, Polly thought. You feel guilty because you've slept with another woman. And I feel guilty because I haven't. It's a joke, really.

"The thing is, Varnie and I, we've been having some rough times lately," Mac said after a pause. "She's a real eighties type: what she's looking for is security, and a father for her kid. She has this four-year-old daughter, see. She wants to get married and set up a nuclear family, but I've been dragging my feet."

"Oh, yes?"

"Yes." He nodded. "Last night, I didn't even go back up there. I stayed at the house we've been working on, here in town."

"Oh." There was an awkward pause. "You don't want to get married," Polly said finally.

"No." Mac shook his head several times. "Not to Varnie anyhow. I know what it'd mean. Life insurance, holidays with the in-laws, what they call a job with a future, and sleeping with somebody twice a week because you promised the State of Florida you would. That's not my scene." He pulled his gin and tonic toward him, but instead of drinking took the plastic straw out of the glass and, holding one finger over the top, released two drops of liquid onto the straw's crushed paper casing. The paper caterpillar squirmed, expanded, collapsed.

"I haven't seen anyone do that since sixth grade," Polly exclaimed.

"Want to try it?" He grinned.

"All right."

As her caterpillar in its turn rose and subsided, she realized for the first time what it resembled. The other kids must have known all along: that was why they had giggled and shoved each other so.

"Hey," Mac said. "Do you really have to go back to New York Sunday morning?"

"Well, I was planning to."

"Why don't you stay awhile? There's a lot here I'd like to show you. And I've got the whole day off Sunday. We could go out to the reef, if this storm blows over." Mac glanced again at the waves, now spotlit to a milky aqua. "You ever been snorkeling?"

"No," Polly admitted.

"It's beautiful under the water. Literally out of this world." He leaned toward her, stroked her arm. "I bet you could change your ticket."

Don't do it, Artemis cried, suddenly reappearing with a swirl of stony draperies. *You've had your fling; if you don't watch out you could become emotionally involved with this unsuitable person.*

"Well; I could try," Polly said, stubbornly refusing to listen to this inner voice. "But I've got to be back by Wednesday, I have an interview scheduled then." What does it matter, she argued; it's only three more days. I just want to get him out of my system. *Yes,* Artemis remarked. *That's what addicts always say. One more fix. Get it out of my system.*

"Great." Mac leaned farther toward Polly; he touched the side of her face.

"I said I'd try, that's all." In spite of her resolve, she smiled. Okay, she admitted. I like him. I could love him, even. What's the matter with that? *It's stupid and dangerous; you'll get hurt,* Artemis replied, but her voice was shrill and faint.

"Great," Mac repeated, putting his hand on her arm. The wind blew harder; the thick pale green lace-trimmed waves churned under the deck. He and Polly gazed at each other, half smiling.

"Hey," he said finally. "There's something else I have to tell you."

"Okay." She laughed.

"It's, uh. This bastard that you're looking for, Hugh Cameron. . . . That's me. I mean, I'm him." In the gathering dark his expression was impossible to read.

"What?"

"I'm Hugh Cameron."

He's kidding, Polly thought. It's another catch-the-tourists tale, like the Sea-Cow Ranch and the five-foot pelicans (both already refuted, with hoots of laughter, by Lee). "Oh, you are not," she said. "You already told me he's in Italy. Besides, you're not anywhere old enough to be him."

"I'm forty-eight."

"Yes, well." She smiled, though it was a few years more than she'd assumed. "If Lorin Jones were alive now she'd be nearly sixty. When she left Wellfleet with Cameron she was thirty-seven; that's twenty-two years ago, and you would've been only —"

"Twenty-six." Mac nodded solemnly, keeping up the joke.

"Right." Polly smiled. "Besides, Hugh Cameron is a poet — he was a college professor."

"Yeah. He was a professor, but he didn't get tenure, so now he's a contractor in Key West." Mac still did not smile; his expression could almost be called grim.

Polly stared at him. "Prove it," she said.

"Okay." Mac sighed; then he reached into the back pocket of his jeans and took out a worn pigskin wallet stitched with thongs, such as Stevie had once made in Boy Scouts. "Here. Driver's license, library card, food co-op, Visa —" He fanned them out on the damp wooden bar.

Cameron, Hugh Richard. H. R. Cameron. Hugh Cameron.

"Oh, my God," Polly said slowly. Then a crazy laugh came out of her. She shoved her stool toward the ocean, away from him.

"I tried to tell you before, back in the house. Only I couldn't. I knew you'd start asking a lot of questions, and I don't like talking about those years now. It was a bad time in my life."

"Yes?" Polly said half-consciously. I was right this afternoon, she thought, feeling disoriented, as if she had made it happen.

"And besides, I figured you wouldn't sleep with me if you knew. You were so down on Cameron, that bastard, that creep, that shit, you kept saying."

"Jesus."

"Y'know, after I saw you on Frances Street, I kept

kicking myself for losing my chance. When you turned up again on Mallory Dock, I thought somebody up there loved me." He pointed at the sooty lowering clouds. "Then when I got to Billie's I found out you were the woman from New York that'd been hounding me, so I decided to get out of there fast. And I started to leave, right?"

"Right," Polly echoed, dazed.

"But the thing was, you looked so great, sitting there. I couldn't let you go. I thought, what the hell, it's karma, as my friend Sandy would say. You've got to play it out."

"You're Hugh Cameron," Polly said, finally taking this in.

Mac nodded.

"So that was your house."

"Yes."

"And it's not for rent; you live there."

"Yes — no. It's rented all right, from tomorrow."

"But nothing else you told me is true." Now she was trembling, furious. "You're not living with a woman called Varnie; and I suppose your name isn't even really Mac."

"Most of it's true. I was living with her, till yesterday anyhow. And Mac is what everybody calls me down here. I never liked the name Hugh, I don't know why I stood it for so long. Back in Nebraska, where I come from, it was a sissy name. I had to take all these jokes at school. 'Who? Who Cameron? You, Cameron.' "

"You lied to me," Polly said, paying no attention to this story.

"Well, yes. But it was in a good cause." Mac grinned, but nervously. "Anyhow, you lied to me too."

"I did not."

"Sure you did. You told me you were a lesbian." Mac was smiling now. "Last night when I took you back to the Artemis Lodge I was almost scared to kiss you. I let go real fast, in case maybe you'd hit me."

"I should have hit you," Polly said, with a short hysterical laugh.

"Come on. It's not as bad as all that. I'm the same guy I was this afternoon."

"No, you aren't." *You see,* the tall winged goddess said in her mind. *You rushed into this like a greedy, sensual fool. Now you are punished.*

"I didn't have to tell you," Mac protested. "I could have kept quiet. Only I thought we should start out straight." He grinned awkwardly.

"It's a little late for that," she said, with an angry tremor in her speech.

"Better late than never."

Polly did not trust herself to answer. She turned away from Mac, staring out over the ocean, milky green near the deck, but dark and shaky beyond the lights, like some kind of poisonous Jell-O.

"Hey, baby." Mac leaned toward Polly and put a strong hand on her arm. "Let's give this a chance. You don't know anything about me really."

"I know enough," she replied, casting a miserable glance at him and then looking away over the churning Jell-O toward other countries full of folly and deception.

"Hell, what do you want? Do you want me to take you back to the guest house?"

"I don't know." Polly's voice shook. "Maybe you'd better."

"Okay." Mac stood up.

"I have to think."

"Okay. You want me to call you tomorrow morning?"

"Yes — no. All right."

14

"That's really wild," Lee exclaimed, laughing aloud as she chopped tomatoes and peppers for a gazpacho and fed them into her blender. The machine's low-pitched pulsing roar syncopated with the snaredrum spatter of rain on the roof of the veranda; the storm she had been predicting had arrived. "And you never had any idea who he was?"

"I did think of it for a moment," Polly said. "But then I decided I was crazy."

"You really liked him, too, huh? You thought he was a nice guy."

"Mh," she admitted.

"Hell, maybe he is a nice guy," Lee shouted over the sound effects.

"He lied to me," Polly said stubbornly, accusing the guest-house manager of moral laxness.

"Still —" Lee broke off. "Well, anyhow you got to see something of Key West. . . . Right, honey?" she added, grinning and starting on a red onion.

"Mhm," Polly agreed miserably. She had spent a hot restless night, broken by thunder, flashes of sheet lightning, and finally the crack and boom of a bursting tropical storm. Again and again Mac's face appeared before her, and his body. *You're really a slow learner, Polly dear,* she heard Jeanne's voice remarking.

Toward morning, the drenched flashlit leaves outside took the form of Lorin Jones's last photograph, which now wore a mocking lizard smile. *You thought he might be yours, but he's mine,* this reptilian Lorin said without moving her lips. *Still mine, always mine.*

"So overall you're ahead," Lee continued. "All you have to do is get the facts out of the guy this afternoon."

"I wish I never had to speak to him again," Polly said with emphasis, trying to convince herself of this.

"Now, honey." Lee turned off the machine with a sinewy brown hand. "I understand how you feel. But after all, if he's got the data you need —"

"And if he'll give it to me." Polly sighed. The rainstorm suited her mood, which was one of streaming depression. She felt like crying, but maybe it was only the onion.

"Why shouldn't he?" Lee threw in a bunch of peculiar-looking herbs: dark blood-red basil and loose uncurled parsley.

"Because he didn't want to in the first place, that's why." Again Polly sighed, almost groaned.

"So what're you going to do now?" Lee asked, pouring oil into the machine and muting its tone to a rumbling whir.

"I d'know. Maybe I'll go look at some more galleries."

"You might as well. There's not much chance of a swim today, for sure." Lee turned off the blender; the spatter of the rain continued, heavier and more insistent. "I'm sorry about the weather, honey," she said. "But you can't say I didn't warn you."

The lesson for today, Polly thought, as she tramped through a dense foggy downpour that afternoon toward the current Revivals Construction project. Last night's lowering clouds had sunk even farther over the island, drenching the loose-leaved unnatural trees, the peeling white-frame houses, and the potholed streets. Expect trouble, don't trust anyone — that was the lesson.

Though it looked finished behind its eight-foot board fence, the house Mac and his crew were remodeling was only a shell. Within, it had been gutted down to the beams and siding; its roof joists were exposed, and its interior walls were mere scaffoldings of two-by-fours snaked with electric cables. The whole back side of the house was gone, covered now only by a sheet of dirty translucent plastic down which the greasy rain slid, giving the skeleton rooms the air of a stage set under construction. A table saw and a jumble of tools and boards sulked under other plastic covers, and a leak over the front door dripped sourly into an orange paint bucket.

"Sorry this place is such a mess," Mac said, spreading Polly's dripping poncho over a stack of boards, above which a bare, lit bulb hung from the end of a cord looped around a roof beam. "I'd like to take you out somewhere, but I'm still waiting for a call from the supplier. I sent the other guys home; there's nothing more they can do until we get a delivery of sheetrock. Here, sit down." He pulled a paint-spattered folding chair toward her. "Like some coffee?"

"All right," Polly said, trying to speak neutrally. She had resolved not to lose her cool or waste time in recriminations.

"So how's everything going?" Mac crouched on the floor to spoon coffee into a battered percolator.

"All right," she repeated.

"Still angry, huh?" he said, glancing at her over his shoulder.

"And why shouldn't I be?" Polly asked, striving to keep her voice light. "After all those lies."

"I could give you a couple of reasons." Mac stood up; he looked at her knowingly, sensually. Then, registering her lack of response, he stopped smiling. "What the hell," he said. "I came clean, didn't I? And talk about lies, you've probably heard some whoppers about me from Garrett Jones and those other New York types."

"I've heard about you, yes," she replied, setting her jaw.

"From Jones?"

"Yes, as a matter of fact."

"And you assume he always tells the truth, huh." He grinned.

"It wasn't only him." Polly glanced at Mac/Hugh, noting with misery that he was still smiling, that he was still infuriatingly good-looking.

"Okay, who else?"

"Well. Mr. Herbert, at the gallery. He told me a few things, too."

"Great. A cuckold and a ponce." Mac rummaged among some hardware on a trestle table and came up with a bag of sugar and a carton of half-and-half. "That's what an art dealer is, you know. When a guy like that watches a painter at work, he doesn't see something beautiful being created. What he sees is shit flowing out of the end of her brush and turning into money."

"That's not fair," Polly exclaimed. "I know Jacky Herbert — and Mr. Carducci, too — they honestly admired Lorin Jones's work."

"Sure they did." Mac sat down cowboy-style on a bat-tered bentwood chair. "As long as she could keep it coming, and they could skim their thirty percent."

"That's not —" Polly began, and stopped. Why should she defend Jacky or Paolo? She didn't owe them, or any man, anything. Besides, that wasn't what she should be doing here; she should be listening, collecting data. "So what's your version?"

"You really want to know?" Mac tipped his chair away and gave her a hard look over the curved back.

"Yes, of course."

"All right." He lowered the chair. "I'll tell you anything you like. Might as well set the record straight."

"Okay," Polly said. "Thanks," she added ungraciously.

"Right." The percolator had stopped bubbling; Mac squatted beside it. "Milk and sugar?"

"Just milk, please."

"So what would you like to know?" he asked, handing her a chipped mug mockingly stenciled in red: KEY WEST— I WENT ALL THE WAY.

"Oh, anything. Everything," Polly said, forcing a casual, friendly tone and cursing herself for not bringing her tape recorder; she was really fucked up today.

"I suppose Garrett's story is that I moved in on Lorin, his sweet innocent little genius, and lured her away from him."

"Something like that, yes," she agreed.

"I bet he didn't tell you that while she was living alone for months at a time in that freezing-cold farmhouse in Wellfleet, he was chasing around the country, sleeping with any broad who would have him." Mac checked Polly's expression and added, "I'm not inventing that. Everybody in the Arts Center knew it. When he was in P'town he was always trying to put the make on the female Fine Arts fellows."

"Yeah?" Polly asked, expressing in her tone a doubt she didn't feel.

"Yeah. He had a standard MO. He'd tell the woman how sensitive and sympathetic she was, and then he'd say how much he could do for her career, if he felt like it. You don't believe me, you can ask anyone who was around then."

"Okay, maybe I will," she said coolly, thinking that Garrett hadn't changed his approach in twenty years. "You knew him yourself?"

"Oh, sure. He was at half our parties and art openings, bragging about all the famous painters he'd met and the important pictures he owned."

"Mm," Polly murmured. Mac was telling the truth, she thought; it was the Garrett Jones she knew, seen through dark glasses.

"He talked a lot about Lorin too. He used to lay it on everybody what a great artist his wife was."

"I think he loved her, you know," she protested.

"If you want to call that love." Mac made a face. "I could tell right away he didn't have any real feeling for her; she was just part of his collection."

"And did Lorin Jones know about her husband's affairs?"

"Well, I think she had an idea. But that wasn't the main problem. What really drove her crazy was the way he interfered with her work."

"How do you mean?" Polly set her coffee cup on a roll of roofing paper and leaned forward.

"Garrett had all these theories, see. He was always making comments on Lorin's paintings and telling her what other artists they reminded him of and how they fit into the developing contemporary tradition. He wanted to look at what she'd done every day. It got so heavy Lorin couldn't stand being with him in New York, and she spent as much time as she could on the Cape. But of course Garrett came up to Wellfleet now and then, and whenever he was there he kept after her. She had to lock herself in her studio sometimes, she told me, to stop his voice going on and on. And even then he'd come and rattle the handle and talk through the door at her, y'know?"

"I can imagine." But Polly didn't need to imagine; she had a vivid memory of Garrett's rattling the door of Lorin's studio. "So when you turned up, she was about ready to leave him."

"Yes, I guess so. She wanted to get off the Cape too; she'd decided that landscape was about used up for her. I used to kid her afterward that she only came away with me so she could see Nebraska. Something I'd said once about the light out where I come from had gotten her interested. Well, I was on my way there, and I had a van big enough to haul her equipment. It was fate." He laughed, not easily.

"So when you left the Cape you went to Nebraska."

"Right. We took it slowly, camping out and sleeping in the van. It was a pretty good time. But then when we got there the place didn't work for her. Something about the colors was wrong. . . . Anyhow, after a few weeks we packed up again and drove back through Canada to the MacDowell Colony in New Hampshire, where I had a summer residency. But Lorin didn't like that landscape either."

"Why not?" Polly asked. Spoiled, restless, picky, she thought.

"I don't know exactly. She said the White Mountains were too green. But anyhow, that fall we went west again, to Iowa City; I'd got a writing fellowship there for the year."

"You had a fellowship in Provincetown, and then at the MacDowell Colony, and then at Iowa?"

"Uh-huh." Mac half grinned. "I was hot back then."

"And how did Lorin like Iowa?"

"Not too well." He shook his head. "It wasn't so bad for a while, but then the winter came, and she caught bronchitis and couldn't shake it. And the art faculty drove her up the wall."

"Really."

"See, they were uneasy with her because she was a New York painter, and most of them were still into regionalism. But we got through the winter. Then a couple we'd met at MacDowell who had a house down on Seminary Street lent it to us for the off-season, so we came to Key West. And Lorin really dug it, even though it was summer, when it can get pretty damn hot here."

"She didn't mind the heat?"

"Not all that much. Up north she used to get sick a lot. And she was always cold in the winter, maybe because she was so thin. In bed in Iowa City her feet were like two beautiful icicles." He laughed.

"You were a lot younger than she was," Polly said, looking at Mac. He must have been beautiful then, she thought. Hell, he was beautiful now.

"Yes. Eleven years. But I never thought of her as an older woman, you know. Now with Varnie Freeplatzer, my friend up on Sugarloaf Key, the age difference is definitely part of the relationship. For her JFK and Martin Luther King and Woodstock are just a chapter in a history text, know what I mean?"

"Mm." Polly nodded. "But it was different with Lorin?"

"Oh, yeah. I never felt she was any age really, or knew what age other people were. Maybe that's why she made the mistake of marrying a pompous old fart like Garrett Jones." He grinned.

"You're awfully down on Garrett," Polly said, feeling her own favorable opinion of him leaking away fast. "But you know, everybody says he was good to Lorin. And very generous."

"Sure, as long as she belonged to him. Afterward —

well, he made damn certain she didn't get a dime in the divorce settlement."

"She didn't get anything?" Garrett lied to me, she thought, at least by omission.

"No. It didn't even occur to her that she might ask for alimony until her father suggested it."

"Dan Zimmern suggested that?"

"Right. He wanted her to hire a lawyer and sue, cite Garrett for adultery if he got nasty. But Lorin wouldn't even discuss the possibility."

"Really," Polly said. "But she already had the money from their Cape Cod account, didn't she?" she added, remembering.

"Yes. Five thousand dollars. Of course, that was more back then; but it didn't last forever. And then she sold some work from her show the next year, her last show."

"And then what happened? Why did she stop exhibiting?"

Mac paused, looking away and then back at Polly. "You've got to understand, Lorin wasn't like other people," he said finally. "She had a real close relationship to her paintings; she didn't want to be separated from them. And it got stronger as time went on. She thought of them as part of her; her children, maybe."

"Her children?"

"Yes. What I think is, a woman usually has this maternal instinct, and if she doesn't have kids it can settle on anything. And then she can't let go. With one of my aunts, it's her furniture: she's nearly ninety, but she's still polishing and dusting, you know?"

"Mm."

"Well, Lorin was like that. Whenever she had to part with a picture it made her really miserable. Most of the time I knew her she was in mourning for the paintings she'd sold when she was younger. It seemed crazy to me at first, but it's logical really. If you're a writer you can keep your work forever; all you need is a Xerox machine. But suppose you could only make one copy of a poem or a story, and if you wanted to eat you'd have to sell it to some rich bastard and maybe never see it again. Shit, it'd be like death, right?"

"Right," Polly agreed.

"After I thought of that, I could understand how she felt. . . . Excuse me." At the other end of the house, where a khaki sleeping bag was laid on the floor, a phone had begun to ring.

As Mac crouched beside it, swearing into the receiver, Polly opened her canvas tote and scribbled on the back of a deposit slip: "Nebraska — May 63 — wrong colors. MacDowell — summer — too green. Iowa 63–4."

"Sorry," he said, as she put it away. "That asshole still can't confirm delivery. I've got to hang around here awhile longer."

"That's okay." Silently, Polly thanked the unknown asshole, whose delay would allow her further questions and — yes, all right — more time with Mac.

"Like some more coffee?"

"No, thanks." Polly drank the last lukewarm inch, then leaned to set it on the roll of tarpaper. Probably thinking she was handing the cup to him, Mac also reached out; their hands collided, and an invisible charge passed between them. Oh God, I still want him, she thought.

"Tell me about those two paintings you still have," she said, her voice uneven.

"Tell you what about them?" Mac asked, also unevenly.

"Well, for instance, how you happened to keep them. We all thought they were lost, you know. Lennie said he'd taken everything of Lorin's away with him."

"Yes; but those pictures weren't Lorin's. She gave them to me." Mac met Polly's stare; in this light, his eyes were more green than blue.

"But you never said you had the paintings. If I'd known, I could have borrowed them for the show."

"Maybe. Only I didn't feel like lending them."

"That's pretty selfish," Polly said, losing her cool. "I mean," she explained, "when you think how many people would really like to see —"

"Sure, they might. But the way I figured it, if I shipped those canvases to New York, I'd probably never get them back. A couple of years before she died, Lorin sent the Apollo Gallery two watercolors she didn't care about anymore. When they were sold she didn't get a cent; her dealer said she still owed him money."

"I see." And that's something Jacky didn't tell me, Polly thought. "So what did Lorin live on after she stopped selling paintings?"

Mac grinned. "She lived on me, mostly." He checked Polly's expression, shrugged. "It was what she was used to, see, having a man support her. That was what men did, in her experience. First her father, and then Garrett, and then she assumed it was my turn. She never worked a day in her life at anything but her art."

A parasite, an exploiter of men, Polly thought. "And you accepted that," she said.

"Sure; I went along with it at the time. I was just a kid; and I was in love. And I already had some idea how good Lorin's work was. I figured that once her money ran out she'd sell some more pictures; I hadn't realized yet how she felt about that."

"I suppose it was fair," Polly said. "You lived on her, and then she lived on you."

"The hell I did!" Mac said, angry for the first time since Polly had met him. "I didn't take Lorin's money; I wasn't brought up like that. I got a job here as a gardener, and I started applying to colleges for teaching gigs."

"And Lorin? What did she do?" Polly asked, suppressing an impulse to apologize.

"She stayed home and painted." Mac shrugged.

She painted, while you dug and weeded, and I typed catalogues, Polly thought, her sympathy veering further around toward Mac. "And how long did that go on?"

"I don't know. Six months, nine months. Then I landed a job up in northern New York State as a visiting lecturer."

"And did Lorin go with you?"

"No. She figured it was too much trouble to move all

her equipment back and forth, and it was only for eight months anyhow." Mac shook his head slowly. "But it was a bad eight months for me."

Selfish and cold and inconsiderate, Polly thought. It was going to be really easy to write a negative account of Lorin Jones's life; much easier than writing a positive one.

"So then you came back to Key West and worked as a gardener again?"

"Yes; and anything else that came along. Carpentry, roofing, repairs, painting houses."

"And you didn't mind that," Polly said, trying not to make it a question.

"It was okay. The trouble was, I didn't get much writing done. A lot of days I was just too wiped out after work; especially in the summers." Mac grinned, narrowing his green eyes.

"I see." Lorin ruined your life as an artist, just as she ruined mine, Polly thought. But wasn't Mac leaving something out? "I expect Lorin did the cooking and cleaning though, didn't she?" she added, trying to keep her tone neutral. "Or don't you consider that work?"

"Don't give me that feminist glare." Mac grinned. "Sure, it's work. Hard work. I should know, because Lorin wouldn't cook or clean. I found that out as soon as we got to Iowa. She claimed she didn't know how, and somehow she couldn't learn. Of course she was brought up with live-in help, and Garrett always had a daily cleaning lady for her. When she was alone on the Cape she just piled the dishes in the sink and waited for the woman to come. She ate crazy things anyhow, mostly fruit and yogurt and soup and crackers. If I wanted a real meal I had to cook it myself. I tried to make her do the dishes sometimes, but it wasn't any use. She'd forget, or else she'd leave food burned on the pans or break something, you know?" Mac laughed.

"Mm." Polly had heard of this ploy; according to feminist rhetoric, it was known as "klutzing out," and was always employed by men.

"See, what you have to understand is, the only thing that

really counted for Lorin was her painting. Nothing else had any importance for her."

"You make her sound rather selfish," Polly said, trying it out.

"Selfish, I d'know." Mac shook his head. "She was always handing out money to beggars and street performers. And she'd give you her last scoop of raspberry sherbet if you looked at it hopefully." He smiled, gazing past Polly. "But she was the most self-centered person I've ever known."

"Self-centered?"

"Mmh. You didn't notice it at first, because Lorin didn't give a damn about money or possessions or being the center of attention. All she wanted was to be left alone to paint. But if anyone got in the way of that, it was too bad for them."

Yes, that sounds right, Polly thought. "But it must have been different with you, because she was in love," she suggested.

"I was in love with her. I never said she was in love with me." Mac shook his head slowly, as if disagreeing with some invisible person.

"You really think Lorin didn't love you?" Polly asked, surprised.

"Not the way I loved her. But it wasn't personal exactly. She just couldn't care much for anybody or anything, not compared with her paintings. Not even sex."

"She didn't like making love?" Polly said, suppressing *even with you.*

Mac looked past her, through the scaffolding of what might one day be a bedroom. "Oh, she liked it all right sometimes. But it was a private thing with her. She never said anything, she just kind of went away into another world. I'm not complaining, though at the time —" He frowned. "I never knew how lucky I was till I had to cope with my wife, and her Guide to Married Love and Four Stages of Arousal." He laughed crossly. "I never had to ask Lorin afterward if it had been all right for her. The only trouble was, when she was really into painting she just tuned out."

"You mean she tuned out sex."

"Yes, that too. For days sometimes. I used to get mad and swear that the next time she felt like it I'd say too bad, nothing doing, I was working on a poem."

"And did you, ever?"

"Well, I tried it a couple times. But Lorin always got around me. She was so beautiful, for one thing. Her eyes and her mouth and her hands and all that long glossy dark-brown hair, that always looked a little wet even when it wasn't. She could charm the seabirds from the air and the tuna out of the Gulf. And by God, she knew it."

Lorin Jones hurt you worse than she hurt me, Polly thought, looking at the strong jutting lines of Mac's averted profile, the cropped curl of piebald hair behind his ear. Never mind. I'll fix you, she told Lorin in her head. I'll tell everyone how you lived off men, how you sacrificed people to your ambition. They'll hear of your selfishness, your slyness, your spitefulness.

"You think she turned on her charm deliberately," she suggested.

"Yes. With me she did, anyhow. Lorin wanted to be sure of me, see; she wanted to be certain I'd always be there, in case she needed something. Once that was settled, she'd leave, without going out of the house, if you know what I mean."

"Mm." You're still angry at her, Polly thought. And no wonder. "How come you never got married?" she added.

"I don't know. I guess maybe it was because Garrett dragged his feet so long over the divorce. When it finally came through, though, I did ask her if she wanted to marry me."

"And what did she say?"

"She said, 'No. Why?' I couldn't think of any reason, by that time." Mac shrugged. "Excuse me."

Again he rose and loped across the raw floorboards to answer the phone. This time, though, Polly didn't make any notes. She sat staring through the nearest skeleton wall without registering it. I see through you now, you cold bitch, she thought. You had a man like this, and you didn't even love him.

"Right," Mac said into the phone on an up note. "Thanks.... Hey, it looks like we've got a delivery for Monday," he called.

"Oh, good," she murmured, her mind elsewhere.

"How're you doing?" he said softly, standing close, looking down at her.

"Okay, I guess." Polly gave him a quick uneasy smile. You ought to go now, you know what could happen if you don't, she told herself. "Well, thanks for all the information." She stood up, holding on to the back of the folding chair, since for some reason her legs felt weak.

Slowly, Mac moved even nearer. "You know, I was in a hell of a panic all day," he said, putting one hand on her bare arm just below the shoulder.

"A panic?" Polly willed herself to take a step back, but couldn't.

"Yes. I was scared you wouldn't come." He took hold of Polly's other arm and pulled her to him.

Wait a moment, for God's sake, she told herself. You said you weren't going to do this again, didn't you?

But it seemed, after all, that she was.

"Why you?" Mac asked presently, raising himself on one elbow to look down at Polly as she lay on his rumpled sleeping bag and air mattress. "That's what I want to know."

"Wha?" Polly did not open her eyes. In a moment she would remember who she was, where she was; but now she floated in a warm blur of satisfaction; she felt like a pile of pancakes in hot maple syrup. The idea struck her as comic, but she was too sleepy even to giggle.

"Why should I like you so much? It doesn't make sense. I mean, you're not the kind of woman I thought I liked. I usually go more for the bohemian ladies."

"Mh?" Polly yawned and slowly opened her eyes. She felt at peace with the world and everyone in it — except for that destructive, hateful bohemian lady Lorin Jones.

"I bet I'm not the type you usually go for either," Mac said, grinning.

She focused on him. "No, not exactly," she fibbed; in the days when she went for men, it was exactly this sort of man she went for. "But at least you're not an artist or a writer."

"The hell I'm not." Mac sat up, half laughing. "What do you mean by that?"

"Well." Polly swallowed another yawn. "I mean, I know you used to write poetry, but it sounds like you gave it up quite a while ago."

"I gave up teaching it, that's all. Hell, I had to. In the poetry business, if you haven't made it on the national scene by forty, you've had it as far as college jobs go. God, you have such wonderful breasts." He bent to kiss one slowly. "No, I'm still writing. I publish something now and then, and I'm getting a new book together."

"Sorry."

"That's okay." Mac stroked the lower curve of her breast meditatively. "I did try to stop once, you know. It was after Lorin died, when I was married and teaching back in Iowa City. I couldn't get my second book published, and I got really depressed. But then I thought, fuck it, why should I quit doing something that gives me pleasure, and I'm not all that bad at? That's how I still feel. And then, there's always the chance that I might strike it lucky. I might write one really good poem, maybe even more. Whereas if I quit, I haven't got a hope in hell. . . . Equal time." He moved to the other breast.

"I used to paint," Polly said suddenly.

"Yes?" Mac raised his head and looked at her.

"I had a show once."

"Uh-huh." He gave her another slow look. "Only now you're a biographer."

"I'm not a biographer, exactly. I'm just writing this one book."

"I'd love to read your biography." Mac grinned. "I'd like to know how you got to be so fantastic in bed." He traced a line of fluttering kisses down her stomach.

"You're not so bad yourself," she replied, raising her hips to meet his mouth.

"You know something, Polly," Mac said, considerably later. "I could get really serious about you." He pulled down a T-shirt stenciled REVIVALS CONSTRUCTION — navy this time rather than green. "What d'you think?" he added, when Polly, bent over her running shoes, did not respond.

"I don't know," she said.

"You mean forget it, huh?"

"No. I mean, hell, I only just met you two days ago. Anyhow, I live in New York and you live here."

"We could fix that," Mac said casually, smiling.

"Yes? How?" Polly tied her other shoe and looked up at him. He's kidding, she thought.

"I could move to New York, for instance. Or you could move to Key West."

"I couldn't afford that," she said, smiling too.

"Sure you could. It doesn't cost much to live in the Keys if you've got a place to stay. Anyhow, you already own an apartment on Central Park West, right?"

"Mm," Polly agreed.

"How many bedrooms?"

"Three. But one is tiny."

"All the same. From what I hear about New York rents, I bet you could let it for enough to get by on here."

"Maybe. But what would I do in Key West, besides making love?" she asked, almost laughing.

"I d'know. Write your book. Or you could take up painting again." He shrugged. "Your kid could come too; I've got plenty of room. I bet he'd enjoy it here."

For a moment Polly imagined herself and Stevie in Key West; they were sitting on the worn front steps of Mac's house, under the orchid tree. But probably he wasn't serious; it was just a way of saying he liked her.

"Think about it, okay?"

"Okay," Polly agreed, aware that she would whether or not she chose.

"Anyhow, you're going to be, around for a while now, right?" Mac said, a stutter of feeling interrupting the casual question.

"I'll stay till Tuesday. If I can change my ticket." Polly glanced at him, then, shaken by what she began to feel, leaned nearer to blur it with a quick caress.

"Good. And I hope I answered all your research questions." Mac put one hand on the bottom of her jeans.

"Yes — well." With a sort of mental shake, Polly recalled herself to duty. "There was one thing —"

"Mm."

"You were saying before, sometimes Lorin was still in the house, but in a way she'd be gone."

"Yeah. I suppose partly it was the drugs."

"Drugs?" Polly echoed, trying — far too late — to speak calmly. That's what Lennie didn't tell me, she thought. Or Jacky or Garrett. Or maybe they didn't know.

"You didn't know she was into drugs?"

"No," Polly admitted. An addict too, a thin mean voice said in her head; you can tell everyone that too.

"Yeah." He cleared his throat. "We both were, for a while. It was no big deal back then, y'know."

"What sort of drugs?"

Mac grinned. "Well, to start with, back on the Cape, it was grass and hash mostly. Down here I mainly stuck with that; you pretty much have to in my line of work if you don't want to fall off a ladder or saw a hole in your hand. And we tried a little LSD and mesc on weekends, to see if it would do anything for our work."

"And did it?"

"Not all that much. I wrote what I thought at the time was great stuff, but when I came down it mostly looked pretty empty. It did more for Lorin, but she couldn't paint what she saw when she was high, she didn't have the coordination. But after a while —" Mac broke off, staring at the rain that sluiced down the plastic back wall of the house.

"Yes?" Polly prompted.

There was a pause. "Well," he said finally. "After a while Lorin got into speed. Nobody knew what it did to you, back then, see. And she liked it because she could work longer without getting tired. Anyhow, at first she just took some now and then when she was really into a painting. It didn't get heavy till I was up in Maine."

"When were you in Maine?"

"Sixty-eight, sixty-nine. I was going crazy because I didn't have time to write, so a pal of mine got me a job at Colby, he —"

"But that was when Lorin died," Polly interrupted. "February nineteen-sixty-nine."

"Yes, I know," Mac said almost without irony.

"I'm sorry. I —" Polly swallowed, then plunged ahead. "You were teaching at Colby College then?"

"Mm. I came down here over Christmas vacation, though, and I could see that Lorin was in a bad way. She'd been working on a series of underwater paintings, and she didn't want to take time off to sleep. So she went to this quack doctor and said she needed to lose weight, she wanted some appetite depressants. And the bastard gave them to her. I tried to tell her it was insane, because she was too thin already; she never ate enough. But she didn't pay any attention."

"Lennie Zimmern told me Lorin died of pneumonia," Polly said.

"Yes. That's right, technically. She caught it going snorkeling. We always went out to the reef a couple of times every summer, but that last year Lorin got really hooked, and started wanting to go every week. She could get high just from lying facedown in the waves and watching the scene underwater. And of course if you were on something it was just about fantastic. There was one sort of little fish she specially liked; it's sort of transparent, with long white wavy fins, and travels in bunches, I forget now what it's called. There's some of them in that picture over my sofa."

"And that's how she got pneumonia?"

"Mm-hm. See, she was impatient, and she went out to the reef in February before the sea had warmed up. And then she stayed in too long. Only I figure probably she didn't realize it, because she was so strung out. She caught a bad chill. But she didn't like doctors, so by the time she went to one it was too late."

"And you weren't here."

"No. I should have been, but I wasn't. I shouldn't have left her alone, the state she was in, but I thought I had to be a good little boy and meet my classes." Mac almost groaned with sarcasm. "I didn't even know Lorin was in the hospital till the day before she died. And by the time I got home it was all over."

"I'm sorry," Polly murmured, silently apologizing for everything she had thought and said over the last months about Hugh Cameron's desertion of Lorin.

"That's okay. It was a long time ago, and, like I said, we hadn't been getting on all that well."

Had he said that? Polly thought not, but she didn't challenge him.

"Only somehow that made it worse, you know?" Mac looked at her. "Hey, Polly," he said, putting one arm around her shoulders. "You okay?"

"I'm okay," she said, wondering if it were true. "Well, I guess I feel a little awful. I didn't know —"

"Nobody told you, huh."

Polly shook her head. In her mind, Lorin Jones floated facedown in the salty aquamarine water of the Gulf, her long thin legs and arms spread in the shape of a pale star; her dark seaweed hair sloshed in the waves. Below her a school of little pale fish swam through branching coral. Her huge wet star-lashed eyes were wide open behind a snorkeling mask edged with white rubber. They did not blink, though, because she was dead.

What the hell's the matter with you? Polly scolded herself. Why should you feel like crying? Lorin Jones didn't drown, she died in the Florida Keys Memorial Hospital.

Anyhow, you don't like her. "It's stupid, I —" she said. Choking on the last word, she stood up and turned away.

" 'S okay," Mac said. He came over to Polly and put his arms around her.

"I didn't —" She choked up again, recovered. "I mean, I didn't even know her." No, an internal voice said, but you're planning to ruin her reputation, aren't you? Pretty soon Lorin's name will be mud, because of the dirt and muck you're planning to spread on it, out of envy and spite and sexual jealousy. She'll be dead and disgraced, isn't that the idea? And you'll be alive and successful. Isn't that the idea? A spasm of self-revulsion shook her. Forgive me, she whispered silently to Lorin Jones. I won't betray you, I won't hurt you; it was a mistake.

"Sorry. I'm all right now," she said, blinking.

Mac kissed her lightly, then looked around the raw, empty, darkening house. "Hey, this is sort of a dreary scene," he said, checking his watch. "I tell you what, let's get out of here and find ourselves some conch chowder, okay?"

"Okay. But I'd better get back to the guest house first and clean up," Polly heard herself say; she was surprised how normal her voice sounded.

"Right. You do look kind of as if you'd been rolling around on the floor. But I don't mind." Mac hugged her again.

Polly held herself stiff for a moment; then she leaned wholly and passionately into the kiss. You might as well enjoy it, she told herself, almost weeping. You haven't much time.

RUTH MARCH,

photographer

Yeah, I wanted to talk to you, like I told Dad. He says you've been getting all kinds of bad news about Aunt Laurie, really shitty low-grade stuff. So I wanted to even up the score.

Sure, it's true she died when I was thirteen. And the last time I saw her I was only eleven and a half. But I remember her just fine. I ought to, because she like changed my life.

What she did was — But you have to understand how it all happened, the whole scene.

Okay, it was Christmas vacation, the last year before my parents split up, and we were all down visiting Granddad and Marcia in New York. It was always kind of uncomfortable there; we didn't go too often, and we never stayed very long. Half the time they were away somewhere, traveling in Europe or whatever. Granddad was a restless type; well, I dig that, I'm kind of like him.

The way it always seemed to me back then, Dad didn't have a real family; not like my mother's folks in Brookline, who've lived in the same house for forty years, with all these uncles and aunts and cousins and neighbors around. Kids like their families to stay put, you know; I can see it already in mine, and he's only three.

Well, Dad's mother and aunt were down in Florida, and all he had left in New York was his father and Marcia, and his sister, Laurie, who was my half aunt. That always seemed kind of weird to me, you know. There was a family joke that when I was real little I asked Ma, which half of Laurie was my aunt?

I don't know. I guess I thought it could be the left side of her, or maybe the part above the waist. I mean that wouldn't have surprised me. Even a little kid could see she wasn't like other people.

For instance, she wasn't like any of the other women in my family. She wasn't really Jewish, only the part that doesn't count according to Jewish law, and she didn't know anything about Jewish things. Then she was real thin, not like the rest of us, and she had all this long shiny hair that always looked a little damp. She never said much, and she had a kind of drifty manner, as if she wasn't even there in the room half the time. If she did notice Celia or me she didn't talk to us the way most adults talk to kids. I don't think she knew what a kid was exactly.

Anyhow, we were all there in the apartment that afternoon. It'd started raining hard, and we couldn't go to the park, so Marcia got out some paper and colored pencils to keep me and Celia occupied while the men watched television and she and Mom made dinner.

You know how kids get typed, one is a jock and the other is a musician, whatever? Well, everybody in my family was good at words except me, so the idea was that because I liked drawing, I might grow up to be an artist like Aunt Laurie. The trouble was, I couldn't really draw worth a damn, and at eleven I was just finding that out.

I was trying to make a picture of two horses I'd seen trotting in the park that morning, only I couldn't get them right. I got more and more frustrated, and started jabbing the colored pencils into the paper. It was one of those soft cheap drawing pads they sell in the ten-cent store; it would have been okay for crayons, but Marcia's pencils were too hard for it. I kept ripping holes in the sheets, then tearing them out, crushing them up, and throwing them around the room. Finally I got so mad I started a fight with my sister.

Aunt Laurie didn't seem to notice anything much, but while Mom was calming us down she put on her duffel coat and went out without saying a word to anybody. About an hour later she came back, dripping wet, and handed me a plastic shopping bag, and in it, all wrapped up, was this expensive camera, a Leica.

Well, the honest truth is, nobody was much pleased. Mom thought the camera was much too expensive and complicated for an eleven-year-old, and she was right, too. "Oh, Laurie, you shouldn't have!" That was what she said, and she meant it.

Aunt Laurie told her it was a Christmas present. That didn't go over very well, because nobody there celebrated Christmas, only Hanukkah. And besides, they all thought, if Aunt Laurie was going to give me a present she should've bought something for Celia too. Celia thought so too, naturally, though she didn't whine about it or anything. But then it wasn't as if she'd wanted a camera.

I didn't want one much either. I felt kind of hurt and insulted really. It was as if Aunt Laurie, the family artist, had been watching me and knew I wasn't any good, not like her, and never would be. So she was sorry for me; and I couldn't stand that, back then. Hell, I still can't.

But, you see, she knew somehow. When she saw me trying to draw those horses — to reproduce exactly what I'd seen, not like a painter but like a photographer — she knew what I needed. Only I didn't understand then. For me it was as if she was saying, You might as well quit right now, baby. I didn't get any other message, because I didn't have any respect for photography at eleven; I didn't know what it was, really.

Yes, after I got home I put in a roll of film, and tried it out, but my heart wasn't in it. I didn't understand the controls, and the camera was too big for me anyhow; I couldn't even hold it steady. The pictures came out a mess, and I shoved the whole thing away in a closet.

Well what happened was, a couple of years later, when I was nearly fourteen, Aunt Laurie died; and Dad went down to Key West afterward to sort out her things. He found maybe a dozen photography books, going back years. All the greats; Cartier-Bresson, and Stieglitz, and Bourke-White, and Walker Evans, and collections from the old *Life*. Sometime before she died Aunt Laurie had crossed out her name in all of them and written in mine. "Laura Zimmern," and later on "Laura Jones" or "Lorin Jones," was canceled with a long stroke of the pen, and "Ruth Zimmern" was written in underneath, in her fine narrow loopy writing, almost like nineteenth-century calligraphy; you've probably seen it.

So Dad sent the books on to me. I'd given up on art by then. The current family idea, and mine too, was that I was going to live on a farm and take care of animals, like my step-father, Bernic.

Well, those books. They hit me like a bank of flashbulbs going off. I hadn't realized photographs could be like that, but once I saw them I wanted to do the same. I got out the Leica, and this time I was big enough to hold it steady and understand the directions, and that's how the whole thing started. I figure if it hadn't been for Aunt Laurie, I'd be a fat contented country vet somewhere now.

Hell, no. Like Marcia always says, I've got no regrets. I just wish I could see Aunt Laurie again somehow and thank her, that's all.

15

In the ill-lit, high-ceilinged hall of a university building, Polly sat on a wooden bench waiting for Leonard Zimmern to join her for lunch. Shufflings and murmurs reached her from the classrooms opposite, and a gust of chill snowy air slapped her face every time the outside doors swung open to admit students in the uncouth dress and weary, wretched expressions characteristic of exam period.

Polly also felt weary and wretched. She hadn't even started her Christmas shopping, and she had another appointment this afternoon with Dr. Bebb. Stevie was coming home soon, which was something to look forward to; but according to Jim he was probably going back to Denver for the rest of the school year.

At least she could congratulate herself on having gotten out of Key West in time. It had been a near thing, though. After she changed her ticket, Polly had all but forgotten her project and given herself wholly up to Mac and to pleasure. They had jogged in a drifting fog by the ocean at dawn, swum in the rose-stained waves at sunset, and made love on the sand (romantically but rather grittily) by starlight. They had gone dancing again, bought palm-leaf hats at a flea market, and watched the shrimp boats unload.

They hadn't been out to the reef, because the sea was still too high; but they'd gone fishing with a friend of Mac's and brought home a six-pound kingfish that Lee had stuffed and baked for them and two of her guests. For three days Polly had hardly thought of her book, and the only work she had done was to help Mac and his crew tape and spackle sheetrock.

It still scared her to think how close she had come to

really caring about Mac — no, she corrected herself, Hugh Cameron — and accepting his version of Lorin Jones. Because of course his story was just as partial and biased a view of Lorin's life as Jacky's or Garrett's. Maybe more so. The trouble was, as Jeanne said, that though she knew all her informants were untrustworthy, whenever she got too close to one of them her vision blurred, and he turned into a sympathetic person; in Mac's case, to worse than that.

But as Jeanne had pointed out, she had to look at the situation objectively. "Polly, dear. You may have had an exciting time in Florida, well, why not? But you know it would really be a mistake to take it seriously. This is somebody who deceived you, by his own admission; who was cheating on the woman he lives with; and who's more or less stolen two very valuable paintings. I'm not blaming you. I know all too well how crazy I get sometimes myself when I'm in an erotic blur, so that I simply won't let myself see what's quite plain to everyone around me."

It was plain to Jeanne, for instance, that Polly had been in a vulnerable condition the whole time she was in Key West: confused and credulous — almost as if she'd been under a voodoo spell of the sort that Ron and Phil had warned her about. Once home, though, she had more or less fallen apart.

It was Jeanne who had put her back together; Jeanne had been wonderful. She had sympathized, understood, and vigorously denied that Polly was in any way responsible for what had happened in Key West. It was clear to Jeanne that her friend had been lured into Hugh Cameron's house, and then practically raped, when she was ill and miserable and exhausted — after all, hadn't she come home with a streaming cold and a temperature of over a hundred? Hadn't she had to be put straight to bed, and nursed back to physical and emotional health by her devoted Calico Cat?

What had happened in Key West was also partly, Jeanne had suggested, a side effect of Polly's long concentration on Lorin Jones: of first a conscious and later and more darkly a subconscious identification with her subject. Finally she had even begun to have Lorin's experiences: she had been exploited by Lorin's dealers, for instance. (Jacky, as Jeanne had pointed out, hadn't offered to go to Key West himself, or contribute to her plane fare, though when the paintings she'd found were retrieved and sold he would get a large commission.) She had been pawed and condescended to by Garrett Jones; she had been deceived and seduced by Mac/Hugh.

And even after Mac/Hugh had, as he put it, "come clean," he was still dirty, still lying, Jeanne was sure of that. The story about Lorin Jones being addicted to speed, for instance, sounded to her like a parcel of lies; why, even Lorin's own sister-in-law had never heard anything of the kind. It was clear to Jeanne that Cameron was a dishonest, dangerous person: superficially charming and clever maybe, but warped. Maybe even a borderline psychopath, she had suggested yesterday. "Gee, yeah, that could be," agreed Betsy, who had been present at these discussions more often than Polly would have liked.

"Oh, come on," Polly had protested. "He wasn't that bad, you know." But at this Betsy and Jeanne had regarded her with identical looks of anxious indulgence, like nurses in a convalescent hospital. *Still a little infection there, I'm afraid,* these looks said; and they were right.

Of course if Polly were to accept their view of Mac — of Hugh Cameron, rather — it would make her task much easier. She could go back to her original vision of Lorin Jones as a woman of genius damaged and finally destroyed by men and the male establishment; she could set aside all that didn't belong in that story. Then her biography, as she had first planned, would be a well-documented assault on the art establishment. It would also be her revenge on the men who had injured not only Lorin but Polly herself — liars, exploiters, seducers. "They'll be sorry when your book comes out," Jeanne had said the other day, smiling her pussycat smile.

Sorry, and also perhaps vengeful in their turn. Polly's biography would be bad-mouthed by Garrett Jones and

Jacky Herbert and all their friends and supporters; it would be badly reviewed in the establishment press, and its sales would be poor; she'd have to expect that. There would be repercussions when she went back to work at the Museum: cold looks, cold words, the chilly withdrawal of her superiors. Gradually, a strong snowy wind like the one now outside this building would cut Polly off from the New York art world; it would blow her even further into a wholly female and largely lesbian society.

But though she might suffer professionally and financially, she would be supported and encouraged by others like herself. The feminist press would treat her work seriously. Ida and Cathy and the rest of Jeanne's friends would accept and trust her, as one who had finally — though none too soon — spoken out against the patriarchal system.

Polly gazed at the stained wall opposite, and saw herself as if in a film of the future, in Ida's living room. She was sitting cross-legged in a circle of women at one of the study-group meetings she had up to now declined to attend. Her hair was chopped short, and she was wearing worn, woolly dark clothes and a serious, determined expression. Next to her on the lumpy braided rug made by a women's commune in Vermont were Jeanne and Betsy. On the other side, holding her hand in a warm possessive grip, was another vague sympathetic female presence: Polly's future lover, whoever she might turn out to be. ("I'm sure you'll find someone nice soon," Jeanne had said the other day, unconsciously echoing Polly's mother.)

But why was this vision so flat and colorless? Maybe just because of the grayed winter light, and the stained plaster on which the scene was projected. Or maybe she was still rundown; she surely shouldn't be depressed by a future in which she would be accepted, loved, and surrounded by intelligent, affectionate women who admired what she had done.

"Sorry about this place," Leonard Zimmern said twenty minutes later, sliding a plastic tray the color of curdled mushroom soup onto a table in a kosher cafeteria. "The thing is, it's the only restaurant near my office that's not choked with tinsel and artificial holly this time of year." He gave Polly a narrow glance and added: "I'm not going all Orthodox suddenly, don't get any ideas. But the older I get, the more all this Christmas crap irritates me. Hope you don't mind."

"No, it's okay," Polly said, setting her coffee and bagel with cream cheese on the damp tabletop.

Lennie sat, and stirred his coffee. "So, you went to Key West and found Hugh Cameron," he remarked.

"Yes," she agreed.

"And I hear that's not all you found." Lennie smiled. "Jacky Herbert tells me you saw two of Laura's paintings there. Including the big one from her last show that he thought was lost."

"That's right," she said. "Cameron has them."

"Really."

Polly gave Lennie a look of ill-suppressed irritation. It was just like him not to show any surprise at her discovery — let alone enthusiasm or gratitude.

"I understand Herbert would like to get those paintings back for his exhibition." He smiled narrowly and raised heavy black eyebrows threaded with gray.

"Mh." Polly did not smile. The discovery of Lorin's lost canvases was her greatest achievement so far; she wanted them in the new show, so that everyone could see and admire them; she wanted them photographed for her book. Yes, fine. But after that what would happen? Jacky wouldn't give them back to Mac if he could help it; they would be sold to collectors who'd never known Lorin. But, as Jeanne had said, that was none of her business.

"Herbert suggested that we should all go together to his lawyer," Lennie said. "He wants to send Cameron a letter demanding that he ship us the paintings, unless he can produce written proof that he owns them."

"Mh," Polly agreed uneasily. She knew all this; only yesterday Jacky had urged her to persuade Lennie to take such action as soon as possible.

"So you think that's what we should do?"

"I suppose so," she said, trying to speak positively, reminding herself that legally the paintings belonged to Lennie; that their recovery would be morally justified and professionally advantageous to her.

"I don't care all that much for the idea of a lawsuit, you know. I always think of *Bleak House*."

"Mmh." Polly had never read *Bleak House* but was damned if she was going to admit it. Of course Lennie would go to a lawyer in the end, she told herself; he wouldn't want to let two paintings worth at least twenty thousand each get away. But first, just for the fun of it, he was going to give her a hard time. He was teasing her now, as he had teased his sister years before. "Excuse me, I forgot the milk."

The trouble is, she told herself as she picked her way between the crowded tables, I don't like the idea of a lawsuit either. I don't want to help take those paintings away from Mac. It's against my own interests and maybe even illegal, she thought, holding her mug under the metal spigot, but I don't want to be part of that.

"Hey, watch it," a voice next to her cautioned. Polly looked down; her mug had overflowed and a puddle of milk was slopped around it.

"Sorry." But Mac said Lorin had given him the paintings, she thought, releasing the lever. And even if she didn't, they mean something to him; doesn't that give him a sort of right to them?

"About those two canvases," she said to Lennie, setting down her mug, now mostly lukewarm milk. "The problem is, they actually belong to Hugh Cameron."

"Really?" This time he raised only one of his theatrical eyebrows.

"Your sister gave them to him, you see."

"Yes? And what's the proof of that?" he asked skeptically and hatefully.

Polly clenched her jaw. "It's written on the back of both of the canvases," she heard herself lie. " 'For Hugh with love from Lorin.' I hadn't seen it when I phoned Jacky," she improvised.

"Really," Lennie said for the third time, now with a descending intonation, drawing his eyebrows together. "I wonder who wrote it."

"That's why Cameron didn't mention them to you when you were there, I guess," she plunged on, appalled at what she had done, but trying to speak casually.

"It could have been." Lennie shrugged. "It could have been anything. He was half out of his wits at the time, in my estimation." He rotated his coffee mug. "Well. I can't say I'm totally unhappy about it. I have enough trouble with the paintings of Lorin's I've got now: the insurance and storage fees are ridiculous. And then, ever since that damned show of yours, some museum or other is always after me to lend them something." He laughed slightly. "I'm certainly not going to get embroiled in a legal squabble. Let Cameron keep those paintings if he wants to."

Well, you've done it now, Polly thought, shocked at herself. "I thought you didn't like Hugh Cameron," she said at random, recalling that Lennie had earlier described him — it was in her notes — as "a typical *faux-naïf*, clinging to the role of artist and the role of child long after that was even faintly plausible."

"I'm in no hurry to spend time with him, let's put it that way. But I've no quarrel with Cameron; he put up with my sister a lot longer than most people would have, and he didn't cheat on her the way Garrett did, as far as I know."

"You've heard about that?" Polly asked.

"Uh-huh." Lennie shrugged. "Most people who knew them have, I imagine."

"Garrett was in love with her, though," Polly said. "I think he still is, in a way."

"Yes," Lennie said savagely. "Lolly had that effect on men. From her earliest years." He took an angry bite of sandwich that left yellow shreds hanging from his mustache and made him look suddenly carnivorous.

"Lolly; that was your sister's nickname as a child."

"Mm-hm." He sucked in the rags of fried egg and wiped his mouth neatly; his expression was in neutral again.

"Do you happen to know how she got it?"

"I'm not sure, really. Probably it was short for what my father used to call her when she was a baby: Lollypop." He took a sip of coffee. "So what else did you learn from Hugh Cameron?"

Polly glanced rapidly at Lennie, then away. Ridiculous to imagine that he knew what had happened in Key West. It was only his suspicious, probing professorial manner, developed no doubt over decades of intimidating students, that had caused her sensation of panic, her visible flush. She counterattacked:

"I learned several things you didn't tell me. Or maybe you didn't know them."

"Really. Such as?"

"I found out how Lorin died, for instance."

Lennie made no comment; he sat with the coarse white mug halfway to his thin, finely cut lips, waiting.

"She got a chill from swimming in the ocean for too long, when the water was still cold. And then she didn't go to the doctor until it was too late."

"Yes. Cameron told me that," Lennie said on a harsh, falling note. "I wasn't too surprised," he added.

"You weren't surprised by what?"

"The whole thing. Lorin was always attracted by water. And she was strange about doctors and hospitals, even as a kid. She didn't like to have anyone poking about in her body. Or her mind, if it comes to that."

"Who does?" Polly asked, wondering if Lennie was getting at her and her project, suggesting that Lorin would have disliked it. "But of course she was very sensitive."

"Yes. Oversensitive, some might say." Lennie gave a narrow smile. "And also I think she was rather interested in death."

"How do you mean?"

"Well." Lennie hesitated, maybe wishing he had not spoken, then continued. "By that time, you know, the few people she'd ever really felt safe with were dead. Her grandmother, and both her parents, and the maid they'd had all her life. Laura said to my ex-wife once that of course you never really trusted anybody you met after you were about ten — as if that were a quite natural human phenomenon."

"That's really sad," Polly exclaimed, wondering at the same time if Lorin had been right.

"And then, the last time I saw her, when she came to New York after my father died, Laura told me this dream she'd had about him." He paused.

"Yes?" Polly prompted.

"She said she dreamed that her father and Celia and all her other dead friends and relatives were moving about at the far end of a grassy school playground that was half-covered in fog, and calling to her. They were calling: 'Rover, Red Rover, I charge you to come over.'"

"Ehh." Polly sucked in her breath. He means, he's suggesting that Lorin's death was a kind of suicide, she thought. Not just the result of exhaustion, confusion, neglect, and self-neglect. "Hugh Cameron claimed that, those last few years, she was pretty heavily into drugs," she said finally. "Speed mostly. But I don't know if I believe —" She stopped, seeing Lennie's face twitch, his head jerk sideways, as if some invisible person had given him a stinging slap.

"You never heard that," she said.

"I — No. But let's say I had my suspicions." He put down his cup.

"So you think it could be true." And if it is, she thought, Mac wasn't lying.

Lennie hesitated. "I think it's a possibility. The last time we met I definitely had the idea she was on something."

"But if it's so, maybe that was why —" Polly said. "I mean, if her mind was confused — she needn't have wanted to die. And nobody really cared, nobody tried to help her. It was such a waste!" she cried out suddenly, causing other people in the cafeteria to look around.

"Yes, you could say that." He nodded.

"With all her talent —" Polly tried to control her voice.

"Such a damn stupid waste. It makes me so angry, that's all."

"Yes. Me too." Lennie sighed heavily. "But then, we're both angry people." He smiled intimately at Polly.

It's true, she thought, meeting his sharp direct gaze. And probably it goes back to childhood, the way most things do. Both of us stepchildren, with younger siblings everyone preferred to us. My father ran out on me and started another family; so did yours. It's you I'm like, not Lorin. For a moment she looked at Lennie not as an opponent and a research problem, but as an ally, a possible friend. No. She mustn't fall into that trap again.

"I suppose that's a matter of opinion," she said irrelevantly.

Lennie's expression changed. "Like everything else," he said. He leaned back and resumed his normal expression, a slight ironic smile. "Well. And are you going to reveal in your biography that my sister took drugs?"

"I don't know," Polly admitted, suddenly weary. Jeanne's idea was that if Hugh Cameron hadn't simply invented Lorin's drug habit, he had probably been responsible for it. But could he have lied so coolly, and in such circumstances? Unbidden, a picture came into Polly's head, of an empty half-finished house in Key West; of Mac's face as he leaned toward her in the hot shadowy light. She blinked furiously, blinking it away.

"I told you you might find out too much," Lennie said, looking at her. "That's the problem with any book, of course. Your kind and mine anyhow. The less you know, the easier it is to write."

He waited a moment; then, receiving no reply, pushed his cup away and crumpled his paper napkin. "Well, I guess I should be getting back to my office. But I tell you what, why don't you come with me?"

"Well —" Polly hesitated.

"If she's around, I'll have my scatty little secretary make you a decent cup of coffee. I can see you didn't care for what they brew here." He gestured at the mug of dirty-looking lukewarm milk.

But the chauvinist remark had roused her to consciousness. "Thanks; but I can't," she said flatly. "I've got too many errands."

On a soggy, snowy afternoon a few days later, Polly unlocked the door of her apartment and slogged in, heavy-booted and laden with parcels. "Hi!" she called.

"Hello there," Jeanne answered from the sofa, which she had as usual converted into a kind of nest lined with pillows and magazines and student papers; with her pink cable-knit cardigan, her needlepoint and colored wools, her filter-tip cigarettes, and her favorite china ashtray in the shape of a scalloped heart.

"Hey, welcome home!" It was Betsy's voice, childishly high and eager, but at first Polly couldn't see where it was coming from. Then she realized that Jeanne's girlfriend was lying on the carpet by the sofa in a yoga position. Her ass was propped on her hands; her long legs, in lavender sweat pants, were flopped back over her head, so that she looked up at Polly from between thin freckled ankles and white knobby feet.

"How's everything?" Polly dropped her packages and bent over the sofa; but Jeanne, unexpectedly, did not turn her cheek for the usual kiss, or raise her eyes from a line of tiny zigzag stitches in bright green wool.

"All right," she said in a manner that instantly informed Polly it wasn't.

"So what happened about the apartment on Twenty-third Street?"

"We didn't get it," Betsy volunteered upside down.

"Oh, hell. That's too bad," Polly said, thinking that this must be their fifth or sixth housing fiasco since she'd returned from Key West. Either the places Jeanne and Betsy heard of turned out to be impossible, or they were no longer available. As might have been expected, Betsy's abusive husband had refused to move out of the apartment in Brooklyn Heights. He wouldn't even talk to Betsy's lawyer; his position now was that she was having an emotional crisis and ought to see a therapist, recover, and return to him.

The trouble was, Stevie was coming home next week. Jeanne and Betsy would be away then: they were spending the holidays in a women's commune in Vermont. But if they hadn't found another place yet, where would they live when they got back?

If Stevie stayed in Denver, which looked more and more miserably likely, they would probably expect to go on living here. Polly wouldn't have any reason to turn them out, though she would have liked to.

Or rather, she would have liked to turn Betsy out. Now that her classes were over, Betsy was around all the time. She seemed to take up more and more room in the apartment, and get younger and more helpless every day; look at her now, rolling around on the carpet like an overgrown child.

"There were ... a couple ... of calls ... for you," Betsy volunteered, breathing noisily between words in a yogic way and pointing her long white bony feet at the ceiling as if the calls had come from there.

"Yes. Garrett Jones phoned," Jeanne remarked tightly, pulling a length of green tapestry wool through the canvas. "He said to tell you he's sending those photographs you wanted."

"Oh, good." Polly unfastened her duffel coat. Obviously her friend was not only disappointed about the apartment on Twenty-third Street, but seriously miffed about something; what?

"And you had another call from that man in Key West," Jeanne added, in a tone that answered the question.

"Yes?" Something inside Polly's chest rose in a kind of excited hiccup, but she swallowed it down. It was over between her and Mac — it was only her weakness, her vanity that twitched to this news, that wanted to hear him say, one more time, *So when are you coming back to Key*

West? ("You let me know before Christmas, and I'll tell Tony not to rent my house in January after these tenants leave," he had added when they last spoke.)

"It was about ten minutes ago," Betsy offered helpfully, moving her legs in a scissors pattern.

Damn, Polly thought. "And what did he say?"

"I d'know," Betsy said, breathing and scissoring. "Jeanne talked to him."

"He left a message, would you phone him again tonight after eight. Again." Jeanne underlined the word with her voice.

"For God's sake," Polly exclaimed. "You don't need to look at me like that. I only called him once." And only because I had to let him know what I'd told Lennie about the paintings, she added to herself — not aloud, for Jeanne knew nothing of this rash lie.

"I think you *should* call him again," Jeanne said. "I think you should ask him to please stop phoning here, because you're not interested in speaking to him."

"I can't do that. He might have remembered something useful to tell me; he might even have changed his mind about lending those canvases for the show."

"If that's really so, he can always write a letter," Betsy said. "You could tell him that."

"I suppose I could," Polly conceded, looking at Betsy, who was now awkwardly pedaling an imaginary bicycle upside down. If it were a real one and right-side up, she would fall off and hurt herself.

"I wish you would," Jeanne said. "You know it really upsets me, having to speak to someone like that. Someone who took advantage of you that way, when you were so vulnerable."

"I know."

"I should think it would be even more unpleasant for you."

Not wanting to lie, Polly made no comment.

"Anyhow, let's forget about that creep for a while," Jeanne said in a different, warmer voice. "Come and show us what you found at Macy's." She shifted her papers to the coffee table to make room, and patted the sofa beside her, ready now to hear of Polly's struggle with the grizzling gray weather and the jammed stores and buses, and to give her an affectionate hug.

"Just a second; I've got to stop in the bathroom."

Polly headed down the hall; but on reaching her destination, instead of lifting the lid of the toilet, she sat down on it and began, very slowly, to pull off her boots.

Yes, it ought to be unpleasant for her to speak to Mac, she thought. She ought to want to put all that behind her. But she still couldn't forget the way he looked, the way his body had felt, the way he had moved, the flat cubist breadth of his chest, his long hard legs, his long square-tipped fingers. Worst of all, she kept thinking of his cock: its length, its strawberry-vanilla hue, its slight upward curve.

After two weeks, she ought to be getting over this. She was getting over it, really; in a few months she might forget the whole thing, as she had said to Jeanne only yesterday. "Of course you will," Jeanne had agreed. "Probably even sooner."

But not everyone they knew was of the same opinion. Ida and Cathy, for instance, thought differently. When Jeanne told them about Polly's adventures in Key West they hadn't been encouraging. Not knowing that she was being overheard, Ida had said she wasn't convinced it had been a temporary aberration, a last bout of fever. "Polly hasn't got it out of her system, dear, and she's not going to get it out of her system," Ida had pronounced. "It *is* her system." And Cathy had remarked that the sad truth was, you could never really depend on a bisexual.

Ida and Cathy were wrong, Polly told herself, lifting the lid of the toilet, for which Jeanne had recently bought a dusty-pink plush cover, and sitting down again. All she needed was a little more time; and maybe a new emotional interest. She stood up, washed her hands, picked up her salt-and slush-stained boots, and started back down the hall. On her way the phone began to ring. With her heart leaping about annoyingly, she answered it in the bedroom.

"Mom? It's Stevie."

"Oh, honey, hello!" Polly's voice eased half an octave. "How are you? Is everything all right?"

"Sure, it's fine. I just wanted to tell you, I'm coming back a day sooner than Dad wrote you. On the twenty-second. Is that okay?"

"Of course it's okay. It's great." Polly laughed.

"And listen, Mom."

"I'm listening."

"I'm going to be bringing a lot of stuff. Well, see, all my stuff."

"You mean, you've decided, you don't want to go back to Denver after Christmas vacation?" Polly gasped.

"No. I mean, yeah. I want to stay home."

Home; the word repeated itself in Polly's head like a muffled triumphant drumroll through the rest of the conversation, which was concerned with flight numbers, arrival times, and contingency plans.

"That was Stevie," she cried, running into the sitting room.

"Oh?"

"He's coming home a day early."

"Ah." It was clear that for Jeanne the time of Stevie's arrival was a matter of indifference.

"And he's not going back to Denver!"

"Not going back?" Jeanne stuck her tapestry needle into the center of a Victorian rose, and sat forward. "Well," she said. "You must be awfully pleased."

"You must be awfully pleased about Stevie," Jeanne repeated an hour later, as she beat lemon juice and egg yolk together for a hollandaise sauce while Betsy, who usually served as her kitchen maid, peeled potatoes.

"Yes, I really am," Polly answered. "But I know you're not," she added.

"Don't talk that way," Jeanne said, her voice rising to a soft quaver. "I'm very happy for you."

"Sure, but I meant — I realize it's going to be inconvenient for you and Betsy, having to move out so soon, I mean. And I'm really sorry. But what else can I do?"

A rhetorical question; however, Jeanne answered it. "Well." She paused to add a lump of butter. "I thought maybe we could stay on for a while anyhow. Until we find something else, of course."

"But there's no place for you to sleep," Polly protested. With a sinking sensation she imagined Jeanne and Betsy camped out in the sitting room: Jeanne on the sofa, and Betsy humped untidily on an air mattress alongside.

"There's plenty of space in this apartment really, you know." Jeanne smiled persuasively. "If Stevie moved into the spare room we'd all be perfectly comfortable."

"I can't turn Stevie out of his own room," Polly protested.

"But it would only be for a little while," Betsy whined. "And it wouldn't be any trouble, really, Polly. We'd move all his posters and stuff, of course. And all our things are there already, and our bed."

My bed, Polly thought. She imagined trying to explain to Stevie that Jeanne and Betsy had taken over his room. Then, for the first time, she imagined trying to explain to him why they were sleeping together in a double bed. "Well, I can't do it," she stated.

"Jeanne said you wouldn't agree," Betsy remarked dolefully. "But listen; there was another idea that occurred to me."

What had occurred to Betsy, it turned out, was that Stevie should be sent away again almost as soon as he got home. It was the logical solution really, she said, because the New York public high schools were so awful, while the private ones were expensive and snobbish. Besides, the city was a dangerous place for teenagers in a whole lot of ways.

What would be best for Stevie, Betsy thought, would be a nice liberal boarding school with high academic standards, somewhere in the real country — say some place like Putney in Vermont, where Betsy had gone herself. There was sometimes room at midterm for new students, and Stevie would probably adore Vermont. After Colorado he'd want to hike and camp out and ski. Betsy thought it was a great idea.

"Well, I think it's a terrible idea," Polly said, trying to remain calm. "Stevie's just been away from me for four months; I'm not going to send him off again, even if I could afford it, which I can't." She looked toward Jeanne for support, but Jeanne only went on stirring the hollandaise.

"My mother was exactly like you," Betsy said in her whining, stubborn way, starting to scrape at another potato. "She didn't want me to go away to school. But I had a really great time at Putney. I think maybe you're putting your own needs ahead of Stevie's, and besides —"

"I am not —" Polly began, seething.

"— besides, it could even be emotionally damaging if you insist on keeping him too close to you; that's what Jeanne and I think."

"I don't see why it should do Stevie any damage to be close to me," Polly said, feeling angry and betrayed. "He's been close to me for fourteen years." Ignoring Betsy, she stared at Jeanne. "Is that really what you think?"

"No, of course not." Jeanne moved the double boiler off the burner and turned around, wiping her hands on her flowered apron. "Betsy's got it quite wrong," she said in an easy, soothing voice. "Of course it won't hurt Stevie to stay here, because you're not a neurotic, anxious mother like hers." She smiled at them both. "Stevie doesn't need to get away from you, I told her so already. And naturally you want to keep him with you as long as you can."

"Right," Polly said with satisfaction, and gave Betsy a scornful look. You see, you stupid preppie, she thought.

"I know you love Stevie and want what's best for him; and so do I," Jeanne went on, smiling fondly. "But I don't see why you can't ask him to move into the spare room, just for a little while. And really I don't imagine it would make all that much difference to him. He might even prefer it, because he'd have his own bathroom."

"But —" Polly began, choking up again. The spare bathroom had been designed for a maid back when maids would put up with anything: it was cramped, unheated, and disagreeable, with cheap rusted fixtures. The truncated and stained tub, with its cargo of discarded canvases, hadn't been used since Polly moved in fourteen years ago. "I think he'd hate it," she said, trying hard to speak evenly. "Having your own room is important for a kid; much more than for someone like you or me."

"You may have a point," Jeanne conceded. "Well, maybe we should move into your room instead. It's not as big as Stevie's, but it's large enough for two people."

"I didn't meant to suggest —" Was Jeanne really proposing to turn her out of her own room? Polly looked at her friend as she stood by the stove. Everything about her was familiar, from her soft pale curls, caught back for cooking with a bit of rose-colored ribbon, to her scuffed black ballet slippers; but Polly felt as if she had never seen her before. "Anyhow, there's not enough space in this apartment for four people," she said. "It's too crowded already with three."

"It is kind of small —" Betsy began, but neither of them paid any attention to her.

"Now Polly, really," Jeanne murmured, smiling. "You mustn't exaggerate. This apartment is twice as big as the house I grew up in, and there were four of us there. I think you're being just a little bit selfish, you know."

"Well, I think you're being a little bit selfish," Polly said, beginning to lose control.

"I only suggested —" Jeanne began, but Polly rushed on:

"— And if you want to know, I don't think you want what's best for Stevie at all. I think you want what's best for Jeanne and Betsy."

"Oh, Polly!" her friend said in a soft shaky overdramatic voice. "Don't talk that way!"

But the storm of flies had boiled up into Polly's head. "Don't tell me how to talk, okay?" she shouted.

Jeanne flinched as if she had been struck, but did not reply. She bent over the stove, her pink lips trembling, her eyes blinking with unshed tears, while Betsy stared at Polly accusingly.

"I'm sorry," Polly said finally. "I didn't mean — I just meant — I'm upset, that's all."

"That's all right," Jeanne murmured, looking up with a wan expression. "I know it's an emotional issue for you."

"Yeah," Polly agreed.

"Kiss and make up?" Jeanne suggested, smiling.

"All right," Polly said.

Jeanne wiped her hands on her apron, crossed the kitchen, and gave Polly a warm hug. "That's better," she said, laughing a little. "Isn't it?"

"Much better," she said, returning the embrace.

"Me, too," Betsy demanded, dropping the potato she was peeling and clumping over to them. Polly pulled back; no way was she going to get into a three-way hug with Betsy.

"And think over what I've said, won't you please?" Jeanne added over Betsy's shoulder. "I'm sure Stevie wouldn't mind switching rooms, even if you do."

"Okay," Polly agreed sulkily.

A bright, diffuse smile broke over her friend's face. Polly smiled back, but as Jeanne returned to her cooking and she to her desk, her mind was troubled. Am I really being selfish? she thought. Or is it Jeanne who's selfish? And not only selfish, but devious and insincere.

She scowled at her typewriter. To suspect another woman — especially Jeanne — of the faults that men had attributed to the sex for centuries was awful; blatantly reactionary. But the idea was there in her head, refusing to leave. She thought that Jeanne wasn't always frank and direct; that in fact Jeanne sometimes treated her the way women were traditionally supposed to treat men: with charm and flattery and guile. The way she had once advised

Polly to treat the men she was going to interview for her book.

She turned and regarded her friend, whose soft ponytail of hair and ruffled calico apron seemed almost a deliberate parody of the female role. How deft and delicate her gestures were as she stirred the thickening sauce, how pretty her small plump hands with their carefully manicured shell-pink nails!

And now it occurred to Polly that the scene in the apartment was like a caricature of a traditional marriage. She was the cross husband, in worn jeans and baggy sweater, owner of the home and its main economic support, working late. The tactful, charming, manipulative wife, in a flowered apron, was making supper, and the spoiled stepdaughter was pretending to help.

Jeanne cares more about Betsy than she does about me, Polly said to herself with an empty, sinking feeling. And she doesn't love Stevie at all. Her sensible arguments and her teary concern were a sham; what she really wants is for me to shove him out of their way into the maid's room, or move there myself. Well, fuck it. I'm not going to.

16

On a dull cloudy winter day, Polly Alter was trudging down Central Park West from her apartment to Jacky Herbert's. Though it was only four in the afternoon, she was exhausted. Yesterday Stevie had come home, and Jeanne and Betsy had moved out, but at a heavy cost.

It had been a week of scenes and silences, of hysterical accusations and failed compromises. Polly had eventually told Jeanne that she could stay on in the spare room for as long as she liked. But when Betsy heard about this she went into a whiny, jealous panic. Polly was trying to separate them, she cried; she had no place to go — she couldn't possibly stay at Ida's by herself — Jeanne didn't love her anymore — nobody wanted her — she would be so lonely and miserable she'd have to go back to her husband. After twenty-four hours of these desperate, contradictory claims, Jeanne capitulated. But Polly stood firm, determined that whether Jeanne stayed or not, Betsy should go.

In the next few days the Gingham Dog and the Calico Cat finally went for each other, both saying things of the sort you can't forget afterward. Polly lost her cool and told Jeanne that Betsy was totally childish and manipulative and always weaseled out of paying for the groceries and left her hair combings in the sink. Jeanne said that Polly was insensitive and selfish and cut things out of the *Times* before anyone else had a chance to read it.

At one point they almost came to blows. Polly walked into Stevie's bedroom and saw her paperback thesaurus lying on top of a suitcase. She picked it up, exclaiming, "Hey! This is mine, not yours."

But Jeanne, unabashed, tried to snatch the book back,

ripping its cover half off in the process. "Why are you always so petty? You might let us have this, at least," she mewed, as if Polly had denuded her and Betsy of all other possessions. "I'm leaving you every one of my houseplants."

"I don't want your damned plants," Polly barked, not letting go of the thesaurus. "You can take the whole lot."

"You know you can't move plants in this freezing weather." Jeanne almost spat. "But you'd like to kill them, I suppose. Anyhow, we need this book."

"I don't know what you need it for," Polly growled, hanging on. "You and Betsy never use it except to cheat on the *Times* acrostic."

"We do not." Jeanne was still pulling on the thesaurus; suddenly she looked as if she were about to cry.

"All right," Polly said, ashamed of herself. "Take it then, what do I care." She let go so abruptly that Jeanne fell over backward.

"Aow!"

"Sorry," Polly muttered.

Jeanne knelt on the floor, holding the torn book to her robin's-egg-blue cashmere bosom. "Oh, this is awful," she wailed. "How can we be fighting like this?" She held out her arms, and Polly, beginning to cry herself, fell into them.

"If it weren't for the damned housing shortage, we wouldn't be," Polly said. And for a moment, as they hugged each other, weeping and laughing, all was forgiven.

"Oh, Polly. I do love you, you know," Jeanne cried.

"I love you too," she gasped, kissing her friend's soft wet cheek. "I'm going to miss you awfully."

"Me too. I mean — you know what I mean." Jeanne gave a sobbing laugh. "But Betsy needs me so terribly."

I need you too, Polly thought, but she didn't say this, because she knew it was no use. The moment passed, and Jeanne went on packing.

But the Jeanne who had left yesterday didn't seem the same person she had known and loved. Polly looked at her as they all rode down together in the elevator, surrounded by suitcases and boxes and shopping bags (one of which later turned out to have contained, as if to demonstrate how stubbornly greedy and childish Betsy was, Polly's thesaurus). For a moment she saw, not her dearest and best friend, but an unfamiliar pretty, plump, frilly blonde woman, nobody she knew. She helped this woman load the taxi that was taking her and her lover to Ida's, and they parted with a long close hug and fervent pledges to keep in touch. But somehow, maybe because Betsy was standing there watching and scowling, it didn't seem real. Maybe it would never be real between them again.

Well, I've won anyhow; I've got Betsy out of my apartment, Polly thought as the yellow taxi drove away down Central Park West under a cold cloudy sky, becoming smaller and then indistinguishable from other taxis. But as she rode the elevator back upstairs alone, she didn't feel as if she had won anything; she felt deserted, diminished, damaged.

That stupid poem was right, she thought. In the end the Gingham Dog and the Calico Cat had not only eaten each other up in the erotic sense, they had almost destroyed and annihilated each other. Maybe they had been, after all, too different in tastes, opinions, and temperament: irreconcilable entities, like cat and dog.

Polly's project had been another casualty of the battle. Without Jeanne's sympathetic encouragement and Jeanne's conviction that she was on the right track, she faltered on the march. The campaign to portray Lorin Jones as an innocent heroine grew harder every day; the stacks of notes in the folder marked DOUBTFUL — NOT TO BE USED grew thicker. Polly no longer felt even for a moment that she knew her subject intimately, let alone that they were profoundly alike. Instead, she had begun to think that her original idea had been a delusion — worse, a projection.

It wasn't Lorin Jones whose life had been ruined by men. Her father had loved her and been proud of her; Jacky and Paolo had supported and promoted her until she became impossible to work with; Garrett, after over twenty years, was still obsessed with her; and Mac too had loved her passionately, even though she didn't love him. Lorin hadn't been deserted and damaged by men, as Polly had; she had deserted and damaged them.

But if this were true, to write the book Polly had planned would be to force Lorin Jones's life into the mold of her own. Not only would it be professionally disastrous, it would be false to the truth.

"Most understanding of you to come round," Jacky Herbert wheezed, holding out a plump white hand to Polly, then subsiding again onto his rouge-and-beige striped Empire sofa. He reclined there like an overweight seal in an Edwardian paisley dressing-gown, against a heap of Art Nouveau appliqué pillows. The entire apartment, or at least the part of it Polly had seen, was an eclectic and rather cluttered mix of all that had been most elegantly mannered in a century of interior decoration. The tide of furniture and objects, however, ended halfway up the graceful, high-ceilinged rooms: above were bare off-white walls hung with Jacky's celebrated collection of contemporary art.

"I see you're admiring our new side table." Jacky nodded toward a scalloped contraption erupting at the joints into swags of sticky gold seaweed. "Don't blame me, my dear; it's all Tommy's doing. He insists I need to come home to this cozy scene to recover from the artistic austerity of the Apollo Gallery." He waved his plump white hand in a gesture that caricatured the costume and attitude he had assumed for Polly's visit — or perhaps always assumed when he was ill — and broke into another series of coughs and wheezes.

"Sorry. I assure you I'm no longer contagious. And I'm positively going back to work Monday. I must, that's all there is to it. I mean, here it is the height of the Christmas season, credit cards boring a hole in everyone's wallets, and that ninny Alan's in charge of the gallery. A sweet boy of course, but he wouldn't know a serious collector if one came up and bit him." Jacky giggled. "Well, let's hear your report, and then Tommy will bring us tea."

"You won't think it's very good news, I'm afraid," she said.

"No?"

"I told Lennie Zimmern I'd found the Key West paintings." Polly took a breath; she wasn't going to repeat her lie about the inscriptions on the back unless she had to. "But he doesn't really want to do anything about them. He says he already has too much of Lorin's work to look after."

"Oh, dear," Jacky wheezed, with a noise like steam escaping from a leaky kettle. "Well, that does rather throw a monkey wrench into our plans. What is a monkey wrench, by the way? Do they sell them at the hardware store?"

"I don't think so," Polly said. "At least, I've never seen one."

"Pity about that. There are times when it would be nice to have something of the sort handy." He sighed, wheezed.

"So you're not going to try and get the canvases back?" Polly asked, trying to speak neutrally.

"Uh-uh." Jacky coughed. "I mean, after all, Zimmern's the legal owner. If he doesn't want to start proceedings, there's not much the gallery can do." He glanced at Polly and misread her expression. "It's a disappointment for you, I know. But really we already have quite enough work lined up for the show, and Garrett's promised to lend us anything we like from his own collection. . . . That reminds me. He told me the other day that you may be collaborating with him on his memoirs."

"Well, I won't." Polly spoke with heat. "He suggested it when I was in Wellfleet; but I said I wasn't interested."

"That's too bad," Jacky wheezed. "You know, you could do a lot worse, my dear. Of course Garrett is rather an old windbag, but he knows absolutely everyone, and he can get his hands on all sorts of funding. I'm sure you'd be paid very very well. I wouldn't be too quick to turn his offer down, if I were you," he added, in the negligent manner he reserved for his most serious remarks.

"I've promised to go back to the Museum as soon as the book is finished, anyhow," Polly said, fighting the impulse to tell Jacky of the other offer Garrett Jones had made her. It would explain her refusal, certainly; but the whole story — very likely in an embellished version — would be all over New York in a matter of days.

"Oh, nonsense, darling. They can get on without you for a bit longer, I'm sure. And I expect Garrett could fix whatever leave or part-time deal you wanted in a jiffy. Why don't you let me tell him you're considering it, at least?"

"Well. Okay," Polly said, thinking that it might be politic to stay in Garrett's good graces until the book was finished.

"No need to make waves unless one has to," Jacky remarked, appearing to read her mind. "Besides, we all know nobody gets ahead in this business without either money or connections. Preferably both."

"I suppose not," she admitted.

"Paolo said that to me the very very first week I came to work for him. Of course I thought it dreadfully crass; but alas, he was quite right."

"How is Paolo, by the way?" Polly asked.

Jacky shook his head, bringing on another attack of coughing. "Not too well, I'm afraid. It's beginning to look as if he won't be coming back to the gallery."

"So you'll be taking over for good?"

"Well, yes; I think so. Paolo's wife wants me to. I told her I'd like that, but I felt that there really had to be some drastic changes. Frankly, just between us, the Apollo hasn't taken advantage of recent developments as it should have done."

"Mm?"

"You know, there are a lot of exciting new artists coming along. And new collectors. For them Lorin Jones is almost an old master. Since you're such a feminist, perhaps I should say old mistress. But somehow that doesn't sound right, does it?" Jacky giggled, wheezed.

"Anyhow," he continued when he had caught his breath, "I'd really like the Apollo to take a few more risks. I even considered whether we should move downtown; but I decided against it. Most serious buyers, you know, especially the foreigners, don't really enjoy the trip to Soho. Even in a limo there's all that awful midtown traffic to fight your way through, and the streets are dirty and full of spaced-out types. So by the time they get there they're already unhappy and impatient, and in no mood to make a commitment. Much better to bring the work uptown." He smiled.

"And you've discovered some new artists."

"Oh yes. For instance, there's this very very interesting woman from California called O'Connor who does pieces that rather remind me of Islamic wall decorations. The ones with all those bits of mirror embedded in plaster to form abstract or floral designs, you know?"

"Mm."

"Well, she's brought that basic idea up to date. I think she's going to be a great success. The work is very strong, and really beautiful. And then it's also metaphorically rather brilliant: the painter orders the world, and the viewer projects himself — or herself, darling, don't get cross — into this new vision. You must come round and see her slides as soon as you have a free moment. How is the book coming, by the way?"

"Oh, all right, I guess." Polly tried to summon enthusiasm, but failed.

"I know how it is," Jacky said sympathetically. "It's always the hardest part, the first draft. If you'd like me to look at the manuscript anytime, you know, I'd be glad to."

"Thank you," Polly said, thinking that if Jacky saw the book she was trying to write he would never ask her to tea again.

"I mean that. I'd really be happy to do anything I can. . . . Oh, Tommy. That looks delicious. Shall I pour?"

In her empty apartment on the day after Christmas, Polly Alter sat moping in front of a work table covered with stacks of notes, transcripts of interviews, filing folders, three-by-five cards, and magazines and catalogues with markers in them. Stevie was off playing Christmas video games with a friend, and she should use the free time to work, but her book was now totally blocked. Whenever she looked through her papers, trying to get a perspective on the project, she became confused and depressed; she felt her subject splitting into multiple, discontinuous identities.

There was the shy little girl Lolly Zimmern; the flaky college freshman Laurie; the bohemian art student; the ambitious, calculating young professional that Kenneth Foster had taught; and the neurotic, unworldly artist that Jacky knew. There was the poetic lost child Laura whom Garrett Jones had married, and the obsessed genius who had died in Key West. According to her niece, Lorin was generous and sensitive; her stepmother remembered her as selfish and spiteful.

And what's more, it was clear by now that none of the people Polly had interviewed were lying, not wholly anyhow: everyone had told her the truth as he or she knew or imagined it. All they agreed on was that Lorin was beautiful and gifted (the two things I'm not, Polly thought sourly). Otherwise, everyone seemed to have known a different Lorin Jones; and most of them also had different versions of the other people in Lorin's life. As Lennie Zimmern had warned Polly, she had found out too much. How the hell was she ever going to make sense of it all?

Maybe what Lennie had said back in September was right, she thought. Maybe I should just talk about the paintings, instead of trying to write the biography of somebody I don't begin to understand; somebody who probably wouldn't have liked me or wanted me — or anyone — to write about her. If the grief and guilt I felt that last day in Key West was real, that's what I'd do. It would be a lot easier besides, and Lennie would thank me. But then all these notes; all these wasted months — Polly groaned aloud.

If only Jeanne were here, she thought, forgetting all that had gone wrong between them, remembering only her friend's intelligence, warmth, and sympathy. Remembering how, long before Jeanne moved into the apartment, back when she had lived three blocks away, they could call each other anytime. *I need to talk to you,* Polly would say. *I'm in a total funk. . . . Oh, my dear,* Jeanne would murmur. *I'm so sorry. Tell me about it.*

Jeanne was up in Vermont now, but Polly could still talk to her on the phone, Ida would have the number. She shoved back her chair and went into the kitchen.

"No, she's not in town," Ida said in charged, emotional tones. "She's in Vermont with Betsy. . . . I don't know when they'll be back. They're with friends." Her pronunciation of the last word suggested that Polly was not in this category.

"Can you give me the number there, please?"

"No," Ida said; it sounded as if she were breathing hard into the phone. "I don't think I can."

Polly suppressed an impulse to swear. "Jeanne promised she'd call when she got there, you see, but she hasn't," she explained.

"No. I shouldn't expect she would."

"Why not, for God's sake?" Her voice rose.

"Jesus. If you don't know that," Ida said, with a slight but marked pause on the pronoun.

Polly gave a loud, angry, uneven sigh. "Well, when you speak to her, tell her I'd like to hear from her."

"Oh, you would." Now Ida's voice began to shake. "There are a lot of people who genuinely care for Jeanne, in case you didn't realize that," she said. "People who respect her emotional commitments, her privacy, her personal integrity —"

"I don't know what you're talking about."

"No. You wouldn't, would you?" Ida's tone had become so sneering that Polly lost her cool.

"Oh, go to hell, you old bitch," she cried, and hung up.

Feeling even worse than before, she began to wander through the apartment, dim now in the fading winter light. There was nothing to see; only, out of one window after another, the backs of other apartment buildings, blurred by the drizzle of snow that had been falling all afternoon. From her bedroom, though, if she stood close to the cold glass and looked sideways, a narrow vertical strip of Ninety-second

Street was visible. Everything in this elongated rectangle was black or gritty gray, like an early twentieth-century Ashcan School etching: a lamppost, a couple of snow-whitened cars, an attenuated Peggy Bacon cat, two figures walking hunched together against the wind. It was as false and limited a version of Ninety-second Street, Polly thought, as each of those transcripts on her desk was of Lorin Jones's life. But it was all she could see, just as to her informants their reports were the whole truth.

Every one of those people expected her to reproduce their narrow vertical view of Lorin Jones. And what's more, if she didn't, they would be angry with her. Whatever she wrote, she would satisfy some of them and enrage others.

Suppose, just for the sake of argument, she were to write the biography of Lorin Jones that Jacky and Garrett expected, in which Lorin would appear as an eccentric, neurotic genius, and they as generous and wise and tolerant. They would be pleased, and reward her; they would see to it that her book was well and prominently reviewed — Jacky had already hinted as much. If she put her career first, this was the choice she would make.

And suppose too, just for the sake of argument, that she were to accept Garrett's job offer. Since she'd told him she was a lesbian, he probably wouldn't bother her with any more sexual advances; at least he wouldn't come on to her overtly. And as his protégée she would have many privileges. She would meet the most important artists and collectors; she would be invited to review for newspapers and magazines.

And let's not forget the money. If she were working for Garrett, Polly would be able to take taxis when the weather was lousy or the buses crowded; she would never have to descend into the dirty, threatening catacombs of the subway. She would travel business class on planes and visit museums in distant cities, and maybe even abroad. She would see the Prado, the Musée d'Orsay, the Hermitage, the Uffizi; famous private collections here and in Europe would be open to her.

She might as well cultivate her professional connections, Polly thought, because it was clear now that after what had happened Jeanne's friends would reject her. In fact, judging from that phone call, they already had. Even if she could write the book she had first planned, Ida would not forgive her. Feminist reviewers might praise and admire her, but she would never again be invited to Ida and Cathy's study group; though she might one day sit on the floor of some other apartment in some other circle of women, with one hand in that of a shadowy lover.

But maybe she wouldn't care; maybe she wouldn't write that book anyhow, but one that would please Jacky and Garrett, and become a success.

Against the screen of grainy, drifting snow, Polly saw herself in this alternative future, at a party in an East Side townhouse. She was elegantly dressed in black, and carefully made up; her hair was professionally styled and smoothly blown dry (in this incarnation she would be able to shop at Bendel's instead of Macy's, and go to the beauty salon once a week). The people at the party gazed at her with interest; not only because she seemed so cool and confident, but because she was a figure of growing importance and power in the New York world of museums and galleries and artists and dealers and critics. Other expensive-looking men and women stood around her, some of them recognizably famous. Maybe she was involved with one of them, though not seriously. If her career really took off, probably she wouldn't have the time or energy for a serious relationship: she would either be celibate or have brief affairs with men or women whom she didn't like or trust very much; who didn't much like or trust her.

Maybe that was why the face of the central figure in this scene showed no joy or ease: her expression was wary, calculating, and self-conscious. She looked like someone Polly wouldn't want to meet, let alone become.

The idea that she was about to choose, not only a version of Lorin Jones's past, but her own unattractive future, made

Polly giddy, as if she were standing on the top of a steep hill instead of looking out of an apartment window in a snowstorm. And what made it worse was the blurry knowledge that, once she had chosen, she would forget that there had ever been a choice. From the crossroads at the crest of the hill you can see in every direction; but after you start down one of the paths the view narrows, and other landscapes vanish.

The Polly in the circle of women and the Polly at the party in the townhouse would forget that there had been any alternatives. They would believe that they had taken the only possible route. The book they had written, the life they had chosen, the person they had become, would seem inevitable; as inevitable, say, as her separation from Jim.

But how inevitable had even that been? Suppose she had agreed to go to Denver; probably she would soon have convinced herself — or rather, she would have become the person who believed — that keeping the family together was more important than anything else. She would have gone on loving Jim and believing that he was decent and trustworthy. Maybe she would have found another job in Colorado, or begun to paint in a different way that had nothing to do with Lorin Jones, and she would have taken that for granted too.

Now, soon, the biography of Lorin Jones she would write, the life she would choose, would seem the only possible one. She would become an angry, depressed lesbian feminist or a selfish, successful career woman. And Lorin Jones would be established in the public mind as an innocent victim or as a neurotic, unfaithful, ungrateful genius; but it would all be lies.

What she'd really like to do, Polly thought, resting her elbows on the crossbar of the window and watching the flakes of snow, like fine gritty ash, whirl and eddy and descend between the walls, was to write a book that would tell the whole confusing contradictory truth. She'd like to put in all the different stories she'd collected, and — as her father used to say — let the devil take the hindmost.

Yes, but who would be the hindmost? Polly Alter would be that; her biography would be called unfocused and inconsistent, and would enrage everyone who was important to her.

The heavy, damp depression that had been hanging above her head all day descended on Polly like a dirty, sopping-wet blanket. She wished to God she had never heard of Lorin Jones, who was responsible for everything that had gone wrong in her life over the last year, right down to what had happened with Mac.

It's too late to brood about that, she told herself. You'd better make up your mind and get started on whichever goddamn book it's going to be; the grant money will run out by May. But she felt too sodden and sluggish to move. Outside the window, the ash fell.

After what could have been one minute or twenty, the buzzer from the downstairs door sounded. Slowly, Polly moved away from the window and the darkening, sliding snow. Jeanne, she thought foolishly; and then, more reasonably, that Stevie must have forgotten his keys. But it was only Federal Express announcing a delivery. "I'll come down," she called into the intercom, thankful for any distraction.

The package turned out to be bulky and, she was surprised to see as she carried it back up in the elevator, from her father. It must be a Christmas present for Stevie. Not the check Carl Alter had said he would send, but almost on time for once in a lifetime. But when she opened the box on the kitchen table, the first thing that fell out was an envelope with her son's name on it. Both a check and a gift, then: extravagant and unnecessary. As usual the wrapping paper was far too childish for Stevie; it was also inappropriate for a boy: cutesy little girls carrying miniature Christmas trees, for shit's sake.

She looked at the card, which had a bird on it, a white peace pigeon — no, a dove, probably; religiously inappropriate, too. "Merry Christmas to Polly."

For God's sake, she thought; it must be twenty years since her father had sent her anything. She pulled the paper apart and drew out a box marked — holy cow! — ETCH A SKETCH. The same damn Etch A Sketch she had longed for when she was eight years old, that her father had so often promised and never brought her. Polly began to laugh; then, surprising herself, to cry.

Weeping foolishly, she took her father's check into Stevie's room, so that he'd find it there when he came home for supper. The sight of his books and posters, now restored to the shelves and walls, restored Polly slightly. Whatever happened to her, Stevie was back in New York.

Yes, but what would he find here? she thought, looking up at an old wildlife poster that hadn't yet been replaced with something more contemporary, maybe because it hung high in a corner. It was a blown-up color photo of a raccoon that Polly had bought many years ago because of the animal's resemblance to Stevie as he had been at four or five: the round dark eyes set in a ring of almost transparent darker skin, the pointed face and clever, inquiring expression. He still looked like that, a little.

The junior high school Stevie was about to return to was, according to report, worse than ever this year. Both his best friends had now left it: one for Ethical Culture and the other for Exeter. But Polly couldn't afford to send Stevie to private school; he would have to stay where he was, in crowded, boring classes, a raccoon child threatened or attacked by teenage pit bulls. After a while, and not such a long while either, he might want to go back to the wilderness, to Denver; to Jim's so-called normal American family, which would soon be even more "normal."

But suppose she were to write the book Garrett wanted, Polly thought, and become his assistant. Then she could afford to send Stevie to a private school, and soon he would be one of those sophisticated preppie kids you see around Manhattan. With an elegant mother who wasn't home very much, because in her new super-career Polly would often be out of town or at parties and openings. She would have to hire a housekeeper, so that when Stevie came home from his snobby school there would be someone here to make his supper.

These visions, and the idea that she now had to choose between not only her own two unattractive futures, but also Stevie's, terrified and enraged Polly. In spite of the warmth of the apartment she was overcome with a kind of feverish shiver, as if she were coming down with the flu.

But was there any other alternative? As she stared up at the poster, its background altered in her imagination. The leaves of the tree became larger and shinier; brilliant tropical flowers appeared among them. The raccoon turned into Stevie at his present age; but barefoot, tanned, and dressed in a pair of cut-offs and a T-shirt, straddling the branch. Below him, on the deck of a house in Key West, Polly herself (equally tanned) sat at a picnic table typing. She wore her old jeans and a faded shirt; her hair was tied back with a piece of red yarn, and she was smiling. It was the real story that she was typing, the whole truth about Lorin Jones, with all the contradictions left in. While she watched, Mac came out of the house, carrying two cans of beer.

That can't happen, Polly thought, it would be crazy, you know you can't trust him. It would be crazy to trust somebody like Mac when every man she'd ever known, beginning with her father, had hurt her and abandoned her.

But Carl Alter had said that she'd abandoned him, that she hadn't wanted to see him. He really believed that. Jim probably believed that too. For them she was like Lorin, a damaging, rejecting woman. And now it was Mac who thought she didn't want to see him again, because she had more or less told him so. He hadn't called in over a week. Maybe he had given up on her.

The way my father gave up on me, Polly thought.

The interviews are finished now; I could go to Key West. I could take a chance, I could do it, she thought, taking in a breath and holding it. But it wouldn't be easy. She sighed, imagining all the anger and trouble she would bring on herself: the scenes, the explanations, the packing; trying to rent the apartment (Jeanne and Betsy would want it, but could they afford it?), telling Jim and her mother and the people at the Museum and everyone else she knew. All of them would think Polly had freaked out. Leaving a promising career, running off to Florida just like Lorin Jones, *and* with the same man — wasn't that really kind of weird and sick? everyone would say. She starts writing about Jones, and ends up living Jones's life, for God's sake! They wouldn't expect it to work out, and maybe they would be right.

But if she didn't try it, how could she ever be sure?

"And when you finish your book, what then?" her friends would ask.

Well, she would say, I'll just have to see. Maybe Stevie and I will come back to New York. Or maybe we'll stay in Key West for a while, living on the rent of this apartment and Stevie's child support. Maybe I'll get a job in a local gallery or something.

It wouldn't be all tropical flowers. She would be a middle-aged dropout like Mac, living a marginal life in a beach resort; she would probably never be well off or well known.

But no matter what happened afterward, I would be with him now, Polly thought, taking a great gasping breath of air as if she had just come up from underwater. I could write the book the way it ought to be. And I could start painting again if I wanted to. Even if it wasn't any good at first, it might get better. As Mac said, you never know; I might strike it lucky one day. And if everything worked out — It was crazy even to think of it, probably, but if I really wanted to I could have another child.

Polly looked at her watch. Half-past five. It was fully dark out now, and would probably be dark in Key West too, though the sun set later there. Mac and his crew would have finished work, and he would have gone back to the room he was renting from friends.

Before she could lose her nerve, or change her mind again, she ran toward the kitchen. She stared at the harmless-looking wall telephone for a second, took a final deep breath, and picked up the receiver.